BLIND SIGHT

BLIND SIGHT

Meg Howrey

PANTHEON BOOKS   NEW YORK

Copyright © 2011 by Meg Howrey

All rights reserved. Published in the United States by Pantheon Books,
a division of Random House, Inc., New York, and in Canada by
Random House of Canada Limited, Toronto.

Pantheon Books and colophon are registered trademarks
of Random House, Inc.

A cataloging-in-publication record has been established
for this title by the Library of Congress.

ISBN: 978-0-307-37916-0

www.pantheonbooks.com

Jacket photograph by Stephanie Cabrera/Getty Images
Jacket design by Abby Weintraub

Printed in the United States of America
First Edition
2 4 6 8 9 7 5 3 1

Probably a crab would be filled with a sense of personal outrage if it could hear us class it without ado or apology as a crustacean, and thus dispose of it.

"I am no such thing," it would say; "I am MYSELF, MYSELF alone."

—WILLIAM JAMES, *The Varieties of Religious Experience*

BLIND SIGHT

CHAPTER ONE

Names are just what we all agree to call things. They have nothing to do with the intrinsic reality of the objects they name.

I have been thinking about names, actually my name in particular, for about fifteen minutes now. What I should be doing is working on my college application essay. That's one of three things I have to do this summer. The other two are running between seventy and seventy-five miles per week, and getting to know my father, whom I just met. I've made a training schedule for running, and the essay only needs to be between three and five hundred words, so those two shouldn't be that hard.

My father flew me out here to Los Angeles five days ago. I wouldn't say that I know him yet.

Anyway, before I get to the essay, I've got to fill out the personal information section on these forms: name, gender, ethnic affiliation. "Who are you? What are you?"

It's a very American kind of question, "What are you?" People are always telling you how they are Sicilian, or Polish, one-sixteenth Cherokee. People might hear my last name, and say, "Oh, is that English? Your family is from England?" And I will say, "No, my family is from America." Because when it was your great-to-the-eighth-power grandparents who emigrated here from England I feel like, "Yeah, I'm not really English, okay?"

I guess this doesn't happen so much in other countries, where they don't have an Ellis Island to chop off two syllables and six letters from your last name. Imagine this kind of conversation going on in Tokyo:

Japanese Speaker One: Hello, my name is Fumio Watanabe.

Japanese Speaker Two: Water . . . NOB . . . hay? Am I saying that right? What is that? Russian?

Yesterday I visited my dad for the first time on the set of his TV show and there was a little confusion at the security booth. I gave my last name, "Prescott," but the ID tag they had for me said "Franco." I guess they assumed that I would have my father's last name. It seems weird that he would have told them I do. Anyway, Mark Franco isn't even my father's real name.

My father's real name is Anthony Boyle. He had to change it when he became an actor because when you do a movie or a television show you have to join the Screen Actors Guild and there was already an Anthony Boyle registered in the union. Two actors can't have the same name, so my father had to change his. He didn't make "Franco" up: it's his mother's maiden name. She is second-generation Mexican. (His father was "maybe Irish and something else.") I forgot to ask where he got the "Mark" part.

My father told me that if people ask him what he is, he says he is Italian. His manager told him to do that because being Italian sounds sexy and being half Mexican and half maybe-partly Irish sounds "kind of random."

If my father *had* kept his real name, then we—my family—

would have made the connection that the guy on television and in movies was my dad. But since he and Sara—that's my mom—didn't really know each other that long, well, not really at all really, and Sara didn't have any pictures of him, and she never watches action movies anyway, and you don't usually consider that famous people's names aren't actually their names, you can see how the whole thing got lost in translation.

Knowing this about my father's background, I see that I could check off the "Hispanic" box right here on my applications, but that seems shady. I just met my father. It doesn't seem ethical to try and cash in on his partial ethnicity, and furthermore out him as a not-so-sexy-as-Italian half Mexican. And like I said, I don't even have his last name, either Boyle or Franco, since he and my mother were never married.

Sara *was* married once and that is how I have my two sisters, Aurora and Pearl, but after she got divorced she took back her maiden name. This was all before I was born. So all three of us kids have always been Prescotts and when we moved in with Sara's mother—my Nana—that really worked out because Nana is also a Prescott.

Nana is a Prescott by marriage, but her ancestors have been in America for a long time too. She has a special Bible from the seventeenth century with her maternal family tree written down on the inside covers. I guess it was a good way to keep track of people. And the family Bible they wrote in often became a keepsake kind of thing, something to pass on to your children, especially if you were poor and the only other things you had to leave your children were, like, a calico blanket and a thimble.

I should say that Nana's family Bible is not a collectible item. It's held together with masking tape, and there is water damage and ripped pages and stuff. Nana has it stored now in a special acid-free box. Before that, she kept the Bible inside a ziplock bag at the bottom of her nightgown drawer.

One night when I was about nine, I guess, Nana said at dinner,

"Well, I suppose after we clear the table, I might show the children the family Bible," and maybe we all said, "Yay," or whatever because we had all heard about it but never seen it. Nana brought it down from her room—at that point it was still in a ziplock baggy—and we all sat around and looked at the names of our ancestors.

Daniel Perkins (b. 1657, d. 1709)—Abigail Perkins (b. 1664, d. 1738)

That was the first line. The dates might be off by a year or two.

"Abigail Perkins," Sara told us, "was one of the women who were accused of witchcraft in the Salem trials."

My sisters Aurora and Pearl sort of oohed at that; so I oohed too even though I hadn't gotten to the Salem witch trials in school yet.

"Did they hang her?" Aurora asked.

"Oh no," Nana said. "She had to go to prison for a little while and then they let her go. She was just fine."

"She must have been *terrified*," Pearl said, liking the sound of that. "Absolutely *terrified*."

"It's nothing to worry about," Nana said. "We don't really know anything about it."

"Aunt Nancy did some research on Abigail Perkins," Sara said. "She thinks Abigail might have confessed and that's why they let her go."

"Not that she really was a witch, of course," Nana said.

"Maybe she was," Pearl suggested. "Maybe she was the one real witch and gave the one real confession."

"That's a very creative idea," Sara said.

"They weren't witches," Aurora announced with authority. "They were probably midwives or healer women."

"Anyway," Nana said.

"Let's read all the names out loud," Sara suggested. "Everybody can do one line." So we did that. They filled the front inside cover of the Bible and continued on the back, right down to the bottom of the page. The handwriting got much clearer, regular cursive mostly toward the end where we got to Nana and her two sisters, and Sara and her two sisters, and then my two sisters and me. Aurora read that one out loud, and we all applauded ourselves.

"I'll just make some tea," Nana said, going into the kitchen.

"There are a lot of Emilys." Pearl leaned over the Bible. "I wish my name was Emily. It's a million times better than Pearl."

"You can be anything you like." This was what Sara always said to Pearl when Pearl complained about her name. "You tell us what you want us to call you, and we will call you that."

"Everybody had girls," I said, looking at the names. "Unless they left out the boys' names?"

"They didn't leave them out," Sara said. "There weren't any boys. Does anybody see another pattern?"

We all leaned in closer.

"There's always three," Aurora said. "Three girls. Unless people are missing."

"No, that's exactly right," Sara said. "And only one person in a generation ever had children. See how there's only one line coming down from every set? Only *one* of the sisters ever had children, and when she did, it was always three girls."

"Oh yeah," Aurora said. "I get it now."

"Pretty cool, right?"

"Is it supposed to mean something?" I asked.

"Well, what do you think?"

"I think it means something," Aurora said.

"It means something if you believe it does," Sara said. "Remember, it's not, 'I'll believe it when I *see* it.' It's, 'I'll see it when I *believe* it.'"

That was when I suddenly thought of the Plinko game. I had played Plinko at the county fair with my sisters that very summer. It's this game where you are given a ping-pong ball to drop at the top of a wooden board with nails sticking out of it. It's like a kind of maze. You drop your ball in at the top and it falls down, bouncing left or right depending on which nails it hits, and what angle it hits them on, and eventually your ball falls into a bottom slot. The object of the game is to have your ball land in the WINNING slot in the middle of the bottom, and if you do, you get a prize. You watch other people do it, and you strategize and think, "Okay, I'm going to start my ball at the far left corner, because then it will have to mostly bounce right, and it'll kind of work itself over to the middle." But of course strategies like that don't work when the game is entirely random. You can't do anything to improve your odds.

So thinking about that, and looking at the names running down the pages of the Bible, it didn't look to me like a family tree. It looked like a family Plinko game, with girls ricocheting off of girls.

A few years later I did a search on Ancestry.com and found out that those names in the Bible are accurate. None of those women had any boys and there were only three girls to a generation and all of those girls always came from a single member of the previous generation.

It's hard to say why. Take Nana and her sisters, for example. Her younger sister Eileen is still alive, but she never visits because she breeds Dandie Dinmont terriers and says she can't ever leave them. She lives in Nebraska, and sends my sisters and me checks for fourteen dollars on our birthdays and at Christmas. "The mystery of Great-Aunt Eileen," Aurora says, "is not, 'Why did she never marry and have children?' but, 'Why fourteen dollars?'" No one has an answer for this. But I guess we can take it that Great-Aunt Eileen's reproductive interests are pretty much canine.

The other of my grandmother's sisters, the one my mother was really close to—Great-Aunt Nora—died the year my sister Pearl was born. It is Sara's belief that Pearl is actually Great-Aunt Nora reincarnated. (Pearl is totally not into this idea and says that it is "an invasion of her free will" and also "gross.") According to Sara, her aunt Nora was very spiritual and had these amazing psychic powers and through those powers she always knew that she was not "the one" of her generation to have children.

So Nana was the one. Not that she would ever describe herself that way. If you ask her about the whole thing she will just say, "Yes, our family has always run to girls."

The precise geometry—not to mention redundancy—of how our family has run to girls is not especially mysterious to Nana because it falls into the general mystery category of God's will, which is also something you will see only when you believe it.

How did it work out for my mother and her sisters? Aunt Nancy didn't really like children. Our aunt Caroline liked children, but she was married to a really old guy, my uncle Louis, who is almost as old as Nana. Not that old men can't have children, but I knew that Aunt Caroline had to have her ovaries removed because they had cysts in them and that you needed ovaries for babies. Sara studied the human body when she learned massage therapy, and so she had this great *Anatomy Coloring Book*, and she would show us all the pictures and explain stuff. I had seen the ovaries. Sara had made them gold. (The testes, on another page, had been colored blue.) Sara left college after two years to get married when she was really young to a guy named Paul. At that point, neither of her younger sisters was married and everybody's ovaries were intact, so the playing field was level. But after a couple of years, Sara got pregnant and had my sister Aurora. By the end of the following year she had my sister Pearl, or, if you will, the reincarnation of Great-Aunt Nora.

So that was two girls down, one more to go. Plain sailing for Sara, you would think.

Except that about a year after Pearl was born, Sara's husband Paul decided to renounce his life in New York City, all his worldly goods (and girls), change his name from Paul to Deepak, and join an ashram in India. Sara, who had met Paul at a yoga retreat in Boulder in 1982, seems to have been generally supportive of all of Paul's previous renouncements: Judaism, grad school, meat, Paul's investment-banker brother Barry, shoes with laces. To India, however, I guess she was not prepared to go or not anyway, as the renounced wife of Deepak.

So Sara had no husband and potential father for the third daughter. If she had never known about the three-daughters thing, would she have decided that two children were enough? She did know, though. And she believed she had a destiny. She's said that.

The actual facts were vague to me up until just a few months ago, but the basic outline is that my mother met my father one day and they spent a magical night together and she got pregnant. They didn't get married, though, or keep in contact, because they were on very different paths and my father was more like a comet that blazed through my mother's sky.

So that is how Sara had her three children: Aurora, Pearl, and me: three children born of (the mystically chosen?) one of three daughters who was herself born of the (randomly selected?) daughter of three daughters and on and on. So it seems like, hey, mystic or random, everything happened just as was expected, just as was planned, just as it had happened before, just as it had always been for twelve, and now thirteen, generations. There's a kind of flow to the whole thing. Or was, anyway. Because just when Sara thought her ping-pong ball was about to go in the winning slot, it bounced off a nail and went left. What are the odds? When Sara's third child was born, she got what she least expected.

She got a boy.

That's me.

As you can see at the top of my personal information sheet, my name is Luke.

It's not like I didn't know I was expected to be a girl.

"Your name was going to be Leila," my sisters liked to tell me.

I just didn't know the extent to which I was expected to be a girl until that day we all looked at the family Bible. My sisters didn't know either, I guess.

"So, Luke messes the whole thing up," Pearl had said after Sara pointed out the patterns.

"It'd be perfect if he was a girl," Pearl said, frowning at the Bible.

"Pearl," Sara said. "I'd like to hear more mindful language from you."

"Luke was sort of a mistake, I guess," Pearl shrugged. "Too late now."

Then Sara and Pearl got into it, and by the time Nana came back with tea Sara had sent Pearl to her room to think about the ways in which words can be hurtful and Aurora had told Pearl that her new name was going to be "Insensitive Jerk" so Aurora got sent to the laundry room to fold sheets and think about how you can defend someone without being hurtful yourself. (Aurora and Pearl shared a room and you couldn't exile them in there together.) Nana put the Bible back into ziplock and went upstairs.

"Pearl likes playing with words," Sara told me, once she had some tea and calmed down. "She didn't mean to be hurtful. You know she adores you."

"Yeah," I said.

"I don't think it means anything," I said, indicating the spot on the table where the Bible had been.

"Then it doesn't to you," Sara said. "And that's perfectly okay."

On a side note: I've done a little research on Abigail Perkins, accused witch of Salem. She's listed in all of the books on the trials, usually with a little parenthetical statement after her name: (convicted, but not executed). There's nothing to indicate whether she confessed or not, although they did let people go if they confessed. I also found out that most of the accused weren't midwives or healers or anything like that. Mostly they were people in the town that no one else liked because they were troublemakers, or argued with their neighbors, or were involved in lawsuits with the parents of the accusers, stuff like that. I actually just read an interesting article suggesting that the hysterical symptoms of the accusers might have been caused by ergot poisoning from the rye bread that was a staple food of Salem.

I don't know that any of this will make a good essay, though. I know good writing is supposed to be showing, not telling, but for the essay it's not really about showing or telling. It's about selling. Selling myself as the possibly gender-confused descendent of a false confessor and victim of rye bread–munching hysterics isn't going to get me into a good college.

And with that thought, Luke pushes himself away from the desk where he has been typing.

Luke slides back (the chair he's sitting on has casters) to the desk, scrolls through what he has written, and makes a few grammatical changes. Luke does not consider himself to be a writer, but he has writers in his family. His Nana wrote a series of books for young adults called *The Mountjoy Girls.* His mother, Sara, is writing a book on alternative healing, and contributes articles to various journals. His aunt Nancy has written a book on Lucrezia de' Medici. His sister Pearl has had her poetry published. His great-aunt Eileen has written a manual on the proper care and training of Dandie Dinmont terriers.

Luke saves his writing under the title "Notes #1."

He wonders how accurately he has remembered that evening when they all looked at the Bible. Luke was the star pupil of his AP Biology class and is a subscriber to *Scientific American,* so he understands the basic synaptic principle of memory creation, and that the act of memory retrieval will—to some extent—alter the memory being retrieved. Deprived of the exact stimuli that produced a unique neuronal sequence, cells will reconsolidate in a new way, depending on where and what and who Luke is at the time he remembers. Luke's brain—presupposing there is a "Luke" separate from his "brain"—can only remember a memory of the memory from the last time he remembered the memory.

Example: Luke did not think of the Plinko game while looking at the Bible that night. He constructed the analogy two years later, under totally different circumstances, but it so exactly suited the bouncing helplessness of looking at three hundred years' worth of girls' names that it seemed as if he had always made that connection: that he must have thought of the Plinko game at that moment, and forgotten about it, and that he was—two years later—remembering it at last.

But he wasn't.

Also, Luke didn't point at the names in Nana's family Bible and tell Sara, "I don't think it means anything." What he said was, "Yeah," and then, "Can I have a small piece of cake?" Luke was both alarmed and angered by the revelation of his family history. Luke knew Sara was worried about how he felt, along with feeling bad about losing her temper and yelling at Pearl. Luke wanted cake and knew that if he asked for a specifically small piece, he would get a larger one than if he had not specified the size. Luke could not stop himself from feeling alarm or anger. He could, however, and did, get dessert.

Luke is on the move now, leaving the bedroom for the kitchen. He does not think of the bedroom as "his" bedroom yet, even though his father introduced it to Luke with: "So this is your room." For four days, Luke has been moving cautiously about his father's house, putting anything he uses or touches back very carefully. Luke does not stand in his father's house and shout, "Who are you? What does this mean? Are we supposed to love each other? Why didn't you ever want to know me before?" Luke puts magazines down at the same angle he picks them up, flattens them into stacks, and says to himself, "I like keeping things neat too."

"What's his house like?" Pearl asked Luke by phone the day after Luke's arrival in Los Angeles. "Is it really fancy?"

"It's awesome. But it's not, like, super huge or anything." Luke looked around the living room where he was standing.

"Well, describe it," said Pearl.

"Um . . . it's really sort of empty."

"Empty? Like no furniture?"

"No, there's furniture. But everything is put away inside it. All the stuff. It's really organized."

"So it's impersonal," Pearl mused. "Cold."

"Oh no. It's really nice. No clutter. I'll take some pictures," Luke said.

Luke is in the kitchen now, which has all new appliances. He admires the refrigerator particularly, which is full of food in clear containers. His father told him to help himself to anything at all, and so Luke forks broccoli salad into a green rectangular dish. Even the dishes are cool: Japanese style, he thinks. Luke munches broccoli, thinks briefly about sex, which he has never had, and then his jeans pocket rings. It is the new cell phone his father's assistant, Kati, gave to him. (Kati, who, three seconds before, Luke was imagining sitting naked on top of the kitchen counter.)

There is a text from Luke's father: *Done in 1 hr. C U at home. Evrythng ok?* Luke smiles. Mark likes texting. Luke is not used to it because the cell phone plan allotted to him by Sara on his old phone has very limited texting. He likes that Mark texts him about ten times a day, sometimes with information, sometimes with an observation, or a description of what he is doing. Luke types back: *Great! See you then.* After a moment he changes this to: *evrythng cool! C U when.*

Luke puts the now empty dish, the fork, and the glass in the dishwasher, closes the door, thinks, takes everything out and washes them by hand over the sink, dries them with a brown dish towel, restacks them in cupboards and drawers.

Luke sees that somehow, in transferring salad from container to bowl, he has left blobs of salad dressing on the marble countertop. Luke grabs a sponge.

Now that he is examining them more closely, Luke thinks that the tiny blobs of dressing look like cells, and the splattered threads of dressing spreading out from the blobs look like the dendrites and axons that extend from a neuron.

Luke separates a dressing axon from a neighboring dressing neuron with the tip of his index finger. He knows that the axons of neurons do not actually touch other surrounding neurons. There is a space between them, a synaptic cleft. This space is where information is relayed from neuron to neuron. Neurotransmitter molecules move across the tiny space (five thousand of which would equal the width of a human hair) to neurotransmitter protein receptors. Electrical signals become chemical signals, and are converted back to electrical signals.

Signals, Luke thinks, sponging up the dressing. He thinks of Nana's family Bible and conceptualizes the names as cells, the lines connecting the names as dendrites, the spaces between the names as synaptic clefts. Signals, he thinks again. Signals being sent. Signals being sent from a mother to a daughter, then another, then another. Electrical signals. Chemical signals. Luke decides now to take his father's copy of *Fitness* magazine outside and look at it on the patio.

It had taken Luke awhile to think through the ramifications of his ancestral history, but once he did it had seemed pretty obvious to him that Sara had sex with his father for the sole purpose of conceiving a third daughter. A Sara in the grips of a mystical idea made more sense to Luke than a Sara who had a random one-night stand. So what happened? Did an embryonic Luke receive signals to become a girl and then ignore them? Refuse in the womb to obey his mother's electrical and chemical desires to produce a third daughter? Whatever happened, Luke has spent much of his conscious life attempting to correctly read and interpret the signals being sent from one female in his household to another. He is very, very good at it.

Sitting in the California sun, looking at a photograph of a man who appears nearly crazed by his own outsized musculature, and reading an article debating the merits of various protein powders, Luke appreciates the feel of the sun on the tops of his feet, imprecisely imagines sex with Kati (now on all fours with the moon-faced serenity of the Kama Sutra), wonders if he should start drinking protein shakes, thinks about sex again, is slightly disgusted with himself, then not. Luke closes his eyes, visualizes the spaces between the neurons in his brain widening and expanding, no longer synaptic clefts but synaptic seas, with room for swimming, floating on his back, letting the water cover his ears, hearing his heartbeat underwater. Drifting quietly, knowing for a quick second himself to be himself, forgetting all his names.

Luke cannot quite believe he is where he is, and for a moment he wishes the summer already over: hours running logged, essay written, father known. Questions begin to form, and so Luke opens his eyes and returns to the article about supplements. He wonders what doubling up on his protein intake would do to his body chemistry and if doing so would make him look more like his father, who is extremely muscular.

CHAPTER TWO

Okay, new plan is to think out stuff for my essay while running, therefore accomplishing two things at one time, instead of letting my mind drift. I don't want to have to worry about writing. It's enough that I've got to answer all these emails from my family.

The conditions for running here are really great: sun without humidity, hills, near-absence of bugs in the eyes, cool stuff to look at. The section of Los Angeles that Mark lives in is called Beachwood Canyon. It's not a scary-rich-looking neighborhood, but a lot of the houses have signs outside them saying they have video surveillance provided by Bel-Air security.

Mark said he could arrange for the studio to send him a car service, and then I could use his car when he's working. They added another week that he didn't anticipate, and he seems worried that I'll be bored or feel stranded, or something. We keep having odd conversations where he'll ask, "So you, like, drive and everything, right? Do you want a car?" And I'll say, "Do you mean . . . like . . . what do you mean?" and he'll say, "I missed all your Christmases and birthdays. Can I buy you a car?" and then we'll both sort of laugh. I told him about Vlad the Impala, and said I would be nervous to drive anything that wasn't already on the short list for the Grim Auto Reaper.

Anyway, we are going to do more stuff together once the show is finished shooting and he has his "hiatus." Yesterday, though, he had a day off and he took me out to Santa Monica beach. Oh yeah, I could tell my family about that. Of course, what they all want to know is how I *feel* about everything, and what it's all *like*, how I am *experiencing* it. That's called "qualia" in philosophy of mind. Qualia is the way things seem to us. It's one of my favorite words.

What's the qualia of being with my father?

I always knew I had a father, obviously, but we've just never had any dads around. Actually I think most people assume that all three of us kids come from Sara's ex-husband. I don't look like my sisters, but they don't totally look like each other either. All of us look a little bit like Sara, especially Aurora.

Sara had a simile for the way we should think about my sisters' father. Paul was like a caterpillar that had become a butterfly.

"You're not sad for a butterfly that isn't a caterpillar anymore, you're happy for it," Sara said.

It wasn't always possible for Sara to get other people—divorce lawyers, for example—to accept this kind of explanation, so my uncle Louis—who wasn't my uncle then, he was just our next-door neighbor in New York—helped Sara with the paperwork and she was divorced by reason of "desertion" as opposed to "metamorphosis." On Sara's advice, Aurora, Pearl, and I use the phrase "moved on" when referring to Paul, which we don't often do.

I knew my father's name: Anthony. In New York City, the building my family lived in came with a doorman who was also named Anthony. I don't have any memory of this doorman personally, but I do remember the sucking air sound that happened when he pulled open the glass entrance doors of our building, and so I guess I've always connected the name Anthony with that sucking air sound. The other thing Sara would say about my father was that he was young and beautiful: "Like an angel," is what she said.

Sara didn't tell me to think of my father as a butterfly, but more as someone who was on his own path, a path that did not include fathering in any sort of tangible way, and that I should choose to honor that path, whatever and wherever it might be. And according to Nana, we all had a father in the Lord.

In actual fact, I saw my father in two movies (*The Fast Lane* and *Night Begins Now*), without knowing at the time that it was my father I was seeing. Of course I had no way of knowing that Anthony Boyle had become Mark Franco, the guy who plays "Miggs," the rookie cop who spills coffee all over himself when Laura Laughton smiles at him in *Night Begins Now*.

My father has told me a little bit about his acting. It took him awhile to get famous. At first he only got small parts like Prison Inmate, or Drug Dealer. Then he said he started really working out hard and his roles got bigger as he did. He's played race-car drivers, assassins, bodyguards, Navy Seals. He's been in a ton of movies.

The Last is a futuristic drama where he plays the role of James Knox: an ex-military astronaut who struggles to lead a band of survivors abandoned by their own government to a place of refuge where they might be able to make contact with the resistance faction still thought to be circling the planet. (The planet is Earth, which has been partially destroyed by nuclear war and where strange things happen due to high radiation levels.) It actually makes sense if you watch it from the beginning.

The Last is the number-one network television drama now. But even when my father began appearing on magazine covers, sides of buses, billboards, Sara failed to recognize him. She doesn't really notice stuff like that. Also, she didn't have any photographs of him around to remind her of what he looked like, and their actual time together had been pretty brief.

Then, about four months ago, Sara got a call. And it was my dad. He said he wanted to get back in touch. If that was okay.

That's what Sara told me when I got back from working that night. I was standing in the kitchen making myself a sandwich and Sara came in and asked me to sit down with her. "So something has happened," is how she started.

"Really?" I asked, when she finished. "Wow," I think I said. I felt a little dizzy, even though I was sitting down, but I had also done a ton of yard work, and was very hungry.

"I know," Sara said. "We didn't talk for that long but he's . . . lovely. Just like I remembered. I think there's something very . . . beautiful here."

Sara held out a piece of paper. In my mother's language, "beautiful" can mean many different things. Sometimes it means that something is very beautiful. Sometimes it means that something is awful, and it's the process of understanding that something, and treating it with compassion and love, that is beautiful. I looked at the paper.

"Mark Franco," Sara had written, with a phone number underneath that.

"Wait, who's this?" I asked.

"That's him." Sara tapped the paper. "Anthony. He changed his name. He said it might be easier if you—we—just all call him Mark."

"Oh," I said. "Okay. Why?"

"He's an actor. He lives in Los Angeles. He wanted to know if I thought you would like to talk to him. I said I couldn't speak for you but that I *thought* you would."

"I would," I said. "I do."

I looked at the phone.

"Well, it's probably too late to call now," I said.

"There's a time difference," Sara pointed out. "It's earlier there."

"Maybe I'll call tomorrow," I said. I thought maybe I should eat first, and think things over. The first time you talk to your actual real-life father you want to be calm.

"Luke? Are you okay, sweetie? This is a lot to take in."

"I'm okay. I'm just . . ."

"I know," Sara said. "I am too."

She got up and put her hands on my shoulders. Among other things, Sara is a Reiki Master. I didn't experience healing rays or light-ning bolts of clarity or anything like that, but Sara has nice strong hands. I asked her to tell Nana about the whole thing because I wasn't quite sure of what my face was doing and because I knew Sara could use someone to talk to about it. It felt weird that I was still hungry, and weird that I still ate my sandwich and did things like flossing my teeth before I went to bed.

I didn't sleep much that night and I woke up really early.

"Your mother told me there was a telephone call," was what Nana said to me, at breakfast.

"My father." I tried to make it sound casual.

"Well," said Nana.

I waited.

"The Lord makes a tapestry of our lives." Nana glanced at the ceil-ing and smiled approvingly, as if she were giving Him a thumbs-up for His needlework.

"Your mother and I trust your judgment, Luke. And you and your father are in my prayers."

Then we worked on her crossword puzzle as usual. Well, I was a little distracted, so I didn't contribute much. But Nana is very good at crosswords. Even though she is someone who believes that the sud-den materialization of my father after seventeen years of absence is the work of a first-century mystic, she is also someone who knows the seven-letter word for the currency of Malaysia.

It was a Saturday, so Sara was at yoga class. I had a ton of home-work to do, which I did while waiting for it to be late enough to reasonably call California. I thought about what message I would leave if I got his voicemail, and decided NOT to leave one if that happened, but my father answered his phone on the second ring.

"Hello!"

"Hi. Hello. Is this, um . . . Mark?"

"Luke."

"Yeah. Hi. I mean, hi. It's Luke."

"Hi. I'm . . . hi."

"Hi," I said, starting to laugh, forgetting what I had planned to say. "Hi Mark, I'm Luke."

"Hey Luke," my father said, laughing too. "Hey Luke, I'm Mark."

Later that afternoon Sara came home and I told her about the conversation. I didn't tell her that I had spent most of the day doing research online about my father. I hadn't ever seen *The Last,* but I had heard about it. It was a strange thing, looking at all those pictures and saying to myself, "That's my dad." And also, "That extremely good-looking guy who is massively ripped is . . . my dad?" and, "That's the guy I just talked to on the phone. Who is my dad."

There were some mini-biographies of him on various websites but there wasn't any mention of me on those. I was prepared for that: he told me in that first phone call that he had always thought a lot about me and wondered and stuff, but that he was careful to keep his personal life very personal.

"And I didn't want to do anything without talking to your mom," he had said. "I wanted to respect her privacy, and yours too, of course. She's great, by the way, your mom. I was pretty nervous and she could not have been nicer or cooler."

At school on Monday, my semi-sort-of girlfriend Amy asked, "What's up with you?" and I said, "What?" and Amy said, "You're weird today," and I said, "Really?" After school, I biked to Kim's Video and searched for every movie Mark Franco had appeared in that I could find from the list I got from the Internet. I rented *The Hard Line* and *Flight of the Phoenix 2: The Phoenix Rises* to start with.

"Did you tell your sisters about your father yet?" Sara asked when I got home that day.

I hadn't. I hadn't even thought about it, which was weird, because normally I thought about my sisters all the time, especially this year since Pearl was away too, and I had been feeling a little lonely.

"Maybe I'll go see them. This weekend?" Aurora and Pearl both go to college in New York City, two hours away by train.

"Oh, good." Sara *was* being very cool about the whole thing, but I could sense anxiety underneath the coolness, and on top of it as well.

Mark Franco was barely in *The Hard Line* but had a much bigger part in *Flight of the Phoenix 2: The Phoenix Rises.* I watched these on my computer, using headphones to conceal all the screaming, shooting, and "Motherfucker!"s from Sara and Nana. His character got killed halfway through *Flight of the Phoenix 2,* and as it was now almost two in the morning, I stopped the movie there. I still couldn't see any resemblance between my father and myself, but I knew that in movies they put a lot of makeup and stuff on people. I also thought he was a very good actor, even in the small part.

In the following week, I rented *Time Out,* and *In the Zone,* and *Goodnight Stranger,* which my father, in an email response to me, had listed as the ones where he had "halfway decent parts." I'm not sure why, but I didn't tell any of my friends what was going on. I actually kind of avoided Amy, really.

At the end of the week, Sara came to my room for a talk. I had been expecting this. The DVD of *Goodnight Stranger* lay on my desk, and I put my American history textbook over it when I heard her footsteps in the hallway.

"Tea?" Sara asked, from the doorway, a cup in each hand.

"Yeah, thanks," I said.

"Okay time to talk?"

I nodded.

"So." Sara handed me one of the cups and sat down on the end of my bed. "It's funny. The moment I heard his voice on the phone all these memories about him came flooding back. Little details, things I had forgotten."

"Really?" I took a sip of my tea, which turned out to be kind of cold. "I thought it was just like . . . this moment that you had."

Sara eyed me thoughtfully.

"Not exactly. There was a little more to it. There was love, for one thing."

That sort of surprised me, because Sara had never said that she loved my father. "You loved him?" I asked.

She blew into her teacup, which must have been as cold as mine was.

"Well, it was a moment of love," Sara said finally.

I nodded.

"He worked in an electronics store," Sara said. "That's where I met him."

I remembered that Sara did actually once describe her brief relationship with my father as "electric."

"Oh," I said. "Like a RadioShack or something like that?" I tried to picture Mark Franco in one of those shirts the employees of Best Buy wear. Maybe with a name tag.

"Something like that. He—your father—helped me with a VCR."

"It was one of those things," I said. I knew the next part. Sara and Anthony—Mark—my father—had made a connection. There had been a spark. It seemed my mother's choice of words in describing the night of my conception had not been entirely metaphorical. I tried imagining my father in a jumpsuit with a tool belt, cords dangling from his hands.

"No, it was a real choice," Sara said. "I wasn't . . . well, I knew that there was a reason we had met, and when a few weeks later I found out I was pregnant, I knew the reason we had met was going to be you."

Sara's had the safe-sex talk with all of us, but to her credit, she's never said, "You have to have safe sex," because she obviously didn't in my case. What she says is, "Be aware of the choices you are making and accept responsibility for them."

"So when you found out you were pregnant," I said, "you called him."

"Well, no." Sara shook her head. "I didn't have a phone number for him actually."

"Oh." I wondered where I had gotten the idea that she called him. It had been a long time since we had had the "your father" conversation.

"But you did see him again. To tell him about me."

"Yes, we saw each other on the train."

"The train?" I asked. "Like, a *train* train, or the subway?"

"The subway, Luke," Sara said, patiently.

"How long had it . . . I mean, when was this?"

"Oh, well, let's see . . . awhile . . . it was a few months before you were born."

I thought.

"So you were pregnant when you saw him again," I stated. "On the subway."

"Well, I was pregnant since the night I had met him!"

"I mean . . . visibly pregnant," I persisted, shaping a phantom hump in front of my stomach. "Big, I mean."

"Mm-hm," Sara nodded.

"So he guessed?" I said. "When he saw you, he was like, Did I do that?"

Sara laughed a little.

"It was funny. He knew. Right away, he knew. He looked at me and he said—oh, I don't remember exactly what, but he knew. And we got off the train at the Sixty-sixth Street stop and we sat by the fountain at Lincoln Center and we talked all about it."

"What did he say?" I thought that the scenario sounded like the kind of movie Mark Franco didn't do. Mark Franco did movies where if people met each other in a subway train, they started fighting, or slipped a tracer into the other one's pocket, or yelled, "Everybody get DOWN!"

"Did he freak out?" I asked. For the first time I was really trying to imagine my father's side of this whole thing, and it seemed like freaking out was probably a reasonable response.

Sara let a little silence elapse before she answered.

"There was no freaking out." Sara leaned back and switched over to her guided meditation voice and started explaining about how my father wasn't in a place where he could be there for me, etc., but how ready and eager for me she was and how they were really honest with each other and how he came to see me right after I was born and held me and some other stuff but I wasn't really listening because I had already heard all of that and I was still trying to picture my father by that fountain.

Also I was thinking that Sara left it all to chance, really, that she would see my father again, and if they hadn't been on the same subway car he might never have known I existed. That part was definitely new. I didn't say anything more to Sara about it, though. What I was thinking was something along the lines of, "Okay, seriously, what the hell," but I needed some privacy to organize my ideas, so I just told her I understood, and stuff like that.

Saturday I took the train to New York City to see my sisters and tell them the news. Aurora, uptown at Columbia, and Pearl, downtown at NYU, met my train in midtown, at Penn Station.

"We thought a walk through Central Park." Aurora waved an umbrella and a Zabar's bag at me. "Kind of a late-winter picnic."

"What's up?" asked Pearl. "Sara called us both last night. We've been told to 'be there' for you."

"Pearl thinks it might be girl trouble," Aurora said.

"Is it SEX?" hissed Pearl, leering at me over her (not Starbucks) coffee.

"Shut up," I said. "No."

"Oh crap," Pearl said.

"Well, I guess it is in a way," I reconsidered. "Just not mine."

Later, camped out on one of the benches in front of Bethesda Terrace, I explained the situation.

"No WAY," said Pearl, when I was finished. "That guy from *The Last* is your DAD? No WAY."

"I know," I said.

"This is so weird."

"And Sara didn't know about him?" Aurora asked. "I mean, she never recognized him?"

"Well," I said, "you know Sara."

We all nodded. Sara loves music, so she's current on that, but she's not into TV. She was once asked to do a yoga series for television, and she turned it down because they wanted it to be like a workout thing, and Sara says yoga is moving meditation, not exercise.

"She recognized his voice on the phone. And they talked about it all."

"God," Pearl said. "I've never really pictured your dad as an actual person, you know? I guess all that celestial talk really sunk in."

"How did he find you?" Aurora asked.

"He said he hired a private investigator."

Pearl looked impressed. She lit a cigarette.

"Apparently it only took him about twenty minutes," I told them. "The investigator, I mean."

"So you've talked to him?" Aurora asked.

"Yeah," I said. "And we've been emailing every day."

"Also he probably has to be careful," suggested Pearl. "I mean, you could sell your story to the tabloids, right?"

"Pearl," Aurora said, "I'm sure it's not like that."

" 'TV Star Abandoned Son,' " intoned Pearl.

"Come on." Aurora stretched out a leg and kicked Pearl. "Luke wasn't abandoned."

" 'No Presents at Christmas, Says Boy,' " Pearl continued. " 'Son Left to Be Raised by Deranged Women.' "

"Luke had *presents*. We gave him presents."

"Okay." Pearl conceded the point with a wave of her cigarette. "Wow. This is huge."

"What's Sara's take on it?" Aurora asked.

"Luke, go and live and breathe freely as I have always done," Pearl said, in Sara's meditation voice.

"Kind of," I said. "Mixed in with a little 'Are you okay/are you really okay/is it okay if I ask you if you are okay.' "

"Sara hooked up with the guy from *The Last*," Pearl said. "That's something to brag about. This is really juicy."

"He seems cool," I said. "He wants me to come visit him in Los Angeles."

I had given some thought to how my sisters might react to the news, and had decided it would be best to play the whole thing kind of low-key. I mean, it wasn't likely that my sisters' father would become a television star in India and would soon be contacting them with offers to fly them to Mumbai for the summer. I also decided that I wouldn't tell them about Sara leaving it all to chance and just running into my father randomly on the subway. Because I wasn't sure I could say it without sounding pissed off about it, and then Pearl would get pissed off on my behalf, and either one of them might tell Sara that I was "upset" and there would be drama. Sara would want to talk more and she might get weird and not want me to come here and I had already decided that I really, really wanted to.

"This is a big deal," Aurora said.

"It's a big deal, Luke," Pearl agreed.

"Well, yeah, it's a big deal," I said. "But it doesn't change, you know, anything fundamental. I'm still me."

Another month of phone calls and emails passed. Plans got made. It was decided by everybody that I would not go to Belize for the summer to build homes and a school with the Helping Hands and Hearts program. I would go to Los Angeles for the summer and get to know my father. The Belize trip—or something like that—could be found for next summer. Sara stopped asking me if I was okay and started leaving me little notes that I would find in my textbooks, or my backpack, or my sock drawer:

"*Accept life whole, as it is, without needing by measure or touch to understand the measureless untouchable source of its images.*"

And,

"*The man of stamina stays with the root below the tapering—Stays with the fruit beyond the flowering: he has his no and he has his yes.*"

I finally told Amy the whole thing. Well, not the whole thing. I didn't say "Mark Franco."

That's when Amy told me she had been spending some time with her ex-boyfriend, Darren Vincz, and they were getting back together. I wasn't really surprised. I guess a part of me always knew that Amy was using me a little. So I just sort of nodded, and then she wanted to make out, and we ended up almost having sex. Sara always talks a lot about the mind-body connection, but your mind and body can act in total opposition to each other. Like, I knew it was ethically wrong to hook up with someone else's girlfriend, and I even knew Amy only wanted to do it because I had been *too* okay with the Darren thing, and so I really thought we should NOT have sex, even though my body totally wanted to. Anyway, it didn't happen.

Later, when I got home, I watched *The Kindness of Strangers* on my computer. In that one my father, hair slicked back and sporting a Middle European accent, manages to kill several FBI agents before being shot himself, in a car-chasing sequence, in Prague. It's really good.

A plane ticket arrived: round-trip, first-class.

"I wonder if you will recognize each other," Sara said to me on the way to the airport in Philadelphia.

"I sent him some pictures," I reminded her. "And I know what he looks like."

"You know, I'm really excited for *him*," Sara said. "It's like I'm sending him the best present in the world."

Six hours later I stepped off an escalator and into the baggage claim section of Delta Air Lines in Los Angeles. I looked around and met eyes with this tiny blond girl—well, *woman,* I found out later—and she came right up to me.

"Luke?"

We shook hands.

"I'm Kati," she said. "I'm your dad's assistant. He's waiting for you right over there."

I nodded, looking around, although Kati's "right over there" had not been accompanied with any sort of gestural indication of where "there" was.

"I'll get your luggage, okay?" Kati patted me on the elbow. That's when I realized I was still holding her hand.

"Oh, I can get it," I said, letting go of her.

"Just tell me how many and what color." Kati smiled over my left shoulder.

That's when I turned and saw my father, standing by a row of metal chairs. That is, I saw the outline of my father: baseball cap pulled low, sunglasses, slightly hunched shoulders. Nevertheless, I recognized him. I would say that this was because of the movies I had rented, the first season of *The Last* my father had sent on DVD, and all the images I had found on the Internet. Sara might say I recognized him from that one and only meeting, seventeen years before. Either way, I saw the man—Anthony Boyle—Mark Franco—angel, comet, cop, bodyguard, bad guy, bomb-squad captain, beautiful person, astronaut with a destroyed planet to navigate, and thought,

"That person is my dad."

So that's how we met. We didn't fly into each other's arms or anything like that. We shook hands. I appreciated that, because I think it's better to not load a whole bunch of feelings on top of things. Like, you could have a bunch of feelings about my family history and say it's very meaningful, or you could say, "Nope. Just random. Doesn't mean anything." You could say, "Oh, my long-lost father, what an emotional moment," or you could say, "Okay, we are biologically related. Interesting." My point is that people act like their feelings are something they can't help, but that's not totally true. Every time you run something over in your head you are firing the same set of synapses into the brain. You can *create* an emotion, is what I'm saying. You have to be careful about that.

Yesterday we went to the ocean and he said, "Do you want to go in?" and I said, "Well, just to feel it?" and he said, "Let's do it, man," and we took off our shoes and socks and sprinted to the water and Mark yelled, "Jesus fucking Christ it's cold!" and we started laughing and trying to jump over the tail edges of the waves coming in and this became a sort of game of who jumped the best and where one would say, "Oh, you are going down, my friend," or "You can run, but you can't hide," right before a wave hit.

And that did have a certain qualia to it, sure, but I don't really know how to describe it. I'm not good with similes.

This is why I need to start organizing my thoughts, while running. Surely I can get three hundred words assembled during a 10-K.

Luke sighs, and stops typing. He did not "space out" while running today, but space in the brain *is* an issue. So is relevance. Luke had passed a rose bush, heard a dog bark, noticed a squirrel dart across the street in front of a Mercedes with a dented fender and a bumper sticker that read "IMPEACH BUSH," and said to himself, "Man, those roses were as big as my head." Luke may use the phrase "roses as big as my head" in the postcard he will write later to Nana, but in summoning the phrase he will probably not ALSO recall the dog barking, or see the squirrel, or the bumper sticker. On the other hand, if he recalls the bumper sticker, he might forget about the roses.

Actually, Luke had spent most of his run trying to remember everything about the moment of being in the ocean with his father— the exact degree of coldness of the water, the way the beach looked, how it felt to say something that made his father laugh. Luke wanted to return to this moment because it had seemed possible then, jumping over waves, shouting at each other, laughing, that they *could* simply be known to each other like this—as two guys, genetically linked, doing something together, isolated from all expectations and desires contained in the words "father" and "son."

But in the car ride home, there had been an advertisement on the radio for "That Perfect Father's Day Gift for That Special Dad," resulting in a heavy wave of silence that, for Luke, drowned out the next advertisement and the latest news of more suicide bombings in Baghdad. A few minutes later, Mark asked if Luke liked Indian food and Luke said, deliberately, awkwardly, "Yeah, Dad, I like Indian food." It was the first time Luke had used the word "dad" in speaking to his father. It came out with an unintentionally italicized sound. After a moment, Mark said, "Me too . . . son," in the same italicized way. They had laughed a little. Mark did a funny imitation of President Bush, and they laughed a little too much at that. Then Mark had turned off the radio.

During his run Luke had also imagined describing the ocean experience to Sara and his sisters. He created responses from his family along the lines of "Sounds like you are creating memories, that is a beautiful moment to share," or "So is it hugely relieving to be with a dad after being locked up with us crazy bitches your whole life?" Luke does not want or need any of those responses. He is determined to maintain a rational, detached, scientific approach.

But sometimes when Luke sees a butterfly he does feel sad for the caterpillar that was lost. And there is no logic that can stop him from feeling this way. The fact that Luke does not acknowledge this feeling only strengthens the feeling, which is allowed to rest in Luke's subconscious, biding its time, as much a part of Luke as his two feet, driving into solid earth, remembering and forgetting with every step.

CHAPTER THREE

I brought a bunch of photographs with me to show my father. It was Sara's idea—so Mark could see me at different stages of my life and get to know my family and where I grew up and stuff. I haven't given them to him yet, though. If someone tells Sara, "I have pictures of my trip to Machu Picchu!" or whatever, she will sit right down and examine each one and ask questions and everything, but not everybody is like that with photographs.

Mark hasn't really said anything about his own family. I'm hoping it doesn't include any strange genealogical patterns.

So these early pictures I have were all taken with a film camera because there were no digital cameras back then. My favorite one would have been deleted otherwise, because nobody in it was ready yet, and also it's not quite in focus. There was another picture taken a few seconds later, once everybody got organized and in position and smiling, but Sara couldn't find it. So this photo is a real "Moment Before" and that's what I like about it.

Mark explained about "Moment Before" to me. It's an acting thing where the actor decides what his character was doing the moment before they are doing whatever it is the audience gets to see. So, like, if you are playing Mr. Jones, and the first time we see you is when you open the door of your house, then you should have thought about all the things you as Mr. Jones were doing before you opened the door. Because if the Moment Before you opened the door was you dancing naked in your living room, then you'll open the door differently than you would if you were, like, cooking spaghetti.

Sara is in bed in this picture. Her hair is long, the way it is now again, and she's wearing a yellow cotton T-shirt with "World's Greatest Mom" printed on it in bubble letters. She doesn't look like how she normally looks. Normally she dominates any photograph she is in, standing really upright with a big smile and kind of intense eyes. In this picture, you can't really see her face because she is leaning a little bit forward, holding on to Aurora, who is half on the bed and half off of it, with her arms outstretched. Aurora has her hair in two curly ponytails. She has really skinny arms. There is something nice about the two of them. Rory already looks exactly like herself and Sara looks soft and you want to tell her that everything is okay, and she should just lie down and relax.

To the left of this action is a white and pink and very shiny cradle. It looks expensive. Next to that is my Aunt Caroline, who is also white and pink, and expensive looking, but not shiny. Aunt Linny usually looks a little bit lost, or confused, which is often the case. She's the kind of person you have to show where the bathroom is in a restaurant. Not just point to it, but actually walk her there. Uncle Louis is not in the picture. He's an important lawyer and very busy and we don't often see him. Nana will always say ONCE in every visit of Caroline's, "And how is Louis"—like that, without a question mark—and then will immediately get up from the table and start clearing dishes, or go to get the mail or something so nobody ever hears how Louis is.

Aunt Caroline is holding a pink and white bundle in her arms.

On the other side of the cradle is my Aunt Nancy. She looks totally different in this picture than she does now. Now she is super thin and has those kind of rectangular black glasses that, like, a German architect might wear. Here, though, she is a little bit heavy and her glasses are these giant red things. She looks like someone who has cats, but she's actually very allergic to them. Aunt Nancy teaches Renaissance History at a liberal arts college in Maine. Because she lived in England for eight years when she was married to an Englishman, she says English-type words like "daft" and pronounces certain other words like English people do. For instance, instead of saying "Renaissance" the regular way, she says, "Re-NAY-sance."

On the other side of the bed (the right side) is Nana, who is holding a giant bouquet of white and orange flowers. Nana looks like the thin version of Aunt Nancy if the thin version were to put on a fluffy wig. Nana is gesturing with her free hand to Pearl, who is in front of the bed. Pearl is almost two here and she doesn't have a lot of hair, but what she has is blond and sticks almost straight up. She is wearing overalls, but no shirt, and tennis shoes. She looks like she is kicking the bed.

In fact, she is kicking the bed. Earlier in the day, Aunt Linny had given presents to Pearl and Aurora. Aurora got a purse with purple flowers on it. Pearl got a bracelet made out of buttons. Pearl had felt that maybe she hated the bracelet. Aurora offered to exchange items. Pearl had agreed to the exchange, and then immediately hurled the purse across the room, dislodging a purple flower. So Aurora got both things. Aurora tells this story all the time, and Pearl claims to remember it too, or at least her profound sense of the injustice of it all.

So in this photograph you get to see the Moments Before people got all sorted out and posed and that's really interesting, because life isn't really like photographs. Life is more like acting, where you want people to see a little bit of what you are hiding so they know you are hiding something and maybe wonder about what is really going on inside you. In life you might want people to see that something is wrong, so they will ask you, "Hey, what's wrong?" In photographs people just want to look good.

But here is Sara, who isn't exercising her usual mesmeric force upon the camera holder, and looks just like an ordinary mom, holding on to Aurora, who is reaching out for something—me, I think, because that's me in the pink and white blanket. And Aunt Linny looks like she wants to hand me over to my Aunt Nancy, and Aunt Nancy looks like she is defending herself from any contact with me by inverting her shoulders and shrinking her chest, sort of, and Aunt Linny is looking at Aunt Nancy, and not at all in a confused or dreamy way. She's actually sort of smirking. And there is my Nana with one hand on Pearl's knee and Pearl is looking at Nana like she cannot imagine how much more she is going to be made to suffer on this day. It's a fantastic picture. The only person in the photograph you can't see clearly is me. But that's cool. I might have been the star attraction, but it's what my arrival meant to everyone else that was the circus.

I asked Sara who took the picture and she said it must have been Joyce. Joyce was supposed to be Sara's midwife for my birth but Sara had me in a hospital because Joyce sort of panicked at the critical moment. I didn't even have a name yet here, since "Leila" turned out not to be appropriate.

So it's a photograph that was taken about five seconds before everyone got ready for it, and one week before I had a name, and nine years before I looked at the family Bible and learned why it was Sara expected me to be a girl, and seventeen years before I met my father in Los Angeles.

I guess every moment in life is a Moment Before, though, and all the moments of your life are one giant Moment Before you die.

Okay, that seems like kind of a dead end. Literally. I'm going to start over.

Let's try this again: I am looking at a photograph of my family and me. My family runs to girls. Everyone thought I would be a girl too, but I wasn't. In the photograph I am looking at, it's impossible to tell both what I am and what I might be.

What's sort of amazing, when you think about it, is that I was THERE for this moment. I know that my brain wasn't totally formed and everything, because brains can't form all the way inside the womb or our heads would be too big to get out. But I had access to sight and sound, even if in a limited way. I don't know how conscious I was, though. How conscious can you be if you haven't yet discovered your own feet?

It's impossible to know how much I know in this photograph. As Sara would say, all the studies and tests that are done are studies and tests that are thought up by people, and are only as good as the thoughts that produced them. There can be no definitive study of how a human being is, because there is no definitive human person to create the right test. She has a point, but it's kind of annoying. Like, you can't even say something like, "Studies show . . ." to Sara because she'll just say, "No studies have been done on the unthinkable, but the unthinkable still exists," or something like that.

I could probably tell you what everyone in this photo was saying right around when the picture was taken. It's not that I have any psychic abilities. But I've listened to all these people talk and I've noticed that people usually say the same kinds of things. I mean, the sentences are new, sometimes, but people don't often suddenly come out with some radical new way of expressing themselves, or have a total personality change.

Sometimes knowing all these people and listening to them and knowing what they aren't saying and why they aren't saying it, or why they're saying what they are, or what they're really saying when they are saying something else, is very . . . tiring.

There must have been a Moment Before for Sara too. A Moment Before it was just wonderful that she had a son instead of a daughter. A Moment Before she had found a way to make it okay that she had failed to live up to the family legacy. Maybe I'll try writing that.

Sara Prescott lies in bed. She feels really alone. Today is meant to be a day of joy for Sara, and she knows this, so Sara tells herself how joyous she really is. She keeps having to tell herself this. Because she cannot help it, Sara also thinks that what she really feels in this moment is not joy but the sensation of being pretty much royally ripped off. It is not in Sara's nature to nurture such a feeling. The worse she feels, the more joy she attempts to radiate.

Sara's mother is speaking now.

"Oh Caroline," Pauline is saying, as she sets a large vase of flowers upon a dresser crowded with statues of Buddha and Ganesh. "Just look at this beautiful arrangement! You have such an amazing gift."

"They are gorgeous, Linny," Sara says to her sister. "Thank you so much."

"Delight, happiness, gratitude," Sara tells herself, because a mantra is a good way to shut out unwelcome thoughts like how her mother always makes a HUGE deal over anything Linny does.

Nancy is talking now.

"I thought you'd be in hospital still," says Nancy.

Sara looks at her sister Nancy, who is sucking on the right earpiece of her glasses as if it were a pipe. Nancy has recently quit smoking so she's gained some weight. Sara now sees herself through Nancy's eyes: tired, messed-up hair, inaccurately fertile. Sara attempts to sit up straighter. Nancy doesn't know her, Sara tells herself. Not the real Sara, the true Sara, the joyous and grateful Sara.

"Oh I was in and OUT!" says Sara cheerily. "You know me!"

"You're a toughie," admits Nancy. The act of speaking flips her glasses up unexpectedly, the left earpiece nearly jamming itself in Nancy's nose.

Sara smiles.

Nancy removes her glasses from her mouth and pushes them into her hair.

"Unfortunately," Nancy says in her clipped way, "I gather your midwife rather bungled the home birth scenario?"

Sara reminds herself she is grateful that Nancy is here, because Nancy is always an opportunity to practice patience and compassion.

"Joyce could have managed everything just beautifully," Sara says firmly. "But she is young in her practice still, and even though this was my third time, it was really her first all on her own. She needs to grow in her confidence level. She did a wonderful job at the hospital. And the girls adore her."

"Oh Joyce," Nancy sniffs. "I saw this Joyce person. She let me in. I must say she looks incapable of delivering a newspaper, let alone a child."

This, although mean, lies close to Sara's own feelings about Joyce, who panicked and called for the ambulance, and cried, at which point Sara said, "Oh for God's sake, pull yourself together, Joyce." Resentment of Joyce is part of Sara's overall sense of being misled and denied. It is a relief to Sara to hear the inadequacies of her midwife safely voiced by her sister.

"Well!" Nancy continues. "You are the expert on popping these children out. One assumes you know what's best."

"Of course she knows what's best," Caroline says.

Caroline says this, as she says most things, vaguely, as if she weren't quite sure of the words, or their meaning, or to whom, in fact, she is actually speaking.

"Of course we are grateful that the child was born healthy and safe!" says Pauline, brightly, from her corner.

Sara wonders why she can never get a feeling of sisterhood going in a room full of women where most of the women are, in fact, her actual sisters.

"I'm going to be sick," thinks Sara. "No," Sara tells herself. "I'm fine. This is such a wonderful moment. I am so grateful for this moment." Sara scrambles for her mantra. "Delight. Happiness. Gratitude. Delight! Happiness! Gratitude!"

"Oh these flowers, Caroline!" cries out Pauline. "I just can't get over these flowers," she almost shouts.

The three sisters now turn and look at their mother, who is not actually looking at the flowers. Pauline is looking at herself in the mirror over the dresser, not in a vain way, but more as if she wants to make sure of what she looks like when she is in a state of not being able to get over the flowers.

"I have nothing to be ashamed about," Sara thinks. "Shame is not a choice I am going to accept. It was not a one-night stand. It was a moment of love."

"Where are the girls?" asks Caroline, looking around the room, as if just now noticing their absence.

"Joyce has them doing a puzzle," says Pauline. "I'll go get them."

"Mother is never as happy as when she discovers a legitimate reason to leave a room," says Nancy, after Pauline has left the room.

Nancy walks over to the pink and white cradle and peers down at its contents. "Do we have a name for the progeny? You were expecting a girl, of course."

Sara glances at a homemade sign scotch-taped to the wall over the cradle. A sign that had once said "Welcome to the World, Leila" and which had had to be altered by Joyce and a pair of scissors.

"I always thought that's why you smoked," says Caroline to Nancy, or rather, in the direction of Nancy. "You wanted a reason to leave a room."

Now the children run in: small Aurora, smaller Pearl. Pauline behind them, steering Pearl by the shoulders.

"Careful," says Pauline to Aurora, who is attempting to climb the bed.

"I know," says Aurora, working her toes into the space between box spring and mattress and hoisting herself upwards. Very carefully, Aurora puts her arms around her mother. Sara pats her daughter's back. "You have a baby brother!" she had told the girls when they were brought to the hospital room. "Are you mad, Mommy?" Aurora had asked.

Pearl stands at the foot of the bed and starts kicking it, not so hard as to be reprimanded, but hard enough to make her presence known.

Joyce comes into the room, carrying a camera.

"Oh, let's get out Baby," says Aurora. "And make a picture."

Joyce presses the shutter of the camera before everyone can get organized. People complain. "Take another one," they tell her. "When we're ready."

Luke is sweating. He deletes the last section of his writing from his computer.

"Whatever," Luke says to himself. "Whateverwhateverwhatever."

Luke feels that he has been very accurate in imagining the conscious and subconscious feelings of his mother. So accurate that it doesn't feel to Luke like imagination, and he experiences a keen sense of betrayal by his mother's Moments Before, by her mantra, by the effort it took her to accept him.

"But it doesn't matter," he tells himself. "Even if it is real."

Luke kicks off his shoes and does a handstand against the wall. He considers the nature of consciousness and the problems of other minds. He thinks that this might be something he could study more in college and he projects an image of himself engaging in serious intellectual debates over coffee, an image constructed out of other images: a visit to Pearl's dorm room, movies, dialogue from books.

It is not difficult, even for Luke, still inverted, to see why natural selection would favor an organism that recognized not only its own mind, but other minds as well: while Caveman Fug is showing his dwelling to Caveman Oog, he senses that Caveman Oog is envying the square footage of his dwelling. Caveman Fug then assumes a defensive posture or, possibly, deliberately depreciates his dwelling by pointing out the mildew and bat guano. Caveman Oog is appeased, and Caveman Fug lives long enough to pass on his genes. Imagination in this sense is useful for a complex organism that needs to defend itself from members of its own species. However, somewhere along the way this elegant and useful design feature of the brain has run a little amok, creating the possibility of an organism that can imagine the subconscious feelings of others in such a way as to inflict useless pain upon itself, and then avoid facing this pain by standing on its hands and theorizing abstractly on the nature of consciousness.

Luke flips himself upright.

Mark will be home soon from the studio. Luke walks into the living room. He likes to be doing something, when Mark comes home, to show that he's not an aimless teenager. He had planned on mowing his father's lawn earlier today, but just as he had begun a text—*where lawnmower?*—a truck had pulled up in front of the house. Jorge and Dave. Mark has gardeners. So Luke had watched two more episodes of *The Last* instead, catching up on the second season, courtesy of Mark's TiVo.

Luke now thinks through possibilities for the next hour: reading, more television, seeing what's in Mark's garage, jerking off, meditation. Luke examines the contents of the refrigerator. Everything, Luke has learned, is delivered premade, from Whole Foods. Tonight the plan is to grill on the brand-new grill: a pre-marinated steak for Mark, already cut-up and seasoned vegetables for Luke.

Luke prints out the beginning part of his Moment Before essay on Mark's printer, and leaves the writing, along with the photographs, on Mark's desk. When his father comes home, Luke is outside, studying the instruction manual he found on top of the grill. Mark puts him in charge of dinner and Luke is glad to have a task to complete for his father. They eat outside on the patio, Mark praising Luke's skill. After dinner they watch *Heaven Can Wait*, on DVD, which Mark has said is one of his favorite movies. They sprawl in separate leather chairs, but share the leather ottoman. During humorous scenes they laugh, turning to see if the other is also laughing.

Mark and Luke's bare feet bump each other when they laugh. Mark's second toe is longer than the first. So is Luke's. Luke notices this and all the rumbling Moments Before of his day vanish with a soundless snap in the joy of this discovered fact. Luke involuntarily makes a sound, somewhere between "Hey!" and "Oh!" Mark, watching the movie, laughs. Their feet bump.

"I know," Mark says. "I love this part."

CHAPTER FOUR

My father's gym is on the top floor of an office building in Beverly Hills. When you pull into the parking structure, the valet attendant asks if you would like the car washed while you are visiting.

"Yeah, it's sort of a funny place," Mark explained to me the first time we went together. "But you have to be careful about where you work out in public. You can't have some idiot taking a picture of you with his phone while you're in the shower and posting it on the Internet."

Exclusive or not, I think that people must still be nervous about this at my father's gym because so far I've always had the entire changing room, shower, and steam room to myself.

I was intimidated, the first time we went together. I'm an athlete, but I'm not a "jock." At school, jocks are the guys who play lacrosse. I considered going out for lacrosse freshman year, but my sisters were against it.

"Only two kinds of guys play lacrosse," Pearl said. "Total douche bags and guys named Chad."

"So that leaves me out," I said.

"Well, you're definitely not a total douche," said Aurora. "But you should know that all Chads are not necessarily named Chad."

"Yeah," said Pearl. "A Chad is basically a decent-seeming guy, not cruel or an asshole. Technically, he never really does anything bad. He's usually pretty hot, too. But he actually has no soul. He is just imitating human behavior. He has no imagination. No real morality. I think you know what I'm talking about."

"Someone like Lee Wedman?" I asked.

"Lee Wedman is a total Chad," said Pearl.

So I joined the cross-country team. I'm also in the Archery Club. We began our workout today by running side by side on the treadmills.

"So I read your essay," Mark said. "What a trip. I love all your descriptions. I love how your aunt has a fake English accent."

We talked about that for a little bit, and then just ran some more.

"So you think your mom was expecting you to be a girl?" he asked.

"Yeah." I explained to him about Abigail Perkins and the legions of sisters, and Paul becoming Deepak.

"What a trip," he said again. "That's a lot of women. What about your grandfather? Nana's husband?"

"Dead for a long time," I said. "Blood clot."

Across the row of machines, I could see our reflections in the mirrors that line the gym walls. We don't look that much alike, although he says he used to be skinny like me. We are both left-handed, though, which no one else in my family is. We both have curly hair, although his is darker. We have the long-second-toe thing. Right now at least, I'm my father's son only at the extremities.

"So you think your mom, uh, got together with me because she really wanted a third daughter?" Mark asked. "Like it was a plan?"

"She's never said that," I told him. "I think it was more of a sub-conscious thing. But it makes sense if you put it all together."

"It wasn't a sleazy thing, you know," Mark said. "I really wasn't that kind of guy. And she was definitely not that kind of . . . it wasn't like some sort of seduction thing. I wanted to be with her. She wasn't bullshitting you when she said it was special."

"No, I know," I said. "She explained it all. Things just happen, you know?"

"There's usually more than one reason," he agreed. "How come she never got married again? She was really beautiful."

"I don't know. There's not really a whole lot of people in Delaware on her level. But she always says that she's happy in her friendships."

"Yeah, I get that. Hey, you're a really good writer."

"Thanks." I know I'm not a really good writer, but it was nice of him to say that. I wonder if anyone in the past seventeen years has said something to Mark like "You'd make a really good dad," or "Do you want to have kids someday?" I wonder what he thought of when that happened, if it happened.

"Hey Dad," I said.

"Yes, son."

Saying "dad" and "son" in funny voices is becoming a thing for us.

"You came and saw me after I was born, right?"

"Yeah," he said. "I did."

"So . . . what was that like? I mean, do you remember it?"

"Yeah, I remember it. Of course. To be honest, I was pretty freaked out.

"It was sort of a weird time in my life," he explained. "I didn't know how to handle it."

"Yeah," I said. "I don't blame you." I had imagined him freaked out. That seemed reasonable. I don't know why it was a little disap-pointing to hear him actually say it.

"I really," Mark looked at me. "I mean . . . I'm really glad you're here, Luke. In Los Angeles. But also, you know, *here*."

"Me too," I said.

"Anytime you feel like letting me read something, that's cool."

"It's pretty unorganized stuff at this point," I told him. "But, yeah, if you're interested, great."

"I'm totally interested. And thanks for bringing those pictures. I kept trying to picture you in Delaware but it was hard because I have no idea what Delaware looks like."

"No one does. People who drive through it don't even know that's what happened."

"Ha-ha. Well, it looks like a great place to grow up."

"Yeah."

"Okay, son," Mark said, in a deep booming voice, clapping me on the shoulder. "Let's get off these machines and later I'll show you how to shave."

Then he worked out with his personal trainer, and I did some free weights and sit-ups and pull-ups and stuff and then went back to the treadmill for more running. He still wasn't done so I hung out in the empty steam room and then sat in the empty Jacuzzi. I thought about what Mark said, and what he might be thinking about my life in Delaware, and what my family sounds like to him.

My family moved from New York City to Delaware when I was four, Pearl was almost six, and Aurora was seven. Sara told us that we were all going to live with Nana and where Nana lived there would be "space" and "nature," and we would be able to "greet the stars at night." Nana had a house with three floors and a yard. She had a dog. We would all have bikes. It was going to be beautiful.

Up until then, we had lived in the apartment that Sara and her husband Paul had lived in. Paul, of course, was gone. Pearl doesn't have any memories of him. Aurora says she remembers crawling under the dinner table in the New York apartment and playing with a man's shoes and of a man swinging her by the ankles, but she thinks these memories may be apocryphal.

"I did meet the Paul person, briefly," Aunt Nancy told me once, "coming through New York, just after Aurora was born. I must say the flat made rather more of an impression than the man. Well, I mean, really, four bedrooms on the Upper East Side. Upholstered walls. Quite gorgeous Chippendale furniture shoved into the corners, and your mother and her Jewish yogi making everyone sit on cushions. Carrying Aurora from room to room in some sort of Mexican basket affair. It was extraordinary. Mad, really."

Paul left us the apartment in New York City, because part of his transformation was to leave behind all the worldly trappings of his life as Paul in order to fully embrace his life as Deepak, and he would have no need of things like sofas or end tables in the ashram.

The problem was, those things weren't really Paul's to renounce because really they all belonged to Paul's mother. Paul's mother lived in Florida, because it was better for her health, so she didn't mind, but Paul also had a brother named Barry.

Barry, it turns out, was a man who had very strong feelings. And one of those feelings was that the apartment should be his now. He didn't choose to honor Paul's final decision as Paul. He chose to have anger.

So Sara and Barry had been discussing this issue of the apartment for many years, and people like How-Is-Louis had helped us very much with people like Barry's lawyer, and now everyone agreed that it was best that Barry should have the apartment back. And this was an extra-good thing because it had created this opportunity for us to go and live with Nana in Delaware, which would be beautiful. Nana lived alone in a big house that was definitely our family's house, and no one else's. Sara had grown up in it. Aunt Nancy and Aunt Caroline had grown up in it. We would grow up in it too. It was really too big a house for just Nana.

Nana's husband, our grandfather Prescott, was dead, like I said, and had been since Sara was little. He had gone to Ecuador to preach the Good News with a missionary group. Unfortunately, upon landing in Ecuador, he became very ill and died as a result of a blood clot in his leg, before ever converting a single Indian.

That was not quite the version I got initially, because it was my sisters who first told me about him.

"Grandfather was killed by Accordion Indians," Pearl whispered to me. We were all standing in the backyard of our new house, having been let out to play. None of us had ever stood in a backyard of our own before until we came to Delaware. There was a fence running the perimeter of the yard, but before you got to the fence there were a lot of trees, and a birdbath, and flower beds. There was even a shed with tools in it, but we had been told not to go inside that without a grown-up. We understood about not going into places without a grown-up. What surprised us was that Sara and Nana let us play outside by ourselves, and only came and checked on us once in awhile. In New York City we didn't play outside without grown-ups.

"Who got killed?" I asked.

"Our grandfather," said Pearl, pulling me by the elbow over to the birdbath, which was too high for me to look into. "Our mom's dad."

Aurora, who was nice about these things, lifted me up so I could look into the birdbath. Disappointingly, it was just a dish with water and a few leaves in it. I thought it might look more like our bath, with toys and soap bubbles.

"Our grandfather was a preacher," said Aurora. "Preacher Prescott."

"He went to preach to the Accordion Indians," whispered Pearl. "But they killed him."

That sounded very bad. Had the Indians squashed our grandfather with their accordions? (We had an alphabet book, one of those ones meant for "gifted" children, which featured the fine arts for the letters: "B" for "Bassoon" and "E" for "Easel." "A" was for "Accordion.")

"They didn't kill him," said Aurora. "He died before he got to the Accordion Indians. His leg got sick and all the blood got stuck in his leg and that's how he died."

"The Accordions would have gotten him anyway," said Pearl.

"Probably," said Aurora.

I wanted to go inside and ask Sara if I could give the birds my Froggy sponge to play with, but just then Aurora and Pearl started hopping around the birdbath and hooting.

"We are Accordion Indians!" sang Aurora. "We are wild girls! Wild girls!"

"And we'll kill you!" shouted Pearl, crouching down on the ground and growling.

Aurora hopped on one foot and looked at Pearl.

"No," said Aurora. "We're shy. We hide in the trees."

And they danced off to one of the trees, and I hopped along with them, but they said no, I had to be Grandfather Prescott. (I was always being given parts like this.)

By the end of the week, we had modified and perfected this game, which mostly consisted of me watching Aurora and Pearl run around and make noises (they were very enthusiastic accordionists) until it was time for my big moment. Then I got to run in front of them and shout, "Good News! Good News!" And then, "My Leg! My Leg!" and fall down. Then Aurora and Pearl would pick me up (my favorite part) and carry me around for awhile and put me behind the tool shed. Then they threw grass at me. At a certain point, Pearl would demand that we leave because the tool shed and everything in it belonged to her. Aurora would pick me up again (hooray!) and then we all went into the side yard, which was "Florida" and which was where you went for better health.

I don't think I got this all sorted out until I learned about Ecuador when we got to Geography in fourth grade.

Grandfather Prescott died when Sara was little, so she never had a father around either. Mark's father left when Mark was four. I don't know if his father is alive. I don't know if Mark even knows.

I guess it's best not to get stuck on what you think things are, or how they happened, or why. We should remain as detached as possible. Maybe for a second, when a caterpillar emerges from its cocoon, there is a moment when it freaks out and thinks, "Hey, what's happened? What are these wing things for? What happened to all my little legs?" but then it just flies away. That's how we should be, as people. We should be ready for everything to change.

After we finished at the gym today, we went back to the house so Mark could shower and make phone calls. I met Carmen, Mark's cleaning lady, and tried out my Spanish on her. Then we went for lunch. When we are out in public Mark always wears a baseball cap pulled low over his eyes. At the restaurant he sat with his back to the other diners, facing me. After lunch, we visited the Griffith Park Observatory. I'm glad he's also someone who likes to take his time looking at things, and reading about them.

"I'm a closet nerd," he said.

"Me too," I told him. "Well, maybe not a closet nerd. I'm probably an obvious nerd."

"You're obviously cool," he said. "They get that, right? At your school? They get how cool you are?"

"Well, it's easy for me," I assured him. "Because of my sisters. Everybody wanted to be friends with Aurora because she's so nice. And everybody wanted to be friends with Pearl because she's scary. So by the time I showed up for stuff everybody just figured I was okay too."

I think this is mostly true. Sometimes girls will tell me that I'm not like "other guys," but that's probably a product of my sisters too. The whole not-being-a-Chad thing. I wonder what kind of guy Mark was in school.

I told Mark that when I was little, I thought the sky was the ceiling of the planet, like a dome that protected the planet from outer space, and us from falling into it. And that I kept on thinking of it like that for a long time, even after I understood some basic science. Then one day, I looked up into the sky and REALLY understood that the only thing between outer space and me was space. And that we are glued to the earth because of gravity and that gravity is a constant force. There was never any dome at all, just a perception of a dome.

"What do you mean?" he asked. "Are you saying there's not a dome? Shit!"

I couldn't help noticing that in spite of the baseball cap there was a certain amount of double takes, nudges, whispered conversations—"Is that . . . ?"—happening around us. A couple of times I thought people were going to come up to Mark, but nobody did.

"God, a totally normal day," he said during the car ride back to the house. "Great, huh? Let's get Slurpees. I haven't had a Slurpee in forever."

I agreed that it had been great although almost nothing about it had really been normal for me. Two weeks ago, I had never sat in a jade steam room, never experienced valet parking, never been taught about the enlivening powers of Tabasco Sauce from my father, never been taught anything by a father. I had never spoken Spanish with someone from Mexico, never stared at live images of the sun, never known how much I weigh on Jupiter, never been sent into a 7-Eleven to get two Slurpees.

"You know," Mark said, when I got back to the car, "back to what you said about gravity? I have to admit gravity kind of freaks me out. I don't get it. I mean, I get it, but it seems impossible, sort of. I would have been one of the people saying, 'Hell no. The earth is flat.' "

"Me too," I said. "Although you have to go with the idea that makes sense of A LOT of things, not just what makes sense for you personally, right? People tell you to trust your instincts, but . . ."

"When people tell you to trust your instincts it just means they have no clue either," Mark said.

"Yeah," I said, sucking at my Slurpee. "Yeah."

The attraction between two bodies is proportional to their masses. This is the law of gravity, but there is nothing in the law that tell us WHY that should be so.

I agree with Mark. Thinking about gravity, really thinking about it, can kind of freak you out.

Actually, Luke *still* mostly feels that the sky is a kind of protective dome. In many instances he has been able to replace intuition with acquired knowledge, but in this case he has failed. However, he is prepared to accept that what he feels is wrong, and what science has proved is correct.

Luke had spent the day watching. He watched his father watch his own reflection in the mirrors at the gym, watched the couple sitting next to them at lunch watch his father eat a frittata, watched his father watch himself, Luke, at the observatory. Luke had watched the sun. He located the signals being sent to him, around him, for him. Luke experienced happiness in meeting those signals successfully. He enjoyed his father's enjoyment of the Slurpee, and his father's enjoyment of Luke's enjoyment of his own Slurpee.

He enjoyed seeing his father recognized, enjoyed feeling slightly famous himself, enjoyed feeling that he was the person whom Mark *wanted* to talk to.

Later that evening, as Luke was getting ready for bed, Mark came into Luke's room holding a leather jacket.

"I just found this in my closet," Mark says. "Here. Try it on."

"It'll be huge on me," says Luke, but, "No, it's small on me," says Mark, and so Luke puts it on. It fits perfectly.

"It's yours," says Mark. "It looks way better on you, man."

Luke has never owned anything made of real leather. His Nana does not have a problem with leather (God gave Adam and Eve coats of skins to wear, John the Baptist wore leather, etc.), but Sara prefers natural or micro fibers. Luke has only bought a few of his own clothes, and he has yet to consider where he personally stands on the ethics of leather.

"Good night." Mark puts a hand on Luke's leather-clad shoulder and jostles it slightly. "Thanks for today." Mark leaves.

Luke stands in the bedroom that he now thinks of as "his" bedroom and inhales the scent of the jacket. He puts his hands inside the jacket pockets, discovers a coin in the right one. He holds the coin hard in his hand, turns it over and over, rubs it between his thumb and forefinger. Luke experiences a sudden rush of emotion: a tightening and throbbing in his throat, as if his throat were a cocoon for something alive, something with a hundred little legs. Luke thinks for a moment that he might cry, half laughs at himself, takes the jacket off, and hangs it carefully in his closet.

CHAPTER FIVE

Okay, so your mom and your sisters," Mark said to me at the gym this morning. "I'm getting them. What about your Nana, though? What's her deal? She's religious or something?"

"They're called the New Plymouth Brethren," I explained. "It's kind of a splinter cell from the regular Plymouth Brethren, who are really fundamentalist."

"You go to church?"

"They call it Assembly. Yeah, I go. We all used to go. Well, not Sara. But us kids. For awhile. It's kind of complicated."

I told him I would try an essay about Nana today, while he was at work. Then I'm going to go for a bike ride in Griffith Park. He's got a regular Schwinn twelve-speed in the garage, along with the most awesome dirt bike ever. I explored the garage yesterday. There are all kinds of things in there. The dirt bike is brand-new. He hasn't even ridden it yet.

"Oh yeah," he said. "That was part of some gift basket."

"Someone sent you the Z250 in a gift basket? That's like a six-thousand-dollar bike."

"Well, not *in* it. You get all this stuff. Kati deals with most of it. Take whatever you want in there."

It's kind of crazy. There are *bags* of stuff in there. Watches, sneakers, cameras, game systems. I might set up the Wii for us later on, if I have time.

Okay. Essay. This will be more fun, now that I know Mark will be reading it.

There was actually an example of a grandmother story in *50 Successful College Application Essays*. But that girl's grandmother had been a Holocaust survivor.

My grandmother was the first adult woman I saw fully naked.

That sounds really bad. It wasn't a sexual thing. I was four and we had only just moved in with her.

All right, so I have an extremely clear memory of my Nana's breasts and pubic hair. Her breasts were oblong. I mean the skin went down a little ways before it made the round part. And her pubic hair was mostly grey, and it spread—or seemed to—across to the tops of her legs.

It was probably about two seconds (maybe less) of actual viewing time and I don't remember feeling alarmed or ashamed or anything like that. But the event must have been sufficiently impressive to the cells of my body, and I guess some sort of learning moment occurred, and I remember it. Not only that, but I assumed, for a long time, that breasts came in an oblong structure and that pubic hair was mostly grey and there was a lot of it. "Assumed" is the wrong word. It's sort of like my early feelings about the dome over our planet. I KNOW that women have different-shaped breasts. I've seen the Kama Sutra, and R-rated movies, stuff on the Internet, and come on, I have SISTERS. It's just that the initial sort of mental picture that often comes up when someone says "nude" or "naked" is this image of my naked

Nana. It's weirdly hard to unknow what you know even when what you know is wrong. Even weirder is: it's MY brain that's making these images of Nana appear even when it's also MY brain that knows better. People write books or make movies about people losing control over computers, and the machines going rogue or becoming evil, but our own brains are computers, and we don't seem to be able to control those very well. Our entire lives are operating, if you really think about it, on a rogue program.

So anyway, there I was, age four, gazing up at her, and Nana calmly whipped out a towel and her eyes sort of swiveled and locked on mine, and there it was for the first time, the special look of Nana's that has since been dubbed the Sword of Silence.

It's like a superpower she has.

<u>Sword of Silence Meanings</u>
NO
I did not hear that
I did not see that
YOU did not hear or see that
To ask further questions would be insanity on your part

Interpreting the Sword of Silence has always been my special knack. Even though I was only four, I knew what it meant. The towel Nana took up was unnecessary—a gesture to convention, or maybe Nana was chilly. Because Nana was not really naked, I was not really looking at her, and even my own existence and hers was in doubt. It simply was not happening. The sword can only cut so deep, though, I guess, since I still remember it vividly, and she surely meant to swipe my brain clean of it entirely.

"The Sword of Silence" as a term came into use a couple of years later between us three kids, once Aurora and Pearl and I had all received the as-yet-unnamed sword and had discussed it amongst ourselves. Pronouncing the "w" in "sword" when we say it is another thing we do, along with using the word "sworded" as a verb. As in, "Nana sworded me." Nana often smiles when she swords you. It's this very helpful sort of smile. As if to say, Here, let me aid you in your confused ways by evaporating them. It's not necessarily violent, but it's powerful. Aurora wore an "Evolution Rocks" T-shirt to the breakfast table once and she swears Nana sworded it so hard she actually faded the material. Aurora went up to her room and put a sweater over the T-shirt before coming back to breakfast.

That's the thing with the sword. Mostly you obey it because you don't want to push Nana. Pushing Nana would be like pulling the wings off a butterfly, or knocking over a little kid's ice cream cone, or something deliberately cruel like that. Sometimes you obey it because you know that Nana really needs it, for her own piece of mind, and since she never asks for anything, you feel like, "Okay, whatever." That's why I obey it, anyway.

I'm not sure that Sara was totally clear on how religious Nana had gotten when we all moved in with her. I don't remember any big discussions about going to Assembly. It was just something that happened. Nana would take us three kids while Sara did other things. Sara is really good at honoring other people's beliefs, though, and for her rare cameo appearances at Assembly she was always very respectful.

Nana hoped that we would all experience getting Saved. My sisters and I heard stories of other Brethrens' Savings. Talking about your moment of Salvation is a big thing in Assembly. Normally the Brethren are a fairly quiet bunch, but they can get excited when talking about their special moment. Once, Mrs. Potts, who was Saved in the parking lot of Linens 'n Things, got so emotional when recounting her tale that she lost her grip on her Bible and it went whipping across the room and smote Mr. Federmeier on the forehead.

But when I about ten, Sara and Nana had some sort of Discussion, and Sara told Aurora that none of us kids had to go with Nana to Assembly anymore, if we didn't want to.

Aurora and Pearl summoned me to a conference in their room to discuss this.

"Sara says we are old enough to choose," Aurora began. "And I guess Nana agreed to that. So who's choosing to go?"

Pearl passed around contraband Twizzlers and we considered this question.

"I don't think we should all stop going at once," Aurora said. "We might want to work into it gradually, one by one."

"Nana is gonna sword us," is what Pearl said. "How bad do you think it'll be? The kind where she just doesn't talk about it, or the kind where she looks at you like you just farted during Grace? Or total silent treatment?" Total silent treatment was the height of swording, and pretty uncomfortable.

The upshot of the whole discussion was that Aurora would leave first. That way, Pearl and I would have a chance to assess the level of swording and weigh the pros and cons of the whole thing. Pearl and I thought Rory pretty heroic for offering herself like that.

At that point I wasn't aware that any of us had any problems with going to Assembly. I didn't think that going was such a big deal. It wasn't like anything was expected of us. In some ways it was like going to a meditation session with Sara: you went, you sat, maybe you repeated some chants or prayers, you listened or thought your own thoughts.

Aurora was the first to really voice philosophical dissent with Christianity, although her objections were more of a style nature: she simply preferred the kinds of things Sara would read to us. So the virgin Mary was visited by an angel and ended up pregnant? So what? A similar sort of thing happens in the Mahabharata, only in a much more exciting way. The mortal Kunti is practicing her mantra and then the God Lord Surya appears and the next day Kunti bears his son, who is born wearing earrings and golden armor.

The swording of Aurora was not terrible. On the next Sunday, Sara and Rory were out of the house early and away for most of the day. Pearl and I went with Nana to Assembly as usual. When one of the New Brethren asked Nana where Aurora was, Nana replied, "Aurora will be spending some time with her mother for awhile." The way Nana said it, it sounded like some sort of grave punishment was being enacted, and no more questions were asked. Later that night, at dinner, Nana did not speak to Aurora. We were all a little nervous about this, but the next morning Nana was her usual self, and treated Rory just like normal.

Pearl stopped going to Assembly once she got to high school, but I think it was almost because the New Brethren weren't Christian *enough* for Pearl. Even though she considers fundamentalism to be naive, anti-intellectualist, and anti-women, it's at least *serious*. Like, she doesn't call herself a Christian, but she thinks if you do, you should pony up and really *believe*.

"Whatever else you want to say about these fundamentalists," Pearl has said, "they are at least committed. They don't pick and choose which parts of Scripture to believe, like they're picking through a salad. They eat the whole thing. Give me an honest lunatic over a mush-mouth pseudo-Christian any day."

Nana and I get along really smoothly. I do a lot of things with her. I'm her helper. Sometimes she says things like, "I rely on you, Luke," or "I know you are going to see the Light, Luke, and I pray for you every day." I don't say anything back to this, but I nod. I see it as a nod of agreement: I agree that Nana prays for me, and I agree she believes I will see the Light. Okay, sure, whatever.

There have been some interesting theories floating around lately about what has been called "the God Gene." Its actual name is VMAT2. VMAT2 codes for a protein that affects levels of serotonin and dopamine in the brain, and studies have shown that it's those levels that might account for mystical and spiritual feelings. If VMAT2 does have something to do with belief in the supernatural, then belief in God is something that could be, at least partially, heritable. And so then you have to think about whether it's something that's been selected because it confers an advantage. Maybe people who believe in God do better than people that don't. People who believe in "Love Thy Neighbor," for example, maybe do better than people that believe in "Tell thy neighbor to suck it." Or, people who believe that there is an afterlife, or a meaning to their existence, are maybe happier than people who think it's all just random and they are food for worms. Happy people have more babies, and therefore pass on more VMAT2.

Of course, when you think about it, the most religious people are the ones who are always telling their neighbor to suck it, if their neighbor doesn't agree with them. Telling someone to suck it in the name of God is, like, most of history. And suicide bombers are obviously not passing along any VMAT2. Maybe suicide bombers have too much VMAT2, or not enough of something else that would regulate it, and the problem should be treated like the way we treat diabetics. If we can capture one before they complete their mission, we shouldn't interrogate them. We should stick them in an fMRI machine, ask them to think about God, and see what lights up.

Of course, you don't talk about these things with Nana, or with Sara, for that matter. There's the whole "Studies show . . ." problem with Sara, and Nana would not welcome the idea that belief in God is something hardwired, like opposable thumbs or hair color. Some Christians argue that a gene for believing in God doesn't disprove an actual God because God could have created the gene to help matters along, like His decision to create the Big Bang and Darwin's brain. So they would say that Darwin's brain is a secondary cause of the first cause, which is God.

My biology teacher, Mr. Stoddard, gave a speech about "non-overlapping magisteria" before he taught us evolution. This is a theory developed by the biologist Stephen Jay Gould. It's like a separation of powers. You say that science and theology have separate areas of expertise, and that you should let each side do its business. Science shouldn't interfere with questions of morality and ethics, and

Religion shouldn't try to explain physical phenomena. Mr. Stoddard said that if everybody agreed to stay on their side of the fence, then there would be no problems. I think it's a pretty flawed argument, but we didn't have any problems in my AP Biology class. However, there were only eleven of us, and we were being graded.

A gene that has something to do with mystical feelings seems reasonable enough to me. And so maybe atheism is an attempt to override a natural instinct. Unless you are missing that gene, and then your atheism isn't a choice, it's biological. But of course having a gene doesn't mean you'll have what it codes for. A whole bunch of other genes have to be in place supporting it.

Maybe Abigail Perkins didn't believe in God and that's why they thought she was a witch and there is a secret history of nonbelievers in my family, passing along a genetic sequence with no VMAT2. Maybe this whole line of thinking is ridiculous.

I think we should all help our neighbors. I am also happy if my remains provide food for worms. Everybody has to eat.

Luke imagines his father reading this last sentence and laughing. He does not think Mark can be very religious, considering the fact that he says things like "Jesus fucking Christ." Luke takes his laptop into his father's office so he can hook it up to the printer.

Mark's office, like the rest of the house, has a surgical neatness to it, although there are a few personal objects in this room. Luke thinks he would like to have an office just like this, with everything at right angles to other things. Luke has already examined all of his father's books, which are mostly about film, or acting technique, or plays, or actors. He has also inspected the six framed photographs mounted on the wall opposite the bookcase: one large photo of the cast of *The Last,* and five smaller ones of Mark in costume for various roles, standing or sitting with people even more famous than he is. Luke's favorite is the one where Mark is pretending to lose an arm-wrestling match to the old British actor whose name Luke always confuses with another old British actor.

Luke sees the pile of photographs he had given his father in a neat stack next to the printer. On top is the one of Luke, in his cross-country shorts and T-shirt, the number 23 on his chest, leading the pack at the invitational against Elmwood High last year.

While the Nana essay is printing, Luke wanders into the hallway and pauses outside his father's bedroom door, which is shut. He had a glimpse inside this room when Mark first showed him around the house, but Luke had been watching his father show things, rather than looking at what was being shown. He can only remember a big bed and some kind of artwork above it.

Luke wants to look in his father's room. He puts his hand on the doorknob. For a moment he imagines that Mark has rigged some kind of booby trap over the door, a jar of marbles, or a net, and that he will get caught snooping and Mark will send him back to Delaware in disgust. Luke tries for a few moments to think of a plausible excuse for going in his father's room, but cannot think of any. He also does not want to try the doorknob, in case he finds the door is locked, which would hurt his feelings.

"I wanted to see inside your room," Luke now imagines himself saying to Mark. "I wanted to find out more about you because you keep asking me about me, but you never really tell me anything about yourself and we're supposed to be getting to know each other, not just you knowing me."

Luke turns the doorknob and opens the door slightly. Nothing falls. Because his father has not rigged the door, or locked it, Luke feels that it would be more noble not to look inside. He shuts the door quietly. You could misinterpret the significance of objects really easily, he reminds himself. If he hadn't known that his father had been given boxes of things as gifts he might have looked in the garage and thought his father was some kind of thief, because who kept eight boxes of expensive watches in their garage? And if he tells Mark later, "I wanted to look in your room, but I didn't," that will be much better. Because that would be evidence that Mark could trust him.

Luke believes in having evidence. Without evidence, you just have hope, which is nice, but not reliable.

Luke does not tell his father about wanting to look in his room, but when Mark informs Luke the following morning that he wants Luke to meet the girl he has been seeing, that he's made plans for them all to go to dinner that evening, Luke feels that his respect for his father's privacy has been rewarded by this inclusion of Luke into Mark's personal life. So far the only friends of Mark that Luke has met have been the people that work for Mark.

"She's great," Mark says. "Aimee. You'll like her."

"My sort-of-ex-girlfriend's name is Amy," Luke tells him.

"Sort of?"

"Mostly we just hung out in a group," Luke explains. "As friends. But sometimes we . . . kind of . . ."

"Does she spell her name with two 'e's?"

"With a 'y,'" Luke says. "Where does your Amy put the 'e's?"

"At the end." Mark shrugs. "There's also an 'i' in there. What happened with Amy with a 'y'?"

Luke shrugs.

"Yeah," Mark sighs. "I hear you. That happens."

Luke is getting ready for this dinner now, physically at least, although mentally he feels a little unprepared. Luke puts on the vintage shirt Aurora gave him for his birthday. Mark had said, "Dinner is casual, jeans are okay," so Luke puts on the nicest of his jeans. He goes back to the bathroom and gingerly applies a few fingertips' worth of Aveda Anti-Humectant to his hair. Mark had stocked Luke's bathroom with a number of products. All his life Luke had shared a bathroom with his sisters, and thus carried a basic assumption that anything with writing in cursive on it was not for him, avoiding pretty much everything but toothpaste, floss, and hand soap. Some of the products Mark has gotten him have writing in cursive, but the cursive says "For Men," or "pour les hommes." Luke really likes his bathroom, and makes an uncharacteristic effort to keep it neat.

Luke decides to wear the leather jacket Mark gave him. He notices for the first time that the label inside the jacket says "Gucci."

In the living room, Luke finds his father sprawled in one of the leather armchairs, watching the Discovery Channel.

"Am I okay?" Luke asks, indicating his clothes. "Do I need a tie or something?"

"You look great. Don't change a thing. Aimee is going to be late." Mark reads a text off his phone. "Traffic."

They are not picking Aimee up. She is driving over herself, and then Mark will drive them all to the restaurant. Luke wonders if this is because Aimee is going to spend the night. His father has not said anything about that, and Luke wonders if he should say something himself, let Mark know it is okay.

Sara has had occasional "men in her life," but they stayed on the periphery of Luke's visual field, in other cities, or mixed in with the group of his mother's friends. They never spent the night. Luke does not think that Sara has ever been actually "in love" with any of her male friends, although he's not sure that he would know what that would look like anyway, since Sara is a very loving person in general. Luke has never seen Nana "in love" except with God, or Aurora "in love" except with ideas. He has seen Pearl "in love," but that had been indistinguishable to Luke from Pearl "in hate." He has not been "in love" himself. Luke is not quite sure how he should treat Aimee, as someone significant, or not.

Luke and Mark watch the Discovery Channel and learn that all the female wildebeests in the Serengeti ovulate in the same week. Luke tells Mark that this can happen with human females that live together, and that the phenomenon is called "the Wellesley Effect," after the college where the research was conducted.

"Does that happen in your house?" Mark asks.

"Around the fifth of every month," Luke sighs. "Everybody gets a headache and cries if they drop something. Sara's got some kind of tea that she makes for it, though."

They watch the wildebeests' annual migration, which includes a dangerous plunge across a crocodile-filled Nile.

"Whoa," they say, simultaneously.

Aimee arrives at last. Mark greets her at the door, saying something Luke can't quite hear. Luke stands up. Aimee is tall. She is wearing shoes with heels, high heels, but Luke estimates that even in bare feet she must be at least five feet ten. She is glossy and gold and white and when she takes the two steps down into the living room, her bracelets jangle, her high heels click.

"A Christmas ornament," Luke thinks confusedly, and then, looking at her slender ankles, "A reindeer with bells on."

"Hey there!" says Aimee. "You must be Luke."

"Hi," says Luke, holding out a hand. "It's nice to meet you."

"It's nice to meet *you*," she says, advancing on him melodiously. Luke wonders if Aimee is going to kiss his cheek, like she had his father's. Luke feels panic, then disappointment, as Aimee simply shakes his hand.

"You look gorgeous," Mark says to Aimee. "That's a killer dress."

"Omigod," says Aimee, launching into a story about the dress. It had seemed so simple on the hanger, but once in the dressing room, Aimee had come undone. She had not known which way was front, which way was back, whether to slide it over her head, or step into it. The dress had a lining too, which complicated matters, and the hooks were meant to go on the *side*.

"I'm used to people just shoving things on me," she says, to Luke. "If you put me in a dressing room by myself I'm a mess."

"Don't believe her," Mark says to Luke. "She's the least helpless person I know."

"Oh shut up, you." Aimee puts her hands on her silky hips.

"Luke, your dad gives me such a hard time. I need you to be on my side, tonight, okay?"

Luke nods. He is trying not to imagine a naked Aimee in a dressing room.

"So is that the real reason you were late?" Mark asks. "You were stuck inside your dress?"

"Hello! Traffic!" Aimee shrieks, launching into another tale, about the guy who had cut her off on Melrose, about how men can never understand the difficulty of driving in heels, about dropping her phone under the seat while she had been trying to text them, about the gymnastic move she had had to execute in order to retrieve the phone.

Luke listens, laughs, relaxes. He does not think Aimee will require complicated signal decoding. She reminds Luke of a certain type of pretty girl at his school in Delaware. He knows girls of this order require a high amount of communication, and it is helpful to keep straight all the subtle fluctuations of friendship that happen with their girlfriends ("I'm over Janis, she's being totally judgmental about Carrie and Kyle"), but that is not difficult for Luke. This Aimee is taller, more glamorous, and older than Delaware Amy, but Luke feels he has got her general archetype in hand.

"Okay, let me look at the two of you side by side," says Aimee.

Smiling, Mark moves to stand beside Luke. Mark poses, shifting his weight to one leg, crossing his arms in front of his chest, raising his chin and cocking it at an angle. After a second, Luke imitates the stance, puffing out his chest.

Aimee laughs.

"Omigod, Mark, he looks just like you. But, did you teach him a face?"

"A face?" asks Luke. He likes Aimee very much, for saying that he looks like Mark.

"A photo face," says Mark. "Aimee showed me how to do it. Observe."

Luke turns to his father. Mark lowers his chin, narrows his eyes, half-raises one eyebrow, and slightly curls the corner of the opposite lip.

"Wow," says Luke. "That's pretty impressive." He thinks that his father looks cool, and tough, and like he's doing you a favor by smiling. Luke would like to have this face in his arsenal.

"See how I maintain photo face while in motion," Mark says, through his teeth, swiveling about on one foot. "Incredibly, I am able to move laterally in a 180-degree arc while still maintaining my sexy eyebrow thing."

"You have to get one." Aimee taps Luke lightly on the shoulder. "Now that you're in LA you need to get your camera face." Aimee rolls her reindeer eyes at Luke. "I'm kidding, of course. Just be yourself."

"It's impossible for Luke to be anything but himself," says Mark. "He doesn't have a fake bone in his body."

"See?" demands Aimee, to Luke. "That's his passive-aggressive way of telling me I'm fake."

"No, that's my way of admitting that *I'm* a fake," says Mark.

The restaurant next to the restaurant they are going to is lit up in front with a row of lights and an abbreviated red carpet, backed by a temporary cardboard wall, advertising something Luke has never heard of. Photographers are clustered around this, and behind them, little clusters of people. Seeing this, Mark says, "Ugh." A valet attendant leaps forward at the car, but there is an immediate swarming action of photographers from the other restaurant toward them.

Two large and impassive-faced men sporting secret service–style gadgetry step forward from behind the valet, holding out their arms, nodding at Mark. Wires connected to earpieces disappear into the back collars of their dark suits.

Luke had constructed a similar device for himself as part of his Halloween costume last year. He had dressed up as a bodyguard to go with Amy's costume as Vampire Paris Hilton. They had gone to the school's "Vampire Dance" as friends, although they weren't really that, either. Luke's social position in school *is* somewhat fluid, and while he was at that point mildly friendly with some of Amy's circle, he had never talked to Amy much beyond a few exchanged quips during English class. Luke had not considered asking Amy out. He had been thinking he might ask out Keiko, who was in the Archery Club with him, and had been his lab partner in AP Chemistry.

But, "What are you going as for Halloween?" Amy had asked him one day in October, before English.

"I don't know," Luke had said. "I always used to do something with my sisters, but they're both at college now. Last year Pearl and I went as Che Guevara and Frida Kahlo."

"Pearl was always really creative," said Amy. "I remember when she and Aurora went as beauty pageant contestants, only they had, like, pieces of meat glued on them."

The meat had actually been soy bacon, and needed to be taped on, as attempts at rubber cementing had failed.

"I was Donald Trump that year," Luke offered.

Amy laughed.

"So what about you?" he had asked.

"Well, Kristin and I were going to go as sort of Vampire Paris Hilton and Lindsay Lohan. But now Kristin is going out with Matt, and they're doing something together. I guess I could still go as Vampire Paris by myself. To school, I mean. I don't want to go to the dance by myself."

"I could go as Vampire Lindsay with you," Luke joked. "That would be scary."

From there it had been a simple matter to arrange that Luke would bring Amy to the dance, dressed as her official bodyguard. She loved that Luke got so into it, getting a huge suit jacket from Goodwill and stuffing the shoulders and chest to make himself appear suitably imposing. Creating the earpiece out of an old rotary telephone cord. Escorting her to all her classes during the day, instructing other students to stand back, keep away, Miss Hilton had no comment. At the dance, Amy had dropped the real Louis Vuitton handbag (containing the fake stuffed dog wearing a rhinestone collar) in order to put both her hands on Luke's back as they slow-danced. She had rested her head against Luke's stuffed chest, and asked him if he would be her bodyguard every day, it had been so much fun.

"Okay," Luke had said, tentatively. "I'll protect you."

And Amy had pulled Luke into her group, where he was generally considered her boyfriend, although Amy herself had asked that they "keep it casual." In practice, this meant that Luke never knew whether an evening with Amy would end with a chaste hug or something more dynamic. The bodyguard image had been difficult to maintain. In his home life, Luke understood that while he was technically "the man" of his house, in reality this entailed not that he protect his women from the world at large, but that he protect his women, systematically and specifically, from each other. Executive power on his part was not needed, nor would it have been tolerated. Luke's dominant attributes—understanding, empathy, compassion, his disinclination to be judgmental or demanding—had never really been the right sort of thing for Amy, who desired firmness, decision making, aggression. He is almost aware of this.

Now, paused in front of the restaurant, Luke observes his father, who is not significantly, in terms of width, much smaller than these actual bodyguards; his father who has impersonated bodyguards in movies without the need of padding; his father who is now confidently presenting his "photo face" for the cameras, one hand on the back of Aimee's slim back.

"Mark! Over here! Mark! Aimee!"

Luke hovers behind, until Mark looks over his shoulder, releases Aimee and moves beside Luke. Aimee, solo, pivots so the paparazzi can photograph the back of her dress.

"Who's the kid, Mark?" someone calls out.

"My son, Luke," Mark answers, and slings an arm around Luke's shoulders, which are still covered by the leather of Mark's old jacket.

Luke smiles blindly into the flashing lights. To his surprise, someone calls out his name.

"Luke! Over here!"

"You okay?" Mark mutters, through his teeth.

"Quiet. I'm making a face," Luke mutters back. Mark doesn't laugh, because he's making a face too, but he squeezes Luke's shoulder appreciatively.

Inside the restaurant, they are greeted by a collection of sari-clad women.

"Good evening, Mr. Franco, we have the cabana table ready for you."

The restaurant is a large square, broken up into different levels by platforms and hanging curtains. The right side of the square descends into a crowded bar area. The cabana table is a three-sided banquette arrangement, with swags of fabric looped back in such a way as to indicate privacy without actually granting it. Mark guides Aimee into the middle seat. Luke and his father sit facing each other.

"Sit next to me," says Aimee, patting the place next to her.

"Not enough room for my manly frame," says Mark, but he scoots a few inches down, and Aimee scoots a few inches left, so they are wedged into the corner. The pose gives them, like the curtains surrounding their table, an impression of intimacy. Aimee shimmies under Mark's arm, and places her cell phone on the table next to her water glass. Mark rubs Aimee's bare shoulder, and puts his cell phone on the table next to his napkin.

Luke asks Aimee some questions about herself. He discovers with minimal prompting that Aimee is from Portland, Oregon, and has three brothers, five nieces, two nephews, and a pug named Misty. She spent a year in Paris, but she's too curvy for runway modeling, is not willing to starve herself, and believes it is better to be in Los

Angeles where there's more work for her "look" and where she can get more into acting. She turns down roles if they are too slutty, but is sometimes told that she is too "sexy" for parts that she wants, so there is a certain amount of frustration involved. She is a Pisces, likes red meat and eggs although pretends to be vegan in public, ascribes her vague religious beliefs to Buddhism.

Aimee checks in with her cell phone repeatedly, reading texts and tapping out replies, occasionally flipping the phone around to show Luke a picture of the nieces, of rock formations in Joshua Tree where she shot a car commercial last week, of Misty. Luke demonstrates an ability to retain the names of Aimee's friends and relatives, and nods sympathetically to the difficulties imposed on Aimee by the vagaries of modeling agents, casting directors, and "the media." Encouraged, Aimee abandons her corner and slides closer to Luke to show him more pictures: of friends, of herself sporting a head full of giant rollers, of Misty in different poses.

Mark orders dessert for Luke and coffee for himself. Aimee slides back around to Mark and pummels his chest.

"You've totally let me talk my head off," she says accusingly. "Look how I've completely bored your son." Aimee shimmies under Mark's arm again, who kisses the top of her head but says nothing.

Throughout dinner, Luke has been thinking over his relationship with his own Amy. He would most likely NOT have gone out with Amy if Pearl had been around to observe and comment. Pearl would have denounced Amy as being vapid and brainless, which Amy was not, and pointed out to Luke that Amy was only using him to get back at her ex-boyfriend, which was partially true. Luke had not even been particularly physically attracted to Amy. He had been attracted to Keiko, whose long black hair and skill at archery Luke had greatly admired. But without Pearl to hector him, Luke had been free to fall into what was relatively easy and carried no potential emotional cost.

Luke will often leave the part of dinner he most wants to eat until he has finished everything else, even things he doesn't like, delaying gratification until he feels he has sufficiently earned it.

Luke has been peripherally aware, throughout dinner, that his father has been systematically ripping the paper napkin his drink came on into little tiny balls, then aligning these balls into a geometric pattern next to his plate. When Aimee busies herself with a text, Luke points at the paper balls.

"What's that all about?" Luke asks with a smile.

Mark raises an eyebrow, lines up a paper ball, and shoots it with a flick of his thumb and second finger at Luke's chest. Mark then picks up his phone and taps out a text. After a moment, Luke's phone vibrates inside his leather jacket. Luke takes his phone out and reads a text from Mark.

Good grub but wish we home watchng Discov Chnl

Leaving the restaurant, they run the same gamut of photographers, shouting, "Mark!" and "Aimee!" just as before. In the car, Mark tells Aimee that he has an early-morning photo call for a magazine interview. Back at the house, Luke engineers a discreet fade into his bedroom to give Mark and Aimee time for whatever private goodbye ceremony they might need. Before he does, Aimee gives him a hug and a kiss on the cheek. Luke does not care for Aimee's perfume, and this distracts him from enjoying the embrace. Walking down the hallway, Luke hears Mark saying, "I'll walk you out" to Aimee, and before Luke has finished reading an email from Aurora, he hears his father reentering the house. Luke listens to Mark kicking off his shoes, tossing keys onto the little mosaic tile table in the foyer, and padding down the hallway to his, Luke's, room.

"Oh man." Mark flops down on Luke's bed. "That girl can talk, huh?"

"She's nice," says Luke, from his desk chair. "I hope I'm not cramping your, um, style, or anything like that. Seriously."

"Seriously," says Mark, "I have no style for you to cramp." Mark props himself up on his elbows and considers the ceiling. "Not in that way."

"Here I was hoping you were going to tell me how to score hot chicks," jokes Luke.

"Well, Aimee is in love with you," Mark says. "But she's too young for me and she's too old for you. I think she might get voted off the island this week."

"Seriously?" asks Luke. "You're breaking up with her?"

"Oh sure." Mark arranges pillows behind his head. "She's gorgeous and sweet and smells good and all that. But did you know she carries an empty purse around?"

"What?" laughs Luke.

"I'm not joking. When she somersaulted over the table to show you pictures of Misty's first Christmas, she knocked her purse on the floor. I picked it up and saw it was totally empty inside."

"Huh," says Luke.

"Yah. I mean, like totally empty."

"How'd she get in her car?" asks Luke. "How does she drive?"

"She left her car key on top of her rear tire," says Mark. "For real. I saw her pull it out. I mean, what the hell? I can see if she didn't have a purse, but that's the whole thing. She had a purse. She had a non-functioning purse. The purse was just for show."

"That's weird," Luke agrees. All the women Luke knows require large purses. His Nana, for instance, is able at any moment to produce from her purse a smaller purse for coins, a wallet, a date book, Kleenex, stamps, a pair of reading glasses, peppermints, coupons for the Kroger paper-clipped together, a ziplock bag with aspirin in it, Band-Aids, Vaseline, hand cream, safety pins, pens, pencils, a pencil sharpener, nail clippers, a calculator, a datebook, emery boards, antibacterial soap, and the New Testament. The one thing Luke's grandmother does not have in her purse is a phone.

"Aimee had a phone," Luke suggests. "She had her phone with her."

"She carried that," says Mark. "In her hand. Not in her purse."

"Okay," says Luke. "So you're voting her off the island because you think she's empty too? Like the empty purse is a metaphor?"

"Yah, but not for her, for me." Mark sighs. "Or, I don't know. How do I put it?"

Luke waits.

"She's my empty purse," Mark says. "She's my accessory. Among other things, it's not fair to her. She could be someone else's full purse."

"I get what you're trying to say."

"You get what I'm saying?" Mark asks. "Really?"

"Well," says Luke, thinking about his own Amy. "I think I've had kind of a similar situation going on."

"Okay, wait." Mark sits up. "What?"

"Well, it's funny how both of our sort-of girlfriends have the same name. And you know . . . being with a girl for the wrong reasons. Well, she was with *me* for the wrong reasons, she was using me, but since I knew that, I mean, that kind of throws my motivations into doubt."

"Wow," says Mark. "Okay."

"I don't mean that your Aimee is using you."

"Oh, she is using me. I'm using her worse, though, because she doesn't know it."

"You think she's using you?"

"Everybody uses everybody."

"Oh," says Luke, who is losing the neat comparison he was in the process of assembling. He is struck now with the thought that perhaps his father's situation is not like his at all, and that actually his father is less like a Luke and more like a Chad. Luke needs to move away from this thought, and so he searches, as he does when he is worried, for a philosophical platform to stand on.

"I guess," Luke says, "everyone has motivations. Every action we take is motivated by some need."

Mark laughs.

"You're a really smart kid, you know that? You're much smarter than I am. You want to play some Scrabble?"

Luke says yes to this. Perhaps it's being an actor, Luke thinks, as Mark gets up to find the game, that makes his father know when to stop talking about whatever you are talking about and talk about something else. Mark surprises Luke with a thorough knowledge of the two- and three-letter words necessary for competitive Scrabble. They play a close game, which Mark wins. Luke takes pride in the fact that his father is smart enough to beat him, and he is a little relieved as well. Luke wants proof that Mark is not a Chad. Frequently, the amount of evidence that Luke requires is in inverse proportion to the amount of hope he maintains. Luke does *not* hope that there is a God, therefore he requires substantial evidence that one exists. Luke *does* hope a great deal that his father is not a Chad, and is therefore almost entirely satisfied on this point by the thought that a Chad could never beat him in Scrabble.

CHAPTER SIX

Kati came early to the house today to make sure "everybody has everything they need" for this interview my dad is doing, and to take him to a photo shoot he had to do before the journalist came over. It turned out, though, that Kati was the one who needed things. She needed Mark to shave. She needed the caterer to have provided decaffeinated tea. She needed me to take the blower to the patio furniture again, because they got leafy. I was doing this when she joined me on the patio.

"So you don't have to talk to the interviewer today," Kati said, helping me with the cushions. "Or answer any questions. You can just do a walk-through."

"A walk-through?" I asked.

"You know, just walk through the living room at some point. Wave. Say hello if you feel like it?" Kati smacked pillows.

She was wearing a chain around her neck with a pendant

attached. This pendant fell forward when she leaned over the chaise lounge. I imagined grasping the pendant with my teeth and pulling, causing Kati's clothes to magically fall off, enabling Kati and myself to immediately have sex.

"So . . . what would I be walking through the living room *for*?" I asked.

"Well, if you get hungry," Kati said, eyeing the pillows critically. "And you want something from the kitchen: something to eat, a soda, whatever. Just don't feel like you have to hide in your bedroom. It'd be nice if you came out and said a quick hello."

"Okay. Sure. No problem. They know about me, right? The interviewer?"

"Oh yes, of course," Kati said.

I actually got an email from Pearl informing me that my name is now included in Mark Franco's website biography. It says, "Mark has a son, Luke, from a previous relationship," but it doesn't say Sara's name.

Kati busied herself with more pillows. I put the table back in its spot.

"It's an important time for your dad," Kati said. "You know, for him to be able to really take it to the next level."

Kati's got really nice hair: blond on top, but darker brown underneath, a "bob," I think it's called. I like how smooth it is. She was wearing a shirt that tied around her neck and came lower down in the back. The small white tag with washing instructions was peeping out of this. Considering the geometry of the blouse, I would say that Kati was definitely not wearing a bra.

I knew Kati wanted something from me, something to do with Mark, and that it was now my job to glean what this was, exactly. I waited for instructions.

"We've got to keep building up the heat," Kati said. "He's got to really get in the game now."

I wasn't sure how providing immaculate patio cushions or faking a sudden need for a soda in order to wave hello to an interviewer sipping decaffeinated tea would help my dad build up heat or get in the game, but I said, "Okay." Then I thought that maybe by saying that I should feel free to "walk through" my dad's interview, Kati was really trying to tell me that everyone would prefer that I didn't. That maybe it wasn't very convenient to have a teenage son about when you want everyone to think you are a dark and dangerous guy that all the women desire, like James, the character Mark plays on *The Last*.

I wondered if I should tell Kati about her tag or just casually reach around and tuck it in myself.

"Your dad seems much more relaxed since you've been here," Kati said. "He's kind of an introverted guy, normally."

I haven't noticed that my dad is all that introverted, but I just nodded because Kati seemed to be on the verge of coming to whatever point she needed to make and I didn't want to interrupt her.

"Anyway," Kati concluded, "I think, we think, that it's best to respect your mother's privacy, and your own, of course, and so it's understood that you live with your mom for most of the year, and you're spending the summer with your dad, and that's it, really, no big deal."

I hope she didn't think I would actually tell some person I've never met about Anthony Boyle and his sudden reemergence in my life as the transformed Mark Franco and freshly minted dad. Although it's nice that Kati wants to make sure Mark looks good and not like an absentee father.

"I see what you're saying," I told her. "I'll just do a walk-through, like you said, and let my dad do the talking."

"Yeah, hey, whatever, just be yourself," Kati said. "Okay, this looks good. Thanks, Luke."

I told her "no problem" and then pointed out the tag thing on the back of her shirt.

Later, after Kati and Mark had left for the photo shoot, I ignored a hard-on and went for a run in the canyon, took care of the second hard-on that occurred after my shower, and then enjoyed the instant access to perfectly constructed food in my father's refrigerator. Just as

I was starting to think about maybe doing a little work on my essay, I heard the sounds of Mark returning: the front door opening, the keys being tossed onto the table, now accompanied by a new female voice. The interviewer, I guessed. After a moment, Mark appeared in the doorway to my room.

"Cool?"

"Cool," I said. "I'm just looking at these websites on essay-writing advice. I'll come say hello in a little bit?"

Mark nodded, making one of his upside-down smiles, and left. I turned back to my computer and looked at the list of writing prompts from EssaysThatDon'tSuck.com.

I just spent a few minutes practicing Mark's upside-down smile. I've almost nailed it, I think.

Okay, time to do a little work.

"What fictional character do you most identify with?" This is supposed to be a creative essay–type prompt, I guess.

I like fiction, but what I identify most with is reading biology or philosophy, because that's what is going on with everyone whether or not they are aware of it. I like poetry if it's short. I've always liked Pearl's poetry. She is really talented. Sometimes she'll just scribble something out and hand it to you, without even taking time over the wording. I still have in my wallet this one she wrote for me on the back of a movie ticket stub.

> I show my brother where I hid the body
> And he tells no one
> But moves it later
> To a safer spot
> I think

I love that last line: "I think."

We have fictional characters in my family, sort of. Nana wrote a whole series based on stories her mother told her about growing up in Littleton, Massachusetts, in the early 1900s. I forgot to tell Mark about those. Maybe I blocked it out.

There are eight books all together, beginning with *Introducing The Mountjoy Girls* (which Nana wrote when she was just seventeen years old) and ending with *The Mountjoy Girls Set Sail* (written just before Sara was born). The Mountjoy Girls are three sisters, surprise, surprise: Sally, Anne, and Eleanor.

Nana got a bit famous from the books. In the attic there are scrapbooks filled with pictures of her in the newspapers and magazines. There's even one of Sara and my aunts in a magazine called *McCall's* with a caption underneath that says, *A New Generation of Mountjoy Girls: Sara, Nancy, and Caroline Duren Prescott.* There are tons of letters there from girls who read the books, too.

The *Mountjoy Girls* books went out of print for awhile, but then they got on those Recommended Reading Lists of wholesome books that Christian organizations put out for parents. So the series got reissued a few years ago in a new edition, and Nana is having kind of a comeback. She gets invited to speak at different places. She goes if it's connected in some way with a Christian organization, because then it is goodly.

My sisters loved *The Mountjoy Girls.* They still do. When Rory and Pearl were home for Christmas last year, they spent a whole week curled up on the couch rereading all of the books. Aurora said that she realized she was old enough now to feel nostalgic about her childhood. Pearl said that Nana's prose was actually quite good.

Sara wasn't exactly thrilled that the girls were having a *Mountjoy Girls* revival. We had a conversation about it, in the kitchen, where I was helping prepare the tofurkey.

"It's nice for Mother," Sara said, "to see the girls reading her books and enjoying them so much."

"Uh-huh," I said.

"Of course, I could probably quote the whole series to them, if I wanted to," Sara said.

"Oh," I said. "Yeah."

" '*Sally pinned her hat so that the brim covered one eye,*' " Sara quoted. " '*She felt this gave her an air of mystery, an air somewhat at odds with her eager smile, which Sally could never quite remember to suppress.*' "

"That sounds like Sally," I agreed.

"For mother, the Mountjoy Girls were the paradigm of the childhood experience. She wanted us to have all those same experiences. She wanted to create a world for us that didn't exist anymore, and she wasn't prepared to accept that it didn't. And you know, we just couldn't be Mountjoy Girls, or live Mountjoy Girl lives."

"Well, no," I said. "For one thing, in the beginning they are still mostly riding around in horse and buggies."

"It didn't help that she all but named us after her own fictional characters," Sara continued. "It was like there was a blueprint already made for us. That's why I've been careful to give all of you room to be yourselves," Sara said. "Not put expectations on you."

I reassured her that we all felt very free to discover ourselves, without a blueprint, but come on. At the very least, there is a twelve-generation ghost posse of three sisters hanging around, wondering why I'm here. That's one of the reasons I never liked Nana's books. I've got enough women around without adding the Mountjoy sisters.

I mean, seriously, even the dog we had was female. It was Nana's dog, Freida, a totally nervous cocker spaniel. She spent most of her time underneath things. When she died, Nana said she was with her Maker, and Sara said she might be reincarnating into a new animal and I was like, "Yeah, probably a mole." No, I didn't say that, of course.

I always wanted a dog of my own.

I think I should do my walk-through now.

.   .   .

Luke moves away from his desk—flees from it, really—and steps lightly down the hallway.

"Well, that's what really drew me to James, as a character," Mark is saying. "He has a lot of demons, but he's been taught to hide those, to wear this mask of control. What's interesting about James, about anybody really, is what's underneath the mask."

Luke takes the last few steps that lead around to the living room.

"Hey there," Mark calls out.

Mark is sprawled in one of the dark leather chairs. The interviewer, an older woman wearing a good deal of makeup and jewelry, sits on the couch, one plump leg crossed over the other, knees angled toward Mark; a large yellow notebook nestled in her lap. As Luke gets closer, he notices a recording device on the coffee table in between two glasses of iced green tea. The woman's glass is almost empty.

"This is Angela Hewson," Mark says. "Angela, this is my son, Luke."

Angela gives Luke her fingers to shake, as if Luke might not know how to deal with her entire hand. Bits of lipstick are missing from her lips. Luke can feel Angela's eyes raking him over.

"It's nice to meet you," Angela says. "You're about to start senior year of high school, right? And you're already working on your college applications? That's pretty impressive."

"Oh, well . . . I'm not working that hard, actually," Luke says.

"Luke is a very disciplined guy," Mark says. "Self-disciplined."

"So where are you going?" Angela asks, leaning forward to take up her iced tea glass.

"Oh, I'm just going to the kitchen," Luke explains.

Angela laughs again.

"Okay!" she says. "I meant where did you want to go for college, but that works too."

Luke thinks Angela can hardly be a crack journalist if she asks vague questions like, "Where do you want to go?" out of the blue in this fashion and expects that he will know in what context she means.

"UCLA," says Mark. "Right, Luke? So I can be an overprotective annoying dad for a couple of years?"

"Definitely UCLA," Luke says. "That way, I have somewhere to bring my laundry."

Everybody laughs at this. Luke wonders if his voice is making it onto the recording device.

"I'm going to get a soda. May I get you another iced tea, Mrs. Hewson?"

Luke is careful to say "may" instead of "can" and to speak in a polite tone. He would like to be helpful to Mark, and show what a well-brought-up young man he is. Luke can tell from Angela's response that his strategy has worked. Mark makes a funny face at Luke and coasting on this, Luke sails into the kitchen, where he finds Kati putting together a plate of fruit and cheese. Kati mouths, "Hey," silently at him. As he opens the refrigerator door, Luke overhears Angela saying,

"Okay, so you must have had Luke when you were a teenager yourself?"

"Yeah, I was young. Not much older than Luke is now."

"How often do you get to see him?"

Luke pauses, one hand on the refrigerator door. He turns and looks at Kati, who has paused in her cheese arranging and is clearly listening too. Kati and Luke look at each other.

"Not as much as I would like," Mark says.

"Good one, Dad," Luke thinks. Kati smiles. Luke pulls a bottle of lemon ginger juice and the pitcher of iced tea out of the refrigerator.

"It's clear you are really proud of him," Angela says.

"He's a fantastic kid. Way smarter and pulled together than I was at his age."

Luke refills Angela's iced tea, and wonders if he should wipe the lipstick smudges off the rim of her glass. This is the first time Luke has heard his father refer, even vaguely, to himself as a young person.

Luke knows that Mark was born in Illinois, that his parents divorced when he was four, and that his mother, Julia, raised him. He knows Mark attended Grover High School, where he played football and was a member of the Grover High Spotlight Players. After graduating high school Mark moved to New York City to study acting professionally. Luke knows these things from the biographical section of Mark Franco's listing in the Internet Movie Database, not from anything Mark has said to Luke.

Luke hears Angela ask, "So what were you like at his age?"

Luke takes his time putting the juice back because he would very much like to hear the answer to this question.

There is a longish pause and then the sound of Mark's voice saying, "Angry."

"Angry at what?"

There is another long pause. Luke pretends to examine the contents of the refrigerator because he can feel Kati watching him. Mark laughs.

"Oh, all teenagers are angry, right?" Mark asks, lightly.

Luke prepares for his second pass. He mimes taking the cheese tray in for Kati, who shakes her head and waves him off. On the way back through the living room, Luke tells Angela that it was nice to meet her. Walking down the hallway, he hears her say, "I'd like to get back to this idea of masks . . ."

In another hour, the interviewer and Kati have left. Mark comes to Luke's room, and flops down on his bed.

"Jesus, God, that was excruciating," he groans. "I'm fucking exhausted."

"It's kind of weird, isn't it?" Luke asks. "Being recorded like that? I guess you get used to it?"

"I'm bad at it," Mark says. "It's impossible to say anything that doesn't sound like . . . I don't know . . . like, 'Listen to these thoughts I have! They're so interesting! Wait! Write this down!' But she's a Golden Globe voter so I had to do it."

"I thought you sounded good," Luke offers. "What I heard of it."

"Oh yeah? Maybe I was okay. But, *you*!" Mark laughs. " 'May I get you another iced tea, Mrs. Hewson?' " he says, in an ultra-suave version of Luke's voice.

"Hey, good job on answering the 'How often do you see him?' question," Luke tells him.

"Oh," Mark says. "Um, okay. Hmm."

"I heard it from the kitchen." It wasn't really eavesdropping, Luke thinks, since Mark was being recorded, and was speaking publicly, as it were.

"No, no," Mark says. "Of course. I'm just not sure what you mean, I guess. What do you mean?"

"I mean it's nobody's business but ours, right?" Luke says. "We don't have to tell people the whole story. You were being interviewed for a magazine; of course you have to be careful what you say. I mean, you can get into a whole argument about moral relativism . . ."

Luke stops talking because he thinks he is starting to sound like he really does mean something else. And that maybe he was eavesdropping, since he wasn't the one asking the questions.

"I don't know about moral relativism," Mark says. "But now I feel like a dick. I didn't mean to pass myself off like some kind of . . . like I'm this great dad and I've always been there for you." Mark looks upset, with himself or Luke, Luke doesn't know, just as Mark doesn't know how eager Luke is to embrace a three-sentence explanation of his father's seventeen-year absence.

"Technically you always were there," Luke says. "You're half of me. The rest is just . . . shared experience, really. And we're doing that now, right?"

"Well, hey, that's solved, then." Mark swings himself off Luke's bed. "Thanks for letting me off the hook of any responsibility. What a relief."

Luke has heard his father be sarcastic about things, and people, but this is the first time that he's felt himself to be the object of Mark's sarcasm. Luke does not know what to do, or say, next. People do not usually require Luke to be *less* understanding.

"Well, I can't act mad at you if I'm not really mad at you," Luke tells him. "I'm not an actor."

Mark sits down on the bed again.

"You can be mad at me if you want to," he says.

Luke wonders if this is like when Pearl wants you to be mad at her, so she can unload whatever monologue she's been devising in her head. You have to throw the first punch, so she has proper justification. But with Pearl, Luke more or less knows what's coming, how long it will stay, and what the aftermath will look like. Luke doesn't know Mark well enough to know what he's going to do. He could walk away entirely, disappear behind glass doors that make a sucking air sound when you pull them apart.

"My dad split when I was little," Mark says. "I wasn't mad at him, for bailing. I never knew him. My mom didn't have anything good to say about him. There's been times that I've been grateful, I didn't have to . . . it's complicated."

Mark's face looks sad.

Luke waits.

"I want us to be honest with each other," Mark says, after a moment. "I think that mostly means that I want to be honest with you."

"Yeah, let's do that," Luke agrees.

"I would like to say that you are a really amazing kid, apart from the fact that you are . . . that you're my son. I'm really glad I'm getting to know you."

"Thanks," Luke says. "I feel the same way about you."

Of course, Luke can't be sure that how he feels about Mark is how Mark feels about him. Luke is reminded of a philosophical thought experiment: if six people are each holding a box, and can only see inside their own box, and they are all asked, "What's in your box?" and they all say, "A beetle," it doesn't follow that they are all seeing the same thing. Because what one person may call a "beetle" may be what another person would call an "apple." Even if everybody speaks the same language they can still be talking about different things.

Luke makes the upside-down smile at his father, who makes it back at him.

"Wanna go see a game tomorrow?" Mark asks, reaching into his back pocket and producing a small white envelope, "Dodgers? Me and you?"

"Seriously?"

"I'm not a huge baseball fan. But one of the show's producers gave me these, and it seems like a classic father/son opportunity."

"That's awesome, Dad. Yeah."

"How 'bout we stay in tonight and watch some movies, play some Scrabble. I had Kati pick up that Japanese film you were talking about. Or you want to go out? We can go out, too."

"Let's stay in," Luke says. "That sounds cool."

The next day Mark takes Luke to Dodger Stadium. Luke has never been to a professional baseball game. It is exciting being there, with his father, in a special section called "The Dugout Club." Luke feels dazed and almost guilty by the sense of privilege and status their seats convey. They sit closer to home plate than the pitcher, close enough to hear the players swearing and talking to each other, close enough to hear the sound of disturbed air in the wake of a flying baseball. So many people want to say hello to his father, or take his picture, that Luke wishes that Kati were with them to be reassured that his father gets a lot of attention and has heat. In between cheering their heads off for the Dodgers, or thinking up what archaic abuse to hurl at the Mariners ("Scurvy curs! Lecherous knaves!") Mark turns to Luke and says, "I meant it. I think it'd be great if you went to college out here. If you want," and Luke says, "Yeah, I've been thinking about that too, I'm going to look into UCLA. Maybe even Caltech."

Luke does not want his father to feel guilty about him. This is not altruism on Luke's part. Luke does not want any potential feeling his father might have for him to be contaminated by guilt. He wants for his father and himself to look into separate boxes and see exactly the same thing. He does not frame these wants into sentences. Instead, he tells himself that if he gets into Caltech, or UCLA, then maybe he will live with his father for a year or two. And maybe they can get a dog together. If Mark likes dogs.

CHAPTER SEVEN

My dad gave me an iPod yesterday. It comes in different colors, but my dad chose the black one, which is what I would have chosen for myself. This was a real gift, too, from him, because there weren't any iPods in the garage. I checked.

My dad doesn't make a ceremony out of giving things. He just does it. With the iPod, he pulled it out of his pocket and handed it to me, saying, "Oh, you could use one of these, right? These are good for working out." He gets embarrassed if you thank him too much, so instead I will just make sure he sees how much I am using and enjoying it. I liked having it at the gym, but I don't think I'll take it for running in the canyon.

We're not allowed to do any of our training runs on my cross-country team while listening to music. Part of it is a safety thing, but also our coach wants us to really forge unity on our team, and not shut each other out with headphones.

It's important for us to forge unity because in cross-country the sum of the top five times of your team makes up your score. But on our team, we only have five runners total. (Our school has a long tradition of barely making up a cross-country team.) So on our team, everybody counts. It also means that nobody on our team can quit the team. Or get sick. Or injured. It's a pretty motivating factor, knowing that if you quit you've just destroyed the team.

I signed up for cross-country freshman year. I was attracted to running because it seemed challenging, and also peaceful. I was pretty heavily recruited too. That's not because I displayed some sort of incredible ability right off the bat. Two members of the previous team had just graduated, and the remaining three members were pretty desperate. At that point, my high school had never won a cross-country meet, ever, and recruitment was difficult. Cross-country is not glamorous, the conditions are often pretty rough, you have to train vigorously, and hardly anybody makes it through a season without finding themselves on their knees trying not to yack. We don't have cool uniforms or a band or cheerleaders. We don't have a bus that takes us to invitationals or meets. We go in Coach's van. We train in the fall, when the other sport that's going on is football. That means our little five-member team changes into shorts and T-shirts in a corner of a locker room populated by the largest guys in our school, whose equipment probably weighs more than we do.

Sophomore year, this guy Ivan Lowell transferred to our school and joined the team, which was great for Tim, because he wanted to focus more on violin, so he was able to quit. Ivan and I started trading off times.

Sometimes Ivan was faster, and sometimes I was. That worked well because whoever was slower in one practice session would then try to be faster than the other in the next one. So we both ended up getting pretty fast and last year we were in the top five of every meet, and that got our team score down low enough to actually win a few.

In fact, we ended up almost winning regionals. Ivan thinks we have a real shot at State next year. It's kind of a long shot, but if Raj and Nick really step up, and Ethan sticks it out, who knows? We might even be able to recruit some of the guys from track to join us now that we've won some meets.

Ivan will be our team captain next year. We voted him that unanimously at the end of the season. Raj said that if I wanted to be team captain the other guys would vote for me, but I thought that Ivan wanted it more than me, and really wanting to lead other people is the one leadership quality I lack. It seems like a crucial one. Also I think I'm going to be running faster than Ivan this year pretty consistently, and being team captain will help him deal with that, so all around it worked out for the best.

Our last team captain was David Pollen, but he just graduated. David always led us in prayer before races. That's not a school thing, praying, but David thought we should pray and nobody really objected (we are a mild-mannered team) and Coach thought it might help forge unity. Sometimes we would pray for specific things or people: "Lord, we ask that you be especially with Raj today as he just had dental work and is in pain." When I say "we" prayed, I mean David prayed and the rest of us said "Amen" whenever he finished talking.

Running can be very meditative, because there is a pain point that you have to work through and if you let yourself get caught up in that, you are toast. I've tried to use some of the techniques you use in yoga. You are supposed to identify what hurts, acknowledge it, and then send it acceptance and love. I can't say that I have ever truly loved burning lungs or quads, or the shooting pains that occur in the ankles, but if love means that you have learned not to resent something, then I guess I have loved.

A more useful technique I use is to call myself different names at different points in a race. You start off all lined up together in a bullpen at the start line and then you run toward the flags that narrow the course down. You want to run this pretty fast to get in with the top guys. It's a defensive kind of sprinting you need to do, because there is some trampling to be avoided. So for this part of the race I call myself Shade of Mercury. As the Shade of Mercury, I have the ability to move past other runners because I am not in corporeal form. Once the course becomes narrower I shift into Bolo Softsole. As Bolo, I can run the first mile and a half at my optimum pace, putting as much distance between myself and the other runners as I can. Bolo handles rough terrain well, due to his very soft soles, which keep him light and agile.

Somewhere between two miles and the last four hundred yards is where Stoke Fireforge comes in. Stoke is a running machine. He churns. He must run because if he does not, the Earth will stop rotating on its axis and darkness will cover the land. He has a task to do and it's not up to him to question the task.

Unfortunately for Stoke, there comes a point where he gets attacked by dwarves. They attach themselves to his ankles in order to slow him down. The dwarves are very, very, very heavy. I don't like to think about this part.

The last four hundred yards is where I became Luke Skywalker. Yeah, I know. But when my sisters came to meets, they positioned themselves at the last four hundred, and they used to scream the theme song for *Star Wars* for me. Even if they weren't there, I would do it in my head. I used to think of the finish chute as that narrow lane that Luke has one shot of firing into in order to destroy the Death Star.

I guess my feelings about being part of a team, and running in general, have changed over the past three years. At first I just really liked running. It was painful, and hard, but it was also pleasantly hypnotic, like a physicalized mantra: one foot in front of the other, the other, the other, the other. I liked the other guys on the team, we were all friends and sat together at lunch and did stuff together away from school. Ivan became sort of my best friend, we got faster, Nick joined the team and he's really funny, and so on.

But last year things started to change, right after we won our first meet. That made it more serious. Before that, there was just no way we were going to win, and it was all about finishing and being these underdogs that were doing it for the love of sport. Suddenly we all got more intense. Coach got excited and started really riding the other three guys on our team. Nick and Raj were okay with it, but Ethan became this, like, miserable wreck. All of us said stuff to him like, "Ethan, all you have to do is finish. Your one job is to make it to the chute. If you give it your all, then you're our best runner, because you're the one it's hardest for, and that makes you the toughest guy on the team," etc. Sometimes I would say to him, "It's okay if you quit," because he would always say back, "I'm not quitting," and just saying that amped him up a little bit. You have to do things like that, because in theory a cross-country team is only as good as its weakest runner. It's not about individuals.

But after I finished first out of all the runners for the first time, I noticed that I started becoming, well, kind of obsessed with winning. With me, Luke, winning, as opposed to our team winning. I don't get upset if our team loses, as long as I'm first. I can't explain it exactly. There's some particular high that I get going into that chute first. I just really want it. Sara would say that it is Ego, and that's probably right. And even though I know I should release my Ego, and still run with the same spirit of the guy I was when I was finishing in the bottom third, I can't help myself. It's almost like a possessive feeling. I want to own that chute, and have everybody else be the people that came after me.

My sisters were both at college last year, so they weren't at meets anymore, and I didn't sing the *Star Wars* theme in my head. To be totally honest, what I'm thinking for the last part of a race now is something along the lines of, "MINE, MINE, MINE."

I think maybe I could do sort of a humorous essay about running and my secret names, but *50 Successful College Application Essays* warns against the humorous essay. Also, it probably wouldn't get me into Caltech.

I should really take a shower.

. . .

By the time Luke is out of the shower, Mark is home, having only been called in to a short day on the set of *The Last*. They are now going to the Los Angeles County Museum of Art, for the Rothko retrospective.

At the museum, Mark rents headphones so they can listen to the audio lecture, but at a certain point they agree that the lecturer's voice is annoying and they want to stop listening and just look at the paintings.

"These," Mark says, "are really great paintings."

"These," Luke agrees, "are now my favorite paintings."

They sit down on a bench in front of the last piece and look at it for awhile: an orange square floating in a larger yellow rectangle, the edges of the paint faintly blurred and thin. There seems to be an additional rectangle floating on top of the orange one, but the yellow has mostly swallowed this.

"I feel like I'm watching it," Mark says. "Do you know what I mean? Like I'm not just looking at it."

"Like you are observing it. Like it's happening right now."

"Exactly," Mark says. "Would this be, like, a Zen moment we are having?"

Luke laughs.

"I don't think so. People think of any peaceful moment as being Zen, and Buddhism as being all passive and gentle, but that's not always the case. It was Buddhist monks that convinced the kamikaze pilots in World War II to sacrifice themselves."

"I love the Nana stuff you wrote, by the way. So your Nana is really Christian and your mom is . . . ?"

"She would call herself a Pantheist," Luke says. "Pearl calls her the Sony Cineplex of belief."

"Does it offend you that I swear?" Mark asks.

"Oh, no," Luke laughs. "Everybody swears."

"You don't," Mark says. "I don't think I've heard you swear yet."

"Well, I swear mostly in extreme situations," Luke answers. "Or just in my head. But I have no problem with it. It's more that I've grown up with this emphasis on words, and word choice, so . . ."

"No, it's good," Mark says. "You speak like a gentleman."

"I say 'yeah,' though," Luke points out. "Nana hates that. It should be 'yes,' not 'yeah.'"

Mark and Luke turn back to the Rothko painting.

"But you never got saved, or born again, or anything like that?" Mark asks, after a moment.

"Well, actually," Luke begins, and then pauses. The gallery is beginning to get more crowded, and Luke thinks that the couple off to their left has recognized Mark. This turns out to be the case, and Mark autographs the couple's museum map.

"Let's go walk around outside," Mark suggests. "The La Brea Tar Pits are next door."

It is possible to wander around cordoned areas of tar pits. Luke is intrigued by their smell, and the proximity of thirty-thousand-year-old Ice Age fossils still unexcavated lying so close to Wilshire Avenue, where you can get Mexican fast food, and office supplies.

"You were saying?" Mark asks, after they talk about the smell. "About getting saved?"

"Well, a weird thing happened to me once," Luke says, slowly. "When I was at Assembly. I was just sitting there, kind of thinking my own thoughts, and I don't know why, but I flipped open my Bible and put my finger down, you know, randomly, just to see what it would land on?"

"What did it land on?" Mark asks.

"'For with the same measure that ye mete withal it shall be measured to you again,'" Luke quotes.

Mark asks him to repeat it, which Luke does.

"So that's, like, you get what you give, right?" Mark asks.

"Yes," Luke says. "And, well, I read it over a couple of times and then I got this really weird feeling, almost like the feeling you get when you are getting the flu. Like your bones and joints ache and you feel about a half step removed from everything around you?"

"Okay," Mark says. "Interesting. Go on."

"It was exactly like what a lot of people describe as a moment of getting saved, but in reverse," Luke explains. "Because you are supposed to have, like, an overwhelming feeling of radiance, or love, or maybe even something happens, and you see something or do something. I mean it doesn't have to be huge, like you lift up a car or anything like that. But your whole body is supposed to respond very intensely and you just KNOW that the moment has come."

"But you're saying that it happened in reverse for you?"

"Well . . . I mean I didn't feel any radiance or light or anything like that. I felt heavy, and tired, but also . . . detached. I felt a certainty, but not the kind of certainty that I was supposed to feel."

Mark and Luke are no longer walking at this point, but standing at the southern end of the tar pits, where a giant fiberglass family of mammoths has been erected in a reenactment scenario: a mother mammoth flounders in the tar as her mate and baby look on from the safety of dry land. An explanatory placard describes the "helplessness" of the father and baby mammoth. The baby appears especially distressed: its fiberglass trunk is lifted in panic.

"You know how if you say a word over and over, a bunch of times, it loses its meaning and starts sounding incredibly weird?" Luke asks.

"Yeah, for sure," Mark says. "It was like that?"

"Well, in a way it was. I read that one verse over and over and I just moved farther and farther away from it, and I thought, 'Well, this is all just *nonsense.*' I guess it finally really occurred to me that everybody else around me, they actually *believed* all this stuff. I mean, really, really *believed* it. And then I knew that I wasn't going to give anything to God, and so I wasn't going to get anything back. I couldn't give anything to God. I didn't believe in God. And it wasn't just a part of me that felt that, or the rational part of me, or the skeptic part of me. It was all of me. My *body* didn't believe. My body was like, rejecting the whole thing. Not just the idea of religion, or organized religion, or Christianity, but the entire idea of God, of anything separate from myself. Of belief in belief without evidence."

Luke is clutching the fence of the tar pits now, in an effort to find the right words.

"But you meditate," Mark says. "And you do yoga. You seem like a spiritual guy."

"I meditate for mental and physical discipline," Luke says. "I contemplate my thoughts. I don't pray. I don't ask anything of anything. I don't believe there's anything out there to ask. I don't think there is a special point to existence, or that there is any plan or purpose beyond what we invent for ourselves. I know ... I know I'm supposed to respect other people's beliefs, but some people believe we are descendants of alien lizards. All of these things that Nana believes, and Sara believes? I think it's all made up. So why should I respect that more than alien lizards? And, and, even if you just think of religion as a metaphor it doesn't mean anything to me. Because for spirituality to mean something you have to believe you have a spirit. And I don't. I don't think I have a soul."

Mark and Luke stand side by side. The fiberglass mammoths look at each other, with fiberglass dismay.

"I haven't ever told anybody that," Luke says. "Maybe it doesn't seem like such a big secret, or anything, but I haven't even told my sisters."

Mark does not say anything to this, but he puts his hand on Luke's back, in between his scapula. Luke releases the railing.

"The joke part is," Luke continues, "that passage I read? It was from the Book of Luke."

"Holy shit," Mark says. Luke and Mark laugh. Then they leave the tar pits, the hidden remains of animals, the helpless fake mammoths, the painted floating rectangles and squares. On their way home, they pick up Mexican takeout.

CHAPTER EIGHT

A car from the studio arrived at five in the morning today to take us to the Mojave Desert, where *The Last* shoots most of its exteriors. This is the final day for the show before they go on hiatus. On Sunday, Mark is taking me to the "wrap" party.

The location we were going to, Mark told me, is popular with film and television companies because of the dry and cracked lake bed, which is very unusual looking. Parts of the area, Mark explained, are designated for off-highway recreational sports like motorcycling or light aircraft flying. He asked if I was interested in trying any of those things. He had warned me that there would be a fair amount of sitting around, waiting, and I should bring things to do. I brought my laptop.

"Maybe not today," Mark added. "But sometime this summer. Whenever. I've been making a list of stuff we could do. You know, suggestions." Mark pulled out his BlackBerry, flipped through it, and handed it over to me. I read:

Ideas

Mexico or Hawaii (Bahamas?)

Camping (Sequoia National Park?)

Road trip up Highway 101 (Redwoods?)

Adventure: Sky diving, parasailing, motorcycling, etc.

Surfing lessons

"I realize it's kind of a physically oriented list," Mark said. "I wanted to put down some more intellectual-type activities. And we could go to concerts, too. We could go to the Hollywood Bowl. The opera. Theater. Anything you want."

"This," I said to him, "is a really great list."

"Maybe you could rank the ideas," he suggested. "In order of interest. Oh, and I wanted to ask you, because I was thinking . . . well, I thought maybe we could go visit my mom. Just a quick trip. A few days."

"Your mom?" I asked, totally surprised.

"My mom," he said. "Your grandmother. She lives in Grover, Illinois. That's where I grew up. It's a completely boring place but I haven't been to see her in awhile, and I thought that maybe you'd want to meet your grandmother. Your other grandmother, I mean. She wants to meet you. What do you think?"

"I'm putting 'Visiting Mom/Grandmother' in the number-one slot," I said, and Mark smiled.

"It should be fun today," he told me. "It's like the last day of school for us."

Arriving at the set, Mark was quickly herded off to hair and makeup, and I was shown to my father's trailer, where I found Kati blending Mark's special protein-powder drink.

"Oh, hey," I said. "Why didn't you ride with us?"

"I came early with the crew," Kati shouted, over the noise of the blender. "So I could hand out gifts he got people. Plus your dad enjoys having alone time with you."

I checked out the books Mark had on the small coffee table. I didn't know that Mark likes to do crosswords.

Kati explained that normally the show had all its exteriors wrapped before June, when the temperature can get up to 120 degrees and the winds set in, but a last-minute script change had brought them all here for the day. Also, she told me, there has been a lot of talk lately about a possible writers' strike, and they wanted to make sure they had everything done.

"Well, it works out for me," I said. "I'm glad I get to see what our planet looks like after a nuclear holocaust." I stepped outside the trailer to take a look around.

Before, I visited Mark on a soundstage at the studio lot. They use that for "interiors," the various semi-destroyed shelters that James and the other survivors of *The Last* take refuge in. I had been surprised that day to see how what looked like really fake sets in real life suddenly appeared totally real on the monitors, from the camera's point of view. Like, artifice was constructed out of real things, but only achieved the appearance of reality by artificial means.

I took a deep breath. It was so arid I could practically feel my gums drying. A short distance from the trailers, crew members were setting up equipment under tarps, running cables, shouting directions. The lake bed was incredible. I shut my eyes, tried to imagine it covered with water, but instead I got this image of a giant prehistoric snake, struck by lightning, left to petrify and decompose, flattening under the sun and trampling feet of people shooting car commercials and television shows. I took a few pictures with my phone of the Joshua trees to send to my sisters. Kati came out of the trailer wearing a headset.

"I'm taking Luke to craft services," she said into it.

I thought that maybe today I should work on forging some kind of relationship with Kati. She might be more of a permanent fixture in my father's life than Aimee. Kati always carries a very large and heavy-looking purse.

"Cool, right?" she asked, waving around at the landscape.

"Very cool," I agreed. "Like nothing I've ever seen."

We started walking and Kati pointed out people and told me who they were, and what their function was on the set. Whenever we passed someone who was not talking into their own headset, Kati either introduced them to me ("This is Mark's son, Luke") or reminded them who I am ("You remember Mark's son, Luke"). When we had moved on, Kati said things like, "That was one of the producers," or "He's the second AD." I'm learning film jargon, who does what and what they are called.

"The wrap party is going to be great," Kati told me. "They're doing this whole carnival thing on the beach."

After assembling a plate of food, we threaded our way back to Mark's trailer.

"You can watch TV if you want." Kati handed me a remote control. She sat down at a small table and opened up her laptop. Kati treats me like a kid, but I don't think she's much older than I am. I put the remote down and opened up my own laptop.

"So, what are you going to do this summer?" I asked her. "Are you going on vacation?"

"Well, there are still things to do. We're hoping for another Emmy nomination for Mark in July. I've been sort of acting as your dad's publicist, you know. I wear a lot of hats."

"Oh. So will he have to do more interviews and stuff?"

"Don't worry," Kati said. "You're his number-one priority. I won't interrupt your plans unless it's totally necessary."

"Well," I said, "you should get some time off. You work really hard."

"I've got the best job in LA. I am the envy of personal assistants everywhere. No two a.m. phone calls. No bizarre requests for things nobody has ever heard of. No screaming tantrums. No drugs. No hookers. No messed-up chil—"

Kati stopped.

"That's good," I said. "I'm glad he's not a tyrant. And that he doesn't have any 'messed-up chil.' Let me know if he steps out of line. I've got your back."

That's pretty much as close to flirting with Kati as I've actually gotten. I tried to think of a way to ask her if she has a boyfriend.

Mark came into the trailer then, wearing a dirty T-shirt and dark military-style pants, the remnants of the uniform James Knox was wearing when he was sent on the mission to Earth that failed so spectacularly and set the whole ball rolling on *The Last.* Mark's hair was scraped back at the sides, there was a faint bruise underneath one eye, and a realistic-looking cut above one ear. I think I've been around actual real-life Mark long enough now that I see the clothes as a costume, and him as an actor dressed up to play a part. When I visited him before, on the studio set, I hadn't really known the difference between what James Knox looked like and what my father actually did.

"Do you need to practice your lines or something like that now?" I asked, since Mark was carrying a script.

"Here are my lines." Mark handed the pages over to me. I looked down and saw three chunks of writing highlighted in yellow in between descriptions of action and another character's dialogue. Sort of like this:

JAMES

You can't change human nature. You should know that
better than anyone, Doc.

JAMES

(his eyes sweeping the landscape)
Take a look at what men do.

JAMES

(level, he means it)

Don't.

"I think I've got 'em covered," Mark laughed. "Want to play some Scrabble?"

We set up the board.

" 'You can't change human nature,' " Mark said. "What do you think, Luke? Is that true?"

"I think so." I selected tiles. "The brain has a lot of plasticity, otherwise we wouldn't be able to learn anything. But we can't change who we are as a species, only how we behave, maybe. And we can't change our genes, although our genes can change themselves. They can mutate."

"We've got some mutating genes this season." Mark pointed at the script. "Although I'm not sure the science on the show is one hundred percent accurate."

"Hey Kati," I said. "Want to play with us?"

"I'll be the judge," Kati said. "In case there's any dispute, I've got wordfinder.com right here."

So we played Scrabble and started up a running joke for Kati's benefit about what we are going to do when *The Last* goes on hiatus.

"Hey Kati, Luke and I are going to take a class in mime," Mark said, very deadpan.

"You are going to do what?"

"Oh cool," I said. "Will that give us enough time to make our own hand puppets?"

"A consideration, for sure," said Mark, peering at the board.

"Very funny," Kati said.

"I was thinking, though," I joked, laying down my word, PRAY, earning myself a triple word score. "We should go to one of those medieval-themed restaurants. You know, where they have jousts and quaff mead and stuff? That could be good research for you, Dad, in case you ever play King Arthur."

"Oh shit, we have to go. Seriously," Mark said, laughing. "Medieval Times, it's called. I think there's one out by Disney Land. No, seriously. I used to know a guy that worked at one of those places. That would be hilarious. Kati, wouldn't that be hilarious?"

Kati agreed, tolerantly, that it would be hilarious.

"Check it out." Mark added a CLEPT after the "Y" in my PRAY.

"Yclept?" I asked. "That's a word? An English word?"

"Are you challenging me?"

"Hold up," Kati said, touching a button on her headset and listening.

"Okay, copy that. Mark, Pete is on his way over. Anton wants to take another look at the fight."

"Yup." Mark stood up and stretched his shoulders, swinging his arms in arcs.

"Can I come too?" I asked. I think if I drink protein shakes until the end of time I still won't have arms like my father.

"Yeah, sure, come. It's hot, though. You're gonna sweat your balls off."

"Mark!" Kati said. "You shouldn't talk like that in front of Luke."

"I think Luke knows he has balls. Do we have a hat for him to wear?"

There was a tap on the trailer door.

"Ready?"

"Let's do it," Mark said. He opened the door. "Oh, Pete, this is my son, Luke."

A young guy, wearing a headset and a sweat-soaked T-shirt, looked at me blankly.

"Oh!" he said. "Oh, hey man." We shook hands. Pete laughed.

"They said your son was here," Pete said to Mark. "But I was thinking he . . . I thought he'd be in a stroller or something."

"Luke was born fully formed." Mark took a baseball cap from Kati with "The Last" printed on it, and handed it to me. "You know, like that God that sprung from the eye of whoever. You know the one I mean. Luke, who am I talking about?"

"Well, there were a couple," I said. "It's kind of a popular form of childbirth in mythology. Saves a lot of time."

"Yeah. And that's why we don't hear about the early years of many gods. Like, 'Zeus: The Teenage Years.'"

"Before he got handy with the thunderbolts," I added. "And just keyed chariots and was really awkward around mortals."

"They're like this," Kati told Pete. "You get used to it."

Mark and I made the upside-down smile at each other, proudly.

Outside the trailer there was a golf cart, which we all climbed into.

"We're moving," Pete said into his headset, as if he were driving a SWAT team–style van. I started to laugh at this, but nobody else did, so I turned it into a cough. Pete drove us about two hundred feet to a canopied area where a cluster of people were waiting. I got introduced to Neal, the actor who plays "Doctor Grant" and to Anton, the stunt coordinator. "This is my son," Mark said again. "My son, Luke."

"Are you ready to watch your father kick the stuffing out of me?" asked Neal, who has a British accent in real life although he doesn't on the show.

"We can stand over here," Pete told me, moving us off a few feet. Neal put on knee and elbow pads.

"Wow," Pete said quietly. "So Mark's your dad?"

I nodded.

"I'm visiting him for the summer."

"I didn't know he had kids," Pete said. "I mean," he added quickly, "not that I would know. I'm just a lowly PA, so it's not like I have long personal conversations with your dad. Not that he's not nice to me. He's nice to everyone. He's a really nice guy."

"Normally I live with my mom in Delaware," I said, in an offhand way.

Anton was telling Mark and Neal to move at quarter speed. The action seemed to entail Neal shoving Mark, then a pause, then Neal raising an arm to hit Mark and Mark making a swift karate-style chop to Neal's arm, then grabbing him by one shoulder, flipping him around, knocking one of Neal's legs out from under him so that Neal twisted and fell with Mark landing more or less on top of him. They rolled over a couple of times, punching at each other, before Mark pinned Neal down on the ground, one knee in Neal's back, one hand holding his neck. Once they had done that a couple of times, Anton told them to move at half speed.

Mark seemed totally comfortable with the whole thing, as opposed to Neal, who needed to talk through the action as they worked: "Right, right, so here I go, and now you spin me, and this one is all me, and down I go, and I let you take that wrist, right-o, that's the ticket, easy does it for safety," etc.

Sara always says that physical violence is a failure of the imagination to settle differences peacefully. She doesn't even like it in sports. She thinks there are more creative ways to release aggression. When I wanted to play on the junior high football team, Sara took me to t'ai chi class instead, and gave me a bongo drum. I liked both of those things, but come on.

When my father and Neal started moving at three-quarter tempo, Neal stopped talking.

I've seen Mark fight in movies—get bloodied and cut up, smash through a window, fire guns, get shot. Mark told me that he almost always does his own stunts. Not that he particularly wants to, he said, but it always looks better if you do it yourself, and anyway, he doesn't want to be sitting in his trailer sipping tea while some stuntman takes the knocks for him.

"This is all going to get changed once we're on set," Pete explained to me. "It's always like that. They'll figure out that half of it won't read on camera, or the angle is wrong, or something. Your dad really knows how to sell this stuff, though. People always ask me, when they find out I work on the show, 'Hey, what's Mark Franco like?' I always tell them that he's actually this really laid-back guy. Very mellow."

I wonder if Mark had been around in my childhood, would he have convinced Sara that it was okay for me to play contact sports? He might have seen that I had aggression, but not an aggression *problem*. Then I would have spent my Saturdays playing football instead of playing the bongo for Sara's Ecstatic Dance Class. At the very least

I would have watched football on television, instead of all that figure skating.

Mark and Neal both started making sounds as if they were really fighting, although the punches were silent, since no connection was actually being made. "Sound effects are all done in post," Pete told me. "But it helps the actors to make the sounds."

It looked like fun. I haven't ever been in a fight. I haven't even wrestled that much, just goofing around. Sara is very huggy and everything, but it's not like she ever initiated mock combat. I wonder if by the end of the summer my father and I will be at a level where we can throw each other around like this, or he can teach me some moves.

It's a good idea, I think, to start at slow speeds, and then work up to real time. For safety.

An hour later I stood next to Kati and one of the producers, watching as they shot the fight scene in front of the camera. There was a lot of stopping and starting. Pete's predictions were correct: most of the sequence got changed. It got more violent.

Actually, in second grade Kyle Grenbacher shoved me down to the ground during recess. I don't think either one of us knew why. I stood up, and Kyle called me "crap head" before running off to join the kick-ball gang. I didn't tell anyone about it, but I think for a long time I sort of replayed the scene in my head, enacting various forms of physical revenge on Kyle. I hope this doesn't mean I have some kind of weird backlog of violence stored in me.

Everyone seemed very professional and serious on the set to me, although the director kept shouting things like, "Okay, the fat lady has not sung, people. Let's stay focused." The director also had a British accent. Between takes a makeup lady would dart in and apply something to Mark's face. It's kind of funny to see someone put makeup on your father, and then see him take a swing at somebody.

I was pretty blown away by Mark's ability to pretend. On the monitor it seemed as if James was looking out at the desolate landscape of ruined Earth when he said to Dr. Grant, "Take a look at what men do," and in reality Mark was looking at the boom operator wearing a *South Park* T-shirt and holding the microphone on a long stick over his head. I don't how my father was able to appear both mournful and cynical while gazing at what was, essentially, an armpit.

I knew that my father was not that person with the scar over his ear, the dirty T-shirt, the battle-weary eyes, but I was impressed all the same.

My dad is the kind of guy other guys wish they were like.

"All right!" the director shouted, suddenly. He hopped off his seat next to the camera and moved over to Mark. They had this huddled conversation, with some arm waving, at the end of which Mark walked away abruptly, as if the director had said something upsetting. Mark walked in circles, agitated.

"Let's try to get this right," the director shouted, I wasn't sure to whom, as he settled himself back in his seat.

"One minute," Mark snapped, in a tone I hadn't heard before. He squatted down, put his head between his knees. I watched the muscles of his back flex and unflex. He looked pretty scary, and everyone got really quiet. I got nervous, and looked over at Kati.

"Is everything okay?" I whispered. Kati nodded slightly.

"Fuck," Mark said to himself.

I looked at Kati again, but she was stepping away, texting into her phone. Crew members shuffled around, looking at their feet.

"Okay, let's go," Mark said tensely, standing up.

They started shooting again, the camera moving smoothly on its track, following the action. Only when they got to the final position, the director didn't yell, "Cut." Mark was breathing more heavily. He made a frustrated gesture, then stopped himself.

"Enough!" Mark shouted. "ENOUGH!"

I looked around at the crew. Everyone on the set was staring at Mark and not moving.

"I said, ENOUGH!" Mark shouted. "Do you hear me? ENOUGH!"

The sweat on my back turned cold. I actually felt it do that. Mark sobbed, out loud, a choking sort of sob, and tears started running down his face. Real tears. That's when I panicked. I felt like I should do something. I mean, everybody was just staring, looking freaked out.

"ENOUGH!" Mark shouted, screamed really.

Then Mark took his knee and hand from Neal's back and neck; he moved a few steps away from Neal, who rolled onto his back and coughed. Mark squatted down and put his head in his hands, like before.

"Enough," he said, quietly.

That's when I realized it was all part of the scene. I think I said the words "Holy shit," to myself.

Mark scooped up some loose dirt and gravel from the ground, held it in his hand for a moment. He threw it angrily away from him and stood up.

"CUT," the director said.

People applauded.

"Got another one in you, love?" the director called out.

Mark, whose nose was running, gave a thumbs-up to the director.

"Lovely," the director said.

"Everyone back to one," the AD shouted. "Fast, people."

They shot the sequence three more times. Mark cried every time. It was totally brilliant.

The producer turned to me.

"You know your dad is a real badass, right?" he asked. "Your dad is the man."

"Yeah," I said. I had gotten this huge surge of adrenaline when I thought everything was going wrong, and I felt it starting to leave my body. I felt a little tired, and almost sad. "He's awesome," I said.

Crew members moved in and began laying down a new track for the camera, fitting it to a longer track that extended away from the set. Mark stayed squatted down.

"However you are moving, move twice as fast," the director shouted. He lit a cigarette, and moved over to Mark, hunched down beside him, said a few words. Mark nodded. The director stood up and bent over Neal, who reached for the director's cigarette.

"Two minutes!" the AD shouted. "I want this done in TWO MINUTES."

The makeup woman came over to Mark carrying an umbrella. She sat down next to him, holding the umbrella over his head. Mark took the umbrella from her, and put his arm around her.

A caterer appeared and offered mini club sandwiches from a tray. Kati materialized behind her.

"I'll get you something vegetarian," she said.

"No, no, I'm okay," I said, but she disappeared again. The makeup woman had her head on Mark's shoulder now, and Neal joined their circle. Neal put his arm around Mark. Someone came forward and took their picture. Mark looked around and spotted me. He said something to the makeup girl and pointed. The makeup girl smiled and waved at me. I waved back. Kati appeared carrying a yogurt-and-granola parfait. We were in the middle of the desert and Kati got parfait.

"We need to be rolling in THREE MINUTES," the AD shouted. "WE ARE GOING IN THREE MINUTES. I AM TOTALLY SERI-OUS."

Twenty-four minutes later they were filming again.

This time, all Mark had to do was stand still while the camera rolled on its track away from him. They did this once and then the director stood up on his seat. Someone handed him a bullhorn.

"Ladies and gents," he said. "Some applause for the actors, please." There was clapping and some cheering from the crew. "Okay," continued the director. "I did my whole big speech yesterday and it's hot as fuck out here and you know I can no longer stand the sight of each and every one of you and I'm only showing up to the party to get the free alcohol that has been promised me. That said, I love you all madly and you sweated blood for me this season and I'm a lucky, lucky bastard and this is . . . officially . . . a WRAP."

People cheered again for a minute and then immediately started working again, dismantling the track and breaking down cables.

"So what did you think?" Mark asked me later, in the car on the way back home.

"You're really, really good," I said. "I know you say that it's mostly just sitting around, but it doesn't look like that to me. It was so cool . . . seeing you do all that. I'm impressed."

"Thanks. It was cool having you there."

"What did the director say to you? You know, when you suddenly got all intense."

"David?" Mark laughed. "He said, 'Okay darling, let's have it. Bring me the juice, baby.' " Mark does a very good imitation of the director's accent.

"You learn to save your moments," Mark said. "For when they'll count."

"You must be really tired," I said.

"I'm okay," Mark shrugged. "I'm a little wired actually."

When we got home, Mark unpacked the two boxes of things from his trailer that he had collected, and I made my special tofu Thai salad for us to eat. He said he had some work to do, and I said I would write even though I didn't really have any essay ideas. I was hoping one would sort of emerge.

I don't know what Mark's doing. I've heard him pacing around the house the entire time I've been writing this.

Luke pauses, listens to the sound of Mark coming down the hallway, turns to see his father standing in the doorway.

"So," Mark says. "I actually have something for you to read. Actually."

"Oh, great," Luke says. "What is it?"

Mark holds out not a book, but a couple of typewritten pages. He hands these to Luke.

"Is it a script?" Luke glances down. The pages look to be in script format.

"Sort of," Mark says. "It's something I've been working on."

"Oh," Luke says. "Wow. That's great. I'll read it right now."

"Actually, give it back to me."

"Really?" Luke holds out the pages to Mark.

"No," Mark says. "No. It's okay. Read it. Come find me when you're done?"

"Sure," Luke says. "Absolutely."

Mark nods, and leaves. Luke settles himself to read.

                    INTERIOR: KARA'S BEDROOM,
                UPPER WEST SIDE NEW YORK CITY

KARA (mid 20s? very attractive, bohemian) lies in bed. Next to her is a fancy pink cradle with a yellow mobile hanging over it. TONY (barely 20 years old, nervous and awkward) stands just inside the door, holding a cheap bouquet of flowers. The sounds of two little girls playing can be heard intermittently throughout.

                            TONY

    Hey!

                            KARA

    Hey yourself! Thank you so much for coming.

                            TONY
                    (waving the flowers)
    I brought you these.

KARA
(holding her arms out)
Oh, thank you so much Tony. Those are beautiful.

Tony moves over to the bed (on the opposite side of where the cradle is) and hands Kara the flowers. She smells them and places them in her lap. Tony retreats to the foot of the bed.

TONY
So . . . Mazel Tov!

KARA
(startled)
Oh! Oh, thank you. I . . . I didn't know you were Jewish, Tony.

TONY
I'm not. I thought you were.

KARA
Really? You thought I was Jewish?

TONY
You said, "Oy vey." When I was . . . you know . . . here. Before. I said something to you and you said, "Oy vey."

KARA
Really? Well, you know lots of people in New York say, "Oy vey."

TONY

People in New York who are Jewish say, "Oy vey."
Everybody else says, "Holy shit."

KARA

Well, those aren't the only options.

TONY

No. I know. I'm sorry. I don't know what I'm
talking about. I'm a little nervous.

KARA
(kindly)

It's okay, Tony.

TONY

Let me start over.
(He smiles)
Congratulations!

KARA
(smiling too)

Holy shit!

They laugh, the tension broken a little bit.

KARA

Oh, Tony. I remember now. It was when you
said . . .

TONY

Yeah. It was when I told you I was gay. I said,
I'm gay, and you said, Oy vey.

KARA

I'm sorry about that. That was really insensitive of me.

TONY

Well, my timing was off.

KARA

I was just a little surprised.

TONY

Yeah, of course.

KARA

Because you know, you didn't seem to have any
trouble . . .

TONY

I'm twenty.

KARA

Even so.

TONY

And I was drunk.

KARA

Off two glasses of wine?

TONY

I hadn't eaten much that day.

KARA

You don't have to apologize.

TONY

I knew any straight guy would jump at the
chance to have sex with you. It was like a fantasy that straight guys talk about. Guy goes
over to fix a lady's VCR ... you know, it was
sort of exciting.

KARA

I can see that.

TONY

It was a classic situation. I had tools in my
hand.

KARA

You did?

TONY

Well, a pocket wrench.

KARA

Well, no wonder I thought you were straight.

TONY

I've done it with girls before.

KARA

I could tell.

TONY

You could?

KARA

Tony, I'm really just incredibly grateful to
you. It's important to me that you know that.

                    TONY
I didn't want to be gay. I still don't. I don't
want to be gay.

                    KARA
Tony, there is nothing wrong with being gay.

                    TONY
                  (sighing)
Oy vey.

Tony moves over to the cradle and looks down into it. It's
clear from his body language that he is conflicted—that he
would like to pick up the baby in the cradle, and also that
he is not sure he has the right to. Instead, he fingers the
yellow cutouts of the mobile.

                    TONY
This is cute.

                    KARA
My daughter Aurora made it. She's very intui-
tive. She could see the baby's aura in the womb
and she made those little drawings for me.

Tony has no idea what Kara is talking about because he's
never really heard the word "aura" before and the only
Aura he knows about is a bar on Avenue A that has hookah
pipes in it and is a place people go to if they want to score
some coke.

                    TONY
            (poking a yellow cutout)
Little peanuts.

                    KARA
                 (laughing)
They aren't little peanuts. It's the shape of
the fetus at seven months.

                    TONY
Oh.

Pause.

              TONY (CONT'D)
What's his name?

                    KARA
Sky.

                    TONY
No, really.

                    KARA
Sky. That's what I'm going to call him.

                    TONY
Really?

                    KARA
I thought it went with the names of my other
two children. Aurora, Pearl, and Sky.

                    TONY
    Wait a second.

                    KARA
    What?

                    TONY
    Is it Sky as in Skywalker?

KARA blushes.

                    TONY
    When I was here I put in a tape to test your
    VCR. *Star Wars.* And you said you hadn't seen
    it, and I said you really should. And I acciden-
    tally left it here. You watched it, didn't you?
    You're naming him Sky after Luke Skywalker.

                    KARA
    You were right. It's a very good movie. I'm sorry
    I didn't return it.

                    TONY
    I guess that makes me Darth Vader.

                    KARA
    Oh, no. Anyway I haven't totally decided about
    Sky. It's just an idea.

Tony knows there is not much he can do for this baby, his
son. He cannot even really take in the fact that this son
is his. He has already thrown up three times this day. He
feels sick and confused and he wants to do something, but

he doesn't know what. He feels that Kara is a good person, a caring person, and that she will love this baby. He also feels that she has hung yellow fetuses over his son's head and what, really, is there to stop her from naming his son Han Solo? Or Yoda. Tony tries to think of something he can do. He wants desperately to do something.

> TONY
>
> What about Luke?

> KARA
>
> Luke?

> TONY
>
> It's a nice name.

> KARA
>
> Yes. It is. I like that name.

> TONY
>
> If you give him a name like Sky, then he's going to have to become the kind of person who would have a name like Sky.

> KARA
>
> Well, that wouldn't be so bad. The sky is beautiful and open and free.

> TONY
>
> Not if you're falling through it without a parachute.

Pause.

TONY (CONT'D)
It's just a thought. I know I don't have a right
to . . . you know, interfere or anything.

KARA
I can call him Luke. I can do that.

Tony reaches down into the cradle and picks up LUKE. He
holds him. Luke opens his eyes and looks at Tony. Tony
holds his son and hopes with everything he has that he
will meet this boy, his boy, again when his life isn't so
fucked up and weird and he isn't living on baked beans.
When he is something his son could look up to.

FADE OUT.

Luke sets the pages down in his desk. He picks them up, sets
them down again. He picks them up, starts to reread them, sets them
down. He stands up. Sits down. He accidentally knocks the pages to
the floor. Luke's physical actions mirror the activity of his neurons,
which are spraying electrical charges like crazy, in all directions. Luke,
mentally and physically rickety, looks for solid ground. He picks up
the papers, makes a neat pile of them on his desk. Mark, he thinks,
will want them back.

Luke moves into the living room. He can see through the French
doors that his father is sitting on the patio. Luke looks at the back of
his father's head.

Luke opens up the French doors and steps outside. Mark, who is
drinking a beer and smoking a cigarette, stands up hastily and faces
Luke. Mark takes a swig of beer and nervously flicks his cigarette
toward an ashtray on the table. Luke can see that there is already one
stubbed-out cigarette in the ashtray.

"Hey," says Luke.

"Hey," says Mark.

Luke thinks of speeds: 25 percent, 50 percent, 75 percent. Luke begins slowly. He does not want to hurt his father. He does not want to lose his father, the half of himself, the identically longer second toe, the possible WINNING slot at the bottom of a Plinko board.

"When I told you that thing," Luke says, "about what happened to me when I was reading the Bible? About how I realized that I think I'm basically physically unable to believe in God?"

Mark nods.

"Well, when I told you that," Luke continues, "I wasn't telling you because I feel like . . . like I want to start telling everyone that. I don't tell people that. I'm not ashamed; it's just that it will make things complicated for me at home. So, it was . . . something between you and me, I guess."

"I won't tell anyone," Mark says. "I won't tell anyone what you told me."

"Is that . . . ?" Luke asks, tentatively.

"I understand exactly what you mean," Mark says. "I feel the same way. I feel exactly the same way. I wish . . . I wish I could tell you how . . . it's just that . . . how do I say this?"

Luke waits.

"Everyone is the person that I haven't told, Luke," Mark says. "Everyone. And I didn't want you to be everyone, too."

Luke thinks that he would like to hug his father. Before he can finish the thought, Luke is hugging his father.

They are slightly different in height. Luke steps forward on his toes an inch in order for his chin to make it past Mark's shoulder. This throws Luke's balance off a little and he leans into Mark, who, after a moment, hugs Luke very hard, almost lifting him off his feet. Releasing each other, they stagger a little, and then stand there nodding, as if they approve of their clumsiness.

"Would you like a beer?" Mark asks.

"Um . . . maybe?"

"It seems like the occasion calls for something a little stronger than water," Mark says. "I'll get you a beer."

Mark goes inside the house and Luke sits down on the bamboo armchair next to Mark's. No matter how hot it gets during the day, it still gets quite cool at night in Los Angeles. Mark has turned the heat lamp on. Somewhere, a fire truck is sounding its alarm. Somewhere in Los Angeles, Luke has noticed, a fire truck is always sounding its alarm.

Mark comes through the French doors carrying two beers, hands one to Luke. Mark sits down. Mark and Luke look at the empty back-yard for a moment. Mark holds out his bottle toward Luke without looking at Luke, and Luke holds out his bottle toward Mark without looking at Mark. They clink bottles.

"So," Luke says. "It turns out you're a smoker."

Mark gives a short laugh, almost a bark.

"Good one."

They sip their beers.

"So," Luke says. "I'm thinking you . . . spiced up the dialogue a little bit from the original version?"

"I was hoping for a sitcom effect. Rather than some sort of Tennessee Williams drama."

"There's some pretty funny lines in there."

"Well, we're known for our sense of humor," Mark says, lighting another cigarette.

Luke takes a sip of his beer. He's only ever had a few sips of beer before, and hasn't cared for the taste, although this one tastes pretty good.

"Sara didn't tell me," Luke says, just now realizing this.

"When I talked to her, you know, when we got back in touch, we didn't really talk about it. I sort of . . . anyway, it's not . . . I don't know.

"On a level of one to ten," Mark asks, after a moment. "How uncomfortable are you right now?"

Luke looks at Mark.

"I'm not uncomfortable at all," Luke says, who is mostly not.

Luke has participated in social and political discussions regarding homosexuality, but has not fully conceptualized the sexual mechanics of it. Luke cannot connect Mark to the one or two vaguely repellant images he does have. He knows that some men are gay and do gay things and Luke now knows that Mark is gay but Mark is definitely not "some men" therefore Mark does not do anything Luke would find repellant.

"I'm something," Luke says, who has gotten a little lost in the circuitous loops of his own logic. "But not uncomfortable. What number are you?"

Mark takes a long drag off his cigarette.

"I'm about a seven, I guess," Mark says. "There is also . . . I'm registering high on the fear factor. 'Cause . . . well . . . I don't know what happens next. And . . . you know . . . did I just ruin something?"

"No way," Luke says. "Not a chance."

"No?"

"No way."

"Does it change things between us?" Mark asks.

Luke thinks.

"Yes," Luke says.

I know him now, Luke thinks. Now, I know him. He wants me to know him and I do. He wants me to be the one person who knows him.

Mark laughs, a genuine laugh this time.

"Yeah," Mark says. "Yeah, I guess it does."

Luke and Mark clink beers again.

"So you can ask questions and stuff," Mark says. "Whatever you want."

Luke and Mark sip beer. Luke listens to the cicadas sing in the yard.

"Oh, Dad?" Luke asks, abandoning, forever, the italics.

"Yes?"

"I forgot to ask you," Luke says. "Is 'yclept' really a word?"

There is a long pause. Luke decides that he will not drink any more beer. Cicadas sing.

"Yes, that's right," Mark says, at last. "That was a really genius move on my part. I'm glad you remembered."

"So, it's a real word?" Luke asks.

"It's a real word," Mark says.

"What's it mean?" Luke is almost sleepy now. It has been a long day.

"Named," Mark says. "It means named."

CHAPTER NINE

N ames can be very deceptive, for they divert our thoughts from what is accurate, to what is inaccurate. Thus one who hears the word 'God' does not perceive what is accurate, but perceives what is inaccurate. So also with The Father, and The Son, and The Holy Spirit, and Life, and Light, and Resurrection, and The Church, and all the Rest. People do not perceive what is accurate, but they perceive what is inaccurate."

That's from the Gnostic Gospel of Philip. Sara was big into the Gnostics at one point, and this was a favorite of hers.

The subject of names has come up in my family over the years. As in, "Why did you name me what you did?" This is inevitable in a family of the twentieth, and then twenty-first, century where one of the family members is named Pearl.

Pearl used to complain about her name, but I guess she got used to it, or grew into it, or something. Now she wears her name with a certain defiant majesty, like the way another person might wear a giant afro. Pearl doesn't have a nickname, although sometimes Sara calls her "Kali." Kali is a Hindu goddess, the one who went into a killing frenzy against a field of demons. Kali is usually depicted standing on top of her husband, Shiva, with a bunch of weapons in her hand and her tongue hanging out.

Aurora we often call Rory.

I don't have an official nickname but sometimes my sisters call me Ribs because I am skinny. I have my collection of running aliases but I don't tell people about those.

All I ever heard about my name was that I was going to be called Leila, because Leila is the feminine form of the Semitic word for night and Sara thought it would be appropriate to go from Aurora (dawn) to Leila (night). Sara did say that "Luke" just seemed to fit me. Personally, I like that it is monosyllabic.

The possibility of being yclept Sky was never mentioned. I'm really glad my name isn't Sky.

I guess I should go and look at that Moment Before picture again, in the light of this new information. Names aren't the only things that are deceptive. Sometimes images are too. You can see the mobile above my crib in the photo, but I thought the little yellow things were snails. Or bananas. I didn't know they were renderings of me and my aura.

A word here about Aurora and auras: yes, she does see colors around things, not around everything, but a lot of things. There is a closet in our house that we call "The Blue Closet" not because it's painted blue, but because Aurora says that it has a blue aura. Interestingly, I was no longer yellow once I was born. I was green, and at a certain point I became orange. Aurora also has a very particular sense of smell. I think these two things might be linked, and that Aurora might have a form of synesthesia, which is where two sensory modalities in your brain involuntarily cross each other. I was reading about this the other day. The most common form of synesthesia is to experience numbers as colors, but there are lots of different manifestations. In fact, synesthetes can go their whole lives undiagnosed, and never fully consciously register the correlations they are making. Maybe Aurora sees the Blue Closet as Blue because it has cedar chips in it, and whenever she smells cedar wood, her brain says: blue. Maybe my colors have changed because my changing hormones have changed the way I smell. Synesthesia is consistent, which is how they know it's not just people being artistic, so it would be simple to test Rory and see if she has it. I'm not going to suggest this to her, though. I think she would prefer to be someone who sees auras, and not have to go back and review her whole life and change all the times she saw an aura into a time she was having a multimodal sensory experience.

I think certain things make more sense now that I know what I know. For instance, Aimee makes more sense now. (Although the thing with her purse is still a mystery.) Why it took my dad seventeen years to get in touch with me makes more sense. You can see how things were complicated for him.

I wasn't sure what the rules were, on us talking about his script, but throughout the past two days my dad and I have kept up a running conversation about things between conversations about other unrelated things in a kind of extended parenthetical statement.

Like, yesterday we spent the day going into all these cool stores in an area here called Silver Lake. There were other people around, sometimes, so we didn't go into details, or say anything if we were in earshot of other people, but we did talk. Mark has a way of creating a kind of bubble of privacy around us when we are in public.

When we were looking at these funny kitchen gadgets in a store called "Eat Me," I said, "Check out these salt and pepper shakers," and he said, "Oh, those are cool," and I asked, (Does Kati know?) and he said, (Nobody knows. Whether or not they suspect is another story.) Later on, at an antique place called "Den of Antiquity," after I explained synesthesia to my dad he said, (Well, I haven't been a monk my whole life, so there are people who know.) And then when we stopped for tea at Casbah Cafe we talked about different foods we don't like and he threw in, (I've been careful. The people that know have just as much reason as I do for no one to know), and I said, (Oh because they are famous too?) and he said, (That, or married.) On a side note: both my dad and I have an aversion to cottage cheese.

The other question I asked him was, (Do you still feel the same way? That it's something you don't want to be?) But for that he had only one answer: (It is what it is), he said.

It's funny how people use that phrase. People say it when they feel stuck, or indifferent, or helpless about something. "It is what it is" is something people say when they want to express, "I guess I can't change it," or "Too bad, but I can't do anything about it," or "I can't think of any adjectives."

By "people," I should clarify, I mean people who are not Zen Buddhists. In Zen Buddhism, "It is what it is" is like the equivalent of, "HUZZAH!"

Last night we had dinner at home, and my dad and I were able to have a fuller, nonparenthetical conversation about things.

"I always knew it," he said. "Even when I was a kid. I just thought it was maybe like a mental thing. Because I can have sex with girls, you know. Well, obviously I can have sex with girls."

"Yeah, no one at this table is going to debate that," I told him.

"And you know," he said. "The gay scene in New York at the end of the eighties? It was a funeral parlor. Everybody had died these fucking awful deaths or watched everyone else die some awful death. I used to pass this gay bar on my way home from work and these older men would be walking in or out and they'd see me and they'd have this look in their eyes and . . . anyway, it just seemed like a whole lifestyle I didn't want. I really just wanted to stay away from the whole scene."

"Things are different now, though," I said. "There's still AIDS, but the stigma about being gay . . . most people don't think like that. You can have any lifestyle you want. And there are some gay actors, right? I mean actors that are openly gay?"

"More in England," my dad said. "Here, not so much. And those don't play romantic leads, or action heroes. Can you name a single A-list American movie star who's gay? It's not a judgment thing, even. People may be totally liberal, have a ton of gay friends, think gays should be able to get married, everything, but they're still not gonna want to see me as a romantic lead if they know that I'm gay. It'll ruin the fantasy. The whole time I'm kissing the girl they'll be thinking, 'But he's really *gay.*' "

"I guess there is a possibility that I could be gay, too," I said. "I've never had sex so I don't have evidence either way."

"You've never had sex?" he asked. "Not with Amy with a 'y'?"

"Well, she wanted to," I said. "And I wanted to, but not totally. I mean I had mixed feelings about it. So, I'm saying that as far as I know, my mixed feelings were because I'm gay and I just don't know it yet."

"Luke, do you look at dudes and think, 'I'd like to have sex with that dude'?" my dad asked. "I'm not talking about random speculation, or enjoying musicals. I'm saying . . . you know . . . bottom line is: do you want to suck cock?"

"Um . . . no," I said. "Definitely not."

"Then you're not gay," he said.

This is perhaps my favorite conversation with my dad so far. It might rank as one of my favorite conversations ever. There is no way I could have had this kind of exchange with Sara, or one of my sisters. With them it would be days, weeks, possibly months of conversation and they would be interested in the entire history of my sexual thought process, and ask lots of questions, and in the end the whole thing would end up in some sort of "Well, you should be open and honest with yourself" and they would never forget that I once voiced doubt and would always and forevermore think of me as someone who is sexually ambivalent, or bi-curious, and would email me articles about this and would stay gender neutral when asking if I am dating someone.

I'm glad I told my dad about being an atheist, if that's what I am, because it seems like we both have a thing about ourselves that we prefer to keep private, but we both know what the other one's is, and we can relate to each other even better. And that's another conversation we can have, in between other conversations. Like, on the way to the wrap party today, we drove past this guy who was carrying a big "Jesus Saves" poster and we were listening to *This American Life* on the radio at the time, but later my dad asked me, "So, you don't believe in Jesus either?" and I knew he had seen that guy and his poster too.

"I don't believe in a supernatural Jesus," I explained. "There *might* have been a guy they based those stories on, but all those stories are basically the same ones you get in every religion, and if there was a Jesus, he had an earthly father just like the rest of us suckers."

That made my dad smile.

And later, at the actual party, when we were on the Ferris wheel, he said, "So, okay, no old guy with a beard in the sky, but what about there being some kind of force in the universe that connects us all?" and I said, "Well, nobody really believes in an old guy with a beard, right? Not really. That's just what people say, like, 'Hey, I'm not a *crazy* Christian! I don't believe in an old guy with a beard! I only believe in a mysterious, unknowable, improvable, eternal, invisible force that is intimately connected with the events of the universe and my personal life and fortunes!'"

"But there's a big difference," my dad argued, after he finished laughing, "between saying, 'I believe in a Universal Force that promotes love' and 'I believe God thinks homos should go to hell.'"

"They sound different," I agreed. "But you're still saying it's something other than you that is handing out morality. A God of Love or a God of Hate is still a God. Your universal life force might as well be an old guy with a beard," and he said, "Huh, I never thought of it like that."

The wrap party really *was* like a carnival. They had all kinds of rides and games set up, and different booths, and a huge buffet under a tent (I still cannot get over how there is, like, delicious prepared food *everywhere* here). Someone on the crew had made a great short film, and they were projecting it on a wall inside the tent. It was set to Louis Armstrong singing "What a Wonderful World" and the images were all of the ruined-Earth sets of *The Last* but with actors and crew hugging or laughing and stuff. It was really nice, seeing my dad smiling and hugging, and funny too, because sometimes when the song went to the chorus and the lyrics were "What a wonderful world" it was just a close-up shot of my dad standing there without a shirt and everybody watching would whistle and say, "Yeah, baby," and stuff.

I teased him a little about this and he said, "I don't think it has much to do with me, really. I've been around for awhile, you know, and nobody put me on a list of hot male actors until now. It's more about fame. And the character I play. Anyway, all this stuff about how 'sexy' or 'hot' famous people are? It's just a sign of how bored people are with the people they're actually fucking."

I suppose people think of my dad a certain way because of who he pretends to be, but some of what he pretends to be is also what he actually is. So some of the symbol of what he is for other people is also him. It's interesting to think about how nothing about his looks, or his voice, or the way he carries himself would change if people knew he was gay, but a lot of people would interpret all those things differently. They'd read the symbol differently, I mean.

I know that some people—including people who are gay— think that you shouldn't discriminate against gay people, because they can't help being gay. "It's how they were made," they say, or, "I didn't have a choice." This may be true, although we don't know whether it's a gene, or prenatal hormones, or whether there are "gay" brains, or "straight" brains. It's a weird argument, though, because you shouldn't discriminate against people at all; whether or not they chose or were chosen shouldn't make a difference. We don't say, "Hey, let's not discriminate against African Americans because they can't help being African American."

We are not supposed to judge other people. If you follow that argument, then not judging other people means you also can't judge other people for being judgmental. People usually don't follow that argument to its conclusion, though, because the sum of it is zero and zero is not a very satisfying number. Unless you are a Zen Buddhist and then zero is, like, awesome.

At best we are getting "truth" in tiny bits and pieces. Faster neurons tell parts of the brain what you are seeing before slower neurons actually assess what you are seeing: like you are watching a movie and someone is leaning over your shoulder telling you about the characters—"He's a villain. She's really an alien"—right as the characters appear, before you've gotten a chance to know them. There is no such thing as total objectivity. We have blind spots, actual ones, because there are no light-sensitive cones where the optic nerve connects to the retina, but we don't experience that because we automatically fill in the blind spot with information surrounding it. We'd freak out and probably fall over if we knew how little we are actually seeing, or how accurately. People put this huge emphasis on being truthful, but our brains are designed to alter reality. We have to tell ourselves lies just to stay on our feet.

Even with observation being what it is (partial and subjective) I'm still really looking forward to going to Illinois and meeting my dad's mom, and getting to see the house where he grew up and everything. We're going in two days. Mark said we should ask Sara if this is all okay with her, but we can't ask Sara about anything right now, because she is at a Vipassana retreat, and you take a vow of silence at those. She'll be there for a month, meditating and not speaking. Knowing how to not speak is something most people have to practice, but I think both my parents have it down pretty well.

. . .

Luke, who has been typing out the better part of these thoughts, stops typing. It is almost two in the morning. Luke knows he cannot use any of what he has been writing about his father in an essay, but he feels that he has made several declarative statements stating his opinion on things, and that this is more the direction he needs to be moving in.

Luke is faced now with the problem of what to do with what he has written. He is not entirely comfortable leaving it on his computer, which could be stolen, or lost, or hacked into. This, Luke thinks, would be bad. On the other hand, Luke does not want to erase what he has written, at least not yet, while there is a possibility that one or two sentences might provide something for an actual essay. Luke decides to download the writing onto a disc. He does this. Luke removes the disc from his computer, and erases the writing from the hard drive on his computer. Luke then picks up a pen, and considers how to label the disc in a way that will prevent both theft and accidental listening. After a moment, he writes "Early Harpsichord Music" on it. Surely, Luke thinks, the mathematical probability of the kind of person who would steal a disc being *also* the kind of person who is an Early Harpsichord enthusiast would be very small. Satisfied, Luke goes to bed.

CHAPTER TEN

Mark and I flew into Chicago yesterday. We checked into this really nice hotel and then went to the Natural History Museum for a few hours. When Mark told me this plan he said it was so that we didn't have to get off a plane and immediately into a car, although we flew first-class which is extremely comfortable. I also offered to do the driving but Mark said, "No, let's take it easy." Later, at dinner, I suggested we take one of the late-night architectural tours you can do in Chicago by boat, on the river that runs right through downtown. There was a pamphlet about it in my hotel room.

"I don't know anything about architecture," I said. "But it looks pretty cool."

"Actually, I'm sort of . . . meeting someone here tonight," Mark said.

"Oh," I said. (That's when I realized why my dad got me my own room, on a different floor from his.)

"It's someone I see from time to time," he said. "When we can."

"Oh, okay," I said. "No problem."

"Hey, I can cancel," Mark said. "Well, not cancel, but push it back till later. That does sound cool."

"No, no, it's okay," I said. "Maybe we can do it on our way back or something."

"Seriously, Luke," he said. "If it's important to you . . ."

"Hey, I can just go on my own," I said. "That's fine with me. I like doing stuff on my own."

After dinner, Mark went to his room, and I went to mine. I thought maybe I would just take it easy and read or something, but I was restless. I was also a little pissed, I guess. Anyway, I ended up doing the boat tour, and I'm glad I did. I think that I will make a good solitary tourist someday, because I have an excellent sense of direction, and I don't have problems talking to strangers. I met a really nice couple from Bangladesh on the boat tour, and they ended up giving me their address and inviting me to their home and everything, if ever I am in Chittagong.

This morning Mark drove because he said getting out of Chicago was tricky. I didn't ask him anything about anything. During the drive, we played music and kind of thought our own thoughts. There wasn't much scenery on the way from the airport to Grover. Basically just really flat fields on either side of the highway.

Grover itself reminds me of Acton a little bit, if you flattened Acton out. Sort of like Acton on a two-dimensional plane.

"You are now officially in suburbia," Mark said, when we entered the town.

"We seem kind of far away from a big city, though," I pointed out. "Like if this is a suburb of Chicago, it's really sub."

"It's super suburbia," Mark agreed. "It's über suburbia."

"Über-burbia," I suggested.

"Über-burbia," Mark said, nodding. "Well done, my young apprentice."

We drove past the hospital where his mom works as a nurse, past a Dairy Queen where Mark worked one summer, and past Grover High School, where he played football and acted in school plays.

"Yeah, there it is," he said, as we drove past the high school. "The scene of my troubled youth."

"How troubled were you?" I asked.

"Oh, I had a ton of friends," he said. "I wasn't this amazing genius student, like you, but I did okay. I hung out with the jocks in football season, and the drama kids in the spring. You're gonna see about ten million photo albums at my mom's of this. Be prepared."

The house where Mark grew up is a regular-sized house on a street called Maple, although I haven't seen any actual maple trees on it. We pulled into the driveway and the front door opened and this really short woman all in pink clothes came out waving both hands and Mark said, "That's my mom."

"What should I call her?" I asked quickly.

"Everybody calls her Bubbles," he said, opening the car door. "Hey, Mom."

I got out of the car. The woman made a little rush at Mark, sort of bumping his chest with the top of her head, and he tried to catch her by the shoulders, but she had already moved away and turned to me. I wasn't sure if we were going to hug, or what, so I just tried to stay physically neutral, and she clasped me by the elbows, and sort of flapped my arms up and down while looking me over. "So you've found Luke," Mark said behind her.

"*You've* found Luke," she said. "*You* found Luke, after losing him all these years, you stupid motherfucker."

She's this little tiny thing, this grandmother of mine, and she looks a lot younger than Nana. She doesn't have any gray hair and she was dressed all in pink, with pink tennis shoes. She is a little bit chubby, or maybe what you might call voluptuous, and what with the arm flapping and her being so much shorter than I am, I found myself, for the second time in my life, sort of confronted with a grandmother's breasts. Only looking down this time, instead of up, and this grandmother wasn't naked, which was a relief. I was still taking all this in, along with the fact that she had just called my dad a "stupid motherfucker," and that I was supposed to call her "Bubbles," when Bubbles released me and said,

"Okay, you better come inside before the neighbors all come out and try to take pictures of my movie-star son. Get the bags, Tony."

"Careful," my dad said to me, when we first went into the house, "we are in a knickknack booby trap."

"I heard that, asshole," Bubbles said.

First she gave us a tour of the house. Mark needed the tour too, because he had to see all the improvements. She has a new couch, a new TV, a new TV stand, a new washer and dryer, a new microwave, and a new shoe rack. I'm thinking that my dad must have given her the money for all these things, because after she showed us each item, she would do that head-butting thing at my dad's chest and say, "That's my good boy." And each time my dad would try to grab her shoulders and she would move away. This seems to be the way they embrace each other. There are indeed pictures of my dad all over the house, in frames with fabric or lace around them. Almost everything in Bubbles's house is trimmed with something, and most surfaces are covered with little figurines. Bubbles has a lot of collections. She has a collection of things that are strawberry themed, and she has a collection of miniature horses. There are groups of china angels, and groups of glass-domed paperweights with skylines of different cities under them. She also seems to like teddy bears, and birds.

In the hallway, there is a lineup of pictures of my dad, class photos and team photos, stuff like that. I can see from these that when he was my age he wasn't some big muscle guy at all, he was actually more my size. Bubbles gave me a high-speed caption explanation of each photo:

"OkaycanyoubelievethisskinnybabyIhadtotiehimdowntocuthis-hairbrokehisarmfallingoffaswingsetatschoolIalmostsuedthosemoth-erfuckersandnowhewouldntsmilefortwoyearsbecausehedidntwant-noonetoseehisbracesokaynowwearesmilingseeandImadeallthecos-tumesforhisschoolplaysseehetookthisgirltopromshewasatramp."

Later we had dinner.

We sat in Bubbles's kitchen nook and drank lemonade out of glasses with strawberries printed on them, eating grilled-cheese sandwiches (according to Bubbles, Mark's favorite food), and talked, sort of. My dad would ask Bubbles how work was going and Bubbles would say something like, "You want see some shit, come to work with me. I got this woman now, whole right side of her body looks like burnt ham. Three kids, husband. Husband is like, What are the options? I'm like, Options? Options are you get in there and tell her you love her, you sack. See, they laid off two of the psych nurses, so there's nobody to counsel these people but us." And then Mark and I would say, "Mhmm" or "Wow" and then Bubbles would say, "We all had to take this seminar: sensitivity training, they called it. I'm like, I've been a nurse for thirty-five years, you think I need to be more sensitive? Let me tell you something, when the shit goes down, you don't need to be more sensitive, you need to act right. This guy, he wants to stand out in the hallway while his wife is lying there half dead, and he wants to know if we can skin-graft her back to normal. You think I should be sensitive with this guy? The other day, Nancy got this guy . . ."

And it kind of went on like that.

So here I am, sitting at the desk in the room that my dad grew up in. It's kind of a small room. It's a little bit sad, in some way. Maybe it's not sad. I don't know. Above the desk is a shelf, with three trophies and two framed pieces of paper. One is a certificate commemorating Anthony Boyle's completion in something called "Polar Bear Swim Camp," and the other is my dad's high school diploma. Two of the trophies are for Grover High City Champs, and the figurines above the plaques are carrying footballs. The third trophy isn't as big as the football ones, and is for Mark Franco: Best Performance by an Actor in a Television Series—Drama. It's a Golden Globe award. There is a photo on the desk, in a frame with gold stars, of Mark standing on a stage holding the award. It looks like the picture was taken off of a television screen. I'm going to go to bed now.

Luke turns off the desk lamp and gets into his father's old twin-sized bed. The sheets have a slightly musty, flowery smell. Mark is sleeping on the couch in the living room, and Luke can hear his father turning over, sighing, thumping a pillow. It is the kind of house in which you can hear what other people are doing in other rooms, quite distinctly. Luke stares at the ceiling. He waits for his eyes to adjust to the darkness.

After lunch, Bubbles went to work. Mark had Luke drive them to a place called Kickapoo Park, where Mark said there were some good running trails. They did not talk much in the car, because Luke was concentrating on driving well, and Mark was pointing out more things along the way: "That's where my friend Brian lived," or "God, they have a Chinese restaurant there now? That used to be a Wendy's."

When Mark and Luke got to the park, they found a trail that looked promising, and ran it fast. Luke noticed the humidity, and the presence of bugs, conditions more similar to Delaware than California. Mark suggested running over to the lake and taking a dip to cool off. They removed their running shoes and socks and their sweat-soaked T-shirts at the lake's edge, and waded in. The water was fairly muddy at first, but refreshingly cool. In the distance, they could see powerboats on the lake, and someone water-skiing.

"On the other side of the lake is where the country club is," Mark said. "We weren't members, though. My friends and I used to sneak in at night and do shit, you know. Drink beer. Get high. Try to scare each other."

"Well, we could do that tonight if you want," Luke said.

"Ha. Can you touch the bottom here?"

"I can kind of bounce off it."

"So you okay?" Mark asked.

"Oh yeah," Luke said. "I can tread water for a long time. Or I can bounce." Luke demonstrated this.

"No, I mean with being here. Meeting Bubbles. It's a little awkward. She's a piece of work, I know. And believe me, she's actually mellowed a lot."

"Why do they call her Bubbles?" Luke asked.

"I don't really know. She used to drink."

"Oh," Luke said. "She doesn't anymore?"

"No."

"She seems nice," Luke said, lying.

"Luke," Mark said. "Really? *Nice?*"

"Well, I don't know," Luke amended, partially. "I didn't actually form a concrete opinion or anything like that."

"She's been a little pissed at me," Mark said. "Because I told her that I knew about you, and I didn't ever tell her, and I didn't . . . you know . . . do anything until now."

"Oh. Is that why she called you . . . ?"

"A stupid motherfucker?" Mark laughed. "No, that's normal. You see where I get my foul mouth now. She'll call you that too, if we stick around long enough."

"How long are we going to stay?" Luke asked.

"Well, I wanted to talk to you about that. The . . . uh . . . person I saw last night? I haven't seen that person in a long time and . . . I kinda want to see that person again. Like maybe on Saturday? Only if that's okay with you, though."

"Oh," Luke said. "Tomorrow? Okay. Yeah, that's cool. Won't Bubbles be upset, though? We just got here."

"Well, I thought I'd just go in the afternoon," Mark said. "And you can hang out with Mom, which is probably better anyway, because that'll give you some time just the two of you. And I'll come back on Sunday and we'll stay until Tuesday if we can both stand it?"

This was not exactly what Luke thought he was agreeing to, as he had imagined that Mark would take him with him to Chicago. Luke had not anticipated being left behind, and tried to think of a plausible objection other than, "Don't leave me here alone."

"What are you going to tell your mom?" Luke asked.

"I'll say that it's a work thing. She won't ask, though. And I mean, it's really you she wants to see, I think."

Bubbles had not said anything along the lines of, "Sit down and tell me all about yourself, my long-lost grandson." Luke had thought she might be more curious about him, but so far the only question Bubbles had asked Luke was if he had any dietary restrictions. Even that had not been phrased in question format. Bubbles had said, "I don't know what you eat," when she gave Luke a grilled-cheese sandwich.

"There's that barbecue on Sunday," Luke reminded his father. Bubbles was planning a sort of Franco family reunion, and several of Mark's uncles and cousins would be there.

"I'll be back Sunday morning."

Later, Mark and Luke had stayed at home and watched TV since Bubbles was still at work. They were unable to sprawl in their usual way in any of Bubbles's chairs, because of the knick-knack element. Mark ordered a pizza.

"Everyone knows about me, right?" Luke asked Mark at one point. "In your family, I mean?"

"Yeah, Bubbles spread the word," Mark said. "And I bet everyone said, 'Oh shit, really?' and that was pretty much it. We're not exactly the Royal Family. I guess compared to your family, we're kinda ... I don't know. There weren't any Francos on the *Mayflower*. Hey, are you really okay with me going tomorrow?"

"Sure."

Luke knew that Mark felt guilty and that "sure" was not a word that normally satisfied people. Luke didn't know if Mark felt guilty about abandoning him with a stranger in a house full of china teddy bears and pillows shaped like strawberries with someone who said things like, "Well, if you ask me you could use a little meat on your bones," when you told them you were a vegetarian, or guilty about going to Chicago to have sex with someone who was either a celebrity or married. Possibly, Luke thought, Mark felt guilty about leaving Bubbles with a seventeen-year-old stranger that she never knew about who didn't have the sense to know a good steak when he saw one. Luke himself felt guilty for not providing the necessary words that would release his father from any of these possible guilt sources. The phrases formed themselves in Luke's head: "Hey, that's great," and "I'm happy to stay here with your mom," or "Don't worry about me," but Luke did not say any of these things.

Luke, listening now to his father turn over once again on the pullout couch, wonders how Mark would feel sleeping in Luke's room in Delaware. Luke wonders how his father would feel if Luke brought him to Delaware and left him there by himself for a whole day with Sara and Nana.

Mark coughs.

Luke stretches himself out, and smacks his ankle against the wall. Mark coughs again. Luke inhales for a count of four, holds the breath for a count of four, exhales on a count of four. He does this ten times, then increases his breath to a count of five, then six. Luke tries to quiet the chemical processes within him. He visualizes the neurons in his brain moving to a resting potential, a quiescent state where the neurons keep their ionic charges separate. There are something like a hundred billion neurons in Luke's brain, working in large network systems: talking to each other, processing information, giving commands, and making associations. Luke does not want them to do this. He does not want chatter. He does not want ideas. He does not want to connect the dots.

Luke can take deep breaths, consciously slow down his heartbeat, relax his jaw. He can visualize running the perfect race and his body can learn this visualization. Luke can think about sex, and then decide not to think about sex.

Luke cannot keep potassium away from sodium in his brain, or sodium separate from chloride, simply by conceptualizing this, and trying to relax. "Resting potential" is a bit of a misnomer. An extraordinary amount of energy is needed to make things still, to keep things separate, to be silent, to think nothing of nothing.

CHAPTER ELEVEN

When I was ten, my sisters and I spent two weeks with Aunt Caroline and Uncle Louis at their house in White Plains, New York. Sara had not come with us because she was in Colorado leading a Rolfing seminar. Nana didn't come with us either. She went to Nebraska to visit her sister. We took the train by ourselves to White Plains, with Aurora acting as our leader, which meant that she got to hold the tickets and was in charge of keeping track of the stops so we would get out at the right one. I remember that she took this duty very seriously.

Aunt Linny met us at the train station in a brand-new car. I remember that because she almost hit somebody pulling out of the train station parking lot, and she got totally flustered by this and made us promise not to tell Uncle Louis.

My aunt and uncle live in a really big house. A deliberately big house, I would say. We live in a big house too, but it's not all fixed up and new, and this makes it seem more accidentally large.

I've never been exactly clear on our family's finances. Sara's sort of a well-known person in the world of yoga and alternative healing, but that's not, like, a high-finance world. The Rising Moon Wellness Center is successful, but it's Sara's friend Lydia that actually owns it. I think Sara still gets some money from Barry, Paul's brother, for my sisters, or maybe as part of the divorce. Nana made money from her books, and also I think my grandfather's family had money, and she got some when he died. My sisters and I earned money by working at the Wellness Center, and Aurora babysat. Pearl and I had our little driveway-shoveling business in the winter. So there seemed to be money around, in a general way, although we don't have a fancy car, or designer clothes, or go on ski trips, like a lot of the kids at school. Well, actually my sisters have some designer clothes, because Aunt Linny always gives them clothes for their birthdays and at Christmas. Our nicest presents always come from Aunt Caroline and Uncle Louis. Not necessarily the best presents, because both Sara and Nana are really good at giving presents, and Aunt Nancy always sends us big gift certificates for books, but I mean my aunt and uncle give us stuff that we wouldn't even think about asking for. This computer I am writing on was a gift from them.

Anyway, Aunt Linny went out of her way to make everything nice for us on that trip. She took us to the swimming pool at her country club and to the Bronx Zoo. We went into New York City for the day and saw the musical *Titanic* on Broadway. Doing things with Aunt Linny is fun because of the element of conspiracy that Aunt Linny creates around her. Standing in front of the concession stand at the Bronx Zoo, Aunt Linny would gaze and sort of murmur, "Things to eat . . . *should* we?" and we would all say, "Yes, let's get pretzels," or whatever and Aunt Linny would say, "Pretzels! Really? Well, I won't tell if you won't," and somehow eating pretzels became this very subversive action.

What I remember best, though, was the Fourth of July party that happened while we were there. That memory has a couple of different parts to it.

The first one is that Aunt Caroline had forgotten something she needed at the grocery store that day and Uncle Louis took me with him in his car to go get it. I didn't really like being in the car with Uncle Louis by myself, because I don't really like him so much. Pearl always says I like everyone, and that I am completely uncritical, but that's not totally true. I have likes and dislikes like everyone else. People often make that mistake about me.

Uncle Louis is not a bad person. It's just that I'm not comfortable around him. He used to pat me on the head. That might not sound like a big deal, but I didn't like it. For one thing, he is really tall, and has big hands, and his hand would hover over my head before he patted it, and so there was a moment when I knew that at any second this hand was going to descend, and there would be three or four pats, of varying degrees of strength, and that I would just have to stand there while it happened, and I never knew what to do, like should I say, "Thank you," or what. What I always really wanted to say was, "Don't touch my head." He also has this way of speaking like he's giving a demonstration of what a powerful speaking voice sounds like, as if we should all be totally mesmerized by how brilliant he is, even if he's saying something like, "Pass the juice."

Growing up, there was always some extra gift for me that was specifically just from him, and it was always some gift that was very "boy" like binoculars, or a compass, or a telescope, and I liked all those things, I was grateful for them, but I didn't like how it made it seem as if Uncle Louis was "looking out for me," or something like that.

I know that Uncle Louis is supposed to be this incredibly impressive person, and people talk about how "charismatic" and "charming" he is, but I just don't get it. Pearl doesn't either, but with her it's more about Uncle Louis's hair. "Uncle Louis walks around like somebody just told him what a great head of hair he has," is how she describes him.

I don't mean to imply that there is anything creepy about my

Uncle Louis. Sara always has nice things to say about him because he helped her get divorced and Sara thought he was so great she introduced him to Caroline, and they got married. And it's not like we see all that much of him, or that he's a major player in my life.

Anyway, I remember being in the car with him, that Fourth of July, and I remember at the grocery store the clerk handed me the bag of whatever it was and said, "Why don't you carry this for your granddad?" And Uncle Louis got *into* it with this clerk, like he reprimanded her about making personal remarks to strangers, and I was just standing there with this bag of groceries. It was very uncomfortable. I guess Uncle Louis is used to people just gazing at him in awe, or admiring his hair or something, but it was an honest mistake and, I mean, he *is* sort of old enough to be my grandfather.

So then we got back in the car and Uncle Louis was totally silent, and then I said something, or did something, and he said, "I understand I have no control over the way you are being brought up, but when you are with me, Luke, you will obey my rules."

I don't remember what I did to provoke that. I felt like I didn't do anything at all and I felt like he was making sort of a slur on Sara, who always, like I said, spoke really nicely about *him*: "He held out a hand to me in a dark hour of my life. He's so good for Caroline," etc. Anyway, just because Sara isn't a big rich lawyer doesn't mean she's not a competent parent or that we didn't have rules.

The party turned out to be fun, though. Right before the guests arrived, Aunt Caroline said, "Wouldn't it be nice if we all played croquet?" and my sisters and I set up a course in the backyard and we had a tournament, and everybody played. We had a good view of the country club's fireworks right from the backyard.

The last part of this memory is of Uncle Louis and Aunt Caroline getting into a fight after the party. They fought in their bedroom, and the three of us could hear it, and so Aurora said we should all go out in the yard and pick up the croquet hoops.

"It's 'cause all the women were flirting with Uncle Louis," Aurora said. "That's why they're fighting. Because Uncle Louis is so hand-some."

"Gross," said Pearl.

"Also they had too much to drink," Aurora said. "When you drink, it affects your judgment." (I totally have to remind her of this conversation.)

"How can you tell if Aunt Linny is drunk?" Pearl asked.

Then Pearl did an imitation of Aunt Linny playing croquet, where she would start to line up her mallet in completely the wrong direction and then go, "Oh, oh, where am I supposed to go now? Which one is me? Am I orange still? What should I be doing?" and then an imitation of how Aunt Linny took these tremendous whacks at her ball, I mean just creaming it, and how we all had to dive out of the way. I remember standing in that yard and laughing so hard I was crying at Pearl doing this imitation. And part of my laugh-ing, and general happiness at that moment, I have to say, was that I was glad that someone was yelling at Uncle Louis and his stupid hair.

I am remembering this because we are having a Fourth of July party here, today, with this other family of mine. It seems weird to call them my family since I'm coming in halfway through the movie, as it were, but Bubbles, at least, seems to feel like I'm as much a Franco as a Prescott. Apparently I am not a Boyle at all.

"You're a Franco," is what she said to me several times yesterday. It's sometimes a little difficult to follow the logic of Bubbles's conver-sation, though.

"I'm the best cook," Bubbles told me, at the Kroger where we picked up two tons of meat and a box of frozen veggie burgers for me. "I don't make fancy things because I don't have time. I had to work full-time and raise a son. But what I cook, I cook good. Every-body loves my cooking. You live with your grandma, right? Your grandma and your mom?"

(Time for me to nod and begin opening mouth.)

"Yeah, I didn't have my mother around to help me," Bubbles continued on. "I had to help her. People say that it's so amazing, how I do everything for everybody, but that's just what I do. I drink coffee late at night and it doesn't keep me up because when you work like I do, you go to sleep when you need to sleep. That's what I do. I sleep when I need to sleep."

Even if you ask her a direct question, you get a lot of other things besides your answer. For instance, I asked her if she grew up speaking Spanish at home, because both her parents were from Mexico.

"Yeah, people always tell me how my son looks like me," Bubbles said. "Let me tell you, I turned heads in my day. I still turn heads. I coulda married, like, five different doctors, but you know what, I take care of enough doctors at work, I don't need to take care of another one at home. You take Spanish at school or something?"

(Nod from me and the beginnings of the idea of opening my mouth.)

"Yeah, if you speak another language," Bubbles said, "it's like a sign of education. If you're white. If you're Spanish and you speak Spanish then everybody's like, 'Speak English, this is America.' My parents both came here when they were little kids. My grandfather said to my father, 'We speak American now.' You know what my mother called my son? She called him "*flaco*," because that means skinny. He was the skinniest baby ever. People thought I didn't feed him. Did I feed him? I fed him every second of the day. Look what happened. Now he's a big star and he eats nothing but those fucking shakes."

I don't think that Bubbles knows much Spanish. She is a Catholic, though. I found that out, and my dad is too because there is a picture in the house (in a white frame with a gold cross on it) of him being baptized. He never said anything to me about that.

I didn't even get a chance to talk to Aurora or Pearl yesterday, even though I had texted them that I would, because Bubbles kept me pretty busy with her, and I didn't feel like I could whip out my phone and make a call. Honestly, I'm not sure if there was even a moment when I could have *said* something like, "I need to call my sisters." Bubbles had me mow her lawn at one point, but I needed both hands for the mower. All in all, it was a pretty long day. I didn't get to run, either. So I'm going to go now. I've charted a little course for myself. Okay, let's kick it in gear now and get out of the house before Bubbles is up.

Luke is about halfway down the block when he identifies the car Mark rented coming up the street. For a moment, Luke thinks about cutting through someone's lawn and avoiding it. The car slows down and Mark rolls down the passenger window.

"Are you running away?"

"Just running. I didn't think you'd be back so early," Luke says.

"Can you wait for two minutes? I'll just park and change."

"Okay."

Luke waits. He tells himself that he is irritated because now he will have to do a shorter run. Mark's knees start to hurt after about four miles. Luke does some squats. After a bit, Mark comes jogging up the street and Luke starts running a little before Mark gets to him. Mark stays a few steps behind until they both have to stop at an intersection.

"How's it going?" Mark asks.

"Fine," Luke says. "How are you?"

"I owe you one," Mark says quietly. "Thank you."

Luke wants to say, "Whatever," but he doesn't. He just nods.

Later in the afternoon, Luke finds himself immediately accepted by and assimilated into the Franco family. He is hugged by all of his father's uncles and cousins and their wives and husbands. He is offered beers and mocked about his veggie burger. Francos instruct other Francos to hold the camera so that Luke can be in the picture. Luke is enjoined to try Aunt Sheila's potato salad, to help Uncle Robbie bring out more ice, to listen to stories of Franco family lore.

So this one time, me and Frankie were driving Pops over to the VA and Frankie, he thought he'd be real cute and tell Pops . . .

No, dude, Robbie was scared of that fuckin' cat, man, he'd be all running away from it, and Trey and me we used to take that cat and . . .

But then I remembered that this chick, she had her name on her license plate, so I climbed out the window, man, and ran out to her car while she was still sleeping . . .

None of the stories Luke hears involve his father. Luke watches Mark listening to these same stories. Mark laughs and says, "Oh shit," or "Oh, man," in response.

Luke has trouble sorting out who belongs to whom in his father's family. Bubbles is the oldest of her four siblings, two of whom are present, with their wives and five of their collective children, who are all Mark's cousins. There is another cousin present from an absent uncle, and two cousins who are honorary cousins, the offspring of an absent aunt's second husband's first wife. Additionally, there are two of Bubbles's coworkers on hand.

There are children of the cousins at the party too, all of them under the age of twelve. Luke watches as Mark's cousin Kerry offers Mark her newborn. Mark handles the baby easily, nonchalantly, bouncing it lightly in his arms as he talks to his Uncle Robbie. The baby reaches out a hand and touches Mark's chin. Luke watches as Mark does his upside-down smile and shakes the tiny hand. Kerry takes a picture of Mark holding the infant up to his face.

"Luke, go bring the cupcakes in from the kitchen," Bubbles tells Luke, and Luke moves into the house. From the living room, he hears the sound of lowered female voices coming from another room. Because of the acoustics of Bubbles's house, Luke hears several sentences quite clearly before he enters the kitchen.

"Does anybody know anything about the mother?"

"No. Who knows what she might be after? She's got other kids from someone else, too. Did Tony ask for a paternity test?"

"Well, Bubbles thinks . . ."

Luke enters the kitchen. There are three women there: Mark's Aunt Sheila, his Aunt Audrey, and one of the honorary cousins. They all stop talking when they see Luke. Aunt Sheila smiles brightly.

"I'm supposed to bring out the cupcakes," Luke says.

"Oh, okay!" Aunt Sheila says loudly. "We'll get them."

The women spring into action. Bakery boxes and more paper plates with American flags on them are produced. "These look good, huh?" Aunt Audrey asks, angling a box toward Luke. Luke looks at the red, white, and blue frosted cupcakes, inhales the aroma of refrigerated plastic, is repulsed, says nothing. He leaves the kitchen, goes to his father's old bedroom, grabs his cell phone from his backpack, and moves through the house to the front door. On the way he passes Aunt Sheila, coming out of the kitchen with a handful of plastic forks. Luke waves his phone at her.

"If my dad asks, I had to make a phone call," Luke says.

"Okay!" Aunt Sheila says.

"I'm calling my family," Luke says.

"Oh!" says Aunt Sheila. "Okay!"

"They live in Delaware," Luke says. "That's where my family lives. I'm calling my sisters now. They're both in New York City. My sister Aurora has a full scholarship to Columbia."

Luke does not wait for Aunt Sheila to reply, but moves determinedly to the front door and out of it. He almost lets it slam shut behind him, but does not.

Luke walks down Maple Street, where there are no maple trees, and calls Pearl.

"Pick up, pick up, pick up," Luke says, into his phone.

Pearl does not pick up, so Luke calls Aurora.

"Luke!"

"Hey Rory."

"I was just thinking about you!"

"Where are you?" Luke asks.

"Montauk," Aurora says. "Dr. June has a house here. There's a big party. It's all feminists and those who love feminists."

"Can you talk?" Luke asks.

"Yes, I'm going outside now. Hold on."

Luke can hear voices, laughter, what might or might not be the sound of a dog attacking a feminist, and the sound of a screen door rattling. Luke sits down on the curb of the sidewalk where the chalk outline of a game of hopscotch has nearly been rubbed away.

"Ah. Here I am. What's going on? How's the party?"

"It's okay," Luke says. "I'm down the street now. There's a lot of people."

"Is it all your dad's family?"

"Uh-huh. Mostly."

"Interesting," Aurora says. "Very interesting. Do you feel a connection to them?"

"Not really," Luke says. "No."

"Well, you're amazing. They're lucky to have you."

"I don't know that they're all that interested in me," Luke says. "As a person, I mean. Nobody has asked me any questions about myself."

"Of course they're interested in you. They might be a little shy, or maybe they want to be polite and not overwhelm you. You have to look at how they are feeling too. It's a lot for them to take in. Just give it a little time, Luke."

"Sure," Luke says. "I'll do that."

"You okay?"

"I'm okay."

"Listen, I read this great thing the other day. 'Are you so afraid of losing your moral sense that you are not willing to take it through anything more dangerous than a mud puddle?' "

"Is this a trick question?" Luke asks.

"It's Gertrude Stein. Isn't that great? It means that your morals have to be able to withstand pressure. It's one thing to have the courage of your convictions in a . . . in a closet. But you have to take those convictions out in the world."

"Funny you should use that analogy."

"What's that? I'm losing you a little."

"What? No, I think Pearl's calling me. Have fun at your party, Rory. Say hi to all the feminists for me."

"I will. Take care, Luke. Call me anytime, okay? Love you."

"Love you too," says Luke.

Luke hangs up his phone. Pearl was not, in fact, calling him back, but Luke could tell that he didn't have Aurora's full attention. Luke watches a line of ants following a crack in the sidewalk into the grass of a front lawn. Luke sighs. His cell phone rings. It is Pearl.

"Luke Prescott here. Man of the hour."

"Luke! You need to come back here immediately and rub my feet for me. Get on a plane. I'm dying."

"Okay, I'll see you in six hours." Luke smiles a little. "Why are you dying?"

"I sling the hash, Luke," Pearl says darkly. "I sling the hash. I serve the eggs. To couples. Reading the newspaper. Couples who have gotten up early on a Sunday morning to go to a restaurant and read the newspaper at the same table. Instead of staying home and having sex and smoking weed like sensible people. I despair for humanity. Seriously. I weep for it."

" 'Are you so afraid of losing your moral sense' . . ." Luke begins.

"Jesus!" Pearl interrupts, screaming. "I know! Gertrude fucking Stein! She was over here yesterday lecturing and quoting at me. Miss Fancy Pants Montauk. We need to stage an intervention. I think she's stopped shaving her armpits."

"Well, I'll come back immediately then." Luke stands up and steps carefully around the ants.

"So," Pearl says. "Tell. What's the family like?"

"They're okay. They're, you know . . . very welcoming. On the surface."

"Are they cool?"

"Um . . ."

"They're not cool."

"Mostly they are nice," Luke says.

"Well, you think everybody is nice," Pearl says. "So that tells me nothing. Would I like them?"

"Well, you don't like anybody," Luke says. "So that will tell you nothing either." Luke begins to feel a little better, imagining what it would be like if Pearl were with him. He pictures his sister, one hand on a skinny hip, the other holding a cigarette, saying something very funny and sarcastic about the cupcakes, and Aunt Sheila.

"True. Very true," Pearl says. "Seriously, how is it, Luke? It's got to be a little weird, even for you."

"It's a little weird even for me."

"But you really like your dad, right? He's still the Best Dad Ever?"

"It's not," Luke says, "like I have a selection to compare him to."

" 'All happy families are alike,' " Pearl says. " 'But each unhappy family is unhappy in their own way.' "

"Is that also Gertrude Stein?"

"Tolstoy. Oh crap."

"What?"

"I've got to get in the shower. Shawn is having a party tonight. The chances that there will be anyone there *remotely* interesting are very slim, so I've got to leave enough time to shower and smoke some pot before I go."

"Is that what Aurora was lecturing you about?" Luke is walking now, back to Bubbles's house. He would like to keep Pearl on the phone with him a little longer, and he would like Pearl to prod him a little more, ask more questions about how he feels. He would like to tell Pearl everything and be able to listen to her reactions, which would be loud and dramatic and indignant. He is not sure how to make this happen without telegraphing his need for it.

"Yes!" Pearl says. "I told her it was a phase and that I am fully cognizant of its dangers and that I believe judicious use of cannabis to be a helpful social aid."

"That seems reasonable enough. What did Rory say to that?"

"That's when she laid Gertrude Stein on me," Pearl says. "I told her it was an inapt quotation. I'm not afraid of losing my moral sense. It's other people's moral senses that are the problem. Hey, can you bring back any California weed?"

"Well," Luke says, "I'm not sure becoming a drug mule is the best option for me at this point. I've . . . you know, I've got enough to worry about."

"Yeah, I hear you. Okay, gotta go, sweetie."

"I miss you," Luke says, hopefully.

"Miss you too. Come back soon, okay?"

"Okay," says Luke. "Okay. Bye, Pearl."

"Love you!"

Luke arrives back at Bubbles's house just as the front door opens and Mark comes out, carrying an American flag.

"I was just looking for you," Mark calls out. "We forgot to hang this. Give me a hand?"

Luke shrugs.

"There used to be a pole in the garage," Mark says. "I have no idea what happened to it. I don't know. Maybe we should just drape it over a bush or something?"

"A bush? No," Luke says. "I don't think so."

"Right," says Mark. "How about over the front window here? Wait. Let's hang it from the gutter. We can put some of these rocks on the edge, to hold it down."

"Is there a ladder?"

"Get on my shoulders," Mark says.

"Dad, maybe we should get one of the kids. I'm too big," Luke says. "You seem to be really good with kids, I've noticed."

"I can't go back there yet," Mark answers. "We've reached the stage where everybody makes a circle around me and asks which famous people I know and what are they really like? And doing imitations of me. Not me. James. And then they want to know how come James didn't do this, or that, or why is he such a pussy; he should have done Naimi when he had the chance. Only for that, they don't say 'James.' They say 'you.' 'How come you were such a pussy? You should've blown his head off.' "

" 'All happy families are the same,' " Luke says. " 'But all unhappy families are unhappy differently.' "

"Who has a happy family?" Mark asks. "Here, take these rocks and put your foot in my hands. We'll do a boosting action. Grab onto the window ledge."

Luke puts the stones in his pockets, takes the flag, tucks it under his arm, and puts one foot into his father's hands.

"One, two, three." Mark hoists Luke up and grabs him around his knees.

"Okay, I got you," Mark says. "This gonna work?"

"It's going to get the flag dirty." Luke peers doubtfully into the gutter. "Is that okay?"

"We're kind of a dirty country," Mark says. "Do it, man."

"Move me to the left."

Mark staggers to the left.

"Too far," Luke says.

"Are you shitting me?" Mark says. "Just do it before anyone catches us. I can't believe you suggested this. What were you thinking?"

Luke cannot help laughing at this.

"Execute!" Mark yells. "Execute maneuver! Hang this bitch!"

"I got it!" Luke yells. "We've got flag! I repeat! We've got flag!"

Mark steps backward with Luke, grabs Luke's waist, and swings him around, tackling him to the ground. They tussle. Even though his father is playing, Luke uses a portion of his actual strength. This, his father counters easily. Luke is torn between enjoying his father's size, the comfortable breadth of his chest, which makes Luke feel pleasingly small and young, and an actual desire to hit his father, for real, in some way. Luke punches Mark in the arm, not as hard as he can, but hard.

"Ow," Mark says. Luke thinks about hitting his father harder.

"Oh shit, I ate too much," Mark groans. "You win."

Mark and Luke lie side by side in the grass. They look at the flag, which is hanging at a slight angle. Luke tears out a handful of grass and throws it at his father, who closes his eyes and smiles.

"We should get back to your family," Luke says.

"They're your family too."

Luke says nothing.

"Yeah, don't worry about it. I don't like them that much either."

"I heard someone," Luke says. "Saying something. About my mom. As if . . . she maybe had some sort of agenda getting you and me together. A financial agenda. It seemed like—"

Mark is up off the grass and at the front door of the house so fast that it takes Luke a second to register what is happening. Luke sprints after his father and catches Mark at the kitchen, which is now empty.

"Wait. Dad." Luke grabs his father's arm. "Wait. Calm down."

"Who said something?" Mark asks him. "WHO?"

Mark's raised voice is so loud it causes a slight echoing bounce off the stainless steel appliances.

"It doesn't matter," Luke says. "It's not a big deal, really."

"I will," Mark says, "fucking KILL whoever said that. I will fucking KILL them."

Full-blown adult-male rage lies outside Luke's experience. This is not his uncle Louis speaking sharply to a grocery-store clerk, or Coach hectoring the team for increased sprint times. Mark's anger: the sight of it, the sound of it, and most of all the unpredictable ramifications of it have caused a sympathetic surge in Luke's own hormonal system. Luke freezes as he hears the sound of the screen door in the living room sliding open and children's voices.

"Tell me who said something." Mark lowers his voice. "I'll take care of it."

"I don't want you to," Luke says. "Really, I don't. Please, Dad. Forget it. I don't want you to be mad."

Two of the cousins' children come running into the kitchen, red, white, and blue frosting smeared on their faces.

"Holly and I had a cupcake fight!" says one, to Mark. "We smashed cupcakes in each other's faces!"

"That sounds like a pretty stupid thing to do," Mark says, after a moment. "You're supposed to *eat* cupcakes."

The children run out again.

Luke looks at his father carefully. He cannot tell if Mark's anger has subsided, or if Mark is shoring up for some larger and more violent outburst.

"It will really upset me," Luke says, "if you say anything. Who cares what they think, right? They don't know us."

The muscles in Mark's jaw move, but the rest of his face remains impassive.

"It's nothing to make a big deal about," Luke says. "Chill."

At this, Mark rolls his eyes.

"Chill," Mark says. "Chill, my son says to me."

"Yeah, Dad," Luke says. "Chill out. It's a fucking barbecue."

"Wow," Mark laughs. "Wow, Luke. You said 'fucking.' "

Luke smiles tentatively at his father, who, after a moment, puts his arm around him briefly. The two move through the house and into the backyard. For the rest of the afternoon, Mark does not leave Luke's side.

The next day Luke and Mark run to Mark's old high school. They jump the fence of the athletic field, where Mark used to play football.

"What position did you play?" Luke asks.

"Quarterback. Second string. Yeah. I had one or two good

moments, but I wasn't, like, the star guy, really. I had a good arm, I guess."

"I wanted to play," Luke tells him. "When I was little, but Sara wouldn't let me. She gave me a bongo drum instead."

"You're kidding me."

"The bongo drum was cool," Luke says. "What was less cool was having to play it for Sara's Ecstatic Dance Class."

"Hey, how come you call your mom Sara?" Mark asks. "And not Mom?"

"We call her Mom sometimes. She once told me that sooner or later you have to see your parent as an autonomous person, and not just an extension of yourself. I guess she figured why not sooner than later."

"But you're close, right? You seem really close."

"We're close," Luke agrees. "Yeah. But it worked, I think, her plan, because I do see her as an individual. I see her as a person first, and my Mom second."

Luke has said this before, but now he wonders if it is entirely true, and if it is, what exactly it means.

"When I was a kid," Mark says, "I think I heard my mom more than I saw her. She was like this constant yammering noise in my head."

"Well that house does echo," Luke points out.

"Does it?" Mark laughs. "I guess it does. Anyway, I just wanted to get away from all that noise."

"How come you wanted to be an actor?" Luke asks.

"My drama teacher," Mark squints into the sun. "He was pretty great. Mr. Holt. He was also my English teacher. That was the only subject I was really good in. Anyway, he got me to try out for the school play. *King Lear.*" Mark shrugs. "A high school production of *King Lear.* He had to make a lot of cuts. Yeah, he wanted me to play Edmund. You know the play?"

Luke shakes his head.

"Well, Edmund is the son of the Earl of Gloucester. But he's the bastard son. There's a legitimate son—Edgar—and Edmund is all screwed up about that. He's mad at his father for loving Edgar more and he's mad at the world for trying to tell him who he is, and what he can have, and what he is supposed to be, and all that. So Edmund plots against his half-brother, and for most of the play you think he's a total villain. But in the end, he redeems himself. Anyway, Mr. Holt said that he thought I had talent." Mark's voice takes on an edge of sarcasm. "He could tell by the way I read things out loud in class and he thought I had a real feel for Shakespeare's language. A sensitivity."

"So you did it?" Luke asks.

"Yeah," Mark says, his tone lightening. "I mean, whatever, a little high school production, but it was the first time I really felt like I was in the right place. I was more excited about rehearsals than . . . God, pretty much anything. And the audience, the first time, I was sorta nervous but the moment I stepped onstage I was just like . . . I just wanted everyone to know exactly what Edmund was feeling and I knew I could do it and . . . I knew I was good, you know? I was so pumped. Best feeling in the world. I kept playing football and every-thing, but I knew that as soon as I got out of school I was going to go to New York and become an actor. I used to talk to Mr. Holt about it. He gave me plays to read and books on acting. He helped me find a drama school. He was like, 'Go for it. You have to follow your dream,' blah, blah, blah."

"So he must be really proud of you." Luke is thinking that he would be really proud of Mark, if he were Mr. Holt. "Do you keep in touch and stuff? Is he still here?"

"I used to call him from time to time. Things were hard, for me, you know, when I was starting out. I shared this shit-hole apartment in New York with two other people. I worked at this restaurant, and an electronics store, moving boxes."

"And helping women with their VCRs," Luke adds, not to be funny, but because that is what he is thinking.

"Yeah," Mark says. "Right. That was then. I was in over my head in so many ways. I got into some . . . I just, you know, struggled. It wasn't like I never thought about you, Luke, or . . . I just didn't know what to do."

"I know," Luke says. He wants to get back to the story. "So anyway, eventually you started acting for real, right?"

"I got a part in an off-Broadway play. Mr. Holt was the first person I called. He was so excited. And he came to see it. My mom didn't even come to see it, but Mr. Holt did. He came and afterwards . . . he . . . well, he . . . I guess you could say that I wasn't the only closet case at Grover High."

"Oh," Luke says. Oh. "You mean . . . he . . . ?"

"It was sort of . . . awful. I mean, I thought of him as kind of a . . . well, not a father, but as, you know, a mentor, or whatever. And I guess I felt a little betrayed or something dumb like that. Anyway, I ended up punching him."

"You punched him?" Luke asks. "Like a real punch? Like, in the face?"

"Sort of," Mark shrugs. "I didn't take a big swing at him. I told him that he was wrong about me, and that I wasn't a fag, and he tried to kiss me and I hit him. And he cried. He stood there crying and saying, 'I'm sorry, I'm so sorry,' in this crappy little hotel room where he was staying, and I walked out and I never saw him or talked to him again. And he died a few years later. From bronchitis. So probably from AIDS, I guess, really. I don't know."

Mark runs backwards a few paces and throws an imaginary football across the field.

"*Thou hast spoken right. 'Tis true,*" he calls out. "*The wheel has come full circle. I AM HERE.*"

"Is that *King Lear*?" Luke asks, after a moment.

"It's a good play," Mark says. "You should read it."

"I will."

"Was all of that . . . was that . . . too much? 'Too much information,' as they say?"

Luke thinks that is wasn't too much. That he's not that sheltered. Or firewalled. That he knows that life can be really messed up.

"Relationships can be very complicated," Sara has sometimes said. "But imagine a world where all people treat each other with love. Isn't that a world you want to live in?"

And Luke had always said yes, because that did seem to be the best kind of world. But now he begins to think this through. Did Sara mean that we should live in a world where we treat all people with the *same* amount of love? Because unless we love everybody *exactly* equally then we'll be right back where we started, only people will be going to war over amounts of love instead of hate, or amounts of tolerance, or compassion. We would have said to Iraq: "Yes we totally love the people who flew the planes into the World Trade Center and we totally accept them and have compassion for them, but we have slightly *more* love for the people *in* the World Trade Center, so we are going to bomb your country." You have to love everybody *exactly* equally or it won't work. Luke concludes that Universal Love, like reincarnation, might be one of those ideas that are just mathematically improbable.

Luke tells his father that he can tell him anything and Mark says, "Okay, but now you tell *me* about playing drums for your mom's Ecstatic Dance Class. Because that sounds like a fucking riot."

And so Luke had told Mark about that. He watched his father throw imaginary footballs. He thinks about this now, sitting at his father's desk, with his father's high-school copy of *King Lear* in front of him. Luke is moved by the sight of Mark's handwriting in the margins, notations in pencil indicating where a teenage Mark had needed to go onstage.

Mathematics aside, Luke simply does not *want* to love his father with no more love than he has for everybody else. He wants to love his father particularly, exceptionally, uniquely. He would like there to be an "us" that is his father and himself, and a "them" that is everybody else. Weeks ago, Luke had wished to render the words "father" and "son" meaningless, beyond their biological markers. Today he wished to throw them across the field to his father, see his father throw them back. Today, Luke was willing to exchange even the idea of Universal Love for an actual game of catch with his dad.

CHAPTER TWELVE

This latest essay attempt is pretty hilarious. My dad helped me write it. I'm saving it under the title "If All Else Fails!"

We're on the plane now. He's asleep.

He totally surprised me at the airport in Chicago. Instead of going back to Los Angeles, we're actually en route now to Hawaii.

"Seriously?" I asked, at the ticket counter. "We are seriously going to Hawaii?"

"You ranked camping in the Sequoia National Forest above Hawaii," he said. "And we're definitely going to do that too. But I thought maybe you were afraid to put Hawaii first 'cause you thought it was too big a thing to ask for? I'm counting on the fact that everybody wants to go to Hawaii, right? Like, you don't have a problem with Hawaii or anything like that?"

I assured him that I have no problems with Hawaii.

"We're going to the main island," he explained. "It's less touristy.

And I rented a little condo instead of doing the five-star luxury thing. I thought you'd like that better. We're gonna rough it. Slightly smaller wide-screen television, ha-ha."

Then he pulled a guidebook to Hawaii out of his carry-on bag.

"You're in charge of itinerary," he said. "Research and report back. I am in your hands."

"Well, what would you like to do?" I asked. "It's your vacation too."

"I would like to know that we are doing what you want to do," he said.

Mark fell asleep shortly after takeoff, and I read the guidebook. I made a list: visiting the black sand beaches, snorkeling, hiking on the volcano. Definitely surfing.

Then I pulled *50 Successful College Application Essays* out of my backpack and read two successful essays. I set up my laptop and wrote things like:

Glugglugglugdugglugglug.

And then deleted them.

Mark woke up and asked me what I was doing.

"Yesterday," I told him, "I had this great idea about how to turn all these random free-writes I've been doing into an actual essay. It's supposed to be between three and five hundred words, right? Well, that's about twenty-five lines if you use four hundred words as a target point. So all I needed to do was extract three of the best sentences from each of the seven free-writes and combine those sentences together."

"Yeah, but your free-writes have all been about different things," he pointed out. "The sentences won't go together."

That's what I found out when I tried it. I don't know why I didn't realize that.

"All the childhood stuff you've been doing is great," he said.

"Yeah, but it's all really rambling," I explained. "Like the other day I tried doing what you suggested . . . on being the one guy in a family of women? And I ended up writing, like, six hundred words about playing Barbies with my sisters."

"You didn't have GI Joe? I had GI Joe," he said.

I had Spider-Man and Batman. The girls just had one Barbie each because Sara didn't approve of Barbie's shape. But Rory got one as a birthday present from her friend, and then Pearl had to have one so Sara got her African American Barbie. For diversity.

"I love your mom," Mark said, when I told him about that.

"Yeah. So they would get the Barbies going, doing something, and then Batman would attack."

"Batman attacked African American Barbie?"

"Well, both of them, because he wasn't always in control of his inner demons. Then Spider-Man would show up, and battle Batman, and then rescue the girls."

I thought I was maybe making an interesting statement about human nature vs. environment. I was taught to be nonviolent. Sara wouldn't let me have plastic guns or GI Joe. But there I was anyway, violently destroying my sisters' peaceful global community.

"You have to let me read that," Mark laughed. "It sounds awesome."

"It's maybe a little dark for an essay." I showed him *50 Successful College Application Essays.* "It's hard to figure out a pattern with these things. This girl wrote how she has learned Important Life Lessons from watching *Star Trek.*"

"I was on *Star Trek,*" Mark offered, yawning.

"Really?" I laughed.

"My first job in LA. I had four lines. They gave me a prosthetic forehead. My name was Tabor. That essay got someone accepted into college?"

"This guy," I told him, turning to another essay, "his sister had leukemia. It's what made him want to become a research scientist."

"Okay, so either you need to sound all academic and ambitious, or you need to show what a wonderful human being you are?"

"Right." He's pretty quick about these things.

"I'd go for wonderful human being," Mark said. "I mean you've got a 4.0, right? And you'll probably ace the SATs or whatever."

"I should do okay," I said. Aurora did tons of SAT prep and she got an astronomically high score. Pearl didn't do any SAT prep and she lost a contact lens on the way to the test and had to do the whole thing with one eye shut. She still did almost as well as Rory. I'll probably do a little prep, but I'm not worried about it. I test well."

"You've got cross-country," Mark pointed out. "And your community service stuff: shoveling driveways and mowing lawns for free for the elderly, the school recycling program. I'm sorry I messed up the Belize thing. That would have looked good."

"I think I can write an academic essay, but I need another one that's more personal. It'd be great if I had one that was both," I said.

"It seems like you've got plenty of material. You just need to, what, narrow your focus?"

"I know," I said. "I just don't know how to do that."

"Well, here," Mark sat up. "Let me help. I'm a totally narrow person. We can write it together."

"Okay." I opened a new blank document on my computer. "What should we write about? You need to give me a first sentence. That's usually where I go wrong. It needs to be exciting so I stand out from the pile of applicants."

"What about Ecstatic Dance Class? That's pretty juicy. I still think you can market this whole being-raised-by-women angle. I've milked the my-mom-was a-single-mom stuff myself. It totally works."

"I see dangers with that," I said. "I mean, what did I really learn from playing the bongo for Ecstatic Women? I learned that women like to run around and yell as much as boys, only they don't shove each other. They like to wave scarves. Some women, anyway; obviously not all women are into scarf waving. I learned that when you are a thirteen-year-old boy, it's problematic to be in a room with adult women in leotards. I learned that the more grounded I am in my yang, the more free I am to experience my yin. But I don't think a college admissions board wants to hear about my yang."

"That chick wrote about *Star Trek*."

"Yeah, but she tied it into lessons about a shared sense of purpose and collective humanity."

"We could all use grounded yang or what have you, right?" Mark asked. "Imagine if that was a thing that everybody did. Like, before the Senate sat down to make laws and pass bills and shit, they all ran around waving scarves while you played the bongo for them."

"That would be cool. Although I'm not sure that the Inner Goddess would be helpful with things like the federal deficit."

"More people would watch C-SPAN, though. Anyway, you learned a life lesson. It's better to hit a bongo drum than a face, is all I'm saying. Your mother did well by you."

"Maybe that should be my first sentence?" I asked. "It's better to hit a bongo drum than a face?"

"It's not bad. Not bad. You want to catch the reader's attention, like you said. Yeah, we could work with that. Put it in quotes and write it down."

So I did.

" 'That is something my mother taught me,' " Mark said slowly. " 'And while she mostly let me learn my own lessons, that was one I was prepared to accept at face value, as it were.' "

"Ha," I said, typing.

" 'I have never hit a face,' " Mark continued. " 'But I've gotten pretty good on the bongos.' "

"Cool," I said. "You're good at this."

"I'm channeling," he said. "I'm channeling you. It's making me more interesting. Okay, now we talk about how you come from a single-parent home."

I told him that it really didn't feel like that.

"Yeah, because you had all these great people in your life," he said. "That's the point of the essay. Okay, so write this: 'I was raised by my mother, my grandmother, and my two sisters. I've had no spe-cific'—um, what'd you call it—'*paradigm* of maleness to observe at close hand, but I think the women in my family did a pretty good job of teaching me how to be a man.' "

"What's a real man anyway?" I asked. "Like, what is the criteria for that?"

"Who knows? Anyway, let's give examples. What did you learn from your Nana?"

From my grandmother I learned that to believe in a biblical God totally requires that you carry an invisible sword with which you can slice off anything that doesn't make sense, seems ridiculous or cruel, or flies in the face of every evidence of the physical world and the conclusions of reason.

"Ummm . . ." I said.

"Write this: 'My grandmother taught me how to change the tire on our Chevy Impala.' "

"You," I said, "are kidding me."

"It's not like they're gonna check," he pointed out. "Keep going: 'She also taught me how to bake a mean pie crust. This may not be a traditional "manly" attribute but it's useful if, like me, you really enjoy pie.' "

I typed that out.

"This is great," Mark said. "I like being you. Okay, how many words we got?"

"One hundred forty-nine. We're halfway there."

"Now you can say what your sisters taught you."

"Oh well," I laughed. "Where to start, really?"

"Highlight reel. Or wait. Just free-associate for a sec."

My sisters taught me that my maternal grandfather was killed by accordion-wielding natives. It's not the bleeding that hurts when you get your period, it's the muscular cramping and the bloating. Some bras have this wire thing that pushes everything up. Girls masturbate too but they like to think of stories more when they do it. Umm . . . how to ride a skateboard, how to ride a bike with no hands. The three parts of the Hegelian dialectic: thesis, antithesis, synthesis. Mrs. Podner gives pop quizzes so always look over your notes. Foreign films are cool. Drawing a horizontal line though the number seven. Don't count on nobody claiming the last piece or bite because someone *always* does and so if you really want it you should say something. I went on like this for awhile and then Mark closed his eyes, sort of conducting the air with his hands while he was thinking.

"My sisters taught me how to dance with a girl," Mark said at last. "This is where the man needs to lead and make all the decisions, but, as my sister Pearl says, the man should never get too used to this idea."

It's not that far off. Kind of like the cartoon version of Pearl.

"In addition to the bongo drum lessons, my mother taught me . . ." Mark prompted.

"My mother taught me that my father was a beautiful comet on his own path and that I should honor him." I raised my left eyebrow at my dad, the same eyebrow that he raises when he raises one eyebrow.

"Your mother taught you to have compassion for assholes."

"My mother taught me not to judge anyone as an asshole."

"Wow, Luke, you said another bad word," Mark laughed. "Good thing we're not talking about what you learned from your father. Okay, let's have your mom teach you dude stuff. Throwing a baseball. Okay, maybe not throwing a baseball. Let's keep it somewhat realistic."

"Installing a ceiling fan?" I suggested. "I did that at Sara's studio."

"With your mom?"

"By myself, but I had an instruction manual." I could see where he was going, though. Yin and yang. Masculine and feminine aspects of a similar action. "How to tie a tie and make an origami crane? How to shave and how to cut flowers?"

"Yes, keep it manly, though. We don't want you to sound like a wuss."

I typed, then showed him what we had so far.

"Good, good. Yeah, how to fix electrical wiring and how to meditate, that's good. See what a great guy your mom taught you how to be?"

"Actually," I told him, "recent studies show that children are mostly influenced by their peer group, rather than their parents. And people often get their data backward. They think that little Jimmie is a rebel because his dad is so authoritarian. But it's just as likely that Jimmie actually *is* a rebellious person, and his behavior is *making* his dad act in an authoritarian way. Little Jimmie would be just as much a rebel if he were raised in a commune. And hey, you didn't have a father around growing up either."

" '*I should have been that I am, had the maidenliest star in the firmament twinkled on my bastardizing,*' " Mark quoted. "You got me thinking about *King Lear* again."

"You should do Shakespeare," I said, making him repeat the quote so I could write it down. I liked the sound of it. "Maybe you could do a production of *King Lear.*"

"I think I'm a little old for Edmund," Mark said. "Although God, that would be great. Anyway, back to you. Now that we've been cute and gotten their attention with some humor, let's go for the deep stuff. Say something about yin and yang and how we need to have both to be complete."

So I wrote about how Chinese philosophy contains the idea of yin and yang, two opposite forces that balance each other and move together as part of a whole: darkness and light, hard and soft, masculine and feminine, and without this unification, one cannot be complete. I read it out loud to Mark.

"And you say you can't write an essay. I could never write that sentence. Wait. Check this out: 'Understanding the flow of yin and yang within you is essential for understanding yourself as a complete human being.' "

"That's perfect," I told him. "That sounds exactly like something Sara would say. Okay, what next?"

"Start talking about how this balance is something that you seek out. That as committed as you are to your academics, and to competitive sports, you know you also need time for contemplation, and for personal relationships. Those are the things that give meaning to the other stuff. Like, enhance it."

I felt sort of in character at that point. Like I could see an alternate Luke who would say this kind of thing, you know, sincerely. Mark read over my shoulder as I typed, saying, "Yeah, yeah, yeah. That's good."

"Okay, I need a concluding sentence," I told him. "C'mon, Dad. Bring me the juice."

" 'So when I really think about it,' " Mark said, grandly, " 'I have the women in my family to thank. Not for showing me how to be a real man, but for showing me the path to becoming a real person.' "

I checked word count. We had 413 words. Done.

"Read it back to me," Mark commanded, settling himself back into his seat.

So I did.

"Wow," I said, when we had finished laughing. "It's totally ridiculous, but I think it might actually work."

"Welcome to show business."

The flight attendant appeared with drinks and a cheese plate. I showed Mark my list for Hawaii. We ate some cheese and he fell asleep again.

I'm glad I have this essay. In case the real me turns out to be too hard to organize, it's good to have backup.

Luke puts his computer away, reclines his seat back. He looks at his sleeping father, smiles, shuts his own eyes.

There had been a conversation, after the cheese eating, which Luke has chosen not to record.

"Hey," Mark said. "Getting back to little Jimmie who is a natural rebel?" Mark had given a quick glance at the passengers seated across from them, an elderly couple who were napping. The two men behind them were both wearing headphones and working on their computers.

"Yeah?" Luke said.

"So say someone is a closet case," Mark said, his voice so low Luke had to lean in to hear. "We think they are a closet case because society doesn't accept their lifestyle, and they are afraid or whatever. But maybe they would be a closet case no matter what."

"Like, there would there still be closet cases in a totally accepting society? Like being a closet case is a state of being, not a reaction to something?" Luke kept his voice low too.

"Right."

"Well, probably," Luke said, who didn't know if this was true but had correctly guessed that Mark would like it to be. "Right?"

"Yeah," Mark had said. "Probably."

Luke thinks now that he and his father might be on to something, but that social activists—including his sister Aurora—would never accept that "closet case" could simply be another delineation of sexuality. Aurora might even say that Mark had an obligation to come out. A flight attendant appears with an extra blanket. Luke takes it from her, and unfolds it over Mark's sleeping form. Tenderly, he tucks his father in.

CHAPTER THIRTEEN

So you know when it's really great weather, really warm and sunny but not too hot and the air is really fresh and you're almost freaking out that it's so nice? Yeah, that's when the weather of wherever you are is trying to imitate the weather of Hawaii. Likewise whenever you see waterfalls or bunches of tropical plants or beaches with clear waters you are probably seeing places that are doing their best to look as much like Hawaii as possible.

My dad says there are other places as beautiful, but that Hawaii is special because it's still America and so you don't feel as much like a tourist here, you still feel like you're home, and that makes a difference.

"I like the idea of being a total stranger, though, too," I said. "Stranger in a strange land. Totally out of my element."

"Everywhere is your element, Luke."

We were originally supposed to be here for ten days, but after the fifth day, my dad extended it to a full two weeks. I'm glad because I really think he needs the vacation.

Anyway, it's like every day here is the best day ever. Every morning we get up and go for a run, or we do sprints on the beach. Then we make each other breakfast at our condo. Then we go for surfing lessons with this guy Edvin, who is totally cool. After surfing my dad and I eat someplace and then we snorkel, or hike, or ride around on these scooters we rented. Every night we go to the same restaurant, Iolani's, which has organic food and where we've gotten to know all the people that work there. They call us "the boys." After dinner we go back to our condo and play Scrabble and talk and just hang out. Mark's been telling me stories: about things he did as a kid, about stuff that happened to him in New York, about making movies and being on television. Sometimes he'll stop in the middle of a story and say, "That was October 1996, so how old were you then?" and it's like we're able to draw this line from the Mark-that-was to the me-that-was. Or we're able to move the parallel lines of our lives closer together.

Tonight we were walking on the beach back to the condo from Iolani's and we passed these two guys who were holding hands, and about a hundred yards after we passed them he said, "What do you think about that?"

"About what?" I said, although I knew he meant those two guys.

"To see two guys holding hands like that. You saw that, right?"

"Yeah, sure. I didn't think anything."

"No, you did."

"Um, well, I noticed it, I guess," I admitted. "You don't see guys holding hands that often. I guess I was glad that they were. You know, that they felt comfortable and all."

"In front of their gay friends they feel comfortable holding hands. When they're at the mostly gay restaurant or the rainbow resort, or the all-gay synagogue or whatever, they don't have to think about it. But I bet when they saw us walking toward them there was some moment where they consciously decided to keep holding hands. Maybe they felt comfortable, but I bet they still had to think about it."

"Huh," I said.

"Luke? I worried that I kind of . . . grossed you out, in Chicago?"

"You didn't," I told him. "You could have told me right away that you wanted to see somebody, but it's okay."

"You were a little pissed at me. For leaving."

"Yeah. A little."

"I'm sorry. I won't do it again. But if I do, tell me right away that you're pissed, okay?"

"Okay."

"I've kinda gotten in the habit of being really . . ." He kicked at the sand. "Secretive, I guess."

"That must kind of suck," I said. "You must get tired of that."

"It is what it is."

"Do you want that?" I asked him. "To be able to walk down the beach with someone and hold hands? If things were different?"

"What things?" he asked back. "The world? Or me? Like if I weren't an actor I wouldn't care about who saw me walking around holding hands with a guy? I think we've agreed that in a different world I'd still be Joe Closet Case. If I came out, it would tank my career. Tank it. Totally. And for what? So I can walk down the beach deciding to hold hands with somebody? For five minutes before I decide I don't really like that person, or find out they're cheating on me, or that the only reason I'm with them is because I'm scared of dying alone or some shit like that? Or I want to go to some freaking pride parade and wear a leather vest and dance around with all the queers and call them my community? NO fucking thank you. I'd rather have a career."

"But if you're not . . . happy?"

"You don't actually die if you don't have sex very often. I should know. And having sex doesn't make you happy."

"I'll have to take your word on that."

"I guess it makes you happy in the moment. Or, I don't know. Happy? That's probably not the right word. Anyway, you came to Los Angeles and it's like I got handed this free ticket to a normal life. I get to be a dad. Just like normal people. And I'm not worrying about whether I'll get any work next year and I'm not broke and I'm with you and I don't feel all lonely or whatever. So now I'm going to watch this sunset with my son and for ten minutes I'm going to believe that it's all solid and it's not going to disappear."

"Ten minutes?" I asked. "That's all you're giving yourself?"

My dad pointed to the horizon because the sun was just about to disappear. You can kind of feel the speed of the planet in these moments, because it would take something like 109 Earths to stretch across the sun, and so a sunset must be the only time we can stop seeing something so big, so quickly. Without shutting your eyes, I mean. Or turning away.

"Ten minutes is a long time for me," he said. "I'm going to really enjoy this. This is me being really, really happy."

And he lay back in the sand and shut his eyes with this very peaceful look on his face and later that night, before I went to bed, he said, "Love you, Luke," and I said, "Love you too, Dad," and that's the first time that we've said that to each other.

Three days later, Luke is sitting in the Green Room of a television studio, watching a giant monitor as a late-night talk-show host interviews his father. There are other people in the Green Room, various people associated with the rock band that will be performing later on the show. Kati sits beside Luke on a yellow leather couch. Kati is wearing a short skirt, which the act of sitting has rendered even shorter. Her legs are crossed. Twice the toe of her swinging left foot has brushed against Luke's ankle. The second time this happened, Kati said to Luke, "Oh, sorry. I keep kicking you," and moved two or three inches further away from Luke, causing her skirt to ride up even higher on her legs. Luke can see a faint blue vein at the top of her right thigh. Kati has the kind of skin that does not tan.

On the screen, Mark is humorously recounting Luke and Mark's surfing lessons in Hawaii.

"My son," Mark is saying, "learned to surf in about five seconds. Which turns out to be the exact amount of time I can stand on a surfboard without falling off."

This is not at all true, but it is funny the way Mark says it, and Luke is very proud of his father, who seems relaxed and confident and has said several things that have made the host and the audience laugh. He has also said "my son" three times.

Luke steals a look at Kati, who has now scooted herself to the edge of the couch and made adjustments to her skirt. Her legs are crossed, her arms are crossed, even her hands are twisted around each other and she is biting her thumbnail. Luke is slightly annoyed with Kati for being so obviously nervous about his father's performance.

"We'll be right back," the host says, "for more with Emmynominated actor and failed surfboarder Mark Franco."

Kati unlaces her hands and heaves a large sigh.

"He's doing well," Luke tells her. "Right?"

"He's doing great," Kati says. "Great."

Now the talk-show band is playing and various people have surrounded the host's desk. The host is talking to Mark, and Mark is nodding his head and smiling. In the Green Room, the rock band people all stand up and pile out of the room, waving unlit cigarettes and phones, in search of cell reception and ashtrays.

Luke catches sight of himself in a mirror above the monitor. Luke is very tan. Mark is also tan. They both have the kind of skin that tans. Luke thinks that he looks pretty good. Luke would like to hold on to the way he looks right now, the way he would like to hold on to every moment of the trip to Hawaii.

But things had been hectic since their return to Los Angeles. *The Last* had received seven Emmy nominations, including the one Mark had gotten for Outstanding Lead Actor in a Drama Series. Kati had a list of appearance requests for Mark. Mark's phone rang or buzzed every five minutes. Masses of congratulatory flowers were sent to the house and then carried away by Carmen. Mark and Luke were trying to keep the spirit of their trip to Hawaii up but they were no longer "the boys" and they both felt it. Still, every night when they said goodnight to each other, they now said, "Love you," and this, Luke thought, was something they could both hold on to, and was something that could not be taken away by other people.

This was Mark's second Emmy nomination. He had lost the previous year, to the actor who played an unscrupulous detective on a crime show and who was also nominated again. Luke had never seen that show, but in his opinion Mark had been especially great on the second season of *The Last* and surely deserved to win. The flashback episodes had been very intense, and you had gotten to see James Knox before he became so hard and guarded, which showed Mark's range. Kati thinks Mark's main competition is the African American actor on the medical drama. Mark himself does not expect to win.

"The show is too popular and too sci-fi," he said. "You get less cred for sci-fi."

"But it's good just to be nominated, right?" Luke asked.

"If you're really hungry," Mark said, "you're happy if someone gives you a cracker. For about five minutes. Then you want more crackers and you want them to put peanut butter on them and then you want the whole box and for it to be delivered to you and pretty soon you're just always hungry no matter what. But yeah, it's good just to be nominated. Up until you don't win. Then it's like, hey you lost and you wish you hadn't even been nominated. If you win, though, then it's something no one can ever take away."

The Emmy Awards show will take place after Luke is supposed to be back in Delaware. Mark had asked Luke if he would like to stay a little longer in Los Angeles, or come back, and go with him to the ceremony.

"It's kind of a long day, though," Mark told him. "And not as much fun as you might think. I guess it's sort of fun but it's also like a really long popularity contest and I'll have to be *on* the whole night. But if you have even the slightest interest, then stay. Or I'll fly you back out. If you think your mom would be okay with it."

"Sara's birthday is that weekend," Luke said. "She'd probably be okay with it, but I think I'd rather save her understanding for something else. You know, like another trip out here."

"Like for Christmas, maybe? Or New Year's?"

"Yeah," Luke said.

"Wow," Mark said. "I think I just looked forward to Christmas for the first time in about a decade. Shit. That would be so great."

"Maybe you should take Kati to the Emmys," Luke had suggested later.

"Kati's probably already set it up for me to go with Aimee."

"Have you talked to her? Aimee, I mean?"

"Here and there. She gets it. Well, I don't know what she gets, but she gets it about the business. Those super-sexy-looking chicks are always really practical."

In the Green Room now, Kati puts her hand on Luke's knee and shakes it.

"You okay? Can I get you anything?"

"I'm cool, thanks."

"Sorry about all this stuff we're having to do." Kati pulls out her phone. "But this is fun, right?"

"It's all fun," Luke says, truthfully, as Kati moves into the hallway to make a call. "All this stuff"—which Kati also calls "visibility"—is important for his father's career, and Luke likes being helpful. He also likes "visibility" when it includes, as it has today, riding in another limousine and meeting the rock band and the talk-show host and wearing a special pass around his neck on a cord.

Luke's own visibility is now an issue. A large picture of Luke and Mark at the Dodgers game was published in a weekly magazine, and there were several more photographs of them on the Internet. People in Delaware had seen these, and word had spread.

Luke had left his Delaware cell phone behind in Los Angeles when he and Mark had gone to Illinois, since his sisters were now using the new one and Sara was at the ashram. There wasn't a DSL line in Mark's room at Bubbles's house, and Mark and Luke had taken pleasure in "going off the grid" in Hawaii, with Mark only checking in with Kati twice a day by phone. So Luke had not looked at any of his messages until they got back. Luke had nine voicemails, thirty texts, and thirty-one messages on Facebook, some from people he didn't even know.

"Everybody is asking me if I knew," Amy had written in an email. "But of course, I understand. I hope you trust me, though. I feel like things ended a little weirdly with us, and your friendship is really important to me. You're coming back, right?! I really hope so. I miss you. I think about last year all the time, and all the amazing times we had together. Remember the night you took me to that Fellini movie? Still wondering what the plot was! Call me anytime. It'd be great to hear from you."

They had both missed the plot of *La Strada*, because just as the film was starting, Luke had put his arm around Amy and she had turned to him and they had started making out. They were in the back row, and the nearest people had been several rows ahead (the Fellini Retrospective at CinemaArts had not exactly drawn lines in Acton). Amy had been wearing a short skirt, although she had on tights underneath that. Blue tights. Luke's hand had gone far enough up under Amy's skirt to reach the waistband of those tights, although once there he had gone no further. Luke had thought it would be very Italian of him to remove Amy's tights, but he knew from his sisters that the putting on of tights was a complicated business, with lots of hitching and wiggling. He had not thought that Amy would want to do that in a movie aisle.

"People from home are Facebooking me," Luke had told his

father. "I told some people at school, my friends and stuff, that I was going to see my father, but I didn't say who you were. But people are finding out now."

"You've been outed," Mark said.

"I guess, yeah," Luke nodded.

"So what do they want?" Mark asked.

"I don't know that they want anything," Luke answered, although he knew this wasn't true. He just wasn't sure what it was that people wanted, specifically, yet.

"Really? Well, let me tell you, now is not the time to make new friends. Just be careful. God, these things are a pain. Don't answer anything from people you don't know."

"So far," Luke assured him, "it's mostly people from school saying, 'Hey, for real? Is that you? That's your dad?'"

"I guess people will be asking you a lot of questions," Mark said. "Shit. Yeah, we should talk about that."

"Okay," said Luke. "But you know I'm not going to say anything, right? About . . . you know. To anyone. Not to my sisters, or anyone." What Luke really wanted to say to Mark was, "As you would not tell, so would I not tell, there is no difference between us."

"You and Sara met when you were young," Luke continued, in a rush. "She didn't know who you were because you changed your name. We just got back in touch. You're awesome. I don't know what happens next on *The Last*. That's it. That's the whole story. That's all I'm saying."

"I trust you," Mark said. "I totally trust you. It's just . . . you know, right? It's kind of . . . it's a lot to ask of you. I know that. I know you would never mean to hurt me. I mean, I don't think you would. It's just. There's sort of a lot at stake, for me, and—"

"Dad," said Luke. "Dad. I hate this. I don't want you to worry about that at all. We don't even have to talk about it because it's never going to be an issue."

Mark had said okay to that. Luke wished they could flash forward to the end of their lives, just for a moment, so that his father could see how Luke never did tell.

"We're back with Mark Franco," the host is now saying.

"Kati," Luke calls out to the hallway. "He's on again."

Kati scurries back into the Green Room and sits down next to Luke. Her bare knee touches Luke's bare knee. Luke can smell her shampoo. Luke moves his knee away.

Luke looks at his father on the monitor. He appreciates that his father told a funny and not especially accurate version of their surfing lessons to this host. Sitting on a board in the ocean, looking at his father sitting on another board, waiting for a wave, smiling at each other, that story belonged only to them.

Mark is talking again now, telling another funny story. The host is smiling, the audience is laughing, Kati is nodding her head. All too soon, Luke thinks, he will be going back to Delaware, and what will happen then? Luke tries to imagine himself telling funny half-true stories about his father to Sara, to his sisters, to kids at school. Luke cannot imagine this, not because he wants to tell the whole truth, but because he doesn't want to tell anything at all.

"Mine," thinks Luke, looking at his father on the television. "Mine, mine, mine."

CHAPTER FOURTEEN

I seem to have a lot more stuff now than when I started out the summer. I have more to think about, yes, but I actually mean physical possessions. I may need another suitcase to get everything back. I think I saw one in the garage. I have only eighteen more days here in Los Angeles, and time, along with everything else, is getting crowded.

Earlier in the week, Kati showed up at the house with this team of people, and they carried three racks of clothes into the living room, some in my dad's size and some in mine. I don't even know how Kati got my size. I wonder if she went into my room and looked at the labels of my clothes, or if that's one of her assistant superpowers. Kati told me to make a pile of things I liked and so I did, thinking that it would lead to some sort of selection process, but everything I liked they let me keep. I don't even know if my dad had to pay for it, or what. Now I have all this new stuff. My suit got tailored for me by a guy named Diamond. It's pretty sharp. Even I can tell that it's significantly nicer than the suit I came with. I've got it on right now because in another hour a limousine is coming to pick up me and my dad and Kati and take us all to the premiere of a movie. After that, we are going to the after-party. All of this seems to be the kind of stuff that people at home who are wondering about me imagine that I am doing and that is, in fact, what I seem to be doing.

Today Sara called me. She's back in Delaware from her retreat. Talking to her made me think about what I've been doing here a little differently. Sara has that effect. The conversation was good when we were talking about her retreat, and what she experienced, and what was going on with Aurora and Pearl, and how Nana is doing and all that, but when we started talking about me, things got a little awkward.

"So," Sara said. "It sounds like you are in a good place with your father."

"Oh yeah," I said. "He's been great."

"You didn't say if Mark has anyone special in his life right now."

Here we entered into that weird infinitely regressive territory of: does she know/that I know/that she knows, etc.

"Um . . . no," I said. "He's pretty busy with the show and everything. We did go to dinner with a girl he's been seeing."

For all Sara knows, I thought, Mark has changed. Sara believes that people can change.

"Oh?" is what Sara said.

"You got my emails about going to Illinois and everything, right?" I said. "I knew you wouldn't be reading them until after, but Dad wanted to keep you in the loop."

"Oh yes, of course I did," Sara said. "I appreciate Mark keeping me in the loop. Nana and I are wondering if you'd like us to invite Mark's mother here?"

I tried to imagine a meeting between Bubbles and Nana. Bubbles and Sara. Bubbles and my sisters.

"No, that's okay," I said. "Maybe at some point we'll all meet, but you know, actually I was thinking that Dad might want to come to Delaware sometime next year. If that's okay with you and Nana. Or maybe I'll come out and see him again?"

"Of course, Luke. He's always welcome here. So tell me more. Give me a typical day in the Life of Luke."

"We're busy right now," I told her. "Because Dad got nominated for an Emmy for his show and so he has to do publicity stuff for that. So I go with him and kind of keep him company at these different events."

There was a little bit of silence on the other end, and then Sara said, "Yes, that certainly is a different world."

"It's fun," I said, firmly, because I wanted Sara to enter into the spirit of it more, even though she sounded like she was still in ashram-induced detachment mode. "Like, we're going to this movie premiere today, and then to an after-party at a big restaurant."

"Pearl told me there are pictures of you on the Internet with Anthony," Sara said. "Mark, I mean."

"Yeah," I said. "There was something in a magazine too, I guess. Some kids at school saw it."

"Yes, I've heard all about that. I haven't seen it."

"People take pictures of him all the time," I explained. "You get that he's kind of famous, right?"

"I'm not entirely out of it," she said. "I understand that."

"Well, I'm just saying," I said. "I know it's not like they have *People* magazine at the ashram. And it's not like any of the New Brethren are surfing the web. I wasn't sure what you and Nana know."

"What I'm interested in is finding out how you are," Sara said. "I think it's wonderful that Anthony feels he's in a place now that he can welcome you into his life, and that you are having a good time. I'm a little . . . I'm a little concerned, honestly."

"About what?" I asked. "Exactly?"

"Yes, well," she said, after a moment. "You know I trust your judgment. I'm sure you won't let Mark put you in a situation you're not comfortable with."

"He wouldn't do that," I told her. "He's always checking to make sure everything is okay with me."

"And what," she asked, "is okay with Luke?"

I could picture Sara's face very clearly when she said that, because the voice she was using comes with a particular look: a stare, really, only she doesn't seem to be staring at you but at some invisible mid-point between her and you that she's substituted for you. It's to this third person—who, coincidentally, shares your exact biology, history, and circumstances—that Sara will express a very measured disappointment or dissatisfaction. It's to this person that Sara has said things like, "I'm wondering how you feel about letting others clean up after you?" or "I'm sure that you are sorry to be causing anyone worry with your lateness." This third person, invisible though he may be, always gets the picture, so I made some noncommittal sound and waited for Sara to tell me whatever she needed to tell me.

"What I've been hearing so far," she said, "is a lot about Mark. What he thinks and what he does and what he wants, and it's wonderful that you are sensitive to that, but I'm not hearing a lot of Luke. I'm not hearing about what Luke thinks or Luke feels. I'm just wondering where Luke is in this picture that you are creating."

"Maybe I'm not expressing myself well?" I said, because you can sometimes cut Sara's "let's try to go to a deeper level" gambits off at the pass with a little speak-for-speak deflection.

"I know that you are not someone who easily falls under the influence of other people or other ways of life," Sara said, getting to the point. "We all have people in our lives who are different from us, and we can participate in their lives without changing who we are."

"Why is everyone treating this like it's all some kind of ordeal?" I asked, because now I was really annoyed.

"I'm not sure I understand what you mean," she said.

"I called Nana when we were in Hawaii," I said. "And I was like, 'Nana, I'm in Hawaii, it's so awesome,' and she was like, 'Luke, I will pray for a safe return journey for you.' It was like I told her I was in Baghdad."

Sara laughed a little at that, but I wasn't finished.

"Listen," I said, "I really appreciate that you trust I can get through this difficult time of having . . . you know . . . a really great time. If everything suddenly reveals itself to not be as totally cool and simple as it seems, and I've been corrupted and blinded without even knowing it, then I'll figure it out somehow and you can be sure, at that point, that I will treat it with total love and compassion just like always."

There is a way of saying things where you can still get away with saying, "Oh, I was just joking," if what you said upsets someone. Both my sisters have it mastered, but I think I might have erred on the side of being irretrievably sarcastic.

"Okay, Luke, my only concern," Sara started to say, and then stopped. I knew that we had probably reached the point now where Sara was going to let her point go. And that is what happened.

"You know how Mother is," Sara said at last. "She can't hear of anyone getting on a plane without thinking it's going to lead to disaster. I'm sorry, honey. You were wanting to tell me all this fun stuff. Pearl said you took surfing lessons and I could just picture you on a surfboard doing great and having the time of your life. I was smiling all day thinking about that."

We talked a little more and then we hung up and of course now I can't help thinking, okay, where am I in this picture I'm creating?

Luke goes into his bathroom and looks at himself in the mirror. Luke goes back into his bedroom, retrieves his phone, and returns to the bathroom. He holds the phone up next to his face, and takes a picture of his reflection in the mirror. Luke looks at the image he has captured of himself, which looks different in a number of ways from how Luke looked to himself while he was looking at himself.

It is difficult to know what level of consciousness nonhuman animals experience. One test for this is to show an animal a mirror and see if it recognizes that the reflection is itself, and not some other animal. Nine animals consistently pass this test: bonobos, chimpanzees, gorillas, orangutans, bottlenose dolphins, orcas, elephants, the European magpie, and humans. Animals that fail include chimpanzees, dogs and cats, and humans before the age of eighteen months.

Luke leaves his bathroom and presents himself in the living room, where Mark is waiting.

"You look like a movie star," Mark says to Luke.

"Spawn of Movie Star," Luke corrects.

"Spawn of TV Star," Mark amends. "There will be real movie stars out tonight. You'll see what small potatoes I really am."

The limousine, with Kati in it, arrives, and twenty minutes later Luke is standing on a red carpet next to his father and he knows that what this experience looks like to him, Luke, is actually significantly different in a number of ways from what it will look like later to other people when they look at pictures of it. Luke sees several famous people he recognizes, even though they too look different than their well-known images. Mostly this has to do with proportions: either their bodies are smaller, or they have much larger heads. Kati, in a black dress with a much smaller purse than usual, moves Mark and Luke to different positions, organizing where they should stand and who Mark should talk to. Mark waves at the crowds of people lined up behind a portable barricade. Luke does not see that his father is small potatoes at all. Once inside the movie theater, before they take their seats, several very famous people approach Mark and tell him how much they love *The Last* and congratulate him on his Emmy nomination. "Really great work," people say, and "I'm such a fan." Mark introduces famous people to Luke and famous people tell Luke their names. They say their own names as if they were not names that Luke already knew.

Luke knows that his father gets edgy and nervous at public events like this, although Mark always appears relaxed. Mark has already told Luke that Luke is hugely helpful to him in these situations because Luke is very calming.

Chimera is a summer blockbuster movie in the science fiction/ fantasy vein. Scientists studying soil samples brought back from Mars find and are able to extract an actual zygote from the soil. A Top Secret experiment is started to fuse the alien embryonic cell with a human one and create a genetic chimera. The experiment is successful and the Chimera grows up in the laboratory with extraordinary abilities and a blue and partially transparent skin. The plot gets more complicated when it is revealed that a second Chimera was started at an even more Top Secret lab (this Chimera is called C-2) and the first Chimera and C-2 eventually battle each other. Additionally there is a romantic subplot, involving the Chimera and a sympathetic woman scientist who loves the Chimera and does not mind the partial sight of his circulatory system. The world is saved from destruction, and the Chimera discovers he possesses a soul (although it's not clear whether this was a biological inheritance or something he developed through love).

Luke enjoys the film. Later, in the limousine en route to the afterparty, Mark is extremely critical of a particular actor's performance. Luke is interested to learn how his father would have played the role. Kati reminds Luke that if anyone asks him, he should say that he thought the movie was great.

"Say that you thought it was entertaining but it also made you think," Mark suggests.

The after-party is being held at a restaurant, redecorated for the evening to look like the laboratory in the film, with servers dressed in white lab coats, and an enormous glass beaker in the middle of the main room with blue liquid bubbling in it. There is a buffet, and tables, but Kati keeps Mark and Luke circulating through the crowd in order to "say hello" to people, some of whom were also being circulated by their own assistants to "say hello" to other people, a situation that Luke judges to be highly inefficient. More photographs are taken. No one lingers very long in one spot and everyone is very friendly and nice to everyone else, in short bursts: an artillery fire of friendliness and niceness. Mark finds a friend in the crowd, an actor he's known for a long time, and when Luke sees his father safely settled into a conversation, he excuses himself to investigate the buffet.

There is a crush of people near the food, and Luke finds himself momentarily blocked in. Treading water, he attempts to sidle into an outside lane. Luke feels his elbow being tugged. He turns and finds himself nearly nose to nose with a girl.

"Are you going to the buffet?" the girl asks, half shouting because they are underneath a speaker playing the *Chimera* soundtrack.

Luke nods. The girl has thick bangs that hang in her eyes, and the rest of her hair is pulled back into a ponytail. She is wearing large and elaborately ornamental earrings that pull the lobes of her ears slightly downwards. Luke cannot see the rest of her due to the jamming situation of the crowd.

"Can you get me something?" the girl shouts. Someone behind Luke jostles him and Luke steps forward and onto someone else's foot. The girl still has her hand on Luke's elbow, and her grip tightens reflexively.

"I'm sorry," Luke shouts. "Was that your foot? Sorry."

The girl pushes her bangs out of her eyes, which Luke can now see are blue, and pulls him down slightly by the elbow in order to say softly and solemnly into his ear, "It didn't hurt." One of her earrings swings against Luke's jaw. Luke smells a spice he cannot identify. The girl is wearing a strapless dress. She releases Luke's elbow and takes a step back as the crowd coagulates into a new formation.

"So can you get me something?" the girl shouts.

"Yes!" Luke yells. "What would you like?"

"God, anything," she yells back. "Anything and crab cakes."

"Crab cakes?" Luke hollers.

The girl tugs Luke's elbow again and he willingly leans his head down.

"They always have crab cakes," the girl says into his ear, signifi-cantly, as if the ubiquity of crab cakes is part of some larger con-spiracy. Luke nods.

"I'm sitting underneath the picture of dancing leprechauns," the girl calls over her shoulder, jimmying her way into the crowd.

The buffet does indeed have crab cakes. Luke fills up two plates with assorted food, taking some care to provide variety and visual interest. He executes a lap of the outer rim of the restaurant, where most of the tables are located. The artwork on the walls is mostly single-colored canvases with different colored dots or circles. Luke stops a lab-coat-wearing server and asks if the server knows where a picture of dancing leprechauns can be found. The server is Spanish speaking and as Luke does not know the Spanish for "leprechaun," he substitutes *"pequeno hombres verde,"* a translation that neither Luke nor the server finds to be adequate. Luke is about to give up when he sees the girl sitting at a table with several older people under a white canvas dotted with off-white circles. The girl sees Luke and holds up one hand in a sort of half wave. A woman with a horn of very shiny blond hair molded on top of her head says something to the girl, who shrugs and stands up, walking toward Luke with her hand still held to her shoulder, palm outwards. Luke sees this: the position of the hand in the traditional mudra of protection and peace, the elaborate ear-rings, the grave expression of the girl, and wonders if he is bringing crab cakes to a bodhisattva.

"Let's sit somewhere else," the girl says. "That woman is crazy."

"How about under the picture of the dancing leprechauns?" Luke suggests, switching gears. He is glad he has this opening line semiprepared. "Where is that exactly?"

"That's it." The girl points to the off-white circles. "Don't you see them?" She grabs two blue drinks off a passing tray. "Or is it just me?" The girl blinks at Luke.

"Oh," Luke nods. "I get it now. I didn't see that they were dancing at first. I thought they were dueling."

The girl smiles slightly, less with her mouth than with the curve of her blinking eyelashes. "Really?" she deadpans. "Weird."

Luke follows the girl over to a small table by a window. Now that they are in a less crowded area, Luke is able to take in more of her appearance. The girl is wearing a short dress with purple cowboy boots. Luke thinks that any heterosexual teenage boy will follow a girl with bare legs and purple cowboy boots. Luke thinks that this might actually be a fundamental law, like gravity, or the heliocentric model of the galaxy.

Luke and the girl sit down, and Luke hands the girl her plate, which she inspects somberly.

"Did I get the right things?" Luke asks.

"Yes," she says. "You did well."

Luke feels his phone vibrate inside his suit pocket. He takes it out and reads a text from Mark.

Where you?

Eating w girl, Luke types back.

"Sorry," Luke says to the girl.

"You are very funny," she says, neutrally. "So, who are you?"

"Um . . . I'm Luke," Luke says.

"Okay," the girl says. "I'm fine with that if you are." She stares at Luke challengingly for a moment, and then smiles a little.

"I'm Leila," she says.

Luke feels a slight physical jolt at this.

"That's . . . funny," Luke says. "That was my original name."

Leila nods. "So you're transgender," she says, not asking, and spearing a crab cake.

"What? No. No, everyone thought I was going to be a girl so they had a girl's name ready. But I'm a boy. A guy." Luke tries to regain his equilibrium by eating a fried risotto ball.

"Why'd they think you were going to be a girl?" Leila asks. "Did your penis not show up on the sonogram?"

Luke swallows fried risotto. This is the first time a girl has directly stated a speculation on the size of his penis, even in the prenatal state.

"My mom didn't have a sonogram," Luke says. "That's how certain she was. For twelve generations there have only been girls in my family."

Luke is surprised to hear himself saying this.

"So . . . oops?" Leila asks.

"Yeah," says Luke. "Oops."

Leila and Luke smile at each other.

"Are you going to drink that?" Leila moves the blue drink closer to Luke's plate.

"What is it?"

"The Chimera," Leila tells him. "Vodka and something else. Who knows? It tastes like facial cleanser. You are now going to ask me how I know that, do I drink facial cleanser. I do not."

"I wasn't going to ask that," Luke says.

Leila dips two fingers in her drink, reaches across the table, and slides her fingers lightly down one side of Luke's face, then up the other.

"There," she says. "You're all clean now."

This action causes a slight stirring in Luke's pants. He is glad that they are sitting down and that he is wearing a suit jacket.

"Thank you," Luke says.

Luke and Leila begin talking. Luke learns that the woman with the blond hair horn whom Leila described as "crazy" is Leila's mother, and Leila's mother is one of the producers of *Chimera*. Leila has two sisters as well. They are twins, and only three years old.

"That's unusual," Luke comments. "Twins."

"Are you kidding?" Leila laughs. "Every woman my mom's age has twins. That's what you get when you go all in vitro. I don't know if she even tried to do it naturally, I think she wanted to stay hip and be a mother of twin babies like all the other mommies. She can't take *me* to Mommy and Me class. The next generation? After us? It will be all twins."

Leila tells Luke that her father lives in New York.

"I wanted to live with him. Because he's not psychotic and New

York is way better than here, but my mom had custody. Not because she wanted me. She just didn't want him to have me. But it actually didn't hurt him at all because he'd rather just have me visit once a year and not have to worry about me. Not that my mom worries about me. Her assistant handles my schedule. Anyway, she could have made him keep me and that would have been worse for him but then she couldn't give all those interviews about how she balances being a high-powered woman in the industry with being a loving and caring mother. Of course, she doesn't need me for that now because she's got the twins. I would get emancipated but it's too much bother and I'll be eighteen in eight months anyway."

Leila says all of this, half laughing as she talks, while delicately dissecting her crab cakes. Luke, practiced and deft at predicting the intended trajectories of verbal arrows, thinks it sounds as if Leila is describing the plot of a movie she knows is silly and totally unrealistic, but cannot help enjoying anyway. On the other hand, when Leila stretches out her legs in front of her, taps the pointy toes of her purple boots together, frowns, and says, "I don't like carpeting," Luke feels as if an intimate moment has passed between them.

Leila asks Luke where he lives, which leads to Luke explaining that he is just visiting his father in Los Angeles.

"How often do you come?" Leila asks.

"This is my first time," Luke says.

"Your dad just move here?"

"No," Luke says. "It's just the first time I've come." Luke wonders if this explanation is enough, but Leila has finished her crab cakes and is still looking at Luke expectantly.

"My dad is an actor," Luke adds, hoping this will help.

"Oh, gotcha," says Leila. "Who's your dad?"

"Mark Franco."

"Oh yeah," Leila nods.

Luke waits.

"I didn't really think you were transgender," Leila says. "That was a little joke of mine."

"Like the dancing leprechauns?" Luke asks.

"No," says Leila. "Those were real."

Luke and Leila talk some more. Luke is intrigued by Leila's way of saying personal or emotional things without emphasis, and giving simple declarative remarks an italicized significance. It is almost, Luke thinks, as if she were speaking in code, although he is not sure whether it is the emotional statements or the non sequiturs he should be paying attention to. Not knowing what kind of reaction Leila needs from him makes Luke feel reckless.

"Do you want to hang out sometime?" Luke asks. "Soon, I mean. I'm not here for much longer."

"People usually do things in groups here," Leila tells him.

Luke thinks of possible group members: his father? Kati? Carmen? Mark's trainer Kyle? Aimee? Diamond?

"I don't have a group here," Luke says.

"Why do you want to hang out with me?" Leila asks.

Luke is prevented from replying to this by the appearance at their table of Mark, with Kati in tow. Luke makes introductions.

"I just wanted to let you know I'm taking off now," Mark says to Luke. "See ya later at home?"

Luke nods, although he has no idea how he will get home, if not with his father, but then the blond woman, Leila's mother, joins their group, and further introductions are made.

"Congratulations," Leila's mother, whose name is Karen, says to Mark. "On the Emmy nod. I love the show."

While Mark tells Karen that *Chimera* was fantastic, and also made him think, Leila leans across the table and says quietly to Luke, "Put your phone by your knee."

Luke takes his phone out of his pocket and holds it by his knee. He feels Leila's fingers against his thigh for a moment before she takes the phone. Luke tries to keep his facial expression neutral. In a moment, he feels a knocking against his knee. He would like to touch Leila's thigh, or anything belonging to Leila, but gets only the fleetest impression of her thumb before his phone is back in his hand. Leila stands up and moves next to Karen, so Luke stands too. Mark gives him a quick glance.

"Well, I've got two little girls at home," Karen is saying to Mark. "So playtime is over for Mommy."

Mark nods and chuckles as if in sympathy. There are renewed congratulations exchanged on all sides. Leila holds up her hand in the bodhisattva salute, smiles, turns, and walks away. Kati makes some gesture behind Mark's back and a photographer comes forward. Mark and Karen stop talking and smile at the camera. Luke looks at his phone and sees that Leila has entered her name and phone number in his contact list.

"You disappeared on me," Mark says, when they are back in the limousine.

"I'm sorry," Luke says. "I didn't think you needed me. You ran into that friend of yours."

"A friend?" Mark questions. "Yeah, I guess he's a friend."

"Karen Michaels's daughter," Kati says. "Nice work, Luke."

Mark frowns.

"Is that a bad thing?" Luke asks Mark.

"God, no," Mark says. "I love Karen Michaels. This is the third time I've met her. She might actually remember she's met me next time. You gonna go out with her? The daughter?"

"If that's okay."

"You hear how Karen Michaels called it an Emmy *nod*?" Mark asks Kati. "Like they had to give me a nomination but of course I won't win."

"I'll rent you a car," Kati says, to Luke. "Something flashy? Or a hybrid?"

"I'll rent him a car," Mark says. "I'll do that."

"Of course," says Kati smoothly. "That's what I meant."

"Did you have a good time tonight?" Luke asks his father, who shrugs.

"God, can you believe Derek Portnoy is now getting all this great work?" Mark demands of Kati. "Derek fucking Portnoy. I used to cater with that guy, and now he's got three features coming out this year."

"Derek Portnoy isn't nominated for an Emmy," Kati says calmly.

"You mean Derek Portnoy doesn't have an Emmy *nod*."

Luke leans back in his seat, slightly relieved that his father is grumpy because of professional jealousies, and not with Luke for abandoning him at the party. Luke looks out the window of the car, but it is dark and all he can see is the blue-black outline of his face in the glass. Luke blinks in time with his reflection. He turns back to his father and to cheer him up begins to tell Mark how Leila described her mother as a crazy woman.

CHAPTER FIFTEEN

Talk about a special trip you have gone on. What happened during the trip? Who was with you? Were there surprises along the way? Did you face any challenges? In what ways were you different at the end of your journey?

I went on a Sacred Journey trip right before my thirteenth birthday, in the Adirondacks. Sara took me. She actually got me out of a week of school to do it. She had done special things with both of my sisters when they turned thirteen, but not Sacred Journey. Aurora had gone with Sara to a spiritual retreat house in Long Island, and done meditation and a whale watch. Pearl got a couple of days in Martha's Vineyard, on some special island where she got to herd sheep and make her own sweat lodge. In most cultures, and religions, there is some kind of "coming of age" ritual or ceremony. That was the idea behind these trips. "Attention must be paid," was a thing Sara said.

Sacred Journey is sort of like those Outward Bound programs, but with more of an emphasis on spirituality. You still hike, and learn survival skills, and do group trust exercises, but every day on your Sacred Journey adventure you focus on a different chakra, and there is a lot of chanting and meditation and stuff like that.

The opportunity came up because Sara became friends with this guy Jeff who was a Sacred Journey guide. He was also a numerologist, which is how Sara knew him. She knows a lot of people like Jeff.

Sara told me that she really wanted to spend meaningful time with me. As it turned out, though, a Sacred Journey is mostly an internal thing, and at best you have adjacent meaningful time together. Also, there were twelve other people in our group, and of course Sara had to get to know all of them on a meaningful level too. People talk to Sara. That's one of her things. If Sara goes to the post office and has to stand in line, by the time she gets to the window she knows all about the marital troubles of the person in front of her and the difficult childhood of the person behind. I know this because I have frequently been the person standing next to Sara in the post office line, listening to all this too.

Jeff gave us a big speech the first day when we assembled as a group at the Sacred Journey Station with all of our gear. I didn't hear any of this speech because I saw a rabbit. I know that sounds ridiculous, but we were all crowded together in this little orientation room, and I was sitting on this window seat, and right as Jeff began his speech I saw a small brown rabbit about ten feet away outside. I had just read *Watership Down*, which was a book my sisters had both loved, and so I saw this rabbit and I started thinking about all the rabbits in that book: Fiver, who was the mystical rabbit, and Hazel, the steady leader type, and Bigwig, the fighter. I stopped thinking about the whole story of *Watership Down* and started listening to Jeff right at the moment that Jeff said, "Okay, while we make our first hike to our base camp, I ask that we all maintain a Noble Silence unless there is an emergency, so that we may all reflect on these four points."

I've always really liked hiking, especially if it's in difficult terrain, and you have to make choices about how you are going to surmount obstacles, but our first hike was pretty easy, and nobody broke the Noble Silence. I had no clue about what four points I was supposed to be reflecting on, but I wasn't particularly worried about this. I figured it probably had to do with creating a spiritual goal, or making space in one's heart for self-love, or something along those lines. When we got to the campsite, though, after we built a fire, Jeff asked us to write "those three things we talked about" down on the pieces of paper he was handing out. When we finished, he told us, we were to cast our papers into the fire.

In situations like these, where you might have totally missed the point or argument of something because you were thinking of something else, like the adventures of fictional rabbits, for example, it's safest to go for broad strokes. Like sometimes after Assembly, Nana might ask me what I thought about the scripture lesson of the day, and if I said something like, "I thought it was about God's love for us," or "It seemed like they were saying we need to trust in God," that usually works pretty well. I was on the point of writing down things like, "I will be a good listener," or "I will help others," when Jeff made a clarifying statement about renunciation, and how we should search inside ourselves for ways of *being* that we were ready to renounce, rather than things like chocolate, or smoking.

So I sat down on the ground and tried to think of three things to give up. I was familiar with the concept of renunciation, because that's in all religions and both Sara and Nana talked about it. A lot of my renunciations had already been made for me: not eating meat or processed foods, not owning any toys or games that were orientated toward war or violence, not playing football, etc., so it was hard to come up with things. Everybody else was busy scribbling away except me. I wrote down "I will give up" three times and waited for inspiration to fill in the spaces. Inspiration did not come. Soon everybody was casting his or her papers into the fire, so I just left mine blank and threw that in. I guess my whole Sacred Journey got off on the wrong foot, with the rabbit.

Each day on the Sacred Journey, Jeff would hand everyone a small crystal on a cord to wear around our necks to help ground us in the day's chakra. The idea of chakras is that there are seven invisible wheel-like things in the body, through which you can receive and transmit energy. People relate them to specific organs or glands, and also emotional states, and colors. Wearing or using a crystal associated with a chakra is meant to help activate or balance it. My sisters and I already knew all of this from Sara, who was as likely to give you a turquoise to help you with your sore throat (fifth chakra) as belladonna or honey. By the third day of my Sacred Journey I was already a little bored with chakras, so when Jeff conducted the meditation, I used the time for experimentation.

For example, when we were doing Manipura, the solar plexus chakra, I did the physical action of fire breathing, but I really tried to shut Jeff out and not see the color yellow or the blue ten-point lotus flower, or recite the names of the petals, or find my inner flame, or any of the visualizations. Instead I concentrated on imagining a green frog with purple spots croaking: *boo-ya!*

I was just interested, you know, in seeing if I could still get all the benefits of fire breath like increased energy and a smooth bowel movement if I was thinking of something totally non-Manipura. What happened was that I got really dizzy, and for the rest of the day I had the sound of a frog croaking—*boo-ya!*—on some sort of auditory loop in my brain circuitry, which was really annoying. But I also did have a smooth bowel movement, which is a useful thing to have in the woods.

Jeff was a good guy, and knowledgeable about things like rope tying and plant life and astronomy, and there were some cool people in our group too, so it was fun. On the sixth day (Ajna, the third-eye chakra), Jeff gave me my numerology reading. That was something he did for everyone in our group, but he had to spread it out over the week, because he couldn't do everybody in one day without exhausting his spiritual resources. Everyone who had had a numerology reading by Jeff agreed that Jeff was amazing.

Jeff did my numbers after we had set up our camp for the night, and everybody was writing in their journals around the fire. I sat with Jeff on a log a little bit away from camp, and Jeff held a flashlight in between his teeth so he could see his notebook while he was writing down my name and my birth date and doing his calculations. He said that he had been doing numerology for a long time, and had a very refined system based on these ancient precepts from kabbalah and other sources.

"Wow," he said, taking out the flashlight and looking at me. "You have a lot of nines. You have an overabundance of nines. You have the numbers of a Universal Sage."

"Hmmm," I said.

"It's a very clear chart," Jeff said. "Extremely organized: groups of nines, groups of sevens, a nice clear thirty-three, a repeating seventy-seven. Wow. Makes a lot of sense."

"Cool," I said.

"I'd like to deal with this thirty-three first," Jeff said. "That is the Christ number, the age Christ was when he died. Thirty-threes can go either way. They can be teachers, and humanitarians in their most positive aspect, but they can also be martyrs. That's what you have to look out for, Luke."

"Okay," I said.

"You are a sympathetic person. A person with huge powers of empathy, you can be a social reformer, you can effect great change on humanity. The work that you do will really change people. On a global scale."

I don't remember what I said to that. I'm not sure that at twelve I had any desire to effect change on humanity, or that I had a concept of global scale. I thought of being things like an astronaut, or some kind of explorer, but I wanted to be an astronaut because I thought it would be cool to travel in space, not because it would be cool to give humanity the benefit of my space knowledge.

"You have trouble granting that your feelings and needs are real feelings and needs," Jeff said. "It's important that you clearly communicate your needs early in your relationships. You are also an adept in the darker subconscious aspects of humanity. That increases your self-knowledge, but it can also draw dark elements to you, seeking your understanding. You have to watch out for that. You'll have to fight that, Luke. I don't say this to scare you."

I don't think I was scared because I don't think I really knew what he was talking about. I wasn't sure what he meant by fighting. I *was* pretty good at t'ai chi. Of course, that's not a fighting martial art, in the traditional sense. If someone attacks you in t'ai chi, you defend yourself with your ability to anticipate and absorb oppositional forces, you don't, like, karate-chop them into submission. (I don't know how well t'ai chi works in some sort of brawling situation. You'd pretty much have to be a Master to stand there in "hug tree" pose fusing your yin and yang while someone came at you with a broken beer bottle.) But of course, Jeff wasn't talking about actual hand-to-hand combat with people.

There was a bunch of other stuff that he said that I don't remember and two other things that I do.

"You are on a thirteen-year cycle," Jeff said. "Every thirteen years you will experience a complete epiphany that will change the direction of your life."

"Starting when?" I asked, since I was just about to turn thirteen.

"From the beginning of your life. Also, 2007 will bring the number two into play for you, and that will be the only time that it does and it will change things at a very fundamental level for you."

So that was my numerology reading, and then we went back to the campsite and Sara asked me how I felt and I said, "Good."

After we finished with our seventh chakra day we had two more days of spiritual integration and some other stuff like rope tying and shelter building and then we did our solo camp.

This was where you went off on your own and spent a night by yourself communing with all your new knowledge and testing your skills. It was also where you might find your totem animal. Sara was really big on my finding a totem animal.

It's hard to induce a coming of age, but I had everything I needed for one. I was in the mountains. I had nothing with me but a small backpack that carried basic supplies. There were a variety of forest creatures about as potential spirit guides. I was totally up on my chakras. I was apparently, according to my divine numbers, on the cusp of a personal epiphany. I was ready.

Because of my youth, Jeff was keeping an eye on me for my solo. He wasn't, he said, going to interrupt me, but he would be within shouting distance and he gave me a whistle that I was to wear around my neck and blow on in case of emergency. I wondered if I would see a bear, and if that would mean that it was my totem animal, and if so, what would it mean if you were mauled by your own totem animal?

I enjoyed the building of my shelter, and of my small fire. I made a little clearing and designed a labyrinth, with rocks and twigs and leaves and things. I walked my own labyrinth, very slowly. I listened to the sounds of the woods. Eventually I rolled out my sleeping bag next to the fire, because it was a clear night and I didn't need my shelter. I looked at the stars. I prepared myself to have deep and powerful dreams and the next thing I knew it was morning and all I could remember of my dream was that at one point Sara and I were driving in our car and we passed a McDonald's and I said, "Can I get some fries?" and Sara said, "No," which was weird only because I would never ask Sara to stop at a McDonald's.

We all reconvened at our group campsite and people were invited to read from their journals or share experiences.

"How was it?" Sara asked me. "Wasn't it wonderful?"

I agreed and Sara asked me if I knew my animal and I said yes and that it was a rabbit. It was what came to mind, I guess, because of *Watership Down*. I didn't want to disappoint Sara. I was taking a bit of a risk, because I had no idea what rabbits symbolize, but I figured there had to be at least one culture where the rabbit was the

ultimate mark of *something* that Sara would read as very significant
and Special.

It was a good guess. When we got back home, Sara did research
on the meaning of rabbits. In some North American native tribes,
Nanabozho—the Great Hare—is a hero and creator of the Earth,
born of a human mother and a spirit father. (In some versions of the
tale, Nanabozho is a very amoral figure, but Sara passed over that.)
Depending on where and who, the rabbit can symbolize fear and
overcoming limiting beliefs, benevolence, whimsy, innocence, abun-
dance, rebirth, and almost always: sexuality. The rabbit was a favorite animal of Aphrodite. Pliny the Elder said that eating the meat
of the hare would increase your sexual attractiveness for nine days.
The number associated with the rabbit is 7997. (Also 58, and 2065.)
The rabbit is also often associated with the moon. The moon goddess Ostara had a magical white rabbit attendant who laid colorful
eggs that were handed out to children during spring fertility festivals.
Early Christians thought the rabbit portended disaster and was the
preferred form of many witches. The Celts said that eating a hare was
like eating one's own grandmother. Chinese astrologers say Rabbits
get along with Goats and Pigs, but on no account should they marry
Roosters. Lord Buddha was once incarnated as a hare, and when he
was unable to procure food for Lord Indra, he threw himself into a
fire so that Indra could eat him.

You can add up all these rabbit things and put with them the
other stuff I'm supposed to be. In astrology, I'm a Libra with Scor-
pio rising. In the Chinese calendar they would call me a Dragon.
Combine these and it means someone who is energetic, brave,
charming, diplomatic, honest, and idealistic. Also someone who is
short-tempered, stubborn, eccentric, and bad with money. I'm des-
tined to be a Universal Sage or a Martyr. I should be careful of my
lower back and my kidneys. I respond best to water and should try
to live near it. I have a fear of knives that I am not even conscious of
having. People are drawn to me.

There is even more stuff. Sara has interpreted my dreams, her friend Eileen has read my tarot cards, and her friend Aju did a past-life reading on me (a monk, a violinist, a healer, a warrior). Then there is Nana, so I've also been reassured that I am a Child of God. Jesus loves me and died for me.

The universe is watching over me. Abigail Perkins and twelve generations of sisters culminated in ME. I have a DESTINY TO FUL-FILL.

Last year I turned seventeen and that is the legal age you can donate blood in Delaware, so I made my first donation. Afterwards I was given a little card that said "I Just Donated!" and listed my blood type: A+. I keep the card in my wallet, not just for a possible acci-dent, but because I like it. I think of it as a sort of private trump card. My ace in the hole. You can think I am a Dragon or a rabbit or a fourth-century warrior or whatever, but I have the evidence: I am A+.

You can take this whole essay and everything you think it reveals about me and shove it up your ass.

"Luke?" It's Mark, knocking on Luke's door.

"Yup," Luke says, jumping up from his desk. "Good timing."

"How's it coming?" Mark asks, as they head out of the house together. They are going to the REI store to look at camping equip-ment for their upcoming trip to the Sequoias. Mark asks Luke to drive.

"I don't even know why I'm still doing it." Luke backs slowly down the driveway. "I think I'm going to use the one we wrote on the plane after all. So it's not me: who cares? Why do we have to run around identifying ourselves all over the place?"

"You're asking the wrong person."

They laugh.

"So you're going on this date tomorrow, huh?"

"It's not really a date," Luke explains. "It's a group hang. I guess a bunch of her friends will be there."

"Ah," says Mark. "A group hang. That's cool. Well, in the morning we will go rent you a car. I assume you don't want me driving you there?"

"Thanks," Luke nods. "I really appreciate it."

"So, this is what kids do, right? I shouldn't have any problems with this or do, like, any parenting thing?"

"You're fine. She said 'hanging by the pool.' I assume that means swimming, right?"

"I hope so. I hope it means swimming in the pool and not standing around outside it, taking Ecstasy and doing tequila shots."

Luke assures his father that he has been around people drinking before, and doing drugs. Luke has not done very much of either of these things. He tells himself that it is because he likes to remain "alert," although it is not that. Luke is afraid of what might emerge if he loses control of himself, and has never been in a situation where he felt comfortable testing this. To be in such a situation is something Luke wants very much.

"You two were sitting there with half-empty cocktails at the party," Mark says. "Don't think I didn't see that."

"They were half full, actually," Luke says. "Don't be such a pessimist, Dad."

"Ha. Well, if you drink, stay away from the pool because you could slip and concuss yourself, or drown or something. And if you do drugs just do a quarter of the amount that everyone else is doing so you don't lose your shit. Just don't drive, is all I ask. If you've had even one drink, call me and I'll send a car to pick you up and I'll be crouched down in the backseat so no one will see me. I'll be very cool."

Luke tells Mark that he has really gotten the hang of parenting.

They enjoy shopping for camping equipment. Mark has never camped before so he leaves the decision making to Luke, who picks out basic items in the mid-price range. Mark attempts to supplement these with more elaborate gear. Members of the REI staff fall over themselves to be helpful. Luke observes that in public, Mark seems to retreat an inch or so inside his own face, leaving a Mark Franco mask.

"It will be good to have all this stuff for the future," Mark says when they are back in the car. The mask melts. "Hey, Luke, we should get harmonicas."

Back at the house, they ready themselves for another event, a charity dinner for the World Wildlife Federation.

"Is this one black tie?" Luke asks, hopefully. Luke really likes the way he looks in his new suit.

"Listen to you," Mark says. "By the way, if this isn't an incredibly gay question: what are you wearing tomorrow? To swim in, I mean."

"My trunks," Luke raises his left eyebrow. "That's what people swim in, right?"

"Those blue-and-white things?" Mark shakes his head. "Yeah, no, you need to upgrade those. I've got dish towels in better shape than those trunks. Let me see what I have."

Mark disappears into his bedroom.

"Um . . . Dad?" Luke calls out.

"Don't worry, they're not Speedos," Mark shouts back, correctly interpreting Luke's concern. "I'm not that gay."

The trunks are plain blue. They're loose on Luke's hips, but he agrees that they are an improvement over his own.

"Kati is a magician," Mark says later, as the limousine pulls up in front of the hotel where the charity dinner is being held. "I don't know how she gets me into these things. I've never even donated to World Wildlife."

"That's okay," Luke tells him. "I have."

Mark blinks at Luke.

"On our birthdays," Luke explains. "One of our presents is ten dollars to donate to the cause of our choice."

"So that's what a good parent does, I guess," says Mark. Photographers, clustered to one side of the driveway, spring into life as the car stops.

"Hey, you've done awesome parenting today," Luke says. "Every day. You are giving me the best summer of my life, Dad."

"Don't thank me," Mark says, sharply. "I haven't done anything. Don't thank me, Luke."

They get out of the car and there's the now-familiar-to-Luke stir of energy, name calling, event-coordinator elbow pulling, flashbulbs. While this is going on, Luke reminds himself to ask Mark what his blood type is. Luke thinks it would be very cool if they had the same. Even better if they had matching bone marrow, so one could donate it to the other if that was necessary. Luke makes his camera face and wishes for a moment that his father could have that opportunity, to give Luke some of his bone marrow, so that he could stop wishing he hadn't given Luke enough.

CHAPTER SIXTEEN

I'm going to drive to Leila's house in about fifteen minutes. I had to explain to Mark that I'm too young to actually rent a car, even though he seemed to think the place would let us anyway. He ended up getting one for himself for the day, and I've got his BMW. This will be my first time driving it by myself. I don't even want to think about how expensive his car is. It has a GPS system, but I'm not going to use it. I've already mapped and memorized the route to Leila's. I was even able to zoom in on Leila's house with Google's satellite system, but mostly all you can see is a gate. I don't know why I'm writing right now. I should just go. Okay, I'm going.

Luke has difficulty finding the house numbers of the houses in Brentwood. He knows he is driving too slowly for the people behind him. "This," he says to himself, "is kind of a nightmare. Wait. Is this it? This is it."

Luke stops at a gate, unrolls his side window, sees that he's too far away from the little white box to reach it, gets out of the car. He notices two video cameras above the gate. He hopes that nobody is watching him, pushes a button on the box, and gets quickly back into the car. After a moment, a woman's voice, not Leila's, comes fuzzily out.

"I'm here to see Leila," Luke says, loudly, toward the box. "She invited me?"

"Okay, Leila, okay," says the box, and the gate opens.

Leila's house is enormous, white with a Spanish roof, columns, and a circular driveway in which several cars are parked. Luke counts two Mini Coopers, an Audi, an Alfa Romeo convertible, and a BMW just like Mark's. He parks and heads for the front door, glad now that Mark counseled him against bringing his own beach towel.

Luke is texting Mark, as instructed, on his safe arrival, when the front door opens and a tiny woman appears wearing pink shorts and a T-shirt. She looks, for a moment, so exactly like Bubbles that Luke almost says, "Bubbles!"

"Hello," Luke says.

"Leila in back," the woman says. "I show you."

Luke says thank you and introduces himself in Spanish. The woman, Elsi, leads him around the side of the house, down a path banked by a tall bougainvillea-covered wall. Luke can hear music playing, a splash, male laughter, a girl's voice, not Leila's, shouting, "No way!" The path leads to steps, into another path, and then down more steps.

"Okay, there." Elsi points through a row of cypress trees that Luke can see lead to some sort of terrace.

"Gracias, Elsi."

"Okay," says Elsi, patting Luke on the arm.

Luke walks past the trees onto the terrace, turns, and is immediately smacked hard in the forehead with a wet Nerf ball.

"Oh shit!"

"Who's that?"

"Hey dude, you okay?"

"Josh, you dumbass."

"Luke!"

Luke can see now, from his doubled over position, two sets of purple-painted toes. He stands up, removes his hand from his forehead.

"Hey Leila," Luke says. "Ow."

Over the next five hours, Luke is instructed in many matters. He is told why the beaches in Bali are preferable to the beaches in Bora Bora, how the Australian Open is much more fun than Wimbledon, and that in the view of Josh, Patrón Silver is superior to several other brands of tequila. Luke is shown things on YouTube: the story of how one girl's hair weave stopped a bullet, a demonstration from a Ukrainian porn star of her ability to projectile orgasm, and a tutorial by a masked man who is able to suck his own penis. Luke has several new sensory experiences: he rinses off in Leila's poolside shower which is nozzled in such a way as to produce three different aromatherapy settings, including one called "Amazonian Rain Forest." Luke eats unagi, and has the toenail of his left big toe painted green by a girl whose Chihuahua has appeared in three feature films. He plays *Guitar Hero* with Caleb, who has an actual band of his own, composed entirely of the children of actual rock stars, one of whom is featured on the cover of the *Guitar Hero* case. He is asked if Delaware is a city or a state.

Luke watches Leila float between her friends, the pool, the white-canopied cabanas; the table filled with sushi and pita chips, the giant stone Buddha heads that bank the hot tub. Occasionally their paths cross, and they speak. The number of people at Leila's house—originally five at the time of Luke's arrival—swells in midafternoon to encompass friends of friends and soon totals almost twenty. Luke does not find himself distinguished by Leila in any particular way over her other male guests, even though on the previous night they

had a two-hour phone conversation which ended with Leila saying, "I'm really glad you're coming tomorrow," in the same mysteri-
ously coded significant way with which she had said, "I don't like
carpeting."

Toward the end of the afternoon, as numbers have dwindled to
half a dozen people, a girl called Michaela offers Luke a blue-and-
green glass pipe filled with medical-grade marijuana. Michaela,
Luke learns, is a backup dancer for a pop star, and has obtained a
card for medical marijuana by a licensed physician, one of many in
California, she informs Luke, who will write you a prescription for
weed if you have symptoms of stress, PMS, migraines, or depression.
Michaela personally suffers from none of these things, but she does
experience quite bad jet lag, which "getting totally baked right before
I get on a plane" greatly alleviates. Luke watches as Michaela peels
off her (apparently false) left eyelash and places it on her knee. At
this point, Leila appears and sits down on the deck chair in between
Luke's straddled legs, pulling her hair over one shoulder and contem-
plating him with her profile.

"Are you going to smoke?" she asks.

Luke, who once smoked pot with Pearl to no demonstrable effect,
who has today refused alcohol and drugs for five hours, and who now
believes his modest claims to Leila's interest to have totally evapo-
rated amidst potential rivals who have gotten tattooed in Morocco,
snowboarded in Fiji, or posed for an Abercrombie & Fitch catalog,
shakes his head.

"I don't have any medical conditions," Luke tells Michaela.
"Unless you count head trauma by Nerf ball."

"Oh my God, you're hilarious," Michaela says. "Leila, I love this
guy."

Leila places a hand on Luke's knee.

Luke imagines pulling Leila back against his chest in the kind
of easy, affectionate, flirtatious way he has observed all afternoon
amongst Leila's friends, but Luke is not sure that Leila's hand on his

knee is enough of a green light for this kind of action. Michaela offers the pipe to Leila.

"I'm going to have one little smoke," Leila says to Luke. "And I will cough and not really be stoned but it will serve as, like, a transition moment."

Leila puts the pipe delicately to her lips and Michaela leans forward and holds her lighter over it. Leila inhales, seems fine for a moment, coughs, and then exhales, frowning. Michaela, summoned from across the pool by Josh to see the hair-weave-stopping-the-bullet video, moves off, leaving Luke and Leila alone.

"Do you smoke?" Leila asks Luke.

"Only once," Luke says. "With my sister. Nothing really happened."

"Do you like Michaela or something?" Leila reaches for a bottle of water by the deck chair and takes a sip.

"They started playing 'No I Never' in the cabana," Luke explains. "So I came over here. There's a lot I've never done."

"You're innocent," Leila says.

Luke sighs.

"It's nothing to be embarrassed about."

"I'm not embarrassed. I'm just tired of not doing things." Luke is surprised to hear himself say this. He asks himself if this is indeed true.

Luke takes the pipe from Leila's hand.

"You don't usually get stoned the first time," Leila tells him, reaching for the lighter Michaela left behind. "So you might now."

Luke inhales as he has observed other people inhaling, and holds his breath for a moment. He can feel a slight burn in his throat, and in his eyes. Luke exhales, coughs slightly, and laughs. Leila hands him the water bottle.

"Okay," says Luke. "Yeah. Don't let me drive until I can do some algebra or something."

Luke and Leila sit in silence for a few minutes, passing the water bottle between them. Luke looks at Leila's hair, because her face is turned away from his. Luke runs a diagnostic check on his senses, noting a slightly elevated heart rate, an increased awareness of his tongue, and muscular relaxation in between his scapula.

"Is there anything," Leila asks suddenly, turning around and putting her hand on Luke's thigh again, "that you are embarrassed about?"

"Um . . . no," Luke says. "Wait. Yes. Probably yes."

"Like what?" Leila prompts.

"Well, give me a hypothetical situation," Luke suggests. "And I'll tell you if I would be embarrassed about it."

Leila slides her hand a little farther up Luke's thigh.

"Would you be embarrassed," she asks, "to walk naked around the pool?"

Luke shifts slightly in the deck chair. Leila's hand on, now, his inner thigh, is causing the hair on his arms to stand up. Luke concentrates. It is hard to concentrate.

"In front of everybody?" Luke asks. "Or just you?"

"Say, just me."

"I don't think so," Luke says. "But if you laughed and said something . . . I don't know . . . mean about how I looked I might be embarrassed."

"What if I just looked at you? Without saying anything?"

"Then no." Luke swallows. He is glad of the extra room in Mark's swim shorts.

"Are you sure?"

"No," Luke says. "But I don't think I'm ashamed of being naked. Like, innately. What I'm saying is that embarrassment or shame, that's something that usually comes from outside forces, like ridicule, or, or . . . religion." Luke is pleased that he is able to draw such a lucid explanation with Leila's hand on his thigh and a narcotic in his system. On the other hand, Luke considers that he might be, just a little bit, babbling.

"What about you?" Luke asks.

"I don't like to be looked at," says Leila, standing up.

"I'm going to get rid of people," she says. "But you are staying."

Leila moves off across to a group of her friends. Luke walks over to the table where he has stashed his phone and texts Mark—*evrythng cool, hangin out fer wile*—and then sits on the edge of the pool. An empty inflatable bed drifts by him and Luke pushes himself on top of it. Propelling himself about the pool gently on his pneumatic cushion, he appreciates the warm temperature of the water, heated, Luke estimates, to something like eighty degrees. Leila's pool, in addition to being heated, is also chlorine-free and tiled on the sides in dark blue squares. Everywhere Luke looks there is something beautiful. The bougainvillea is beautiful, the Buddha heads are beautiful, Leila's friends are beautiful, Leila is especially beautiful. The negative spaces between all these things are beautiful, and should not be called "negative." Luke hopes that all this seen and felt beauty is causing positive spikes in his neuronal sequencing, to countereffect whatever damage the marijuana might be doing to his brain, and that he is breaking, on a cellular level, somewhat evenly. From his floating vantage point, Luke reviews the events of the afternoon. He allows them to fall gently through his mind, kaleidoscopically, in patterns.

The last of Leila's friends and friends of friends leave.

"Luke," says Leila.

"Leila," says Luke.

"Want," Leila asks, standing on one foot at the pool's edge and looking down at Luke, "to get in the hot tub?"

Luke executes a slow fall off the floatation bed, surfaces, and swims to the edge of the pool.

"Yes," he says. "Okay."

"Now is your big moment," Leila says, "to not be embarrassed."

Luke watches Leila's feet walk away. He looks at his fingers. He lowers his chin into the pool until his lips are level with the water. He blows bubbles. He pulls himself out of the pool. He looks around and sees Leila is already seated in a corner of the hot tub. Leila waves something white in her hand. Luke realizes that this is her bikini. He stands, dripping, for a moment and then takes off his (Mark's) swim trunks, places them jauntily on the usnisa crown of the nearest Buddha. Luke realizes that heretofore, his total nudity has mostly taken place in transition moments: from one set of clothing to the next, or from clothing to shower to towel-around-waist to more clothing. Luke finds the experience of open air upon his genitalia pleasant. Luke walks naked to the hot tub and gets in it. He supposes that Leila is watching him for all of this, but he does not directly look at Leila until he is submerged in the water. He feels he does this only slightly more quickly than he would have if dressed.

"And to think," Leila says, "you went to church every Sunday."

"And my Nana prays for me every day," Luke answers. He has, he finds, been holding his breath.

"Guess it's not working."

"Have you ever noticed," Luke muses, squaring himself opposite Leila, "that people only pray for things that could happen through some other physical cause? Like, people pray for rain, or for the infidel to be killed, or for the sickness to go away, but they don't pray for rabbits to start speaking English, or for an addition on their house to be built overnight. If you really think prayer works, you should pray for rabbits to start talking. Because that would be cool."

Luke tells himself to be calm and maintain a certain detachment. Leila is naked. He is naked. Nudity might not necessarily imply sexual activity. Luke resists the temptation to put a hand under the water and touch himself.

"That's a very good point," Leila says, extending a leg and placing her foot on Luke's chest. This causes a slight contraction in Luke's penis. Luke, who wants to touch something, puts his hand on the top of Leila's foot.

"It's the same with the power of positive thought." Luke examines Leila's toes. "People might tell you that if you release positive energy into the universe about getting into college, then that will somehow help. But they don't suggest you release positive energy into the universe about rabbits being able to recite Shakespeare."

"I guess people don't think that would benefit mankind," Leila says.

"Think of all the things rabbits could teach us," Luke answers. "And think of an all-rabbit *King Lear*."

"I asked the universe for you to get naked in the hot tub with me," Leila says. "Actually, I prayed to Jesus Christ for it. So maybe God does exist."

"You took off your clothes too," Luke points out. "That slanted your odds. That's like praying to God to kill the infidel you are about to shoot in the head."

"That feels good." Leila wiggles her toes against Luke's chest. "I like having my feet held."

Luke takes hold of Leila's foot more firmly. He wants to put her toes in his mouth. He wants to put himself inside her. He wants. He wants.

"Were you bored?" Leila asks. "With my friends? I was suddenly totally bored by everybody today. You were the only person who wasn't, like, boring me stiff."

"I wasn't bored." Luke puts his thumb into Leila's instep, which is a thing that Luke likes particularly to be done on his own feet. Luke wishes Leila hadn't used the word "stiff."

Leila shuts her eyes and rests her head back on the edge of the hot tub.

"Talk some more," Leila says, "my little infidel."

For a moment, as Leila adjusts her position, Luke is able to see through the water to the top of Leila's left breast. Luke is very glad of the suggestion to talk more. Luke thinks maybe he should hold off, for the moment, on more intimate contact with Leila, until he has submitted the idea of more contact with Leila to reasoned thought, or at least until he is more accustomed to what is now, he knows, a full hard-on.

"Where is your mom?" Luke asks. "And your sisters? Where is . . . where is everybody?"

"Malibu," Leila says. "They come back tomorrow morning. We're going to London tomorrow night. Did I tell you? My mom wants me to go with her to the *Chimera* premiere. I think I might be slightly more useful to her than the twins for the next few months. She can be the mother of a hip teenager with her finger on the pulse of the youth culture. I'm only going because my stepfather is staying here with the twins and he's always wanting to make sure I know that he loves me too. It's really tiring. I'm like, listen, you don't have to love me. I don't love you. I don't say that because my mom gets incredibly happy when my stepfather and I say 'I love you' to each other. Seriously, she tears up. She's like, 'It makes me so happy that you are happy,' and I'm like, 'Be serious. It makes you so happy that *you* are so happy.'"

"It could be both, couldn't it?" Luke is not really feeling stoned anymore, although his mouth feels very dry.

"It could," Leila says. "Let's not talk about family."

"Okay. I'm sort of thirsty."

"Are you still stoned? There's a bottle of water right next to your head."

Luke drinks about half the bottle. He moves cautiously, not wanting Leila to remove her foot from his chest.

"I don't think I'm stoned."

"Me either."

Leila tightens her grip on the edge of the hot tub, extends her other foot, and puts it gently and precisely in Luke's lap. Luke stops rubbing Leila's foot.

"Don't stop," Leila says, tracing the outline of Luke's erection with the side of her foot.

"Um . . . Leila?"

"Well then," Leila says, seriously. "Sometimes being in a Jacuzzi makes my skin itch."

Leila removes both her feet from Luke and floats forward, placing her hands on the edge of the hot tub on either side of Luke's shoulders, and bringing her face close to his. Luke licks his lips, leans forward, and kisses Leila. Luke judges the extent to which Leila is kissing him back to be enough that he can extend an underwater hand and touch Leila's underwater hip. Leila moves closer, and Luke can now feel her breasts against his chest. Luke tries to angle his hips away from Leila so that his erection is not touching her, even though he wants to pretty much mash it against her. He's not sure where Leila's legs are. He's not sure what can, or could, or should, happen next. For several minutes, Luke is almost content with what is happening in the present, but this ends, and Luke, deciding that he would like to be an agent of whatever happens next, stands up, pulling Leila with him, who grabs his shoulders and moves her mouth away. Luke's hard-on is at an uncomfortable angle against Leila's stomach.

"Shut your eyes," Leila says. "Please."

Luke shuts his eyes. Leila detaches herself from him. Luke can hear the sound of her stepping out of the hot tub.

"Okay," says Leila. "You can open them."

Luke turns around. Leila has wrapped a towel around herself, and is holding one out to Luke.

"Come on," she says.

Luke pulls himself out of the hot tub and takes the towel. Leila walks to one of the cabanas. Luke follows her, awkwardly, on account of his erection. Without the buoyancy of the water, his penis feels extremely heavy, and not quite a part of the rest of his anatomy. He tries holding his penis with the towel in such a way that it looks like he is just casually holding the towel.

"Can you pull this out?" Leila points to the white futon couch inside the cabana. Luke secures his towel as best he can, all things considered, and pulls the futon out until it is flat.

"So, shut your eyes," Leila says again.

Luke shuts his eyes.

Leila takes off Luke's towel.

Luke feels his penis jump slightly, of its own accord. He wishes, for a moment, to cover himself.

Leila kisses Luke's stomach.

Luke thinks he might, actually, fall over. He separates his feet into a wider, more secure stance. He wishes he had something to hold on to.

Luke's eyes are closed and he is not sure where exactly Leila is, or in what position, other than in front of him, because her hands are not touching him, but he can imagine where the top of Leila's head is relative to her mouth, which is now moving lower, and slightly to the right of his penis. Luke reaches out and touches what he feels to be Leila's ear. Is she going to . . . ?

"Whatever you do," Leila says. "Do not open your eyes."

Luke is about to ask why when Leila puts her mouth around Luke's erection and her hands on his hips. Luke grabs Leila's hair with both hands. He is worried for a moment, about Leila's teeth, and then, quite soon, worried that something, some force of nature, a rogue comet striking the pool deck maybe, will stop Leila from doing what she is doing. Luke's erection no longer seems foreign to his body, but connected in some deep and significant way to every part of it and now especially to a sound coming from the back of his throat. He can feel sweat on the backs of his knees. His stomach is jumping. Luke remembers the moment when you feel the wave lift the surfboard, lift you, realizes he is clutching Leila's hair very hard, and releases it. For a moment his arms flail, pinwheeling.

"Wait," Luke says, before he drowns.

Leila puts one hand on the base of his penis and slides her mouth away. The cool air is not as pleasant, now that he knows better. With his eyes shut, Luke tries to imagine what his face looks like with his eyes shut.

"Can I open my eyes?" Luke asks.

"No."

"Well, then you have to let me touch you."

"Okay. That's fair."

"I don't want to presume," Luke says dizzily. "But . . . do . . . you have a condom?"

Leila giggles.

"I love that you are standing there naked with a hard-on and you don't want to *presume*. Presume away. I have a condom. I put one under the futon about an hour ago. Because I, unlike you, am a big presumer."

"Am I supposed to search under the bed with my eyes closed?" Luke asks, trying to calm himself.

"Would you?"

"Yes," Luke says, thickly. "Yes. Totally. I would. Yes."

"No, I've got it," Leila says. "Don't worry."

Luke leans down. Leila guides his hands to the top of the futon. He can feel her moving backward, on her knees, he thinks. Luke kneels down on the bed. Luke reminds himself that his brain knew how to see before his eyes ever saw anything, that he can do this, he will do this. He leans forward, reaches out a hand, which Leila guides to her waist. Luke pulls her to him and kisses her as hard as he can, which Leila seems to like because she pulls Luke down on top of her.

Leila's rapid breathing, thinks Luke, is a sign that he is doing something correctly. He is momentarily flummoxed by the desire to do everything all at once, everything he has ever thought of, or imagined, and the desire to slow each moment down, to better imprint it on his memory. They roll, this way and that, on the futon. Luke tries to position himself in such a way that his erection is not touching Leila, because he is not sure if that is something she would like and because his penis is now so sensitive that he is afraid of what any friction or contact with Leila might do to it. Luke puts his hand in between Leila's legs. Leila makes sounds, which seem to Luke to be like the sounds he is making. Luke wonders why people ever do anything but this, really, when this is so clearly the best thing anyone can do, ever. Eventually, Luke finds himself on his hands and knees, above Leila. He hears Leila opening up the wrapping of the condom. Yes, thinks Luke. Yesyesyesyesyes. Leila slides the condom on Luke, who hopes that Leila will also guide him through the next step. Leila, one hand on Luke's hip and one hand on his penis, pulls Luke downward, and, after a moment of angling, into her. Luke drops down to his elbows. Leila brings her legs up, her knees hugging his rib cage. Luke begins moving back and forth. Okay, thinks Luke. Okay, this is this is this is this is this, this, this, this, this. After awhile Luke senses, in the distance, a moment where he will no longer be able to contain all of this and its this-ness within his own body. This moment comes sooner than he thought, then comes, quite literally, in a series of jagged and contracted pulses. Luke's shoulders jump toward his ears, he says, "Yah," and "Shuh," and "Guh," with no intention of saying any of these things. He feels a singularly pleasant burn at the point of ejaculation, and a shuddering in his stomach. The front of his head throbs. Luke collapses on top of Leila, his open mouth in her hair, completely stunned.

Luke tastes Leila's hair and is filled with a profound gratitude: to Leila, to the Japanese who invented futons, to Google maps for successfully navigating him to Brentwood, to BMW, the makers of fine and reliable automobiles, to Mark for bringing him to Los Angeles, to Mark and Sara for having conceived him, to his twelve generations of ancestral women, to women in general, to the quarter of a million years of human evolution and the gradual selection and adaptation of human beings, to meteorites, gases, molecules, atoms, subatomic particles, and the accordion big banging and crunching of the universe. To all things known and unknown that have led to the perfection of this particular moment.

CHAPTER SEVENTEEN

People who don't believe in God but who think that there "must be something bigger than us" should go to the Sequoia National Park. There is something bigger than us. There are these trees. And you can see them and go right up to them and touch them and some of them are over two thousand years old and they are alive. They are real.

It was cool leading my dad through the mechanics of camp making: the setting up of the tent, hanging a line for drying clothes, building a fire, the rules for proper food storage, the mysteries of the butane cookstove. At the beginning of our trip, I was worried that Mark might be bored, with no activities other than hiking, and looking at trees, and swimming in streams, but on our very first night, as we settled into our sleeping bags in our new two-person tent, Mark said,

"This is just . . . perfect."

We spent the second day hiking up to a fire lookout station.

We wanted to do all the hikes labeled "strenuous" in the trail guide. When we got back to our camp, I got the vegetarian chili started and gave my dad my latest essay attempt, and he read it out loud, which was pretty hilarious.

"I'm telling you, Luke," Mark said, once he finished, "this is good stuff here. I think you have the makings of a great screenplay. I can totally see this whole Sacred Journey thing."

"Can you go and read it to the college admissions board?" I asked, spooning out two bowls of chili. "It's a lot funnier with you doing all the voices."

"I feel like I really nailed the Jeff character," Mark said. "And your mom."

"You've got her down," I told him. "She sounds exactly like that. It was spooky."

"Hey, Jeff said the number two would be significant in 2007, and here we are. The two of us."

"Well, that proves it, then," I said. "Numerology is accurate. We should call MIT."

"What should I do?" Mark looked at me over his shoulder. "Should I be doing something?"

"We're all set. You're doing the dishes later."

"So what was the question that you were supposed to be answering with this one?" Mark asked, about the essay.

" 'Talk about a special trip.' I decided to do that one instead of 'Describe your strongest character trait.' Although I sort of got to that one too." I brought the chili over to the campfire and handed a bowl to Mark.

"You think your strongest character trait is your blood type?" he asked. "What do you think my strongest character trait is?"

I ate some chili while considering this.

"Wait, don't answer," he said. "I don't want to know. What are some other questions?"

" 'What do you plan to do with your college degree?' " I tried to remember what on my list I hadn't gotten to yet. " 'Where do you see yourself career-wise ten years from now? Reveal your life philosophy. Do you maintain strong beliefs and adhere to a philosophy? How do you solve moral dilemmas?' "

"Jesus. I'm glad I don't have to answer any of that. How *do* you solve moral dilemmas?"

"I guess I pretty much go with the basic system," I said. "If you say to yourself, I don't want to do that, but it's okay if other people do, then it's not a moral thing, it's a matter of personal taste. But if you say to yourself, I don't want to do that and I don't want anybody else to do it either, and I think people who do that should be punished, and I would be wrong not to punish them for doing that, then that is something that's a moral absolute."

I'm not actually sure whether I do this or if it's just how I *think* I should do it.

"What if there is something that you feel is right but everyone else thinks is wrong?" he asked.

"Then you're a psychopath," I laughed. "Or a genius. But people like Galileo, they had evidence for believing that something was right even though almost everyone else thought it was wrong. That's why I think you should have evidence for all of your beliefs. Otherwise it's more just a hope."

"So, okay," he said. "Your being a vegetarian, is that a moral thing? This chili is kick-ass, by the way."

"Thanks. Actually no, I'm not even sure that I can say absolutely that cruelty to animals is morally wrong."

"Hold up," Mark said. "What?"

I like testing out ideas on Mark.

"Well, animal testing was used to come up with a vaccine for polio and smallpox, and all kinds of other medical breakthroughs. I guess lab work on animals isn't quite as gruesome as it used to be, but people are still giving animals diseases and removing parts of their brains or other organs. And if you are a vegetarian because you don't believe in cruelty to animals, then you shouldn't accept vaccines made through animal-testing technology. And if someone said,

'Hey, we might have a cure for spinal meningitis but we need to test on a couple of hundred rats first,' you would have to say, 'No, I don't think you should, and I hope you lose all your funding and your lab is shut down.' You would have to say that even if you had a kid with spinal meningitis who was in agony. I don't think I could do that."

"Yeah, that's pretty intense."

"And you know, there isn't anything on this planet that actually wants to be eaten," I continued, getting into it. "A head of broccoli doesn't want to be eaten any more than a cow does. If it didn't, it wouldn't produce toxins. But even organically grown vegetables have toxins because that's how plants try to protect themselves."

"So this chili I am enjoying contains beans that you murdered," Mark said thoughtfully. "You boiled them alive, in cold blood, you bastard."

"I'm a mass murderer of vegetables," I agreed.

"So why are you a vegetarian, then?"

"I guess I've only really thought it through recently," I admitted. "So I'm not sure. I don't know where I stand now actually. At Leila's house I ate an eel."

"You ate an eel?"

"She had sushi," I explained. "I always thought that sushi looked really interesting. Like, a big plate of ham, that looks weird to me, and I don't like the smell, but I like the smell of seaweed and wasabi."

"How was it?" Mark asked. "The eel?"

"It was really good," I sighed. "Actually."

"You don't think vegetables have a soul or anything like that, though?" he asked.

"I don't think I have a soul, remember," I reminded him.

"Okay, this conversation is getting really deep. Let's talk about sports. Or sex."

I tried to make my face blank.

"You going to tell me about how you had sex or not?" Mark stood up to get another beer from the cooler.

"Okay," I said, after a minute. "How did you know?"

"I'm psychic. No, kidding. It was in my numerology reading. I have the numbers of a Universal Sage and I was told that in 2007 my son was going to get laid."

"For real, how did you know?"

"My swim shorts have hetero vibe on them now."

I laughed, a little bit hysterically maybe. Mark settled himself back down in his camp chair.

"I guessed," he said. "And you had that look in your eye the day after."

"What look?"

"I'm just giving you a hard time. You don't have to tell me."

"Well," I said, hesitating. "Well, yeah, I did."

"You wear a condom?"

"Yeah."

"You had a good time?"

"Yeah."

"I actually wasn't sure if you did it or not. Because you still wanted to go camping. I thought maybe you'd be all about this girl now."

"She left for London. But I would have wanted to go camping anyway. This is almost our last week together."

"For the summer," he said. "But we've got the rest of our lives, right?"

"Yep," I said. "You're stuck with me for good now."

"You're stuck with me too," my dad said.

"Good," I said. "Good."

When we got back from camping, my dad decided to get a dog. We were running together in the morning, and he said, "Hey, let's go to the pound and get a dog today.

"My life has been so up and down," he said. "But now I feel sort of . . . steady, you know? I feel grounded. Actually, for the first time I really feel like an adult. Even when I bought a house I still felt like I was getting away with something, like someone was going to come along and say, 'Who you trying to fool?' But now I really feel like I've got it together."

"You've got it together, Dad," I agreed.

"I wanted to get a dog before you left," he said. "So it will be ours."

We ended up going to three different animal shelters before we found the right one. There were a lot of pit bulls available, but my dad said he didn't want an aggressive dog.

"I want something I can take around with me," he said in between the second and third shelter. "Maybe have in my trailer at work and stuff. What do you think?"

"I've got a great-aunt who breeds Dandie Dinmonts," I told him. "If we don't find anything today."

"I don't know what that is," Mark said. "But it sounds really gay. Do you think I'm manly enough to have a purse dog? If I don't put it into an actual purse?"

"You can borrow Aimee's," I said. "Since she's not using it."

"Oh fuck, I'm gonna miss you," he said.

We found the perfect dog at the last place: a small terrier mix of various somethings, about eight months old, that had been found in downtown Los Angeles. He was recently rescued, underweight but healthy, a little brown-and-gray guy with a tail that curled over and a natural mohawk thing going on top of his head. We were pretty wrecked at that point, because all the people at the shelters were really wanting my dad to adopt from them, and it's hard to look at needy dogs and walk away from them because they aren't the right kind of needy dog.

"His name is Humphrey," the shelter worker told Mark. "We found him on Humphreys Avenue."

Humphrey, released from his cage, ran right over to me and started licking my hands.

"Hey," I said. "Hey Humphrey. Who's a good boy? Hey. Hey there. Go say hi to Dad."

When Mark picked Humphrey up, Humphrey put his paws on either side of my dad's neck and licked his chin.

I thought the adoption process might take some time, but we were able to walk away with Humphrey right then, after Mark posed for pictures with the entire staff of the shelter. He gave them a nice donation check, I think.

"Okay, let's go get the stuff," my dad said.

I held on to Humphrey in the car on the way to Petco, where we got a name tag, food, bowls, bones, a new collar and leash, a traveling crate, gates for the kitchen, a dog pillow, toys, and training manuals. We got the nicest of everything. There was another customer there with a big fluffy chow, and my dad talked to the owner while the two dogs did their sniff thing. The guy was about my dad's age, I guess, and good-looking. He seemed like a really nice guy, too. He recognized my dad but he was cool. I didn't get that the guy was gay, but he gave my dad his card in case my dad needed "the name of that dog-walking service" and after we had left the store and loaded up the car, my dad tossed the card onto the dashboard and said, "Tempting, but no."

"What?" I asked. "The service? Or you mean . . . ?"

"At this point that guy is going 'maybe,'" my dad said. "Maybe I'm gay. Maybe I'm just gay friendly. Maybe I was flirting, maybe I was just being celebrity nice."

"You don't come across gay," I said. "You seem totally—"

"Normal?" my dad laughed. "Yeah, I know. To you I do. But queers can smell you out, so you gotta be really careful."

"He seemed cool," I said. "He had a sense of humor, too. And a dog. You don't want to go out with him?"

"Like I can go out with a guy," Mark said. "No. When he tells all his friends at the gay bar tonight, they'll speculate, but he'll say, 'Well, I don't know, he had his son with him,' blah, blah, blah. I can't hook up with guys like that."

"You can't invite him over?" I asked. "Or, you know, meet him in a hotel in Chicago?"

My dad gave me kind of a look then, like I had gone too far.

"Um. Sorry."

"You punk," he said.

"Sorry," I said again. "I didn't mean to—"

"Actually it was funny," he said. "Normally I would say, 'Good one,' but I just feel like being an authority figure right now. You're going to be gone in five days. I need to parent."

I held out Humphrey, who was squirming like crazy to explore the car.

"You can discipline our dog," I said. "It's like a substitute."

"No kidding."

My last few days went by really fast. I finally got another text from Leila, who was in New York at that point. She was coming back to LA on the day I was leaving. I was happy to hear from her, though, because her other text, in reply to this kind of romantic thing I wrote her after our night together, was either equally romantic or one of those random gnomic things she says. I still have no idea what she's thinking, but my dad had some good advice for me about that.

"So what's the deal with the chick?" he asked. "How'd you leave it?"

"I'm not sure," I said. After, we had made out for a really long time, which was almost as amazing as everything else. She had pulled this blanket over us too, which meant I was able to open my eyes and look at her. Then we had sort of fallen asleep for a little bit, and then she said her mom would be back soon, and I got dressed, and she wrapped a towel around herself and walked me to the side gate. It was dark by then, and all these little solar lanterns were glowing and she looked, like, so pretty, and I didn't want to go, or let go of her, and then I did, and was back in my car and we really hadn't said anything.

"I feel sort of in love with her," I said. "I know that's lame."

"Nah," he said. "Love isn't like this thing that people say it is. Like some big thing that only happens once in awhile when you really get to know someone and share the same life goals and all that. That's something else. Love happens all the time. Don't worry about it."

"So what's the other thing? The something else that isn't love?"

"Contract negotiations."

"I just don't want her to think it was just the sex part," I said. "Like I was using her or something."

"It is the sex," my dad said. "It's the sex and the why you wanted to have sex, and wanting to see her again is about the sex too."

"It's about her as a person, too," I said. "I liked her a lot before I had sex with her."

"You liked her a lot *because* you wanted to have sex with her."

"No. Wait. Really?"

"Otherwise you would've just hung out at her pool and come home.

"Using somebody is when you have sex with somebody you don't really want to have sex with," he said. "Or you're only doing it because you want to get something out of them. You had, like, this pure thing with her. Don't worry about why."

"So what should I do?" I asked.

"Just text her every now and then something sweet. I'm not saying play it cool. I'm saying just let it flow."

"I did that," I said. "A sweet text. The day after. She didn't get back to me for four days."

"There you go," he said. "That's her pace. I like this girl. She doesn't sound all needy. Good for you, Luke."

"I'm gonna let it flow," I repeated. "Love happens all the time."

"That kind does," he said.

It makes sense, the way he said it. Scientists haven't been able to isolate the physical properties of "being in love" in the brain. No distinct neuronal sequence or protein has jumped out and declared itself. All the tests people think up are pretty crude: like giving people photographs of someone they say they are in love with, and then giving them photographs of friends, and seeing what happens differently in the brain. But presumably if you are in love with someone you also want to have sex with them, so you can't isolate sex from love in that test. Maybe you can't isolate it because it doesn't exist. Maybe love in the brain is something like black holes, or dark matter, something we think is there because of the strange way things behave around it.

We went to another movie premiere. We had dinner with two really cool friends of my dad's: a married couple, actors Mark knows from New York. They had been away doing a play in Florida for most of the summer, and it was nice to meet them and see my dad hanging out with people he really likes. Geoffrey and Amelia asked me lots of questions about myself, and I ended up sort of telling stories about my life in Delaware, and we all laughed a lot.

"They're great," I said to my dad, on the way home.

"Yeah, they're family," he said. "Sometimes you get born into a great family, and sometimes you have to make one up.

"I guess it's never exactly the same, though," he said after a moment. "Family is family. But now I don't have to be all wistful about not having a real family. Because I have you."

My dad and I shopped for gifts for me to take home to everybody, and things for Carmen and Kati, as a thank you. We got a second suitcase out of the garage for me. We worked on Humphrey's obedience skills. I borrowed Mark's car and drove to the modern art museum, and got the book on the Rothko retrospective to give to my dad. "Happy Father's Day, past, present, and future," I wrote, on the inside cover. Father's Day was back in June, but I had only been in LA for about two weeks at that point, and we were still saying "Dad" and "son" in funny voices. Mark asked me if I wanted to do something special for my last night, but I said, "Just hang," and so that's what we did. We grilled vegetables and watched a documentary about the making of *Star Wars,* and played with Humphrey. I did a last load of laundry, and Mark helped me pack. I gave Mark the Rothko book. He asked me if he could get me a car for my birthday in October.

Kati came to the house this morning to say goodbye. It's kind of funny that I had a crush on her at the beginning of the summer.

She asked Mark if he wanted her to drive us to the airport and Mark said, "No, because I am going to cry like a girl."

I said goodbye to Humphrey.

We had agreed that my dad wouldn't walk me into the airport, so we wouldn't have to have a public goodbye and stuff, but when we got to LAX, Mark said, "No, fuck it," and parked the car. I let him check me into the airline and wheel my suitcases over to security. He offered to buy a ticket just so he could walk me to my gate, even though he knew that was sort of ridiculous.

"Before you came," he said. "I was nervous. I was like, what if we don't like each other. It's going to be a long summer. Now. Shit. I almost can't stand this." He teared up a little, which made me tear up a little too.

"Wait, it's cool, I'll see you soon," he said.

"Definitely."

"Text me random things," he said. "Call me late at night and wake me up. Email pictures."

"I will," I said. "You too."

"I love you, son."

"I love you too, Dad."

Then he practically ran out of the airport.

Just before I turned off my phone, in preparation for takeoff, I got a picture text from him. He was holding Humphrey and a sign that said, "We Miss Luke!"

I feel like I was in Los Angeles for about five minutes, not ten weeks. And now I'm going back to Delaware, going "home," and everybody will want to know how it was, and what my dad is like, and how I feel. And I will have to say something about that.

Maybe in another language, one of those really old ones like Hindu or Farsi or something, there is a word for how I feel. Or a mathematical equation.

Maybe it's like that thought experiment, "The Mary Problem." Mary is a scientist and lives all her life in a black-and-white room. She learns everything there is to know about the physics of light and color from the black-and-white room via a black-and-white television. When she is finally let out, and she sees an apple for the first time, she discovers that she did NOT know everything there is to know about color. She did not know the qualia of color. She did not know redness. This is supposed to show how the physics of something only tells us about the physics of something, and is not the whole story. There is how something feels to us, how we experience it: a kind of knowledge we can only have through experience. Qualia.

So now I know the qualia of being a son, and the qualia of having a father. So I should, like Mary, realize that there were things I didn't know before. But it doesn't feel like that. I don't feel like I've acquired some new special knowledge. I am going to make a guess here and say that hypothetical Mary didn't either. She didn't see an apple for the first time and stare in wonder and say, "Ah, so THAT is red! I never knew! You bastards!" I think hypothetical Mary saw the red of the apple and just thought, "Yes." It didn't shock her, or alarm her, or enlighten her. Because all that time in the black-and-white world, without being conscious of it, she had a space in her mind all prepared for red. Red was there, it was always there. Mary just didn't know that space inside her was called red. Now she knows.

Now I know.

CHAPTER EIGHTEEN

Sara is waiting for Luke in the arrivals section of the Philadelphia airport. Luke sees her first because she is standing apart from a cluster of people and staring very hard into space. Luke thinks that he should have spent the plane ride thinking about home instead of writing about the last couple of days with his father, because he doesn't feel ready for Sara, for her attention, for her scrutiny, for her knowledge of pre-summer Luke and her expectation that post-summer Luke will be identical.

When Sara sees Luke, her face lights up.

"Here you are," Sara says. "Here you are!"

Sara hugs Luke hard, then leans back and examines his face.

"Yup, it's me," Luke says.

"Well!" she says. "Well!" She presses her thumb briefly against Luke's forehead, which is something she always does to Luke, who always says, "Sheeeyaaangh," when she does it, like a gong, as if Sara were ringing his third-eye chakra.

"Sheeeyaaangh," Luke says.

They walk to the baggage claim area. Sara puts one arm around Luke tight, and hip to hip, they match strides.

"Was it hard saying goodbye?" Sara asks, at the carousel. "It sounded like you two really found each other. I was thinking, Soul mates. That's what it sounded like to me."

"Mhmm," Luke says, who is thinking that when someone says something close to what you're feeling, but not exactly right, and not in words you would use, it becomes TOTALLY wrong.

"You tired, honey? You must be tired."

"No, I'm good."

"You have pictures, right? I want to see everything. I want to hear about everything."

"Like, right now?"

A fault line appears in Sara's smile.

"Okay, but first fill me in on what's happening here," Luke says, trying to sound enthusiastic. "Aunt Nancy's here?" Aunt Nancy always visits for a week before her semester starts in Maine.

"Yes, since Monday."

"How you holding up? She driving you crazy yet?"

"Not at all. We've been having a great time. The girls are coming tomorrow. In your honor. They've both been working their pants off this summer. Although apparently Pearl's been stoned half the time."

"Oh," Luke says, startled into actual interest. "Um. You think?"

"Aurora told me," Sara smiles. "And I talked to Pearl about it. I smoked a little at her age. I get it. We all have this desire to transcend out of ourselves, and sometimes we take short cuts. Ultimately, I know Pearl is way too creative to be satisfied with artificial highs."

"Yeah."

"Of course Rory told me because she knew I'd be cool about it to Pearl, and that Pearl would hate that!" Sara laughs. "I'm on to their ways."

"Ha." Just hearing this much makes Luke feel claustrophobic.

Home. Signals being sent from one woman to another. Electrical signals. Chemical signals.

"What about you, though? You have a good summer?"

"A good summer," Sara nods. "A thinking summer. I'll tell you all about it, after you've told me all about yours."

"Dad said he was going to call you. To let you know I got on the plane okay and all that."

"He did. He did call me."

"What did he say? I mean, did you guys talk, or . . ."

"Of course we talked. Of course."

There is a loud honk and a subterranean growl as the carousel begins to move. Sara and Luke spring forward. Luke's suitcase (the new one) is the first to fall down the slide.

"This is actually mine." Luke hauls it off the carousel. "I had gifts and things to bring back, and some other stuff. My bag going there was pretty full, remember?"

Sara raises her eyebrows, but says nothing.

Luke had promised Mark he would text him when he landed, but he waits until he retrieves his other bag, then goes to the men's room, where he sends his father a quick message from a bathroom stall.

"So tell me," Sara says, once they have left the airport and are on the way back to Acton.

Luke has to shout because Vlad's air conditioning doesn't work and the windows are down, but he begins describing bits and pieces of his summer to Sara. He finds it difficult to keep to a chronological order and it all gets jumbled together: descriptions of Bubbles are scrambled into the mechanics of surfing, the paintings of Rothko collide with watching *The Last* be shot in the Mojave Desert, the wrap party on the beach trips into the Sequoia National Park. Luke is not aware of how much he is saying "my dad" and "my dad and I," until suddenly he is very aware. Luke shouts into the wind thundering through the car, feels his words boomeranging back into his face, but does not stop shouting.

When they get off the freeway, Sara tells Luke that she's been thinking about where she'll go after Luke leaves for college.

"Go?" Luke shouts, with unnecessary volume, as they are at a traffic light.

"I'm thinking about Colorado," Sara says. "I might open a Wellness Center there, in Boulder. I've always loved Colorado."

"You'd move there?"

"Well, I never planned on living my whole life with my mother! I think it's time for a new journey. I think I've spent enough time trying to open minds in Delaware. I wouldn't mind living in a community of like minds."

"Wow. That sounds . . . great."

Luke scrambles to process this new information: a Sara not satisfied with her life, waiting for Luke to leave in order to move to a like-minded community in a city named after a large rock.

"It's just something I'm thinking about," Sara says. "I want to hear everybody's ideas about it, since it would affect all of you."

"You should do what you want," Luke says, somewhat blankly. Sara had always talked about the "beautiful opportunity" of living with Nana, and although Luke was used to the myriad meanings of "beautiful" in Sara's lexicon, he had accepted that one as literal. Luke is trying to remember if he has ever heard Sara express dissatisfaction about living in Delaware before, but now it is Luke's street, and then Luke's house, and then what looks to Luke like the back end of his Aunt Nancy.

"Luke." Aunt Nancy straightens up from the flower bed as they pull into the driveway.

Luke gets out of the car.

"Aunt Nancy!"

"My God, look at this child." Nancy advances on Luke, kissing him on both cheeks, European-style. "You have changed once again."

"So what am I now?" Luke stands up straight and submits himself to Nancy's annual classification.

"Hmmm . . . a Murillo. You should not be wearing jeans. You should be wearing a cape, and holding the leash of a greyhound, and looking self-contained."

"I'll try to come up with something."

"Do," Nancy says, drawing the word out to two syllables, turning back to the asters.

Luke knows that for all intents and purposes, Aunt Nancy is now "done" with him, so he turns back to the car, where Sara is unloading his luggage. Nana comes out the front door wearing gardening gloves.

"Well!" Nana says.

Nana squeezes Luke with the tops of her arms, because her gloves are dirty.

"Here you are. Safe and sound."

"He's taller," Sara says. "Luke, your Nana was convinced that two men couldn't possibly be eating properly and she's been worrying all summer that you've been starving."

"Historically, we are hunter-gatherers," says Luke. "How are you, Nana?"

"I've taken Paul's letter to the Thessalonians as my inspiration for August," Nana says. " 'Aspire to live quietly, to mind your own affairs, and to work with your hands as we have charged you.' " Nana holds out her garden-gloved hands. "The Lord has blessed us with a glorious summer, but we've had such winds in the past three days and all my asters are in a terrible state."

"I'll get my bags inside and come help you."

"Oh no, you visit with your mother and Nancy and I will set everything aright and join you later."

Sara and Luke take the suitcases inside the house and up the stairs.

Luke has not—for a long time now—particularly noticed the colors of his room, the shapes of the furniture, the quality of light coming through the windows, etc. Or, for that matter, the front of his house, the street he lives on, and most of Acton. All of these things look slightly different to Luke now. He asks himself if they are familiar without being recognizable, or recognizable without being familiar. He looks at the green curtains at his window, the green-and-brown blanket on his bed, the rug, the bookshelf, the reading lamp, the bike lock on the closet doorknob, the two framed posters on the wall: a photograph of Earth and another of deep space taken from the Hubble telescope. The smell is disorienting. Luke cannot smell anything but the way things smell after vacuuming. On his desk is a brown box, tied with a ribbon.

"What's this?"

"A little gift for you," Sara says. "Open it up."

Luke opens the box. Inside is a piece of blown glass sculpted to look like a banyan tree, which Luke mistakes for a cauliflower.

"It's a banyan tree," Sara says.

"I know," Luke says. "Wow. It's great. Thank you."

"I met an artist at the Vipassana retreat that makes these. And of course I thought of you. You remember the story in the Upanishads, when the father has the boy get the fruit of the banyan tree?"

Luke nods. In the story, the boy is instructed to break open the fruit, and then break open the seeds within it. Finally the boy has split the tiniest part that he can, and the father asks him what he sees. "Nothing," says the boy, and the father tells him that this nothing cannot be seen with the naked eye, it is so small, but it is there, and it is the true essence of the banyan tree, without which the tree could not exist. "That is the Self," the father says. "And you are that Self."

"Thank you so much," Luke says, again. "I love it."

"I was thinking of how you have a lot to process right now, and how that might be like breaking open the seeds of the banyan tree."

Luke's jeans pocket buzzes, loudly, in the quiet room. He takes out his phone and reads a text from Mark.

Humphrey just took a dump the size of Ohio.

Luke laughs. Sara smiles a question mark.

"He just . . . sent me something funny."

"Is that the phone he gave you?"

"Yeah, he said I should keep it so we could talk and text and stuff without . . . you know, he doesn't mind paying for the service."

"He offered to pay for your college tuition," Sara says, abruptly.

"Oh," Luke says. "Oh yeah, he said something about that to me, but I didn't really . . . I mean, I'm still going to try for a scholarship and everything. He just thought, with Rory and Pearl both at school, even with their scholarships, it must be a lot . . . for you, and he didn't want me to . . ."

"Caroline has already told me that she and Louis would like to contribute to whatever you need."

"Wow, that's really nice. How IS Louis?"

Luke says this to make Sara laugh, but she doesn't laugh. She jerks Luke's new suitcase onto his bed with some force.

"I'll help you unpack."

"That's okay. I've got it."

"We can do it together."

"No, I have your gift in there and it isn't wrapped."

Sara opens up the suitcase and pulls out the first item on top, which is the leather jacket Mark gave Luke.

"Well, I know this isn't for me." Sara holds it out. She looks down at the contents of the suitcase, fingers the suit jacket of Luke's new suit, the stack of new T-shirts, the new shoes.

"Luke, what is all this?"

"People came to the house," Luke takes the jacket away from Sara. He does not want her to see the label. "People give him stuff, and I got some too. It's not a big deal. I wasn't like, 'Buy me clothes.' It just sort of happened. I told him he didn't have to."

"I don't understand. Were you planning on not showing me these things?"

"I just got here," Luke points out. "I've been here for, like, two seconds."

"I'd like to see all the things your father got you."

Sara pulls out a long pale blue shawl.

"That's your gift," Luke tells her. "It's made from hemp. He drove me all the way out to Venice Beach to this special store he looked up that sells natural products, just so I could find the right thing for you."

"And did he buy this for me?" Sara asks. "Or did the store give it to him for free?"

The question hangs in the (unfamiliar, unrecognizable?) air of Luke's room, for a moment.

"We bought it together. It's from both of us," Luke explains. "I would've gotten it myself but he said he wanted to help. He wanted to give you a thank-you gift, for letting me come."

Luke steps forward and slams the suitcase lid shut. It's made of a soft material, so it slams quietly. Luke tosses the leather jacket on top of it, crosses his arms, and looks at Sara.

Sara fingers the shawl.

"This," she says, "is lovely. It's perfect. I'm sorry if I intruded upon your privacy, Luke. I'll let you unpack."

She puts the shawl across her shoulders.

"What a wonderful gift. And my favorite color. This is very thoughtful and generous of you both."

Luke wishes he had not slammed the suitcase.

"It looks good on you," he says.

"Grrarggh," Sara mock-growls, after a moment, shaking herself like a dog. "I'm full of emotions today. The biggest one is happiness at seeing you."

She steps back and twirls.

"Well, I have my son's favorite four-mushroom lasagna to get started on. So I better get chopping. You can settle in up here."

"I'll be down in a little bit."

Sara leaves and Luke sits down on his bed next to his suitcase.

His phone rings. It is Pearl.

"You better get here quick," Luke tells her. "The Lord smote Nana's asters, Aunt Nancy thinks I should get a cape, and I've become an asshole. Conditions are tense."

"Ah," Pearl says. "Welcome home."

Luke talks to Pearl for a few minutes. He knows he should go downstairs and help Sara with the lasagna. He opens his suitcase again. Sara's ruffling has displaced the orderly folds Mark had organized. Luke looks around his room. He thinks that it might be some sort of evolutionary brain function that makes you stop really *seeing* familiar things and that this is because you need the brain space to notice new stuff—potential fight-or-flight situations—like, say, the appearance of stampeding mammoths on the savanna. Luke hangs the leather jacket in his closet, where there are no mammoths, and goes downstairs.

"Now, I haven't seen the program your parent is on," Nancy says to Luke at dinner that evening. "Have you seen it, Mother?"

"No," Nana says. "I understand it's very popular."

"Is it one of these reality entertainments?" Nancy asks.

"It's kind of a futuristic drama." Luke explains the basic plot line of *The Last*.

"Right." Nancy draws the "r" from the back of her throat and bites it off at the "t." "One of those."

Luke is already hearing himself replay this exchange to his father. Mark loves Aunt Nancy stories.

Conversation moves to local topics: Nancy's new book, a raccoon that was spotted in the backyard, Aurora's internship, a new acupuncturist at the Wellness Center. Luke, homesick now for dinner-table conversation less blandly familiar and a lasagna more recognizably delicious, imagines himself suddenly saying, "Jesus fucking Christ!" or "I had sex!" or even "Can we talk about how Aunt Nancy pretends she's English?"

"Awesome lasagna," Luke says to Sara.

After dinner, Luke calls Ivan, who tells him that tomorrow's run is at six a.m. Raj, Nick, Ethan, and a new guy, Matt, from track will be there.

"We're doing a ten-K," Ivan says. "You up for it?"

"Totally."

"So your dad is super-famous, dude."

"Yeah, pretty much."

"He going to get you a car so you don't have to drive that lame piece of junk?"

"You dare to insult Vlad?"

They exchange a few more jokes, and Ivan tells Luke about the training regimen he has been leading the team through all summer.

"You better bring it," Ivan says. "You better not have gotten all soft. We've got a new chant before we run. No more praying. We all just go, '*State, State, State.*'"

"Good," Luke says. "I like that better."

He hangs up the phone, decides against calling Amy, skirts the living room, where Sara is giving Aunt Nancy reflexology, and finds Nana on the stairs with her arms full of sheets.

"There's my helper," Nana says. "Let's get these on your sisters' beds. We've had quite a to-do over the rooms. Nancy doesn't care for the attic room, she feels it's too confining, so Sara is in there and Nancy has her room. The girls will have to share again."

Aurora and Pearl had originally shared a bedroom. This had been fine, and then not fine, and battle lines had been drawn: literal lines, with Aurora roping off their room into yours/mine quadrants. When Aurora was granted the attic bedroom, Pearl's sense of injustice at being denied the attic room for herself lasted even after she installed herself in the attic once Rory left for college. Various remnants of both sisters have now been reunited in their old room, haphazardly. Luke helps Nana with the fitted sheets, and then sets about sorting stuffed animals, books, and other historic girl paraphernalia to their correct places.

"It's always the same." Nana sits down on Pearl's bed. "One girl wants what the other has, or wants to be different. Not just different, but better. More."

"Do you mean Rory and Pearl?" Luke asks. "Or Sara and Nancy?"

Nana swords this question away, lightly.

"I hope that you will be coming to Assembly with me on Sunday," she says.

Luke arranges Aurora's shells on her dresser, lining them up in an ascending scale according to size, which is not something Rory did. It's what Luke did, when he was allowed past the barricades.

"Yes," Luke says, absently. "Sure."

In the morning, Luke bikes over to Fishers Park and meets the team in the parking lot. He exchanges the cross-country team greeting with everyone: two high fives followed by a double fist bump. Ivan gives Luke a one-armed hug.

"Good to have you back, Hollywood."

"Okay, no way am I going to let any of you call me Hollywood," Luke says. "That stops right here."

"I saw the picture of you at the Dodgers game," Raj comments. "Sweet."

"Yeah, I saw that too," Ethan says. "You know, a whole bunch of pictures come up if you Google 'Luke' and 'Mark Franco.' There's, like, pictures of you going to *lunch*, dude."

"Did photographers follow you around and stuff?"

"Not really," Luke tells them. "I mean, sometimes people will see him on the street and pull cameras out."

"Seriously," Ethan says. "Everybody is talking about it."

"Yeah, your dad going to visit?" Nick wants to know. "Because we could get mass turnout if he comes to a race."

"We can use it as a recruitment tool," Ivan says.

Ivan begins leading the team in warm-ups. It is already too hot to wear anything but shorts.

"You start eating meat?" Raj asks, looking at Luke. "You look . . . bigger."

"I'm on steroids," Luke says.

"C'mon," Luke says, when no one laughs. "I started drinking protein shakes."

While they stretch, Luke is asked more questions. They want to know what famous people he has met. They want to know if Luke knows what happens next on *The Last*. They want to know what kind of shakes Luke has been drinking. Luke tells a few anecdotes. He describes Mark as "actually a really mellow guy," and does not realize that he is borrowing this phrase from Pete, the golf cart–driving assistant on *The Last*. He believes the team wants to be reassured that he is the same old Luke, and this makes him feel like he is producing an imitation of himself being natural, which makes him uncomfortable, rendering the imitation useless, as well as inaccurate.

Ethan says, "So I'm sorry, but it's kinda weird, right, that you didn't know who your dad was?"

Everyone falls silent and looks at the ground and Luke guesses that this is something that they have all been discussing.

"Well, not you, but your mom," Ethan says. "I mean, she didn't know, right? Or like, she knew but she didn't know or something? I'm not saying that's bad, I'm just saying that's kinda weird, right?"

"It's kinda weird," Ivan says, looking at Ethan, "that *your* mom doesn't know you are an idiot."

"I didn't mean . . ." Ethan turns to Luke. "You know I didn't mean anything, right?"

"Here's the deal," Luke says, who has anticipated this moment. "They had a brief thing and he knew about me but he was really young and he couldn't be a dad. Then he changed his name for acting. If Sara watched TV she would've known it was him, but she doesn't. Once things were good for him, he got back in touch."

"Yeahyeahyeah," Ethan says, hastily. "Totally."

Luke had planned this explanation but not the sharp and slightly aggrieved way he has delivered it. In the silence now, he hears the echo of this, feels exposed. He dons self-deprecation, like camouflage.

"Hey, I know I don't look like him. But I saw pictures when he was my age. And he used to be just, like, this skinny nerd guy too."

"So there's hope for all of us," Nick says. "That's good to know."

Six sets of clearly visible ribs expand and contract with laughter.

"State, State, State," they chant.

Ivan waits until about a mile in, after they have broken into pairs, with Ivan and Luke leading, to say, "I saw Amy last week. She said she and Darren were breaking up. You going to get back with her?"

Luke thinks about lying curled up with Leila, after they had sex. He thinks about the text Leila sent him from London: "Ur sweet. I love umbrellas." He thinks about Amy's email. He thinks that Amy wanting to be with him because his dad is famous is worse than her wanting to be with him because she wanted to get back at Darren. He hears Mark say, "Everybody uses everybody."

"Nah," Luke says. "We're not really a good match."

"People are gonna be jealous," Ivan says, after a moment. "And you know people are going to want to be your friend now, just because."

"Which is totally ridiculous," Luke says, firmly. "It's not like *I'm* famous."

"Yeah, but it's f-ing Delaware, dude. What else are we going to talk about? Cheese sale at the Amish Market?"

"True."

"Yeah, listen. Don't worry. You'll be news for a little bit but then something else will happen. I'm not gonna lie. I think it's cool your dad is Mark Franco. But I know you haven't changed or anything. We all know that. Everybody was psyched you were coming today. Not because your dad's famous. Everybody likes you for you. We just wanted you back."

"Thanks," Luke says. "It's good to be back," he lies.

Once they stop talking, though, Luke does begin to feel good.

He enjoys running in a pack again, in the soggy honeysuckle and dog crap–scented air of an August Delaware, and maintaining a pace he can tell is just a little bit faster than what Ivan expected. He tells himself that he is going to look sincerely at everything he passes, in anticipation of the time when he will once again stop really seeing what is around him. He tells himself that he is going to stay present and focused in the moment, discounting those moments where he looks at his watch, which is still set to Los Angeles time so he can more easily estimate what Mark might be doing.

After the run, Luke bikes slowly to the Wellness Center. He takes the longer route, in order to coast down the hill on FairView Road, and catch a breeze.

Outside the Wellness Center, he parks his bike next to Sara's, puts on his T-shirt, and drags himself up steps he has painted and repainted for the past five years. He pushes open the door. The aroma of the Wellness Center is the aroma of Sara's room, of Sara herself: orange, lavender, sandalwood.

At the front desk is Lydia, Sara's partner, whom Luke has known for most of his life, and whose Philadelphian accent and speech pattern is one of the highlights of Pearl's repertoire of imitations. It was Lydia's money, settled on her after her divorce from one of the DuPont heirs, that made the Center possible.

"Luke!" screams Lydia, in a whisper. She holds up her hands and shakes them, the gesture for applause in sign language—learned by Sara at a two-week ASL workshop—and the Rising Moon Wellness Center greeting when a class is in session.

Luke takes off his shoes and Lydia gives him one of her two-second, rib-crunching hugs—less an embrace than a chiropractic adjustment.

Luke can hear Sara leading her students in the larger of the two studios through most of the conversation with Lydia. He can also hear Sara in Lydia herself, whose feeling toward Sara borders on the worshipful, and whose imitation-Sara responses—"That is beautiful" and "What an interesting journey"—slide in between Lydia's more natural exclamations: "wowie-wow" and "geez Louise."

The class reaches the final pose, savasana, and falls silent. Luke cannot see Sara, but he can picture her, walking lightly in between the aisles of yoga mats, occasionally bending down to place her hands on someone's feet, or forehead, or abdomen, her eyes shut, breathing through her nose. Later, those who have been touched by Sara will tell each other about how powerful that moment was for them. Luke has heard how Powerful–Healing–Wise–Compassionate–Beautiful–Special Sara is for all his life, by people who are envious of Luke for being Sara's child, and therefore a part of all that Specialness.

Lydia says she's thrilled with the idea of sending the spirit of Rising Moon to Colorado, but, "Holy shmo, Acton won't be the same without Sara." She puts her face close to Luke and says into his ear, "I am so proud of her. For once she is thinking about her own happiness." Luke only just stops himself from jerking his head away from the wetness of Lydia's consonants.

A loud and reverent "Namaste" comes in a chorus from the other room. It is Sara's advanced class, and always crowded. Soggy and blissful women begin to filter out of the studio. Many of them spot Luke and want to hug him. They say, "You've had quite the summer!" or "I guess you've been busy!" in a way Luke does not know how to answer. In order to give himself something to do, Luke moves into the studio, grabs the floor duster, begins sweeping.

"There's our famous Luke," booms Howard, Luke's least-favorite Rising Moon regular. Howard's lack of genital support underneath his thin sweatpants and his scraggly shoulder hair have bothered Luke for nearly a decade.

"Hi Howard." Luke sweeps around him.

"Oho!" Howard cries. "Glad to see you haven't forgotten all the little people!"

Luke looks at Sara, whose usual after-class crowd of devotees has now all turned to him, grinning. Sara's face is smooth, impassive, a visiting queen. Luke has always assumed that Sara liked it, being queen. He has never thought that a Sara-who-is-queen was a Sara who was not "thinking about her own happiness." Luke uses the floor sweeper more vigorously.

Sara rolls up her mat and Luke helps her restack the blankets and then idles outside, waiting. Sara appears and they mount their bikes. For awhile they ride in silence and then Luke asks, "Oh, so, what are you telling people? About the whole situation . . . with Dad?"

"What are *you* telling people?" Sara counters, her eyes on an approaching car.

"I'm just . . . what do you mean?"

"Did the guys ask you about it?"

"Kind of."

"I let people know you were spending the summer with your father," Sara says. "It's actually been very enlightening being asked questions. Very revealing, in some ways, don't you think? Of course, I freely admit that I didn't know that your father had become a well-known actor. I suppose that reveals something about me."

The light has changed, but they remain where they are, each with a left foot on the ground, anchoring the bikes.

Luke takes a breath, plunges forward. "I guess we should . . . um, he told me about coming to see me after I was born, and what you talked about . . . I mean, what he told you. About himself. The thing he said he didn't want to be? That he was . . . you know . . ." Luke, who has not thought out how to approach this topic with Sara, fumbles.

"I'm not sure what you are referring to," Sara says.

"Oh." Luke thinks. "Oh, um . . . never mind. I just—"

"At that time he expressed some confusion about his sexual identity," Sara says, evenly. "Is that what you want to talk about?"

"Okay—" Luke looks behind them. A woman is walking her dog, toward them. Cars are passing with their windows down.

"You know you can't say anything about it," Luke says, in a rush because the woman with the dog is getting closer. "I mean, not even that he was . . . confused or whatever. Just. You know. You haven't said that, have you? To anyone? Like, Lydia, or anyone?"

The woman with the dog passes them. Sara smiles brilliantly at her and wishes her a beautiful afternoon. "Oh! Oh, you too," the woman says, momentarily confused and then pleased by Sara's radiance, as strangers generally are.

"It's just," Luke says, quietly, "he's like, struggled for a long time to get where he is. If anything got spread around, that could hurt him. You know what I'm talking about."

"Actually, I don't," Sara says. "I hope you don't either, really, because I hope that I've taught you not to care what people say about you."

"It's not for me." Luke kicks the spokes of his front tire in frustration. "It's for him. I don't care at all. But other people will."

"And is that how we introduce change in the world?" Sara asks. "By keeping secrets and—" she stops and fiddles with the basket on her bike. "I'm sorry, Luke. I do know what you're talking about, but if you remember, I didn't ever tell *you* about Mark's sexuality. That information wasn't mine to tell, and I didn't tell it. I do think people have a right to privacy."

Sara reaches out and touches Luke's shoulder.

"Luke, you seem . . . is there something you want to talk to me about?"

"No," Luke says. "I'm fine. I just . . . I just wanted to get that clear, I guess. I feel a little protective of him."

Sara lets go of Luke and straightens out her bike. She looks like a queen again, smooth faced, ramrod-straight spine, shoulders back.

"We should get home," Sara says. "You said you wanted to pick up the girls at the station."

She kicks off her left foot and crosses the street. After a moment, Luke follows her.

.   .   .

An hour later Luke is leaning against the front door of the Impala, holding up his sign: "GODDESSES REPORT HERE."

Aurora and Pearl, backpacked and sunglass-y, practically tackle Luke, who is relieved to feel that his sisters, at least, are entirely recognizable and familiar, even though Pearl has cut her hair short again.

"Luke!" Pearl screams. "You are a STUD! Look at him, Rory. He is gorgeous!"

"Since the day he was born," Aurora says, kissing Luke on the cheek.

"Yes, but now . . ." Pearl steps back and examines Luke. "Now he's . . . what?" Pearl narrows her eyes at Luke, holding up her thumb like a painter considering perspective. Aurora joins her sister and flutters her fingers against her pursed lips.

"Hmmm . . ." Aurora says. "Yes, definitely something different."

Luke does his camera face for Aurora and Pearl, complete with eyebrow lift and half smile.

"You've lost your kid thing," Aurora says. "I'm sad."

Pearl pulls a magazine out of her backpack. The cover photo is a close-up of Mark Franco's face, staring skeptically at an invisible viewer.

"We think he looks like you," Aurora says. "Not really so much in the features, but the facial expression. This is totally a Luke expression."

"Really?" Luke looks at the photo.

"They talk about you in the interview," Pearl says. "I mean, you were there when it took place, apparently."

"Oh yeah," Luke says. "That one. Wow. What's it say?"

Pearl reads portions of the interview out loud to Luke in the car. Luke takes the long way home, around the cemetery, so they have more time to themselves.

" '*He's the biggest sweetheart you'll ever meet,*' says costar Joelle Fox. '*And yet, he's definitely got a dark side too. I think that's what makes him so sexy,*' " Pearl reads. "*Dave Sonderson, who directed Franco in small roles in two features before casting him on* The Last, *agrees.* 'He has this tremendous quality,' *Sonderson says.* 'He's an observer, a watcher. And then suddenly he explodes with all this energy and passion. And you know he hasn't missed a beat. He carries himself with ease, but you know that there's dynamite in there too.' "

"Is that accurate?" Aurora asks.

"Ummm," Luke says.

" '*But it's not until Franco's teenage son makes an appearance,*' " Pearl reads, skipping to a new section, " '*that something like a genuine smile appears on his face.*' "

Luke smiles, himself, at this.

"And then this is in parentheses," Pearl continues. " '*Luke is Franco's son with Sara Prescott, a yoga instructor whom Franco met in New York City in 1989. The two were never married.*' "

Luke whips his head around to look at Pearl.

"I know," she says.

"It's so interesting," Aurora reaches into the backseat to take the magazine out of Pearl's hands. "To hear her sort of dismissed as that. I'm sure Sara won't take it personally, but it's funny. She's spent her life healing people, but it's your dad who's famous, just for being an actor, and so she becomes just a yoga teacher from the eighties."

"She's stuck inside a parentheses," Pearl says, from the backseat. "Like Abigail Perkins. Accused of unmarried sex, New York City, 1988. Convicted, but not executed."

"Women always get stuck in parentheses," Aurora says.

"Read the part about how wonderful Luke is."

" '*To all appearances, Luke seems an exceptionally bright and polite young man,*' " Aurora reads, " '*And the rapport between father and son is evident.* 'I think I'm more myself around my son,' *Franco says.* 'Than around anyone else. He keeps me honest.' "

Luke can't help laughing at this.

"I know," Pearl says. " '*To all appearances.*' Who else would write a crappy phrase like that but some celebrity journalist? It's sort of a boring interview, really. But those pictures of your dad are ridiculously hot. Very Heathcliff meets James Bond."

"He wants to meet you two," Luke says. "He's already heard a lot from the Aurora and Pearl archives. He thinks you both sound awesome."

"Well, we are that," Pearl says. "Would we like him?"

"Actually yes. You would. You will."

"Poor Sara," Aurora says. "She does all the work of raising you, and your dad gets to have this amazing rapport with the results. Maybe we should all meet our parents for the first time when we're seventeen."

"We should go on a manhunt in India for the father formerly known as Paul," Pearl says to Aurora. "Get the whole band together back in Delaware. Cut an album."

"There aren't enough swords," Aurora says, "for Nana to survive that."

The house changes with the addition of Luke's sisters. Nancy, amused by Pearl's imitations of bourgeois brunch patrons and their nanny-raised children, and treated to a mini lecture by Aurora on the differences between gender and equity feminism, becomes almost jovial. Nana assumes a Mountjoy-style grandmotherliness, and retreats largely to the kitchen for the production of baked goods. Pearl explains to Sara the difference between having read a novel and *knowing* a novel. Sara, who never reads novels, smiles vaguely and opens a bottle of wine at dinner. Luke is aware of Sara's tension, of his growing irritation at Sara's tension. He half hopes one of his sisters will say or do something outrageous, to divert Sara's attention from him, which he can feel coming at him in waves, like sonar. After dinner, Luke goes to the backyard to call his father. There must not be, Luke realizes, lightning bugs in California, because he is now noticing them again.

Mark picks up on the first ring.

"Luke!"

"Hey!"

"Okay, I was just sitting here wondering what I did before you came," Mark says. "What the hell did I do? How are you?"

"I'm good. How are you?"

"Good. Here, Humphrey wants to say hi."

Luke listens to the sound of Humphrey's metal name tag clinking against his collar, and what sounds like Humphrey's jowls.

"Who's a good boy?" Luke shouts into the phone. "Who's a good boy?"

"So what's going on?" Mark asks. "Down, Humphrey. Down."

"Just finished dinner. My sisters are here."

"Whole family, huh?"

"Well, almost. I miss you!"

"I miss you too."

"I saw the magazine. With you on the cover."

"Oh yeah. Pictures are good, huh? I don't sound like too much of a jackass?"

"No, it's good. Our rapport is obvious."

"You keep me honest, ha-ha."

"Ha-ha."

"You get the copy of *King Lear* I put in your bag?"

"Yes! Thank you! I'm definitely going to start reading it."

"Do it in front of your family. So they can see that I'm a cultured type too and give you books on Shakespeare."

"Ha-ha."

"I had a nice talk with your mom. She's funny."

"You mean strange funny, right?"

"No, but I have more of an idea of her now from your essays."

"Yeah."

"You think she'll let you come out for Christmas? Or New Year's Eve? It might be easier for you to come out here than for me to go there. I mean, with your mom and grandmother, and stuff. Although I'm definitely coming to your graduation. I'm gonna get the day off written into my contract."

"Yeah, I haven't talked to her about it yet. She's kind of . . . you know, my sisters are here and Aunt Nancy. She's a little distracted."

"Feel her out about it, okay?"

The screen door of the back porch opens, and Luke hears Sara's voice call out,

"Luke?"

"I should go."

"Okay, yeah, me too. I've gotta go shmooze a party now."

"Luke?"

"Yeah, I'm on the phone!"

"Okay, go shmooze. Be nice."

"Love you."

"Love you too."

Luke hangs up his phone and jumps up the steps to the porch. Sara is standing there, holding the door open.

"I was just checking in with my dad. He says hi."

"Wonderful."

Luke puts his hand over Sara's and shuts the screen door behind them.

"You're letting the bugs in," Luke says.

"Luke . . ."

But Nana is calling them now, to dessert.

Later that evening, Aurora, Luke, and Pearl convene in the girls' room. They lie on their backs, legs in the air, Aurora and Pearl on their separate beds, Luke on the floor. All three have their hands crossed under their heads. They juggle and toss Aurora's bear, Cinnamon, between them, with their feet. Cinnamon, matted and dilapidated from such treatment over the years, is now perched precariously on Pearl's right foot.

"So what does she look like?" Pearl is asking.

"Umm," says Luke, thinking. "She's about your height. Dark hair. Blue eyes."

"Pretty?" Pearl asks, bringing her feet together and vaulting Cinnamon across to Luke. "Sexy? Cute? Sultry? Goth? Geeky?"

"Definitely not geeky." Luke sends the bear over to Aurora. "She's . . . not like anybody I've ever met, really."

"Ohhhhh," say Aurora and Pearl, simultaneously.

"So you went to her house," Pearl prompts, while Aurora twirls Cinnamon on one foot, her signature move. "Following the trail of her purple cowboy boots. The trail of crab cake crumbs. A little Hansel without his two Gretels to protect him. And lo, the witch's cottage was filled with junior Hollywood hipsters who got you high."

"Will you let him tell the story," Aurora asks, "before you rewrite it?"

"I was only a little high," Luke says. "Anyway, so I stayed after people left."

"Hey, are you going to tell Sara about Luke getting stoned?" Pearl interrupts, half sitting up to face Aurora. "Because I so appreciate your telling Sara about me, by the way. That was just a beautiful conversation."

"Oh please, you practically told her yourself. I'm surprised you didn't light up during dinner." Aurora sends Cinnamon hurtling to her sister, who neatly catches him by one paw.

"I'm not even smoking anymore, you Judas. And did we not just hear how you can get a prescription for it in more enlightened States? I was waiting tables all summer! I wasn't researching for the Queen of Equity Feminism and freakin' networking lesbians in the Hamptons."

" 'Feminist' and 'lesbian' are not synonymous."

"No, lesbians are less irritating."

"Oh, so now you're not a feminist?"

"Of course I'm a feminist. Oh, look at Cinnamon's nose."

"Poor thing."

"Nana will fix it."

"Why do I still love him so much?"

"I know what you mean," Pearl says, bringing Cinnamon down to her face in order to kiss his nose.

"Anyway, Luke, go on."

"Yeah, so I ended up staying, at Leila's house, after everybody left."

"And . . ."

"Well," Luke says. "How shall I say this?"

Pearl sits up.

"Did you . . . ?"

Luke nods.

"Luke!"

Aurora sits up now too.

"Okay, tell us everything," Pearl says. "Don't leave anything out."

"Ugh, Pearl! Luke, tell us whatever you feel comfortable with."

"Hey, I told you everything about my first time. Both of you."

"From which we are still recovering," Aurora says.

"And you didn't tell everything," Luke says. "You were more flowery about it."

"Oh please, when have I ever been flowery?"

"You didn't give anatomical details."

"I don't want to know who did what," Pearl says. "Well, I kind of want to know but I don't want to picture it. Anyway, you are horrible at describing things. Okay. Let's ask questions."

Luke crosses his legs and waits.

"Who initiated it?" Pearl asks.

"It was a mutual thing," Luke says. "I think."

"Why her?" Aurora asks. "I mean, were you just seizing the opportunity or was there some special quality to the whole thing or you felt this intense connection?"

"It just happened naturally," Luke says, thinking. "There wasn't this big buildup or anything. We were in the hot tub—"

"Of course," Pearl says. "Of course you were in the hot tub."

"I wasn't sure how far things were going to go. She actually . . . she asked me to keep my eyes closed."

"Wait," Aurora says. "She asked you to keep your eyes closed? The whole time?"

"Um, yeah," Luke says. "That's what she wanted."

"Why?" Aurora asks. "Did you ask why?"

"She said she doesn't like to be looked at."

"Okay, whoa," Pearl says. "What?"

"She's a little unusual," Luke says. "That's what I like about her."

"She gets you to her house," Pearl says, recapping. "And she gets you stoned with her fancy friends, and then everybody disappears and she lures you into her hot tub and makes you have sex with her with your eyes closed?"

"It wasn't freaky," Luke says. "It really wasn't. There was no luring. And we didn't do it in the hot tub. She has these cabana things by her pool. With futons."

"What was she hiding, is the thing I want to know. Like some weird rash or something?"

"There wasn't anything weird."

"How would you know, your eyes were shut."

"I was touching her."

"It's something else," Aurora says. "It's something psychological. It's about control, maybe. Or shame."

Luke had wanted to tell his sisters about Leila in order to keep her real, and in the present tense. He does not want to have to revise his memories now with things like shame or control.

"So what happened after?" Aurora prompts. "How did you leave things?"

"She left for London," Luke says. "The next day. I texted her, she texted me. We're texting."

"What did you say?" Pearl asks. "In this text."

"I could tell you were beautiful even with my eyes closed," is what Luke had texted Leila. A phrase that had felt really right at the time, and then increasingly wrong during the four days where Leila had not replied, and then right again when he got the umbrella text.

"I told her she was beautiful."

Aurora and Pearl smile.

"It really wasn't weird."

"So," Aurora says, "here's the thing, Luke. Sex is totally different for girls. It takes forever for girls to even have a proper orgasm, usually. And so that means there's always an emotional component for girls. Because the pleasure part isn't even totally there."

"Most girls have sex so guys will like them," Pearl says.

"You've told me all this," Luke says. "A million times. Believe me, I was just happy that I could do it without the thought of you two standing over me screaming, 'It's different for her! It's different for her!'"

"So what are you going to *do*?" Pearl insists, once she and Aurora have stopped laughing.

"I'm not doing anything. I'm just going with the flow."

Pearl and Aurora groan.

"You've got to assert yourself, Luke," Pearl says. "Otherwise you are going to be doomed to a series of ambiguous relationships with crazy girls who look down on you for being so nice and don't appreciate you."

"Like all of Pearl's boyfriends," Aurora says. "I'm sorry. I mean: slaves."

"Yes, like all of my poor slaves."

"Okay." Luke stands up. "I'm never telling either of you any of my personal business again."

Aurora and Pearl tackle Luke. Luke is forced to repeat, "I embrace the mystery of women," and "I will not fall for psychos." Also, "Pearl is an unqualified genius."

Later, in his own bed, Luke curls himself around one of his pillows, imagining it is Leila, the one who does not need to be explained to anyone. Luke waits for sleep, for dreams, for a form of consciousness with no responsibility, for images, desires, connections that do not need to be justified with the rest of his mental life. Asleep, Luke can already be in college, be back in Los Angeles, can have had Mark with him from the very beginning.

Luke thinks, while he is waiting for this state, of Aurora saying, "Poor Sara." Luke knows he has been punishing Sara since he has been home in various small ways, although he does not articulate the reasons why to himself. Instead, he decides that tomorrow he will be a very good son, the kind of person Sara raised him to be, and tell Sara that she should think about her own happiness. After all, a Sara fully engaged in her own happiness will be the one most likely to let Luke go to Los Angeles for New Year's. A happy Sara doesn't need him as much as Mark does.

CHAPTER NINETEEN

Luke oversleeps. When he wakes up he's not sure where he is, the pillow that was Leila is on the floor, and his alarm clock says 10:21. He bolts out of bed. The house is silent. He pulls on a pair of sweatpants and moves down the hallway, bumping off the walls. He checks his sisters' room—empty—pit-stops in the bathroom, then continues down the stairs to the kitchen. Sara is at the counter, cutting up fruit.

"Good morning, sweetheart."

"G'morning. Where is everybody?"

"Nana's at Assembly. The girls took Aunt Nancy to the Amish Market. We all thought we'd let you sleep. I heard you and your sisters giggling till all hours last night."

"Whuh."

"You were tired. Nana understood. Have some fruit."

Luke takes a peach.

"I had an idea this morning, and if you're up for it, I thought maybe we could do a meditation together," Sara says. Luke remembers his intention of being a good son today.

"Sure, just let me wake up a little?"

Sara hands Luke a mug of tea.

"Come up to the attic when you're ready."

Luke eats his peach. His quads are a little sore. He eats two bran muffins and a banana, goes back up the stairs, stops at the bathroom again, splashes water on his face, brushes his teeth. He looks at himself in the bathroom mirror, noting that his reflection is different in this mirror than in the one in his bathroom in LA, although his face has not changed. Luke leans closer to the mirror, then farther away. He bares his teeth at himself, tries smiling. Sighing, he leaves the bathroom.

Sara has lit candles and set up two of her meditation pillows on the floor. She is already seated at one, legs folded in full lotus pose, palms facing up on her knees. Luke takes the same pose, yawning a little.

"Thank you for doing this with me," Sara says.

"I'm a little out of practice," Luke says.

It's almost eight in the morning in LA. Luke thinks his father might be at the gym. Or walking Humphrey.

"I thought we might do a mandala meditation," Sara says in her low tone. "Just spend a few moments clearing a space in front of you."

Luke feels a slight twinge in his neck. Sara continues talking, and Luke ignores a desire to rub his neck, scratch his knee. After a bit, he is able to conceptualize an empty space in front of him.

"Let that space become a square. See the edges of the square, and the empty space it contains."

Luke decides he needs a bigger square. He remembers the Rothko paintings, debates the desirability of a rectangle over a square. Settles on a square.

"Put yourself in the center of the square," Sara is saying. "You are the center of this universe. All else radiates from you. Choose an image for yourself: a perfect circle, or a triangle, or a sun, or a star. Anything you want."

Luke selects and discards the suggested shapes before settling on the image of a single cell.

The standard method for drawing neurons is to draw them left to right: first the cell itself, the axon cable running west, the dendritic spines branching off of it. Wrapping around the axon are glial cells, which form a myelin sheath, an insulation cover to help speed up electrical charges along the axon. Myelin sheaths are not present when we are born, we develop them, and they help us learn language and regulate our behavior. For Luke the finest moment so far in his formal education was the day he was told that these neurons, and dendrites, and axons—how many we have, how they interact, how they deal with our environment—are what make us different as individuals. Sara is still talking, but Luke ignores her because he is repeating the words "myelin sheath" to himself, with great satisfaction.

Reluctantly, he tunes back into Sara. She is instructing Luke to think about the events of the summer, and his emotions, and form them into symbols. Luke listens to this, and tries to remember what the little pipe devices that monks use to shake sand into mandalas are called.

"When you become distracted by other thoughts, acknowledge them gently, and let them go," Sara says. "Focus on the images you are creating in your mandala."

Luke, concentrating, adds another cell in the center next to his own. He imagines some silver mammoth tusks, a series of Braille-like dots, in purple. Gold arrows, pointing upwards.

"Chakpur," he thinks, happily. "That's what they are called. Those little pipes."

That settled, Luke becomes slightly more interested in his mandala. He puts in satellite bursts, canyons, green squares, waves, a red carpet.

"Nothing is unimportant," Sara says. "Everything is central, and unique."

Luke swivels his mandala in his mind, mapping it from new angles, memorizing it. For a second, his square elongates into a rectangle, then back to a square. "What a trip," he hears Mark say.

"Experience the image in its entirety," Sara says.

Luke wishes Sara would stop talking, actually.

Luke admires his mandala.

He adds sequoia trees. Sara keeps talking.

"And now, begin to detach yourself from its design and observe it quietly."

"Wait, detachment already?" Luke thinks, annoyed because he is not finished creating. He puts a Joshua tree in each corner of the mandala, for symmetry.

"Observe the pattern and your place in it."

Luke tosses in some dancing leprechauns, tries hard not to think about Leila.

"Observe."

"I could do an essay about symbols," he thinks.

"Observe."

Luke begins composing an essay: "The act of observation affects the outcome of an event. Total objectivity is impossible."

"Detach your emotions from your symbols. Let them exist in their own reality."

Luke gets stuck inside this thought. What reality could these symbols inhabit, without him? And emotions inside symbols? That wasn't real. At some point the meaning of an arrow was agreed upon, but an arrow by itself was nothing. It was lines.

Occasionally, in meditation, Luke will get a little claustrophobic. That is happening now.

"When you're ready, Luke, reach out your hand in front of you."

Luke knows in a moment Sara is going to ask him to destroy his mandala. Because that is what you do with mandalas. Luke feels a little nauseous.

"Reach out your hand," Sara says. "And gently, and with compassion and love, sweep it all away."

The moment she says "sweep," Luke opens his eyes. Sara has her eyes shut and is leaning forward, swaying slightly.

"Sweep your hand across it," she says. "Let it all go from you. Sweep until there is nothing left but that pure and empty space. Sweep the space and release yourself from it." Sara's own hand reaches out, wiping the air before her. Luke decides that enough is enough.

"Hold on a sec," he says.

Sara jerks upright, opening her eyes.

"Why," Luke asks, "are we doing this?"

Sara's mouth opens a little.

"Maybe," Luke tells her, "I don't want to erase anything. Maybe I'm not ready for that."

"Okay," Sara says, nodding. "Okay. Talk to me about that."

"You talk to me." Luke stands up. There is a buzzing feeling occurring in his sinuses. "You talk to me about why it's so important for you that I let it all go. It's my mandala. My summer. My father. You can't make it all go away with a meditation and some candles."

Luke is not really certain of the words coming out of his mouth, but they seem to be still coming.

"If you have something to say to me, just say it," he says. "Don't make it into some Buddhist visualization. I'm not a Buddhist. You're not a Buddhist. Why are we doing this?"

Luke stands up and walks out of the room, moving quickly down the stairs. He is not sure of where he would like to go next. He goes to his room. He is, he finds, experiencing some sort of adrenaline rush, and his hands are shaking. When he hears Sara's footsteps coming down the hallway after him, he knows that there will now probably be a fight of some kind. But he decides he will not fight with Sara. He will listen to whatever Sara wants to say, and he will manage it. He walked away from her guided meditation and that was exciting, and a little dramatic, but not really necessary. It was the kind of thing Pearl would do. Luke knows that in a few minutes he will calm Sara down, and it will all be over.

Luke turns to the doorway just as Sara enters his room.

"You want to talk?" Sara demands. "Or do you want to walk away from me?"

Sara shakes something at him: the magazine with his father's picture on the cover.

"Is that what this is about? That interview?" Luke almost laughs. "Rory said you wouldn't take it personally. She said—"

"This is not," Sara says firmly, "about me. This is about you, Luke."

"Really?" Luke folds his arms. "Really? 'Cause I think it's about him. Actually." Luke knows that challenging Sara will not calm Sara down, but he can't help himself. Now that he has said that, Luke thinks, he will start calming Sara down.

"Well, let's talk about him, then." Sara tosses the magazine on Luke's bed. "And how he's had you participating in all of his . . . whatever. Going on television. And talking about my son all over the place. Taking you to baseball games and parties. And dressing you up, giving you a new expensive thing every time you turn around—"

"Okay, dressing me up? That's crazy. So he took me to a baseball game. That's hardly corruption. He wanted me to have a good *time!*"

"Yes." Sara's voice races up an incline. "In front of as many people as possible."

"Okay, you don't know what you are talking about." Luke shakes his head. His voice has an unfamiliar pitch. He hadn't known he could make this sound. "It wasn't like that AT ALL. He didn't buy me. It wasn't a STUNT."

"I don't know what it was." Sara points at the magazine. "But nobody asked me about this! And now people are coming up to me, in *grocery stores,* and in my own *studio,* asking me about my private life."

"Oh, so that's it." Luke kicks the bed lightly, just below the magazine. "That's what you're worried about? What happened to not caring about what people thought? Are you ticked off because a magazine didn't list all of your healing arts?"

"That is NOT what I am talking about—"

"Or because it says you weren't married? You weren't married! You didn't even know him!" Luke believes this is a very reasonable point, but maybe he should lower his voice now, because things are starting to get out of hand.

"You don't know anything about it," Sara says, sharply. "You don't know what I was going through—"

"Yeah, what did you go through?"

Luke tosses this off, casually, but once it's said, it seems to require something else.

"You got what you wanted," Luke continues, gaining velocity. "You got pregnant. That was the plan, right? Get the third daughter and fulfill your destiny. Sorry I screwed that up. Sorry I wrecked your whole mystical ride. I apologize on behalf of my father for the chromosome that made me a boy. Maybe you should have been more careful."

"Luke, you can't possibly," Sara stutters. "You don't. . . ."

"You had two girls." Luke shrugs. "You needed the third. You got my dad to get you pregnant."

"You think my husband left me and I WHAT?" Sara's voice starts to shake. "I just went out and found someone to get me pregnant?"

"What was I supposed to—"

"You don't know what it was like." Sara is fully shaking now. "Paul WALKED OUT ON ME. He turned to me one day and said, 'This isn't the life I need to be living,' and twenty minutes later he was out the DOOR. My whole world . . . everything . . . just collapsed.

And you think my family rushed in to help? Like, they didn't just all take it as another opportunity to sit around and JUDGE ME?"

"What does that have to do with anything?"

"Everything has to do with everything else, Luke. And I am trying to tell you what was going on with me—"

"Yeah, what the hell *were* you doing?" Luke backs away from Sara, from a Sara abandoned by Paul, holding the collapsed cocoon of a butterfly. "You didn't even TRY to give me a father. And if you hadn't run into my dad again on a . . . on a TRAIN, he wouldn't even know he *had* a son."

"So that's it?" Sara is shouting now. "You've got all the answers now after spending ten weeks with some man—"

"Some man?" Luke says, shouting now too, because he wishes Sara would go away and maybe if he shouts that will happen.

"Some *man*? That man defended you! His stupid aunt and her stupid friends in Illinois, they were talking behind our backs, saying Dad should take a paternity test, and he defended you! He was ready to rip their heads off!"

"Maybe we should have started with a paternity test!" Sara throws up her hands. "And then we'd all know exactly what we were talking about."

"What's that supposed to mean?" Luke can't believe Sara is still here. Doesn't she notice that he is yelling? "I'm telling you he defended—"

"And I'm telling you, you don't know everything," Sara yells back. "You don't know what it was like for me—"

"Stop saying that!" Luke kicks the bed again, but harder now, which hurts his foot, but he'll deal with that later because . . . wait.

What?

"What do you mean we should have started with a paternity test? What's that about?"

"Your father doesn't know what I went through! He disappeared for seventeen years and thinks he can just show up and—"

"Don't you—" Luke's hands are in fists. Like he might hit someone. Like he might hit Sara. "Don't you say ONE MORE WORD about my father. You don't know my father!"

"No, YOU don't know your father," Sara shouts. "You don't know that Mark is your father any more than I do!"

"Wait. Wait." Luke starts to laugh. He feels strange. Is he laughing? No. No, he's actually almost screaming. "WHAT?" shouts Luke. "WHAT? Mark is my father! Who else could he BE? What are you TALKING about?"

"There was someone else."

Luke, who has never been punched in the stomach, feels as if he has been punched in the stomach. He tries to force another sound out of his throat, but nothing comes.

"There was someone else. And I knew . . . we knew . . . right away that it wasn't right. And then there was . . . Mark."

"SOMEONE ELSE?" Luke can barely hear himself over the pounding in his head. He can barely hear Sara's next words.

"I know this is hard to hear, Luke, but you need to understand that this was a different . . . I . . . I was struggling and I thought I couldn't do it on my own. Take care of my girls, myself. Everything. So there was someone that I thought . . . I was wrong, and then the thing with Mark happened. It was just a . . . I wasn't planning ANYTHING, he was so young . . . But yes, it could have been . . . either one . . ."

"Either one," Luke repeats. "EITHER ONE?"

Luke thinks for a moment, wildly and absurdly, that he would like to go back to bed now. He would like it to be the Moment Before he woke up, or any Moment Before this Moment. Luke decides that he will go back to bed. Except.

"So, what, you were like with one person one night, and then with my dad . . ."

"Things happen, Luke." Sara's jaw is clenched so tight there is barely enough space for the words to emerge and they come now jaggedly, between her teeth. "They just do. And I was wrong about that . . . other person . . . in one way, but he was a friend to me and he helped me so much . . . and what happened with Mark was like—"

"So this someone, this OTHER person . . ."

Luke stops. Luke stops because he feels something shift now, inside his brain. It happens so suddenly, so sharply, that he nearly sits down under the weight of it, almost covers his head with his hands to protect it.

"Luke—"

But Luke holds up a hand, stopping her. It almost hurts his arm to hold it up like this, like his arm is a metal rod, hit by another metal rod. Luke tastes iron on his tongue.

"This person was a friend to you." There is something coming toward him now, something gaining speed, starting to stampede. He needs to keep his arm up. "Paul left you and you were scared and things just happen, and you had this person. But you had *Uncle Louis* to help you with all of that. The divorce. The apartment. The money. That's what you've always said. *Uncle Louis* was your friend. You've always been like, 'Oh, he held out a hand to me in a dark hour,' you SAID that, and . . ."

Luke drops his arm. It's too heavy. He thinks of falling, of bouncing off nails. Axons. Dendrites. Arrows. Symbols. Charges. There was a hand that was held out in a dark hour. The wrong hand. Luke feels this wrong hand descending toward his own head, slowly, inevitably. *Don't touch my head. Please don't touch my head.*

"It was one time," Sara whispers. "One time with Louis. I thought . . . he would . . . but right away he said . . . he didn't feel . . . and it was just one moment. He had already met Linny. But she was so much younger, I didn't think. I . . . Caroline never knew. After awhile I saw that they were right for each other and I didn't want to . . ."

"You're making this up." Luke thinks he'll just go outside for awhile, maybe. So Sara can stop making things up. Then he'll come back. He'll come back later when it's over.

"But at the time," Sara continues, "I felt like . . . NOTHING. Invisible. I'd never . . . I felt so old, like I'd never be young again, and all of a sudden there was your . . . there was this beautiful young guy treating me for a moment like . . . he really was like an angel. I know that doesn't make sense to you now. It all happened so fast—"

"No," Luke says. "No."

"Luke, I feel—"

The thing that was stampeding, falling, crushing Luke is now Luke himself. He stands up under the weight of it.

"Get out," Luke says. "Because I don't give a SHIT how you FEEL anymore. Get out."

Sara doesn't move.

"I told Louis that you weren't his son. He asked me if I knew for sure and I said yes and he believed me. The timing . . . I wasn't sure. I'm *not* sure. I don't know if Louis is your father, but he is a good person, Luke, and he's always—"

"I don't want to hear what a good person your sister's husband is," Luke says. "I don't want to hear another fucking thing. I want you to get out of my room."

"They had just met. I had no . . . I didn't think . . . Luke, it has never mattered to me how you got here. Just that you did. You were a gift to me. You have to believe that. That is the truth."

"That's nothing." It's so nothing, Luke thinks, that it's not even nothing.

"Belief is not truth," Luke says. He cannot understand why Sara is standing there like she has a point.

"Belief is NOT TRUTH." Luke wonders how he can make this really clear to Sara. Perfectly clear. Painfully clear.

"Everything," Luke says, "EVERYTHING about you is a LIE. Get out of my room."

"Luke—"

"GET THE FUCK OUT OF MY ROOM."

"You are MY SON," Sara says, covering her face with her hands. "MY SON."

And then Sara looks up at Luke and she says, "Oh God," and something in her face implodes, caves in, collapses, and Sara begins to sob. She doubles over, grabs her ribs, as if the force of her crying might crack them. Luke watches her in silence. Sara sobs violently for several minutes and then stops, still bent and shuddering: a boa who has lost the power to constrict.

Luke goes to his desk, grasps the glass sculpture of the banyan tree, turns, chooses a spot on the wall in between the poster of Earth and the one of deep space, takes a step back, aims, and hurls the sculpture as hard as he can. It hits the wall and shatters, instantly and completely, as if the molecules that bonded it together were expecting this to happen all along.

CHAPTER TWENTY

S ara? Luke?"
    It is Nana's voice, in the hallway. Sara and Luke freeze, and look at each other.

"Don't—" they say to each other, simultaneously.

"Luke?"

Nana appears in the doorway, one hand holding her maroon leather Bible to her chest.

"Mother." Sara holds out a warning hand, stepping forward as if to push Nana out of the room. Nana catches Sara's hand and looks at Luke, at the shards of glass on Luke's floor, back at Luke's face, and then at Sara.

"You told him," Nana says, on a sigh.

"You know?" Luke asks, at the same time that Sara says, "Oh my God."

"She knew?" Luke asks Sara, who shakes her head no and backs away from Nana's grip.

"Oh, Sara," Nana says.

"Who else—" Luke begins shakily, but Nana turns to him, fiercely. "That's enough now." It is not the Sword of Silence. It is far heavier, and sharper: as if all previous swords have been mere practice for this moment. Luke steps backward onto a piece of glass, which cuts his foot.

"Careful," says Sara, automatically.

"Come with me." Nana puts her arm around Sara tenderly. Sara submits to this, her tall frame shrinking to fit under Nana's arm. Nana puts her Bible down on Luke's bed in order to put both arms around her daughter.

"Mom," Sara says into Nana's chest.

"Luke is going to stay right here," Nana says. "Let's go downstairs now."

From below, the sounds of the front door, of Pearl's laughter, of Nancy's thick-heeled sandals, can now be heard.

"I don't know what happened here just now," Nana says to Luke. "But I suggest that whatever did stays in this room."

"We're home!" Aurora calls out. "Hellooo!"

"I'll get the dustpan," Nana says. "Sara, come with me."

Sara lets herself be led out of the room. Nana shuts the door softly behind them.

Luke sits down on his bed. He examines the bottom of his foot. A piece of glass, not large, is stuck in the callus of his heel. He pulls it out, watches a tiny pool of A+ blood well up, and tosses the shard back into the pile under the posters. Luke presses his thumbs against the sides of the hole in his callus to force any remaining glass out that might be embedded. Blood spills over onto his thumbnails. He wipes this away on his sweatpants. Luke shuts his eyes.

"Hey." It is Pearl, tapping at Luke's door. "You in there?" Pearl opens the door. Luke bends quickly over his foot again.

"You missed it!" Pearl cries out. "You would not believe what— whoa, what happened? You drop something?"

Luke says nothing.

"Is Nana back? Oh yeah, I guess she must be." Pearl picks up Nana's Bible. "She left her instruction manual. You get sworded for missing Assembly?"

Luke begins to look around, for socks, for shoes, for a T-shirt. He needs to get out of this house.

"Did you and Nana have a fight?" Pearl asks. "She was going to wake you up but Sara was really adamant that you be allowed to sleep. I'm so used to getting up at the butt crack of dawn on Sundays that I couldn't sleep in. So Rory and I hauled Aunt Nancy off to observe our local marketry. Please don't tell me you had a fight with Nana and I missed it. Not even Aunt Nancy versus that really cranky Amish guy with the tomatoes is worth that."

Luke turns to Pearl, takes a step toward her. Luke is taller than Pearl by several inches. He looks down at her, and he can tell, in an instant, that for the first time in his life he is making someone physically afraid of him. Pearl's mouth opens, and she takes a step backwards.

"Leave. Me. Alone," Luke says.

Pearl turns on her heel and runs out of Luke's room.

Luke pulls a T-shirt over his head, shoves his feet into running shoes, and heads into the hallway, down the stairs, past Pearl on the landing, past Aurora at the foot of the stairs, past Nana, who is coming out of the kitchen holding a broom and dustpan, past Aunt Nancy, who is by the front door holding a cloth bag. Luke leaves his house and begins to run.

Luke knows these streets so well he runs without destination or direction. For lengths of time he runs and knows with absolute certainty that his Uncle Louis is actually his father. Louis is tall. Louis is thin. Louis has a precise, questioning sort of mind. Louis wanted to touch his head; Louis didn't like the way he was being brought up. Louis looks to grocery-store clerks like he resembles Luke in some way.

Then this switches, and Luke knows with absolute certainty that Mark is his father. Mark is left-handed, Mark's second toe is longer than his first. Mark has green eyes. Mark was once a skinny guy, and Mark hates cottage cheese. Mark was younger than Uncle Louis at the time of Luke's conception, possessing more viably potent sperm. Mark has a sense of humor. Mark needs him. Mark loves him.

There is no evidence to suggest that handedness is genetic.

Luke thinks that he doesn't need Uncle Louis. He doesn't care if Uncle Louis needs him. He doesn't love Uncle Louis. He never will.

"Mark is my father," Luke says. He repeats this. Mark is my father. Mark's my father. Mark's my father. He's my father, he's my father, he's my, he's my, he's my.

Luke stops running for a moment, sucks in air. He has no evidence. And without evidence you only have belief. Luke, panicked, wonders what else he is blindly believing, taking evidence for granted. He starts running again.

Luke thinks that he has had it all wrong, even from the very beginning, even from the Moment Before, and that he has never known what Sara was thinking. And that everything, every moment before every moment would have to be reconsidered. Every mandala swept away.

Luke thinks about the things he shouted at Sara. He would not have thought he was the sort of person who could say those things. He would not have thought it *probable,* based on the evidence of himself that he has. He would not have thought it probable that, having said those things, he would not regret saying them. Not totally. Not yet. Luke thinks of additional things he could have said. He continues the fight in his head, sometimes saying worse things, sometimes not.

He tries to argue rationally:

Was Mark using him?

Did Mark tell him he was gay because he felt guilty about using him, putting Luke on his website, talking about him to interviewers, taking him everywhere? Maybe Mark wanted to be honest about one thing, because he was being dishonest about everything else.

Kati could have been in on it too. She asked him to do a walk-through. She wanted Mark to be "out there" but not "out." The whole summer she and Mark could have been working together.

But Mark had made lists of things he thought might make Luke happy. Private things, for just the two of them. Like Hawaii.

Which had become a story that Mark told on television. "My son, my son, my son."

But he was his son. Sara wanted him to doubt his father. He was not going to doubt his father. He was on his father's team, forevermore. He would stand by his father, even if his father never knew it. His father could never know it.

Sara didn't really want him to doubt his father, did she? She wasn't that kind of person. Maybe he has no idea what kind of person she is. Maybe no one knows anyone at all.

Luke thinks of his mother sobbing, waves this thought away, continues his argument:

Sara taught him to be compassionate.

No, that was wrong. He was compassionate. He would have been a compassionate person no matter who raised him.

Mark was his father.

But that was just hope. It wasn't truth.

Sara had slept with Louis. Apparently Nana knew this, or had guessed it. That was why Nana never wanted to know how Louis was. Nana didn't blame Sara. She blamed Louis. For marrying Caroline instead of Sara? And Sara hadn't known that Nana had known. And did Louis really believe Sara? Did Caroline really not know? Aunt Linny couldn't find her own way to the bathroom, but maybe she just preferred not to know.

Mark slept with people who were married. People had sex. You might think you knew the reason why, but maybe you didn't.

You could have sex even if you knew it was the wrong thing to do and would never stop being wrong.

So he wasn't intended to be a girl. He wasn't intended at all. He wasn't the Chosen One. He was the Accident. He was the thing that made Sara feel she wasn't invisible? He was something Mark could think about, and stop worrying for ten minutes?

It would be a simple thing, to know the truth. They swabbed the inside of your cheeks with a Q-tip and you could know your DNA. Soon they will have sequenced the entire genome and there will be no more mysteries.

But of course there will always be mysteries. Because people lied.

But he could know who his father was. That was something that could be known.

Luke hears a car behind him, and he moves to the right of the road. The car passes him, then slows down, pulls over, stops. Aurora gets out of the front seat. Luke stops. He is almost at the cemetery now. If he turns and cuts through the woods behind him and runs north for about fifteen minutes, he'll be out of the state of Delaware. Aurora walks toward him. Luke, breathing hard, puts his hands on his hips, walks in circles.

"Luke."

Luke, breathing too hard for speech, nods at Aurora, acknowledging her.

"Luke, sweetie. Are you okay?"

Luke sucks in a lungful of air.

"What happened?"

Luke shakes his head.

"I'm fine," he says, before he starts to cry.

Aurora has her arms around him in an instant. At first Luke does not want this, does not want contact, can't breathe, does not want to be still. After a moment, though, he holds on to Aurora as hard as he can. His sister's arms act as a kind of myelin sheath, accelerating Luke's sorrow, and he cries harder. Aurora pulls Luke down to sit by the side of the road and settles his head on her shoulder. Luke cries into this while Aurora rakes through Luke's hair with her fingertips.

Aurora's hands are Sara's hands: large, wide, always warm and dry. Luke reaches an end of crying but remains in the curve of his sister's shoulder for awhile longer. A car comes down the road. Luke can hear it slowing down, can feel Aurora waving it away. Luke listens to the gravel sound of tires on road. Luke can hear some kind of warbler singing in the woods behind them.

"I scared Pearl," Luke says, sitting up.

"It's good to know someone can," Aurora says. "She's fine."

"I don't want to go home right now."

"So we won't go home," Aurora says. "We'll stay right here. Or I'll take you back to New York with me."

Luke nods.

"Did Sara tell you what happened?"

"No. She and Nana are having some kind of a talk. Pearl's getting Aunt Nancy high."

Luke finds half a laugh coming out of his mouth.

"No, I don't know what they are doing," Aurora says. "I've been driving around looking for you. I remembered you like to run up here. Do you want to tell me what happened?"

"No."

"That's okay."

Luke takes off his left shoe, then sock. He looks at his heel, where the glass puncture is now a little inflamed. Aurora leans forward to examine it.

"Does it hurt?"

"No, but I should put something on it," Luke says. "Or clean it or something."

"There's a first-aid kit in Vlad."

Luke walks with Aurora to the car, keeping his heel off the ground. Aurora opens the trunk, starts searching beneath dusty blankets, folding camp chairs, a yoga mat, reusable grocery bags, beach hats. Aurora pulls out a battered white first-aid kit. Luke sits on the fender and holds out his foot.

"Remember when Pearl got all those splinters in her feet?" Aurora asks, crouching down.

Luke shakes his head.

"When Mr. Pollack redid the porch? You remember."

Luke shakes his head again.

"You were so cute. The porch was falling down, so Nana enlisted Mr. Pollack and he came over and tore it all down and rebuilt it. You followed him around everywhere. Sara made you a little tool belt, and you walked around with, like, a little plastic ruler, measuring things, telling everyone that you were helping. You don't remember that?" Aurora dabs some alcohol on Luke's foot.

"Ow. No, I don't remember that."

"I guess you were too little. Anyway, when it was done, Pearl went running across the porch. In her bare feet. And it hadn't been sanded yet. She got about halfway back before she realized what had happened and then she started screaming. Sara came rushing out and hauled Pearl off to the bathroom. They were in there for hours, Pearl screaming the whole time, while Sara pulled all the splinters out." Aurora laughs, shaking a bottle of Mercurochrome. "Then Sara coated Pearl's feet in tea tree oil, or something like that, and gave her an amulet to wear, and a little sign that said, 'Pearl is a brave girl,' and that night Nana came tiptoeing into our room with a tube of Neosporin."

"I don't remember that."

"Classic Prescott stuff, really. You remember Mr. Pollack, though? He died the next year. Heart attack. I think he had sort of a Brethren crush on Nana. He was always asking us if we needed any help."

"Really? I don't remember any of this."

"Well," Aurora says, putting a Band-Aid on Luke's heel, "I remember."

Aurora smiles up at Luke, looking for a moment so much like the Sara that Luke loves that his chest hurts. He can see the red imprints of his hands on Aurora's arms. He has gotten stronger over the summer.

Luke thinks of his sisters' father, Paul, who *does* seem likely to be their real father, although possibly not at all like the Paul Sara has told them about. Even Aurora's memories of her dad—the man picking her up, the shoes underneath the table—might not actually be memories of Paul. Sara had said that Paul never wore shoes with laces. Those feet could have been anyone's feet. Aurora could have been playing with Uncle Louis's shoes on the night that Sara took hold of the hand that was held out to her.

"You want to get some ice cream or something?" Aurora asks.

Mary lived in a black-and-white world and then they let her out of her room and showed her a red apple. She was conscious of red now. But maybe she didn't want to know red like that. Maybe she liked it better the other way, with red inside her mind, without a name, without anything at all.

Luke does and does not want to get ice cream. He does and does not want to go home.

"I don't know," Luke says. "I don't know what I want to do."

"Okay," Aurora says. "Let's just sit here for awhile then."

Luke thinks.

Luke thinks he will go home and talk to Sara. He thinks he will not talk to Sara, he will go to New York with Aurora, with Pearl. He thinks he will tell his sisters what happened. He thinks he will never tell anyone.

Luke thinks he will go home and call his father, in Los Angeles.

Luke thinks he will win races this year, go with Nana to Assembly and not be Saved, go to Los Angeles for Christmas, ask Leila to let him keep his eyes open. He will write his essay, and get into college.

Luke thinks he will do none of these things, he will sit on the side of the road wondering if there is glass in his foot, and who his father is, for the rest of his life.

Luke thinks he will not do that.

Luke thinks that there is truth, and there is belief, and there is hope. There are the things you are. And you don't really have a choice about what you are. You might not even have much of a choice about what you *do* with what you are. Everyone would like to think they had a choice. You couldn't help wanting to think that. You couldn't help wanting to believe. We are designed for belief. Belief was a feature of the brain, like consciousness.

Although we were still evolving, perhaps. Evolution is very, very slow.

The brain has evolved, not just from childbirth, but from our primitive selves. Like any device, there have been system upgrades, improvements, and modifications. Our brains are like computers, but we don't discard our old models, no matter how clunky or inefficient. Our old systems move into a state of semiretirement, reemerging into fame only when the star systems fail, are injured, or destroyed. Shattered.

There was a time when humans used the midbrain for sight. But we eventually developed a higher center: the primary visual cortex, a faster, better model. We use that now to process all our visual information. The midbrain still functions, but it doesn't communicate with our systems for consciousness.

How do we know this? We know by examining people who have lost the use of their primary visual cortex, usually through damage or trauma of some kind. Such people experience blindness. If you were to put a pencil on a desk in front of them and tell them to pick it up, they would probably say something along the lines of, "Hey, I'm blind. I can't see a thing." But if you encouraged them to take a wild guess, a stab in the dark, and they agreed to try, they might be able to reach out and pick up the pencil just perfectly. They might be able to do that ninety-nine times out of a hundred. That's because while their primary visual cortex no longer functions, their midbrain still does, and is capable of basic operations like orienting on an object placed within their visual field. They can, in fact, still see. What they lost was not their sight, but their *consciousness* of sight. This phenomenon has been observed, and documented, and is called blindsight.

We don't always know what we know, in other words. We don't know what we know.

But if you understood all of this, really understood it, would it make any difference? Because there would still be . . . everything. And there would still be . . .

Everything, Luke thinks. Everything, everything, everything. Every. Thing.

Everything. Or nothing. What would make him believe? Evidence.

He couldn't know everything. He never would. He would be specific. He would be very specific. You only had one father.

He knew the qualia for being a son. He knew the qualia of having a father. That was what he knew.

He wasn't done yet. There were parts of his brain that weren't even fully online yet. He was only seventeen.

For a moment Luke sees in its entirety a perfectly constructed three-to-five-hundred-word essay describing the phenomenon of blindsight and drawing a line—an axon—from it to him, stating his intention to follow the lines of consciousness, wherever they may lead. To pluck a shiny red apple from the giant Sequoia tree of knowledge, and eat it, and be unashamed.

"Okay," Luke says, standing up. "Let's go."

Acknowledgments

Thank you to agent and lodestar Sally Brady, and Shelley Wanger at Pantheon for taking care of this book. Thank you to Adam and Jen—beloved first readers; Lauren—most wonderfully generous and loyal from start to finish; and Chris—for well-timed notes and kindness. Thank you to Gary, Blair, Nick (muse), Kari, John, David, Marty, Emily, Daniella, Jad, staff and writers of the Stone House Retreat—for advice, inspiration, and support.

Meg Howrey is a dancer and an actor who has performed on Broadway and toured nationally. She currently lives in Los Angeles.

A NOTE ON THE TYPE

This book was set in Minion, a typeface produced by the Adobe Corporation specifically for the Macintosh personal computer, and released in 1990. Designed by Robert Slimbach, Minion combines the classic characteristics of old-style faces with the full complement of weights required for modern typesetting.

Composed by North Market Street Graphics
Lancaster, Pennsylvania

Printed and bound by Berryville Graphics
Berryville, Virginia

Designed by Soonyoung Kwon